Shores of our Forefathers

Sacred places of Valor, Determination and Liberty

Shores of our Forefathers

Sacred places of Valor, Determination and Liberty

Joseph Akoi Zeze

© 2024 Joseph Akoi Zeze. All rights reserved.

No part of this book may be reproduced, stored in a retrieval system, or transmitted by any means without the written permission of the author.

Printed in the United States of America

ISBN: 979-8-89114-080-6 (hc)
ISBN: 979-8-89114-079-0 (sc)
ISBN: 979-8-89114-081-3 (e)

Library of Congress Control Number: 2024907513

2024.09.18

MainSpring Books
5901 W. Century Blvd
Suite 750
Los Angeles, CA, US, 90045

www.mainspringbooks.com

Although this is a fiction, the names of some characters were persons who actually existed. This novel is dedicated to the many abolitionists and philanthropists who dedicated their lives to the emancipation of slavery and championing the dignity of negro and colored people. Among them was is Rev. Dr. Lott Carey, the first black missionary to Africa. Also, to the patriots who lay down their lives to establish the Republic of Liberia that mushroomed from a tiny colony to a commonwealth and now a thriving democracy.

Prologue

Autumn, 1827. A small plantation of about 25 slaves with 5 overseers, located somewhere near Gunston Hill, Fairfax County, Virginia.

Robert Bob-bob Douglass dashed across the newly planted tobacco field, trampling on the young crops that were recently transplanted from their nurseries. He didn't care about what master Perry Cottonwood would do to him as his troubles were going to be grievous, if caught.

But he doubted that he was going to be caught in the first place, and so destroying high grade tobacco seedlings, which the Virginia plantation and slave owner spent close to $15,000 to purchase, as he raced across the field, meant nothing to him. What matters most was to earn the freedom he had recently been made to value, by running away from the plantation he has known and labored, since the day he was born.

Bob-bob Douglass, as he was known on Cottonwood Plantation, was one of master Cottonwood's favored slaves. He was regarded as an overseer, a preferential treatment no slave has had in 50 years throughout the county and all of this slave state. His fellow slaves saw him as the black brother of master Cottonwood and his wife, Mary Ann.

Now racing towards the middle of the field, where it'd take him a few seconds to disappear into the woods, he would never look back to be reminded of his slave brothers and sisters he was leaving behind. Luckily for him, he had no one to worry about. He didn't have a wife, children, mom or dad to tempt him to look back at the place that he now loathed, as he had so far, seen his first glimpses of freedom.

But the only person for whom he would have definitely looked back, was the woman he loved. If she had not been part of his escape plan of meeting her at a discreet location, his entire quest for freedom would've been meaningless.

This beautiful colored woman, brought to the plantation many years ago from Georgia, was known as a sister of Mary Ann Eagleman Cottonwood, whose father, James Chrystal Eagleman, was a successful slave trader who roamed the coast of West Africa and the East and West indies, purchasing slaves all his life. He had her by a former slave of African and Spanish descent. At least that was the only way her cover was going to fit, as the half-sister of Mary Ann.

Everyone knew that Eagleman had fathered many kids by African and other biracial women of Spanish and African descent while on his expeditions. But the true story was, she was the daughter of the retired US Navy Admiral, Charles Norman Drake by a free negro of Latino decent, only known as Maria. She had given birth to the love of Bob-bob's life, and died before the child was a teenager. And the Admiral, who saw this child as the clone of the woman he loved, took her in, and provided all her needs. But when he later entered into politics, and was running for the governorship of Georgia, his opponents somehow managed to concoct the true identity of the child.

One day the Georgia Gazette ran a story that the child was not the beloved slave girl who he had freed, and opted to keep her of her free will. She was indeed his biological daughter by Maria, a Spanish of African descent, and that the child was held out of wedlock. This put the Admiral's credibility into question, slightly plummeting the respected naval officer's rating against his opponents. Moreover, Elijah Poe, the paper's editor, even went as far as suggesting that Maria practiced Voodoo, the dark magic and she had the ability to seduce men, and her daughter may have probably inherited this dark art.

For fear of proving his enemies right, which would have automatically ended his political career, he secretly sent her to his trusted and old-time friend, and comrade at sea, James Crystal Eagleman. Eagleman then confided in his in-law, old Master Cottonwood, and the child was sent to live with the successful plantation owners in Virginia as the half-sister of his daughter Mary Ann.

The child had since lived with the Cottonwoods, as Mary Ann's half-sister and had grown up to become a strikingly attractive young woman. From her youth, Bob-bob, born in the plantation by a maid of the old master's wife who died during childbirth, was her chaperone, even after the old slave master retired from running the plantation and handed it over to his son, Perry. Most times he rode her in her two-wheeled coach, wherever she went.

On the day she turned 19, a week after the mysterious death of Perry's mother, she was in the room of the old master, serving his tea, a new role she had assumed. The old slave owner, now in his mid-sixties, was suddenly besieged by an invisible force of ecstasy. With trembling hands, he suddenly found himself undressing her. And while sitting in his rocking chair near the fireplace, he sat her on his lap, using his knees to open her legs to ease her close to his abdomen. He'd first massaged her full breasts and then buried his face between them, at the same time gently easing her up and down.

The young successor himself, afflicted by this surge of enticing concupiscence, often stole out of his wife's bed, and sneaked into his colored sister-in-law's room at night. Now in her early 20s, she would be far asleep while he knelt between her magnificent thighs, meticulously pulling away her underwear and night gown to reveal her irresistible breasts, perfectly protruding out of her bony chest. He'd then caress her genitals while gently caressing her breasts with his lips until her entire body started to jerk in complete ecstasy. Then he thrust his manhood into her and continued to caress her breast and stroke deep into her.

Sometimes, Perry would wonder whether the young woman was fully awake and in compliance with the entire fantasy or did she think that she was having a wet dream? She never protested or even made any mention of their nightly escapades. But one night the exact opposite of these thoughts were revealed while the additive brother-in-law was on top of her, when she suddenly awoke, urging him to continue, and ended that night's escapade on top of him.

One day in the summer, Bob-bob had ridden her in her favorite two-wheeled wagon to Silver Creek, some two and a half miles into the woods north of the plantation. To Bob-bob's astonishment, he embarrassingly turned around, when she unexpectedly loosened the royal red bristle Victorian dress she was wearing, stepping out of it, naked, when it slid down her enticing body that outlined the morphology of her African ancestry.

He remained standing with his back turned, when she plunged into the water, swam for some time and got back on shore. She called his name. Thinking that she had finished swimming and had put her clothes back on, he turned, but suddenly froze. Wet and naked, she was standing before him, wiping her skin with her shining-long black hair, and her avocado shaped tickling breasts. Then she held and squeezed them with both hands, at the same time licking her pink nipples.

Invoking a sensation that he could not resist, she had him locked with a seductive gaze. Unexpectedly, she pushed him to a tree, dropped on her knees and pulled down his pants. As she aroused his sexual drive with the smoothness of her mouth, the next moment he was convulsing and emitting deep grunts and moans.

Suddenly, he saw himself positioning her against the tree holding her waist, as she bent over. Initially hesitant, he inserted his large genitals into her, and began with some light strokes which later gained momentum with well-coordinated and sustained rhythms until there was a climax.

From that day, he was enthralled by the orgasm he had never experienced. Being a slave with preferential treatment or not, was only on the plantation but it was no longer in his mind. They have since planned to be together forever, and hoped that one day, they would flee to a faraway place.

One day she read about a place along the West African Coast famous for its trade in the Malagueta pepper spice. Many free black slaves had ventured there and there were stories of absolute freedom. She and Bob-bob Douglass then sought the opportunity to forge out a plan to escape to this new land of liberty.

Even after the United States had abolished slavery, and as most southern states were loath to honor such a proclamation, Robert Bob-bob Douglass was not going to get his freedom from the Cottonwoods, and so he must flee with the woman he loves to this Pepper Coast.

30 minutes later, he was far across the field, sprinting into the woods. A quarter of a mile away from the plantation, he was in high spirits. Any attempt to capture him now was impossible. Another 30 minutes into the woods, he was making his way to Manassas, sprinting on an unfrequented wagon passage, known as Snake Trail.

He heard something approaching from his rear and suddenly took a dive behind a dead oak tree lying a few meters from the edge of the trail. With his head sideways and lying flat on his belly, he perfectly concealed himself, and listened to the sound of hoofs and neighs of horses, and the wheels of a wagon. It was a four-wheel wagon, judging from the rhythm of the clattering hooves on the dirt trail. Bob-bob Douglass was good at telling whether it was a single horse, or a two-wheeled wagon or the four-wheeled ones, just by listening to the clatter of hoofs.

Rightly, it was the four-wheeled wagon of the Stewards passing by, when he tilted his head a little above the dead oak to see who it was. Humphry Steward, his wife, Marylin and their two children, Lorie his 13 years old son, and his little sister Annabel, who had just turned 9 were on their way that late Saturday evening, from Leesburg, Loudon County to Heathsville where they often spend the night at a family house to get ready the next day for the Sunday morning service at the Ellis Haywood Presbyterian Church in the coaster town. Prescott and Darrel, two of their trusted slaves, and another one, plus Dick and Terry, their two overseers, were traveling along.

"Hey George!" poking his head out of the back of the wagon and almost falling off, Lorie screamed at the other slave riding on a horse back close to the back of the wagon. "I saw a runaway slave, hiding behind the dead oak over there. Go and check it out now."

"I see no one, young master," replied the young slave who looked in his late teens.

"No! Come on! You got to go and check it up. I did see someone, behind that oak," shouted Lorie, making his way to the front of the wagon to inform his father.

Humphrey nodded to Tom, his coachman to stop the wagon, which he did. With his rifle in his hand, Master Stewart jumped down and went for his black stallion, tied next to the right side of the wagon and mounted it. Then he rode to the back of the wagon and gestured to Lorie who had also rushed to the back, to mount on the horse. Very eager and excited, the kid jumped on the horse back behind his father.

"It's going to be bad for you, George, if you also saw that runaway slave and tried to hide it," warned master Steward, pointing his rifle at George.

George attempted to ride along, but Master Stewart told him to stay put. Instead, he told his other slave, Prescott, to join them. Little master Lorie Steward directed as his father and Prescott, who looked in his forties, rode towards the oak tree, and got there but saw no one.

"Did you really see anybody hiding behind this oak?" Master Steward turned sideways to his right and asked his son.

"Yes dad, as soon as the wagon passed this area, I saw a head with an afro lifted above the oak. I caught his eyes, but as soon as I could call George, he disappeared," answered Lorie, his tone assuring.

"Let me take a look around," suggested Prescott, who went galloping around the immediate perimeter of the area when his master nodded in approval.

Prescott sprinted around the place on his brown horseback, expanding the perimeter for every round he made, until he was a bit far from Master Humphrey Steward and his son, who were still waiting near the dead oak. The Leesburg County slave owner, holding his rifle upright, kept swinging his horse in all directions, with his son firmly holding onto him, to make sure to spot anyone who would be getting away in the woods.

Prescott had expanded his perimeter some more, and came across a big hemlock tree and saw hiding between its huge roots, the run-away slave, Robert Bob-bob Douglass. When he and Lorie's eyes met, he rolled from behind the dead oak, and sprinted to this area before anyone could see him.

The Leesburg slave watched, never taking his eyes off his fellow slave who remained hiding between the roots of the large tree. Both looked at each other for a while as Prescott fought to keep his horse stable. Douglass looked like a well taken care of slave, Prescott thought, judging from his opulence.

Meanwhile Annabel suddenly appeared and stood behind her father.

"Daddy," she crooned. Lorie always imagines seeing a runaway slave whenever we pass this route. He's been hallucinating, lately."

"No! I had not," protested Lorie, before his father, who was startled to see that Annabel had left the Wagon and had come running to them, could say a word. "I saw the head of a slave above this dead oak, Dad."

"He's lying, Dad. He has been drawing a slave with an Afro hiding behind a tree in the woods as a coach passes by."

"No, I had not."

"Yes, you did."

"Okay, that's enough. Let's wait for Prescott," their father was trying to calm them down when the slave scout came galloping towards them.

"Didn't see anyone, sir," he informed his master.

"No!" Shouted Lorie. "He was right here!"

"There was no one here!" rejected Annabel, shouting back at her brother.

"Okay that's enough!" shouted their father. "If it was anyone, he wouldn't get far. He will be caught, okay? Let's go, we have more distance to cover."

Bob-bob Douglass waited until the Stewards had left and then continued running along Snake Trail. Sometimes he would rest and then resume until he reached a junction where the trail splits into two, with one heading west while the other headed east. From the wheel tracks on the ground, he deduced that the Stewarts headed east. He took the one headed west, and within minutes he was in the woods of Warrenton.

He rested again for some time to allow the fast-approaching evening to provide him with the cover of darkness to make his way to Owl Hill where a coachman will be waiting near Morrison Farm. He will huddle at the cargo area at the back and the coachman will take him all the way to Owenton where the love of his life will be waiting for him at an inn. From there, both of them will go to Richmond. Douglass will not have to worry here because he will be her chaperone with a special pass to accompany her.

The ploy was, he was accompanying her, with the special pass to prove this, to the city to pick up an important parcel on behalf of her father, James Eagleman. While at Richmond, they will board a vessel for New York, and then sail across the Atlantic Ocean.

Late into the night, he reached Owl Hill, and saw the coach waiting at the edge of Morison Farm where a track at the west of the gate, headed into the woods. He remained in the woods, hiding behind a tree to study whether it was the two-wheeled coach the love of his life often uses. Satisfied that it was the identical one, he rushed out of his hiding place and climbed into the back. Next, he felt the coach moving. He was told that the coachman will be an old white man, dressed like a Quaker, and he was a secret member of a sect, organized to help runaway slaves escape.

For about two hours, he lay face up. Clung to his chest was his bundle which included the coachman outfit he would wear while he chaperones Master Perry Cottonwood sister-in-law all the way to Richmond. He unwrapped a small parcel he took from the packet of the old but neat blue-black double breasted frock coat he was wearing and was munching on a piece of cornbread, he had asked Miss Mason, the most senior maid in the house of the Cottonwood to prepare for him the morning before he ran off. He took from the bundle, a flask with Kool Aid inside and repeatedly took sips while munching on the cornbread.

He was almost about to doze off when he heard a knock on the wooden trunk of the coach, which told him that he had finally reached Owenton. As planned, the coachman had reached him at the inn where his love was waiting for him in a room whose number he had committed to memory. They would make love the whole night and then leave for Richmond the next morning.

He majestically disembarked from the trunk of the coach, but to his horror, he was back at Fairfax. His heart leapt like it was going to jump out of his throat when he turned and saw Master Perry Cottonwood, Mary Ann, and the rest of the plantation, including the overseers and slaves looking at him. Realizing that he had been tricked, Robert Bob-bob Douglass flunked his bundle to the ground, dropped down on his knees and bowed his face to the ground.

"You are going to pay for this, you ungrateful animal," snared Master Perry Cottonwood, grabbing the once favored slave by his collar and pulling him to his feet. "Take him away while we think about what to do with him."

Another wave of horror overwhelmed the runaway slave when the Quaker stepped out of the coach and began to remove his hat and the wig from his head, thus revealing his true identity. He was not a member of the secret underground sect that helped slaves escape as was planned. He was James Burk, one of the overseers in the fields and a relative of the Cottonwoods. He walked over to Bob-bob Douglass who looked spooky as James Burk and two other white men grabbed him.

"Let him get some lashes, first," Master Perry Cottonwood instructed.

Bob-bob Douglass was taken to the pole where they flogged slaves. His clothes were torn off him and he was strapped. Bob-bob cried out loud as every whip of the 50 lashes, given to him by James Burk and the overseer, named Alan Smith, tore his flesh. After the vicious strokes on his back, causing huge blisters and deep wounds covered with blood, he was thrown into the room at the back of the stable where they kept the disgruntled slaves, and remained there until the following week.

It was early on a Saturday morning, Robert Bob-bob Douglass was led to the gallows where they hung runaway slaves. The entire plantation was made to gather around the tree as the condemned slave was placed on top of a platform built for such a purpose. The other slaves watched, with some of them weeping, especially the women as James Burk tied a rope around his neck. Pitying himself, he bowed his head in shame, but he soon felt the presence of his love and suddenly lifted his head.

Wearing a red gown, she strode near Master Perry Cottonwood. Looking in the eyes of the man she told she loved and wanted to spend the rest of her life with, she held the master's hand and Bob-bob Douglass watched how she squeezed it. Bewildered and feeling betrayed, he looked into her eyes and suddenly, a strange feeling took hold of him.

He could see himself through her eyes walking in this strange alley full of activities. He looked to his right and was stunned to see her as the little teenager who was brought to the plantation preparing tea for Clara, the old master's wife. He looked on as she poured a substance into it and brought it to her. Then Clara drank all of it and started feeling sick afterwards, and never recovered till her death.

Spooked, Bob-bob Douglas closed his eyes tight and opened it again. Appearing to him was the 19 years old daughter of the Admiral, riding old Master Cottonwood as he held onto her breasts, occasionally burying his head between them while sitting on his lap. He ran from there and entered another alley, but saw himself standing in Master Perry Cottonwood bed room lying beside his wife. He watched how he got up and sneaked into the room of his sister-in-law and saw how she came from behind him, naked and pushed him on the bed, loosened his robe and climbed on top of him.

Frightened, he stormed out of the room and ran outside, but saw her coach near the stable. He ran to it and got inside, but soon heard moaning and grunts at the back. He looked behind. To his astonishment, he saw his love lying on her stomach with her legs spread apart, and her buttocks slightly akimbo. Pulling her hair while she enjoyed it, James Burk was ferociously doing her from the back.

Bob-bob Douglass jumped down the coach and ran aimlessly into the woods. He had seen too much of what the plantation looks like from the inside. The woman he loves is dirty and evil, and he should have known better to avoid her the day she undressed herself before him and plunged into Silver Creek.

He continued running until he suddenly froze when he saw what looked like a glow of dim orange red light ahead of him. Mary Ann suddenly stood before him, naked. Then the love of his life appeared from her rear also naked and held Mary Ann by her breasts. She gently turned her around to face her and they started kissing. Shaking and convulsing hysterically, Bob-bob again shot his eyes and started shouting.

Then he saw what looked like a shrine. The love of his life was dressed in a white translucent garment, kneeling before an altar decorated with candles, and all sorts of scary artifice. At the foot of the altar were different kinds of bottles filled with different kinds of drinks, with some, half emptied. Right before her knees were 4 dolls with the image of old Master Cottonwood, his son Perry, Mary Ann and James Burk.

He also saw another doll that looked like Clara lying in an open coffin. What startled him most was when he saw a black one, just like him, hung to a tree with ropes tied around its neck. Horrified, he watched how the love of his life took one of the bottles of dark red wine from the base of the altar, uncapped it and poured some into her mouth.

For every time she spat out the wine from her mouth on a doll, the candle's flames would violently pop. Then she took a dagger laying at the foot of the altar and stabbed one of the dolls in the chest, the one that looked like old master Cottonwood, and blood poured out. Bob-bob Douglass started screaming when the love of his life had stabbed all the dolls. She suddenly threw herself into the pool of blood and started rolling into it.

He opened his eyes and saw everyone watching him, including his love. He looked up and the ropes were still tied around his neck. It was time to be hanged.

"She's evil!" he shouted, taking his eyes off the love of his life, who was still standing by master Perry Cottonwood, squeezing his hands. "She will kill all of you. I have seen it. I have seen it all."

Instead of Master Perry Cottonwood showing a little concern, even though he was still going to hang Bob-bob Douglass, he became infuriated by the comments from the slave he used to love. Bob-bob felt a strange force compelling him to look into her direction and into her eyes again, as the love of his life looked at him transfixed. He screamed as he struggled to avoid eye contact with her, but he was suddenly overpowered by this invincible force and again he was looking directly into her eyes.

Through them her true identity was revealed. She was Rebecca Drake, the daughter of Admiral Charles Drake from the Voodoo queen, Maria, but was brought to the plantation as the half-colored sister of Mary Ann. She had inherited the dark art from her mother and it has taken roots.

"Master Perry," frightened, Bob-bob Douglass opened his eyes and spoke. "I know you will still hang me, but there is an evil in your mist. It's bent on destroying your entire generation. It will destroy you, your wife and old master Cottonwood. It killed your mother. It thrives on seduction, manipulation, death and destruction. We are all going to die."

Every one witnessing the execution of Bob-bob Douglass was shocked when they listened to him. To them, he was saying that he loved Mary Ann's sister and had vowed upon his life to escape with her to the new free world beyond the Atlantic Ocean; the land of his ancestors-the Malagueta Coast.

"Oh my God! Bob-bob!" Miss Mason came before the condemned slave, holding onto the platform, weeping. "You couldn't keep your dick for them beautiful slave women, but to stick it out for Master Perry in-law. Let God have mercy on your soul, Bob-bob."

"Why are you not listening to me?!" screamed Bob-bob Douglass. "She's the daughter of the dark queen. I am not the only one dying here, today. She will kill all of us. I didn't put myself upon her. You got to believe me. She did. Like she did old Master Cottonwood and Master Perry, himself…"

"Do it now!" interrupted Master Perry Cottonwood, commanding.

A slave was standing by a stallion strapped with leather fasteners attached to the level on which Bob-bob Douglass stood. The condemned slave looked and was surprised to see that it was Prescott, the slave from Leesburg who saw him hiding in the woods.

He caught the eyes of Rebecca Drake, the love of his life again, and saw little Master Lorie Steward standing with a folded poster in his hands. The kid suddenly unfolded it and held it up for him to see. Bob-bob Douglass was looking at the drawing of himself hiding behind the dead oak tree.

He resumed his deafening screams, when he saw the love of his life, pulled the robes around the neck of the doll that looked like him, just as Prescott lashed the horse with a whip in his hand, causing the animal to neigh and gallop in one jerk, pulling the level and releasing the ratchet. Bob-bob's weight caused the trapdoor to fall and his legs sank, knee level, beneath the scaffold.

The noose suddenly squeezed and choked him as the notch at the back of his neck reduced to a firm and nasty grip. With his hands tied behind him and eyes jutting out of their sockets, Robert Bob-bob Douglass convulsed violently, fighting on the robes as it swung with him.

At one moment his tongue lolled out of his mouth. Then foamy saliva flowed out. As his convulsions diminished, like a silk of slime, more were dropping to the ground. Finally, Robert Bob-bob Douglass was dead, hanging on the robes as Rebecca Drake, the love of his life, looked on with a broad grin on her face.

Chapter 1

Sixteen days at sea, since leaving New York harbor, the Freedom Star has been on a steady course, sailing west of the Atlantic and heading straight for the West African Coast. On board were 101 former slaves, among which included 45 women, 30 men and 26 children. These free slaves, along with their families, were being repatriated to the Malagueta Coast, a conducive stretch of territory along the Western Atlantic Coast, east of Sherbro Island, Sierra Leone, extending from Cape Mount to Cape Palmas, now the Republic of Liberia.

It was discovered in the late 15th century by Portuguese explorers, but not until the 18th Century, it was being resettled by free slaves, through the instrumentality of the American Colonization Society (ACS), an organization which purpose is to relocate free slaves back to Africa, when slavery was abolished in America. It was the Freedom Star's first voyage across the Atlantic. All of its previous ventures were around the Caribbean, transporting free or recaptured slaves back to the northern part of the United States, and Canada.

Also, on board was the abolitionist Elijah Burgess, co-founder and chief executive officer of Color Purpose, a humanitarian organization whose aim was to promote the advancement of free slaves and colored people. He was accompanied by Angela Draper Burgess, his beautiful colored wife. They have been married for little over three months, and as part of their planned honeymoon, they were accompanying the free slaves to ensure that they re-settle on their anestrous land, by negotiating with the ACS agents and native chiefs on the ground.

Elijah Burgess was the mulatto son of a well-respected Virginian plantation owner, who himself had abolished slavery a few years ago, after the proclamation by the federal government, but encouraged and hired free black men to work on his plantation at their own volition. He encouraged his cherished son to help organize the Color Purpose organization.

It was approaching the evening hours, as the azure skies were turning dark gray to the disappearance of the gradually setting sun. The sea was calmed and the weather has been good all week. The wind was blowing gently, flipping the sails and flying jib, as the vessel plowed through the gentle waves.

The 12 crewmen, a quarter of which were experienced British sailors, had all done their work for the day and most of them had retired to their quarters, except 4 of them who were still on the quarter deck along with the captain, the former United States naval hero, James Newton Summerville.

The retired Navy officer has spent most of his career intercepting slave vessels heading to the United States from the West African Coast, and the Caribbean, since the United States proclaimed the abolition of slavery. Due to his experience, he was recently hired to steer the Freedom Star across the Atlantic. Standing at the rail of the bow, he was peering into a long telescope, scanning the vast blue sea ahead of him. And when he had finished, he nodded to his coxswain. Then he gave some instructions to his Boatswain, while the two other crewmen stood by. After that he went into his cabin.

"Come-on," suddenly whispered Henrique Cassel, a fair 13 years old lad, and a son of one of the free slave families on board the vessel.

He signaled to a group of boys of similar age and complexion, hiding beneath a wooden staircase that led up to the main deck of the ship.

"Are you sure that the captain has gone into his quarters, and there's no crewmen on this side of the deck?" hissed, Daniel Roberts, the fairer and taller of the boys with curly hair, pointed nose, and brown eyes.

"Yeah. Hurry up," Henrique Cassel hissed back.

"Where are the saints?" asked Albert Coleman, one of the boys. "Are they afraid of us, the Yankees, or What?"

"They'll come," assured Daniel Roberts. "Remember their cabins are all the way down the hull. And they need to tip-toe to come all the way up here, or else Ben will notice them and alarm the captain. This would jeopardize the match we 've been planning since we boarded this ship."

"No one will see them coming," Joel Findley, another kid, assured the others. "I don't think Ben will be making his rounds, anytime soon."

"Did the plan work?" quizzed Daniel Roberts, studying Joel Findley.

"Rest assured," crooned Harold Findley, Joel's junior brother. "Our mother's specially brewed ale can pass for a sleeping pill."

"How come they and their families are cramped all the way at the bottom of the hull while we are up here, near the deck? I always wanted to ask," wondered Gabriel Phillips.

"I think because they are from down south. Where the plantations are," scorned David Coleman, Albert Coleman's brother.

"I think it's because their skins are darker than ours," offered Henrique Cassel. "Did it ever occur to you that we who have fair skins are given preference?"

"But we are all negroes, though," chuckled Daniel Roberts. "Even though the dark-skinned ones are mostly from the rural plantations down south, while the fair skinned ones are from the urban areas and the cities where mixed breeding isn't an issue."

"Hey guys. Cut off the crap," suddenly hissed, Henrique Cassell. "Here come our dark-skinned boys."

Just then, Prince Royce, one of the saints from down the hull, opened a center panel door half way, and peered through.

"Are the rest of the Saints with you?" asked Daniel Roberts. Prince Royce nodded, looked behind and signaled to the rest of his team.

The boys from down the hull, all within the ages of 13 and 15, came from behind the middle door and stood before Daniel Roberts and his friends, and soon the hull way beneath the middle deck was crowded with a group of boys.

They all started arguing as to which team was going to win, when Daniel Roberts gestured to the group to keep it quiet by putting his index finger vertically across his lips. When there was silence, he crept up the stairs, and slowly opened the door to the deck and scanned around him. Satisfied that none of the ship's crewmen was on the deck, he signaled to the group to come up, and beginning with the Yankees, each came on the deck, one after the other.

The sea breeze was warm and gentle, and the ocean was still quiet as the Freedom Star gently rocked through the calmed waters. The boys grouped themselves. The Yankees were gathered at the left side of the deck, with the quarter deck at their rear, while the Saints were huddled at the right side, with their backs facing the bow spirit. In silence, both teams stared at each other.

"Are we going to play this game or what?" Prince Royce asked, breaking the silence, his southern negro accent audible in the mist of the wind that suddenly began to gather. He was the taller of the dark-skinned lads with a bigger body, and a well combed afro hair style.

"Well," sighed Daniel Roberts, looking around, studying the wind as it gradually gathered speed. "Why shouldn't we, when the wind is still good?" Now studying the dark faces before him, "But I don't see your bats and gloves. How are you going to play us?" he queried, raising both shoulders.

"We got them," responded Prince Royce, and then signaled to one of the Saints, Hebert Tolbert, a 13 years old stocky kid, who stepped forward, holding a sac filled with baseball bats, caps, helmets and gloves.

At their respective corners, Joel Findley of the New York Yankees handed his teammates their caps, gloves, and jerseys while Harold Tolbert of the Saints distributed theirs to his teammates.

James Cooper, one of the boys who looked older than the others, was wearing the referee outfit. He carved off the pitch by marking the bases with a chalk, restricting it to the area from the main to the foremast, and all the way to the forecastle.

When he had finished, he clapped his hands twice, and immediately the captains of both teams jogged towards the center of the main deck, now the center of the baseball pitch. Daniel Roberts was representing the New York Yankees, while Prince Royce represented the Saints.

"Okay Guys," after clearing his throat, the referee addressed the two captains before him. "Watch how you strike, and how you make a catch, too. Remember we are playing baseball on the deck of a moving ship. Don't make an attempt when the ball is flying too high over the stern. When it flies overboard, it will be counted as off limits. Hope we've got lots of balls. And so there will be no home runs.

When a team strikes the ball and is missed by the other team, home runs will be given to the batting team, even when it lands on the stern, the port side or the starboard. There will be two outs for a count out."

Looking at the captain of the Yankees, and then the saints, "any question?" he asked.

"Why two outs for a count out, instead of the regular three outs?" queried the captain of the Saints, looking at referee James Cooper with suspicion.

"The late evening hours are fast approaching. And pretty soon, it's going to get dark."

There was silence.

"Okay. If there are no further questions, let's cast lots to determine which team will bat first," said the referee who took a piece of chalk from his pocket.

He turned his back to the two captains, and repeatedly flipped the piece of chalk from one hand to the other. With clenched fists, he faced them, and stretched his hands forward.

"The captain who will select the fist with the chalk, his team will be the first to bat," he said.

Without hesitation, Daniel Roberts was the first to choose a fist, which did not have the chalk, and so the Saints were the first to bat. Then there was the exchange of handshakes between the two captains, and then the referee. After that, the two captains returned to their corners to brief their teammates.

"I am not sure about Cooper," speculated Anthony Russel, the pitcher for the saints.

"Why?" asked Edwin Hayes, a tall kid with large arms, who was the main batter for the Saints. "You think he's going to cheat us?"

"Yeah, he's an urban kid, probably from New York, too."

"Not what I heard his parents told mine," Hebert Tolbert cut in. "I heard them say they are from Mansouri. That's way down south. Never mind he's got fair skin like them too."

"That doesn't mean he will not cheat us," insisted Anthony Russel.

"No, he will not," pressed Herbert Tolbert. "His family has some integrity. His father, once a butler in the house of his slave master, witnessed a murder of his master's father by one of his sons, and testified the whole truth in court. He was later granted his freedom by the young master for such bravery as many slaves won't, on grounds that it was a white man's matter. For fear of his and his family's life, they decided to be re-settled at the Malagueta Coast."

Just then they heard the referee calling the teams on the pitch. Immediately the Saints were gathered at the Mainmast, where they were hitting the ball, while the Yankees took up defensive positions.

Henrique Cassel was the first base man and his substitute in that position was Joel Findley. Albert Coleman jogged to the second baseman position while his brother, David, took Shortstop and his substitution was Harold Findley. Harold Wilson, a tall and lanky kid, took the right fielder position towards the Starboard, while Daniel Roberts took the Center fielder position, at the forecastle deck.

Gabriel Philips became the left fielder towards the port side and Stephen Gardner became the third Baseman. Theodore Johnson, the pitcher for the Yankees, was ready, waiting for referee James Cooper to commence the game.

As for the Saints, Herbert Tolbert, holding his bat with both hands and test swinging it, was set to be the first to strike for his team. It was at the port in New York when the families were boarding the Freedom Star when Tolbert overheard Henrique Cassel telling his friends that the boys from the plantation didn't know how to play baseball because all they did down south was work and get flogged. He told Prince Royce about this and quickly a challenge was sent to Henrique Cassel, encouraging him to organize his team so the boys from the south can teach the boys from the north a lesson.

Referee James Cooper blew a whistle for the match to begin. The pitcher for the Yankees, Theodore Johnson, positioned himself and pitched. Tolbert let the ball pass, because it was not good enough to hit it, and so the referee counted one throw against the Yankees. Three faulty throws will be counted as an out against them. Also, missing three good throws would be counted as an out against the batting team.

Theodore Johnson positioned himself and did another overhand throw. This time Tolbert got it with a decisive hit. The ball flew low and bounced on the wooden deck. it slipped past the pitcher and Stephen Gardner who dived for it, but bumped into each other instead. Henrique Cassel, seeing Tolbert running for first base, yelled, calling for the ball in time to secure the base and make one out.

Before his team mates could scramble for the ball and throw it to him, Tolbert had already touched the first base and took off with an impressive speed for the second base, reaching it in time before Daniel Roberts caught the ball Henrique Cassel threw to him. The first strike of the Saints got them to second base.

Anthony Russel hit the ball, after Theodore's first throw. Its flight was low and tricky. Henrique Cassel ran from first base and dived for it, but it slipped past his hands. The agile Anthony Russel jumped over him and headed for first base, then second base. Tolbert, taking advantage of Henrique Cassel's miss, made his home run, scoring a point for the Saints, amid cheering from his teammates.

While Tolbert was making his home run, Theodore Johnson, who had also made a dive for Anthony Russel's strike, caught the ball before it touched the floor, thus earning one out in favor of the Yankees, who also cheered.

13 years old Horatio Teage struck for the Saints, after a second throw from the Yankees' pitcher. The ball flew high, at the same time spinning. It passed over David Coleman at Shortstop, who jumped for it, but missed. It then headed towards Daniel Roberts, but landed short, before the Yankees' Captain could make a catch while Russel, who was on second base sprinted for the third base and made an inn.

Horatio Teage made it to first base, and attempted to make it for the second base, had Daniel Roberts not finally scooped over for the ball, caught it and ran back to the second base in time to secure it.

Lawrence Freeman for the Saints made a powerful hit at the Yankees' pitcher's first threw. The ball flew low at knee level and spun towards Gabriel Phillips at the Left Fielder position. Staggering backwards towards the port side, he jumped but missed it. This gave Russel the opportunity to make a desperate inn for fourth base, thus earning the second home run for the Saints.

Teage also made it to the second base, leaving the first base for Lawrence Freeman who made an inn, when Henrique Cassel, receiving a long throw from his teammate Daniel Roberts, stepped on the first base, seconds after Freeman landed on it with a long jump.

With Horatio Teage on second base, and Lawrence Freeman on first base, it was time for Edwin Hayes, the marksman for the Saints to bat so that his teammates on the bases should make home runs. On the other hand, the Yankees, down to two runs, were all set to prevent that from happening and to earn the second out, which would be their time to bat.

Just then, the door of the cabin where Elijah Burgess and his wife were lodging, was flipped open and the co-founder and Chief Executive Officer of Color Purpose came hurrying out. Looking disappointed, his face was red. He appeared frightened and confused, like he had discovered something horrible.

He sat on the wooden stair, the same one used by the lads to get to the deck, and buried his head in his palm, sobbing. Rubbing his teary eyes for a while, he winced with disappointment, at the same time pulling his curly hair in frustration. His continence was full of awe.

"How did I get to this point?" he cried. "Oh God! What was I thinking?!"

He looked up at the doorway, brooding over the questions and struggling for self-explanation. Instead, getting on deck to watch the vast Atlantic Ocean which would help evoke a piece of mind, was the only option he considered. So, he got up and climbed the stairs that led to the main deck. But when he got there, he was surprised to see a group of kids who had sneaked out of their cabins, playing baseball.

The Findley brothers, squatting at the far side of the mainmast, reserved for substitutes, were the first to see him. Then he looked at both teams on the deck field pitch. Suddenly, a gust of wind blew his face.

He was startled; this was leading to a gradual build up which in no time would turn into a strong ocean wind. It wasn't safe to be on the main deck at this time. The kids were in danger. Before he could tell them to call off the game and hurry back inside, Theodore Johnson had thrown the ball, and Edwin Hayes made a powerful hit.

The ball flew overhead, far beyond the reach of the Yankees, as they jumped, stretching their hands to catch it. Then it flew towards Daniel Roberts, who kept skipping backwards towards the forecastle deck to catch it while Anthony Russel, Horatio Teage, and Lawrence Freeman made home runs.

But instead, the ball flew over the Yankees' captain, and took a right turn as it spun and started descending and appeared like it was going to land on the top of the gunwale. The referee James Cooper, the rest of the Yankees, including the Saints who were celebrating their home runs when Edwin Hayes finally made it home, suddenly stopped and started yelling, calling unto Daniel Roberts to leave the ball as it was going to pass over the gunwale and drop into the ocean below.

But the Yankees captain, racing sideways, had followed the ball, and had jumped too high, and caught it. But while landing, the back of his knees hit the starboard, causing him to flip overboard. He went down somersaulting and yelling with the ball in his glove, and then plunged into the water.

"Get the captain!" screamed Elijah Burgess, running across the deck, towards the starboard.

Immediately, Prince Royce and Henri Cassel raced towards the quarter deck, screaming the captain's name.

Breathing heavily, he looked down into the water and saw the kid struggling to keep himself afloat, calling up to him for help. The Color Purpose CEO looked around him to see whether he could find a robe, tie a knot at the end and throw it into the water so the kid can swim towards it and grab it. Then he would pull him out of the water.

Unfortunately, there was none, but only the rigging supporting the masts, and holding the seals tight against the poles. He looked down again into the water, when he heard Daniel, again calling for help with an increasingly frightened voice.

"Oh no!" he cried as the vessel was sailing away from the kid who was desperately swimming toward the lower stern to keep a safe distance.

The sea breeze was now blowing heavily, and the gentle waves were getting rough, and Daniel was battling with them, as he frantically threw one arm after the other at the same time kicking his legs back and forth to try to catch up with the vessel.

A huge wave was formed coming his way, but the lad took a dive so that it could roll over him. He emerged, spitting out a huge quantity of salt water, and again looked up to Elijah Burgess and cried for help.

"Get back to your parents! It's getting dangerous out here!" he yelled at the rest of the boys, fear stricken and huddled at the Starboard.

They were standing on their toes, with their cheeks pressed against the gunwale, trying to see what was happening to Daniel Roberts in the water.

"Where is the captain?" he looked back towards the quarter deck and asked, when he did not see the captain and any of the crewmen.

Some of the boys attempted to run across the deck to the door that led down to the hull way to the cabins, but the ocean winds had gathered strength and the waves had risen to new heights, causing the Freedom Star to rock violently.

As the rigging rattled and slapped against the masts, the sails and flying jibs were now flipping intensively, putting pressure on the main and foremast. Elijah Burgess' heart suddenly leapt, when he heard the top mainmasts and the top foremast cracking like they were going to break.

If this happens, the lower masts will follow, and fall overboard. This will create a drag for the vessel and it will lean sideways and eventually capsize. It was then he realized that captain James Newton

Summerville would not come. He was heavily engaged, trying to steer the Freedom Star out of the coming storm while the kid was still in the water, battling against the angrily rising waves.

The winds were now blowing heavily, causing splitters of water on the deck as the ocean waves got angrier and were smashing the hull of the vessel. Again, Burgess' heart leapt, this time more severely when it occurred to him that continual splattering of cubic centimeter of waters will flood the deck and add more weight to the vessel which will cause it to sink.

The boys, full of fear, were now sitting on the floor, drenched. Their hands folded. They were shivering so severely that their teeth were chattering as the weather turned cooler by the minutes.

Extremely wet, himself, Elijah Burgess again looked down the water, and saw that the Vessel was leaving Daniel Roberts behind.

The kid now looked exhausted and panic stricken. For every rough wave he encountered, he would go under and emerge back on the surface, spitting out water, sometimes lung full. This was getting dangerous for the kid, and any moment, he was going to drown.

The successful colored business executive looked back towards the quarter deck again, and yet, no member of the crew had arrived. Then he noticed that the vessel was slowing down, and then it occurred to him that they were dropping the anchor. But he needed to do something fast, as the situation in the water below was becoming fatal by the minutes. He took out his shoes, and left his socks on him.

"When the crew comes, tell them I am going to save the boy. They will know what to do," he said to the frightened boys.

Then he climbed on the gunwale of the starboard, folded the sleeves of the white square Cut Frill Lawn cotton shirt he was wearing, and took a frog leap into the rough ocean.

With water flashing in his face, and making it impossible to see and to breathe, he managed to swim towards Daniel. Sometimes a wave would build up and become rough, and when it had swollen to full height and rolled, the force would drift the kid further away from the Freedom Star, which dangerously swayed from one side to another. But Elijah Burgess continued to swim towards the kid as the swelling waves would raise them up and down like they were riding a swing.

"Keep using your legs, and rest your arms," he called out to Daniel, who had gotten too exhausted from throwing his arms.

He had gotten near the kid, and was surprised that so far Daniel had done well to keep himself afloat, battling against the angry waves. His objective now was to circle around him to hold him from the back, a safe thing to do when rescuing someone from drowning or else the panic-stricken person would hold firmly unto you and pull both of you under the water.

Applying a great deal of effort, he finally managed to achieve his objective by reaching him from the back and gently grabbing the kid under his armpit.

On the deck, some of the sailors arrived, and quickly two of them were helping the rest of the boys to safely get back inside the ship, two at a time. The other sailors were at the coxswain assembly, trying to release one of the lifeboats to lower it down into the water, which they quickly abandoned because it was too dangerous. In such a storm, the situation was severe; any attempt to lower the lifeboat, the ferocious waves hitting the hull of the ship would wash away the rescue crewman.

However, Jack Duvall, one of the crewmen who was noted for hunting sharks at deep sea, suddenly came up with an idea. Before inserting an arrow into his crossbow, he tied a white deflectable circular tube to the head of the arrow with a long rope. Then, the experienced underwater fisherman climbed on the bow spirit, with ropes tied around his waist to hold him firmly against the strong winds. He carefully crawled almost towards the end while the other crew were at the upper stern holding the end of the long robe attached to the arrowhead.

He waited until the rocking of the ship eased a bit. Then he shot the crossbow. It flew with the deflectable circular tube towards Burgess and the boy and landed close to them. The crew at the stern holding the robes, tied the end to the foremast so that it doesn't drop into the water. Holding Daniel Roberts under both armpits with one hand, Elijah Burgess made frantic effort to swim to the tube. When the kid had held onto it with both hands, the Color Purpose CEO took a dive and emerged from Daniel's rear. With his head between the kid's legs, he shoved him into the tube.

"You gotta hold on tight to the robes. They will pull you out of the water," he assured the kid, wiping the water from his face with his right hand, while the other held onto the tube.

Watching this development from the bow spirit, Jack Duval signaled to the crew holding the robes to start pulling. As they did, Elijah Burgess, with the rest of his body still in the water, held onto the tube as it was gradually pulled. Because of the strong wind and rough waves, causing them to rise, sometimes about 20 meters high and down into the water, it took little time for the crew on deck to pull them to the base of the stern.

Burgess then left the tube, when Daniel clung on to the robes with both legs wrapped around it. Carefully, the crew began to pull him all the way up the gunwale, and the kid finally landed on the deck. Next, a thick blanket was wrapped around him, and he was hurried off to the infirmary.

Seeing that the kid was finally rescued, while he remained in the water flipping his hands and throwing his legs to keep him afloat, Burgess closed his eyes and took a deep breath of relief and waited for his time to be pulled out of the water.

The tube was lowered half way down the stern, when suddenly he noticed that he was unable to move his legs which he was using to keep him afloat. The next moment he felt a cramp at the back of his neck, and soon his arms became heavy and he was unable to move them. The tube landed next to him, but he was unable to swim to it.

"Hold onto the tube, so we can pull you up, sir!" cried Jack Duval.

But the Color Purpose CEO was unresponsive. His eyes were stretched with bewilderment. A powerful wave came and rolled him, tossing him up and down. Jack Duval, and the other crew were screaming as the motionless body of Elijah Burgess rolled with the wave for some time and then went under.

Captain James Newton Summerville was at the quarter deck, standing at the observation post, mounted midway of the mizzen masts with his left leg curled between the robes that hoisted the Mizzen Sails. He was scanning the rough and open sea ahead of him, spying into the telescope he held to his right eye with his right hand, while the other held firmly onto the wooden rails barricading the cubical frame of the post to balance himself against the stormy winds.

Standing by him, firmly holding onto the robes with both hands, as it swayed in obedience of the winds, was his boatswain Jimmy Penhurst, waiting for orders. Down at the wheels was Alan Gables, the coxswain, steering the Freedom Star as he struggled to navigate the vessel through the storm that had dramatically gotten more severe.

The retired Navy officer looked up at a homemade wind vane, a small rotor made of fine wood, fused into what looked like bearings, with a 15 inches long pole inserted into it and attached to the mast. He was studying how fast it was spinning as a result of the strong wind, to enable him to estimate the wind speed. The rotor was spinning faster than before, as the little instrument emitted a whining sound. This was enough to inform the captain that there was a buildup of an extremely powerful wind ahead. Very soon, they are going to expect a massive storm.

"Maintain course anti-clockwise, and steady the bow towards the tide," drenched, and with his brown lawn ruffle shirt and Callard flipping to the gusting wind, he called down to Gables, who could highly hear him.

"Aye, Captain. But we do need speed, sir!" shouting back, acknowledged the old and experienced British Coxswain.

"Pull the anchor," the captain then instructed Jimmy Penhurst. "And add more flying jibs. We need full propulsion to get out of the way of the storm that's coming."

Penhurst hurriedly, but carefully descended the ladder that led up to the captain's observation post to convey the orders to the crew at the Forecastle deck who were working to rescue Elijah Burgess.

Gables executed the captain's instruction to steer the vessel to where the wave and wind were less intense. Plowing through the rough tide with the bow head on, may prevent the angry waves from striking the hull of the vessel, and adding more pressure on the masts.

"Initiate the drag," again commanded Captain Gables, who in turn signaled to two crewmen, Lien Dole, and the American, Alex Cox, standing a few feet from him.

They hurried to the middle of the bow. The next moment they were winding a double pulley which loosened a neatly arranged series of robes whose end was fastened around a heavy and gigantic iron bulb. As they did, the bulb was rolled into an opening and lowered all the way down to the bottom. It passed through an opening and entered the water beneath the keel.

"Pull the anchor! Pull the anchor!" yelled Penhurst, entering the forecastle desk through a narrow hallway compartment that separated it from the main deck.

"Burgess is still in the water!" cried Howard Lustig, one of the British crewmen. "He couldn't hold the tube. I am afraid something must have happened to him just when it landed in the water."

"What?!"

"I think he got a seizure and was unable to throw his arms and legs and went down!"

"What about the boy?!"

"He's safe."

"We got to pull the anchor," Insisted the Boatswain, with his face sunken and tears in his eyes in reaction to the bad news. "There's a far worse storm ahead which is going to crash upon us in the next 20 minutes." We got to save the people on board."

Lustig ran towards the stern.

"We are about to pull the anchor," he called out to Jack Duvall, who was still lying-in wait on the bowsprit with his crossbow in aiming position. Should Elijah Burgess emerge, he would aim for his thigh, the only option available, and try to pull him towards the stern and figure out a way to get him back on deck.

"Need a little time to see whether the CEO will emerge. He would not be drifting too far as the waves are circling," the shark hunter partially turned sideways and responded.

"There's a far worse storm coming. We cannot risk the boat, the crew and passengers."

Duvall then pressed his head against the wooden pole of the bow spirit and closed his eyes in respect to the fallen CEO of Color Purpose who he had worked with for many years. Then he signaled to the crew to pull the ropes tied around his waist, at the same time gently easing himself backwards towards the forecastle deck.

"Drop the buoys," Penhurst managed to say, when Duvall had descended the bowsprit, looking dejected. "With luck, we will be able to find his body floating when the storm subsides."

The crewmen were now working frantically to protect the vessel from the coming storm. Some of them were at the quarter deck, pulling the anchor out of the water, while the others were climbing the foremast to hoist the additional flying jib. Duvall and three other crew men were throwing buoys into the water to mark the spot where Burgess went under. When the storm subsides, they will row back in the life boat to search and pick up his body, which they hope would be floating in the water in the immediate perimeters around the buoys.

Jimmy Penhurst then ran down the hallway to ensure that Benjamin Coffey, the Ship's Steward boy was up and down the cabins warning people to stay inside and remain stripped to their bunks. He was surprised that the kid, who is seldom idle, was nowhere around, prompting him to marvel at the question: how come the boys managed to sneak all the way to the main deck to play baseball, unnoticed.

"Hey open up, Ben," reaching the steward's quarter, the boatswain pounded the door, but there was no response from inside the cabin.

After some vigorous hammering, Benjamin Coffey suddenly unbolted his cabin door and waddled before the Boatswain, almost stumbling when the vessel rocked.

"Aye, Sir," he said in a drowsy voice and then belched, his breath, oozing out a stench of strong liquor.

"You smell of stale rum, and have abandoned your duty in the midst of a deadly storm."

"Sorry, sir. I was tricked by the Findley brothers who told me that their mother produces non-alcoholic rum."

"The captain will hear this. But for now, put yourself together and go down to the passengers to advise them to remain confined in their cabins. There's a very dangerous storm approaching."

"Aye, sir," said the Steward boy who then rushed to his face basin, grabbed and turned the faucet knob clockwise and water came pouring out.

Jimmy Penhurst watched, as the 18 years old steward boy washed his face, and brushed his teeth like he had just awoken from bed early in the morning. Then he reached for his Oil Lantern, hanging at the far-left corner of his cabin, and sat it on the small round table. He hurried into the small compartment where hung his clothes and got his black frock coat and flung it on.

Penhurst had already left when Ben reached his door with his lantern in his hand. He shut it and made for the passengers' lodge close to the upper deck.

Ben, as Benjamin Coffey was called, was born into slavery. He was just two years old when his mother died and his father ran away, leaving poor Ben with his slave master, John Coffey, an old and frail apple merchant who owned a large apple farm near the state of Maine.

At the age of 14, just before old John Coffey died, he and the other slaves were sold to a slave merchant, but Ben freedom was bought from this slave merchant by Captain Summerville, once on a summer day while the retired Navy officer visited a secret slave trading site somewhere in New York, just before the state had started enforcing the slavery abolition laws. Captain Summerville took to him and the boy has since been part of many of his voyages intercepting slaves' ships on the Atlantic.

He reached the first layer of the cabin quarters, just before the quarter deck and knocked on the door of the Burgess, but was surprised to see it open. He peeped through the narrow space between the door and the frame, and saw Angela, the wife of the Color Purpose CEO sitting with her face down at the mahogany desk. Like a peacock's tail, her long hair was spread all over the desk.

"Mrs. Burgess," he called, but she did not answer, and neither lifted her head to look his way. That was odd, he thought, but he must do his duty.

"Please remember to be strapped to your bed. There's a bad storm coming," he said and closed the door with ease.

Still on this level of the ship, he hurried past the crewmen's cabin. He didn't need to stop and knock on each door to warn or possibly drill an occupant on what to do about the coming storm, because he was going to find none of them. They were all on deck, doing what they do best, bracing the vessel for the monstrous winds.

Just before entering the little hull way to his right to get to the other quarters, located directly beneath the main deck, he felt the vessel swayed. He buckled, and almost threw the lantern down, but quickly balanced himself by holding the wooden wall of the hull way.

"The storm is fast at hand," he muttered.

The first cabin door he knocked on was the Findley's. At the third knock, he heard the hitches cracking and then the door was flung open. Mrs. Pricilla Findley, a fair and puffy woman with gray hair pressed and folded at the back of her neck forming a ponytail, stood before him. With her meaty hands stretched, she was holding both sides of the door frames.

"Good for nothing Ben," she barked. "Where were you when my boys were on that God forsaken deck, playing baseball?"

The Steward boy did not flinch, but rather looked over her shoulders. He saw Joel Findley and his brother, Harold kneeling down, and sweating profusely. Their hands were stretched, holding tons of books they were struggling to prevent from falling, or else, it was going to be a long and difficult night. Their little sister, Aberdeen Findley was at the table near what was used as the kitchen, rolling dough.

"That's not necessary now, Maim. There's a nasty storm coming and it's best that your kids are strapped to their bunk beds."

"God damn-it," she wailed, almost tumbling, before Ben could end his words, when there was a violent shake, and the vessel appeared like it was about to capsize.

Mrs. Findley slammed the door, with a force so severe that it hit the door frame, rattling it, and flinging it open again. With her heavy footsteps stomping the wooden floor, she raced to her bed, yelling at her children to stop what they were doing and hurry to their bunk beds.

"You need to shut your door, Mrs. Findley," the Steward boy suggested, calmly.

"You devil of a Harold, get up and go shut that door," she screamed.

Immediately, Harold Findley, who was fastening his bunk belt around his waist, suddenly stopped, jumped down from his bed, and raced towards the cabin door.

"I am sorry," he whispered, looking nervously at Ben.

Benjamin Coffey looked back at him with no expression on his face. The Findley were the first family to arrive at the New York Harbor to board the Freedom Star, a week before the time for departure. Harold and his brother were the first two lads he met and made friends with them.

Their Father Joseph Findley, a free man, had died two months earlier, and left his family a huge fortune. He was a successful wine brewer, whose father was a Sailor named Owen Findley, who served for many years in the British Navy. He had Joseph Findley by a beautiful recaptured slave girl in the mid-Atlantic when a fleet of British and American war ships intercepted a band of slave ships sailing from the West African Coast.

He married this slave girl who he named Amanda because he was unable to pronounce her long African name and took her to his uncles' Sir Edwin Findley, who owned a large grape vine in the hills of Massachusetts. Few years after Joseph Findley was born, his father, now Sir Owen Findley, was killed in one of the fiercest battles at sea when the British frigate, the Royal Blue Oak he was commanding was plowed into by a huge slave vessel. Joseph Findley grew up with his mother and his Grand uncle Sir Edwin Findley on the orchards where he learned to prune grapes and later brew wine.

Joel and Harold, learning that their grandfather was a sailor who died at sea, loved ships and the sea and so Benjamin Coffey, their new friend, showed them in and around the Freedom Star. But when the lads met to discuss how possible it is to play a baseball match on the deck without being caught, the Findley brothers offered to seduce the Steward Boy with a specially brewed wine that their mother made for reducing stress by keeping people at sleep for long hours. The boys also offered to show the teams how to get to the deck.

"You need to hurry back to your bunk," responded Benjamin Coffey, plunging Harold into a few seconds of thought, his expression apprehensive that he and his brother had lost a good friend and their dreams of knowing more about the sea, squashed. He was about to close the door and bolt it, but Benjamin Coffey held it.

"You and your brother should have just told me, if you wanted to play baseball on the deck," he said with a faint smile, turned and hurried off.

Not sure that Benjamin would forgive them for their actions, as he may not have yet known that Daniel Roberts fell overboard, Harald closed, and bolted the door. As he hurried to his bunk bed, his eyes, full of regrets, were on his brother Joel. They had screw up with their friend.

In the cabin of the Roberts, Mrs. Mary Roberts, Daniel's mother, stood at the opened door, after Ben's second knock. She was slim and fair in complexion with a white hair pressed down the side of her face and the back of her neck. On the sides of her neck were the green outline of her veins.

The steward boy peeped into the cabin to observe whether the Roberts were observing precautionary measures for the coming storm, which he thought by now they should be aware of as the vessel continued to rock and sway. He saw Daniel lying on his bunk, wrapped in a thick quill. His father, Mr. Jason Roberts was sitting on the table with his reading glasses on, writing something. The fair and tall old man looked towards the door, then focused back on his desk, and continued to write.

"Had it not been for Mr. Burgess, our son was going to drown today," she said with a worried face. "We wanted to go and thank him."

"I am sorry to hear this, Mrs. Roberts, and thank God. But that won't be necessary now. There's a dangerous storm coming, and I advise that you be strapped in your bunks."

Mrs. Roberts nodded and shut the door behind her.

Ben had covered the entire first and second layer of the ship, making sure that the passengers were observing safety measures and embracing themselves for the coming storm. He was now down at the hull. He first met two teenagers, around 18 years, Derrick Hart and Henrietta Patmore, standing opposite each other at their respective cabins doors, conversing. He told them it was dangerous to be standing outside of their cabins. It was best to get inside with their parents and be safe.

After the two love birds had reluctantly parted ways, he entered the cafeteria of the main hull. He was startled to see some of the passengers, mainly women and children, gathered, singing and dancing. There were few men among them, beating drums and playing guitar.

Benjamin Coffey tried to call them to attention, but they kept singing, dancing and jumping around. Very disappointed that they were making his job difficult, he stood watching, until they were finished singing and dancing. Then, Charles Gooding III, a young, tall man with bushy hair, wearing a black frock coat and white ruffle shirt stood on a table in the middle of the gathering. He held a black Bible in his hands, which he opened and began flipping through the pages.

"My fellow brothers and sisters in the Lord," he called unto them. "We must keep our faith in what the scriptures say, and never be deterred, no matter what."

"Excuse me, sir," Ben interrupted, after a roar of Amen.

"You shut up and listen to the word of God, little man," in her heavy southern accent, hissed, Barbara Newland, a woman who was standing next to him.

"The Bible says in Psalm 23 verse 4 that 'Even though I walk through the valley of the shadow of death, I will fear no evil, for you are with me,'" The man resumed, sounding like a southern Baptist preacher. This was followed by a roar of 'Amen', again. "And it goes on to say," he continued, "for your rod and your staff, they comfort me." There was another roar of Amen.

"But let me assure you, my dear brothers and sisters. This vessel will never capsize in the mist of the coming storm. For I know our Lord and Savior Jesus will deliver us through this danger, just as he calmed the storm when He and His disciples were crossing the sea of Galilee in a boat. So, you have to hold on to your faith."

"Hold on," the group responded.

"Hold on to your faith," the man said and continued in a melodious tone. "For the devil is using this for you to lose your faith in God. Hold on to your faith, as it may seem gloomy now. For a brighter day is ahead."

"Hold on."

Benjamin Coffey stood looking at the group as the man continued to preach while his audience, mainly the women, were jumping about and shouting as they responded to him in a frenzy.

Because the planks that formed the hull of the ship were fitted with cotton and long fibers that trap bouncing sound waves, it was difficult to hear the angry waves crashing on it. And so, the passengers down the hull did not know how rough the sea was becoming. With this thought and still holding his lantern, the steward boy made his way through the group and stood at the table where the man was preaching.

"Please give me your attention," he screamed, suddenly cutting the man off. "There's a dangerous storm coming and it's safe that you get to your respective bunk beds.

Everyone stood and looked at Benjamin. Part of what they were told before boarding the Freedom Star was to listen to the steward boy and any of the crewmen, whenever there was an emergency.

Suddenly, there was a howl, causing everyone to gasp, and hold their breath when the vessel turned in a zig, toppling Charles Gooding III from the table, and landing on the plank floor on his back. There was another one, rattling the shelves in the small kitchen behind the counter where food was served. The plates, spoons and forks were falling.

Benjamin docked, halfway scooping and gestured to everyone to do likewise and to remain calm. Charles Gooding III attempted to get off the ground, but Ben beckoned him to remain where he was.

"The coxswain is dodging the dangerous waves," he hissed, his voice calmed, and audible in the now quiet cafeteria. "Okay, you all can now go to your cabins and be strapped to your bunks. Make sure no sharp object is hanging on the wall, lest they fall off and wound you," he instructed, after waiting for a few minutes and was sure that there wasn't going to be another swing.

"Take your time; take your time," he repeated as everyone rushed through the door of the cafeteria.

Ben remained in the cafeteria after everyone had left. He reached over to the serving counter. Stretching his lantern forward, he peered into the kitchen. Something on the wall near a wooden box caught his eyes, causing him to raise the wick to see clearly.

He walked slowly towards the passage that led to the kitchen, lifted the bar, entered and got behind the serving counter. He then made his way to the box, at the far-right wall that also formed part of the ship's inner hull, skipping over the wooden bowls, spoons and cups scattered on the floor.

Crouching, he brought the lantern close to the wall to clearly look at what he saw. It was a splash of cooking oil that may have spilled when a bottle fell from the shelf. Ben had thought that the outer hull had started to leak which could have been strange, because the hull was reinforced with tar made of tree resin, solid enough for waterproofing.

After looking around for some time, satisfied, he walked to the pantry, tested the door and saw that it was opened. He entered, and walked to a small door ahead, opened it and descended a narrow wooden stair that curved its way down a basement where he could hear the underwater hitting the kneel of the ship, wondering why this part of the vessel did not have sound proof.

From the stairs, he reached a narrow hallway. He walked through it for some time, at the same time inspecting the wall for leaks, until he reached another door, opened it and entered the cargo hold.

"We need a hand here, kid," Owen Duffy, one of the crewmen who was responsible for the cargo hold, looked up to him and spoke.

He and three other crewmen, John Macalister and Terry Pipes, both Americans and Jerry Smith, a British, were re-arranging the cargo, by rolling and placing on top of each other, equal number of drums filled with oil, on either side of the hull to help balance the vessel, as it swayed in the midst of the storm.

Benjamin Coffey lent a helping hand. In a couple of minutes, they had finished arranging the remaining drums, covering them with nets made of thick robes whose ends were attached firmly to hook-like fasteners on both walls to bind them together to prevent the drums from slipping off when the vessel rocks.

The Freedom Star began to sway and rock more violently. Duffy and team, bracing themselves by holding onto the hook-like fasteners, waited to see whether the drums and the rest of the cargo were tightly held together in the nets.

Satisfied, and with their eyes still on the drums, they retired to a compartment that was separated from the cargo area by a waist-high wooden wall where they strapped themselves to rows of small bunks. Should the rocking of the vessel become too severe for the nets to hold the cargo together, they would hurry there in time to re-enforce the grip by adding and fastening another layer of the nets.

In his final sweep of the vessel to ensure that all was intact, Ben had left the cargo hold and made his way back to the passengers' section in the hull, taking careful steps and occasionally holding the hook-like fasteners on the wall with one hand, while the other held onto the lantern, as the vessel continued to rocked and swayed.

As he did, he would reach an Oil Lamp hanging on the wall and blow the flames out so that when the vessel sways and rocks, they should not fall off and set the wooden floor ablaze.

When he had swept the entire passengers section from the hall to the ones near the upper deck, he reached the door of the Burgess, tested it and saw that it was now locked; Mr. Elijah Burgess may have left the deck while he was down at the hull, and bolted the door, he thought. He yarned and made his way to his cabin as the Freedom Star continued to sway and rock violently.

Deep into the late evening hours, the forces of nature had risen to an unprecedented level. The sea breeze had taken the form of a hurricane, drifting the Freedom Star from its westerly course. Exerting the adrenaline to overcome fear, anxiety and exhaustion, when facing danger at sea, Captain Summerville and his crew were against all odds, working overtime to save the ship and the passengers on board.

The Navy Cross and Purple Heart veteran was still at the observation post, along with one of his crewmen, his fellow American, Harry Reginald, observing the rough and dark open sea. The wind vane was spinning ferociously, whining and deafening to the ears as the wind intensified. It was battering the captain and his crew, twisting the flesh around their faces, making it difficult for them to breathe, and almost tearing off their clothes. This was enough to tell Captain Summerville that more severe storms were on the way.

He nodded to Reginald, who looked to be in his early twenties with brown hair and spotty face. The young crewman was fastened to a bar attached to the mizzen mast by a belt holding him firmly from the back to prevent him from being swept away by the strong wind.

Receiving the signal, he turned the mouth of a 4 feet long movable cannon towards the sky. Then he inserted a small combustible canister into the mouth, wound a zigzag shaped winder attached at the end, four times, and then there was a pop.

A fireball was shot and later exploded into flares that lighted the skies, enabling the captain and crew at the wheel to clearly see ahead of them. With the flying jib, and the rest of the sails, not fully completed to gain full throttle, Captain Summerville wasn't sure how far the winds have drifted them off course, but he was aware that they were sailing in the none-sea route of the Atlantic, where mountainous rocks and huge reefs were abundant. At any moment the Freedom Star will crash on one of them, if care wasn't taken.

The captain was also certain of another thing. This was the part of the sea where pirates and slave vessels, evading the joint patrol of British and American Battleships, docked or lay in wait. Or, in some instances, from where they stage attacks on re-captured slaves' ships at high sea.

For now, that was the least of his worries, as it would be foolhardy for pirates or rogue slave merchants to launch an attack in such a vicious storm. He would worry about the pirates and slave merchants later, when he had dealt with the most pressing challenge, saving the Freedom Star and all on board.

Unfortunately, the vessel was not designed to fight off such attacks. His only reliance was the possibility of the British or American Navies, intercepting and preventing the attacks, should they occur.

Before setting sail, the sea route and possible alternative routes were communicated to both navies, a procedure set to save guide against the pirates and rogue slave merchants. Now that they have drifted far from their course, the captain wasn't sure that they would be on time to rescue them.

Just before the first one doused off, Harris Reginald had fired another bulb, which exploded into another flare. All still looked good, the captain observed. He looked down at Gables and the other crewmen at the quarter deck and nodded to them, with the continence on his face conveying the 'so far so good' message.

The coxswain nodded back at the captain, as he spun the wheels, and occasionally bracing himself against the winds. The oversized clothes on his lean body were drenched and flipping in the direction of the winds, when suddenly there was a heavy downpour.

"Sea mount ahead! sea mount ahead!" suddenly shouted Reginald, pointing ahead of him.

Captain Summerville also saw it through his telescope, but could not make it up entirely, when the flare doused and it got dark again. Reginald fired another one. By now the visibility of the huge rock protruding out of the ocean was clearer. it was about 40 feet ahead of them. Frightening of all, the vessel was heading directly towards it, and, worst still, the flare doused prematurely as the rain intensified. This doesn't occur, unless the particular canister that was fired, had malfunctioned.

The downpour became heavier. The droplets were pelting and pricking their skins like needles. Immediately, another one was fired, but this time it failed to explode in the air as the vessel sailed faster towards the mountainous rock.

The captain however spotted another sea mount through the emittance of the glow when the flare canister was fired. It stood about 30 ft apart from the first one.

The Freedom Star was now sailing blindly in the heavy downpour, and would crush into the mountainous rocks on either side and smash the bow into pieces. In split seconds, Harris Reginald hastily inserted a piston mob into the flare cannon. The 4 ft rod with a thick round sponge at the tip was designed to drain out the water droplets that may have entered and caused the fireball not to explode into flares. Not sure whether he had drained out all the droplets, as time wasn't in their favor, he hurriedly inserted another canister and fired it.

The ship was about 20 ft away from the rocks, when the flare lit the sky. Any attempt to dodge either sea mount, the vessel was going to crash on the other one, which the flare has clearly shown to be a twin rock fused together and covered with seaweed.

The situation was dire. There was limited time for the coxswain to estimate, by instinct, the angle, and the exact path to take to maneuver the ship through, without crashing the keel on the under-water rocks attached to the big ones, and damaging the rudder. This would cause leaking at the bottom, and with the loss of propulsion, the Freedom Star would be left to the mercy of the wind. It would sink very fast, with no time to lower the lifeboats to get the passengers out.

All sailors have no fear in their DNA, but at times, fear beseech the bravest of them, when women, children, the sick and or the elderly are on board in such a situation, unlike when piloting a battleship with only trained and experienced navy personnel on board. This was the first time in the captain's career to have experienced such fear.

In his own view, the accolades of a decorated retired Navy Officer were at stake, when the essence of which was now about to be put to test. From spending a chunk of his career intercepting the slave vessels across the Atlantic to now embarking on another aspect of the noble cause, repatriating free slaves to the land of their forefathers, a success of his first mission, ever, was the ultimate accolade he had envisioned.

As Harris Reginald, popped another flare in the torrential downpour that was rapidly flooding the deck with cubic of centimeters of sea water, adding more weight to the vessel and compounding the dire situation at hand, the captain closed his eyes, as Gables, unsure that he had gotten the right angle, steered the vessel between the two mountainous rocks.

"I think we've got it, Captain," shouted coxswain, breathing with relief.

The captain opened his eyes just as Reginald fired another flare, and saw that they were sailing through the seamounts safely, but listening attentively to detect whether both sides of the vessel's hull were scraping against the wall of the rocks. He could see the twin rocks, and sea crabs and other small crawling sea creatures on them. He wouldn't be surprised if they were part of the menu of pirates and rogue slave merchants. After a few minutes, they safely sailed through the rocks.

"Steer 90 degrees west," commanded the captain, squinting his eyes as he looked at a compass. "And activate the drainage."

"Aye, sir, " responded Gables, and signaled to Lien Dole and Alex Cox who suddenly got on their knees at opposite sides of the ankle-high flooded deck, locating and removing the 24 square inches wooden slats that covered the drainages.

As the other crewmen at the forecastle deck got the message, and did likewise, water from the deck began to flow through openings beneath it, and poured out through tiny holes on both sides of the hull, located beneath the gunwale. The water began to recede rapidly, even with the continuous downpour, and the once ankle-level inundated deck was visible again.

Captain Summerville's aim was to direct the vessel back on open sea. Sailing in the mist of mountainous rocks can be dangerous because the strong winds can force the vessel to drift off and crash on the huge rocks. And this is not a safe place to be when encountering a severe storm.

The Freedom Star had turned westward and had gained full propulsion when the crewmen had hoisted additional flying jibs and top foresails. At the same time Captain Summerville was on the lookout for where the wind and storm were building to avoid them.

Ahead of them, he saw a heavy storm fast approaching in their direction, causing the buildup of huge waves of more than 50 feet high, but the vessel was at its full throttle and was sailing fast and out of its path. Thanks in part that they were now in the open sea.

Unfortunately, Gables was slightly changing course southwest when the bobstay, holding the bow spirit down, snapped. This caused the spar to latch upwards, taking the bobstay with it and wrinkling the flying jibs and the top foresails. With the loss of buoyancy, and the diminishing of propulsion, the Freedom Star suddenly spun, its stern now facing the coming storm.

The passengers who were awake and experienced the sudden spin of the ship, started screaming. This made the others who were asleep, mainly the children, to awake and also started screaming. Captain Summerville estimated that the storm had come within 50 feet of the vessel. With the stern, the weakest part of the Freedom Star in its path, the entire quarter deck would smash in, taking with it the cabins below, and washing away the occupants, if the waves splashed against it.

"It's the bobstay, sir," shouted Howard Lusting, looking up at the bobstay hanging on the bowsprit. He had to cup his hands around his mouth so that the boatswain who was standing behind him should hear his voice through the gusting wind.

"We need to pull the bow spirit back and reinforce the bolts," suggested Jimmy Penhurst, also looking up and cupping his hands around his mouth to be audible.

Lusting wasted no time to adjust the safety belt around his wrist which was fastened on the wooden bar beneath the gunwale from within to prevent the wind from blowing him away. Secured, he struggled to climb the wooden ladder attached to the mizzen mast. With great effort, he managed to reach the top.

He stretched his hands down to Penhurst, who handed him a long pole with clippers at the end. Lusting managed to fasten himself to the pole of the mizzen mast with the safety belt, and then tried to get hold of the two small irons attached to the bolt from both sides. But it was proving difficult because it was still raining and the wind was blowing heavily.

The storm was now some 40 ft within reach of the ship while Lusting was still struggling to grab the irons attached to the bolt with the clippers. After several pain-taken efforts, he finally got it. The next moment, he used a robe from around his waist to tie the end of the pole that held the clippers and sent it down to the Boatswain. Three other crewmen joined Jimmy Penhurst to pull the bobstay down along with the spar of the bowsprit.

Fortunately, they managed to re-enforce the bolt by adding a bigger one to make it heavy enough to hold the bow spirit and the spar down. When they released it, the flying jib and top mizzen sails unfolded. The Freedom Star was now able to regain full throttle just in time when the storm was within 20 ft from the ship.

With no time to veer from the path, Gables, on Captain Summerville's orders, engaged the battering waves with the bow head on. All the sailors on deck were strapped to their safety belts, including Lusting who had hurriedly slid down the mast to embrace himself for the impact of the huge wave.

It finally landed, crashing on the bow, causing no damage because this was the strongest part of the ship. Gables plowed the vessel through the descending waves, raising the Freedom Star into the air, and back down its crest.

The vessel swayed, leaning on one side to the other, causing objects hanging on the walls to fall as women and children screamed. If Owen Duffy and John Macalister had not re-arranged and balanced the cargo, the vessel would have had no center of gravity, and it was going to capsize.

On the deck, some of the sails hoisted on the main, fore and mizzen masts began to shred, due to tension from the strong wind. Again, the vessel began to lose full propulsion, slowing it down. But Jimmy Penhurst and crew were working tirelessly, taking them down one after the other, and in some cases, patching some of them, and replacing the severely damaged ones by hoisting the ones they managed to patch, back up on the masts.

Meanwhile in the ship, Benjamin Coffey was again making his rounds, this time with Doctor Lewis Reid, the ship's physician. From floor to floor, they were roaming the hallways, opening cabin doors to check on the frightened passengers.

In such a storm, in which the motion was rough and unbearable, it sometimes causes vomiting, and shock, and in many cases can lead to fatality. Some of the passengers were already experiencing these sea-hazards symptoms. Where the situation wasn't grave, Dr. Reid would allow Ben, who he had trained to certain extent, some sea-hazard first aid techniques, to do the checks alone, but the situation at hand needed the intervention of a certified sea physician like him.

The old and frail physician, who hours earlier had worked on Daniel Roberts when he was rescued from the sea, was taking careful steps behind Ben, as both held onto the wooden rails on the wall to brace themselves whenever the Freedom Star rattled and swayed.

Strapped on Benjamin's back was a brown wooden chest with a white inscription, 'Medic Kid' etched on the lid. Hanging around his neck was a black lace with a myriad of keys attached to them. These were the emergency keys of the cabin doors that allow the steward access to passengers in time of emergency.

At the second level, beneath the quarter deck, they reached the door of a cabin, and suddenly braced themselves, with the old physician almost tumbling, when the vessel rattled and swayed again, lasting for about 3 minutes. Certain that the heavy rocking was over, Benjamin sought from the dangling keys around his neck, the right one for the cabin door.

"Hello, Doctor Reid and I Ben are at your door and about to enter," he first announced himself, then waited for about a minute and a half and inserted the key into the door and opened it.

They entered the cabin of the Flowers, a quiet family and met Timothy Flowers, an enormous and dark-skinned man lying on his back, on his bunk bed with his eyes stretched and looking confused. He was staring at the ceiling at the same time clenching his teeth and was having uncontrollable muscle spasms. Saliva was oozing out of his mouth and rolling down both corners of his lips.

His wife, Suzannah Flowers was by his side, also confused and weeping, at the same time wiping the saliva from the corners of his lips with a small towel. Frightened, their two children, Timothy Flowers Jr, their oldest son and his little sister Debbie Flowers, were lying strapped on their beds.

"He got a seizure," lamented the old physician, hurrying to the bunk bed, with Benjamin Coffey following him.

"It just happened," cried Mrs. Flowers when Dr. Reid looked at her inquiringly.

"Okay, we got to leave him be for a few minutes. But first we need to make sure he's comfortable. We are going to gently prop up his head, and slowly close his eyes."

Mrs. Flowers watched, as the doctor and Ben gently turned her husband on his right side. A pillow was gently placed under Mr. Flowers' neck. Having observed him for some time, Dr. Reid covered his eyes with the bedspread to stop him from looking at the reflection from the burning Oil Lamp on the table. Prolonged staring at light at a rough and high tide often causes drowsiness, resulting in seasickness. In Timothy Flowers' case, this was the cause of the seizure.

He also shoved two thick pieces of cotton balls in Mr. Flowers' earlobes to break the disturbance in his inner ear which affects one's sense of balance and motion when sailing. He was observed for another 5 minutes until the once motionless man began removing the bed spread from over his face.

Dr. Reid gestured to Benjamin who immediately opened the lid of the medic kit, and removed the upper crate containing small vials. He rummaged through the second one, taking out the medicine bottles one after the other and reading the labels. A small white plastic Jar labeled, 'Ginger Powder,' was sorted out and handed to the ship's physician.

"I need a cup of hot water," Dr. Reid said, looking at Mrs. Flowers.

Holding the small table, then the wall to brace herself when the vessel trembled and rocked, she took careful steps to the kitchen compartment. She opened the small cabin shelf hanging over the kitchen sink, found a medium sized cup and a brass metal flask and made her way back to the bunk bed.

"For every two hours, give him a cup," instructed the doctor, when he had uncapped the small white bottle and slid a quantity of ginger powder in the cup of hot water and gave it to Timothy Flowers to drink. The ginger ale will help with the seasickness and prevent him from vomiting. "In 2 hours, we will come back to check on him."

Dr. Reid and Ben left the flowers when they had observed that Timothy Flowers was moving his hands and legs and began to mummer some words to his wife, with a facial expression, asking her what had happened.

At the Roberts', they checked on Daniel, who was sound asleep, unaware of what was going on. The medication the ship's physician gave him was working.

"Ben wasn't around when the lads were playing baseball on the deck," complained Mrs. Flowers.

"It's your responsibility at all times that kids don't roam the vessel at certain hours in the evening," muttered the ship physician. "Ben is just a boy, who sometimes needs to rest."

From the Roberts, they attended to many of the other passengers who were seasick and vomiting. They met the licentiate, Charles Gooding III strapped to his bunk, holding his Bible firmly to his chest. His eyes were red and tears were rolling down both cheeks. It was difficult to tell whether the redness in his eyes was due to praying and weeping all night or just weeping out of fear, Benjamin thought.

The doctor and the steward boy left his cabin when they saw that he was okay and did not want to be bothered. After making a few more rounds, administering medication to the passengers that were experiencing the sea hazard symptoms, they retired to their respective cabins.

The storm continued throughout the night rocking and swaying the vessel from left to right, and raising it up and down the huge waves. The sailors, weary and drenched, were still working to keep the Freedom Star safe. All the damaged sails were either mended or replaced with storm sails. With pains-taking efforts, they were hoisted back up. As the drag held the rudder deep beneath the waves, the required propulsion was gained, enabling the vessel to plow through.

Captain Summerville was still at the observation post, occasionally spying through his telescope, expanding and contracting it to adjust his view as Reginald, who still stood by, fired a flare.

A few hours later, the wind vane was whining down, indicating that the storm was abating. Tension was lessening on the masts. The impact of the waves crashing against the bow had reduced.

As he maneuvered the Freedom Star anticlockwise, this time with ease, Allan Gables got the hint that the worst part of the storm was over. At the observation post, Captain Summerville breathed with relief when he saw, far ahead, through his telescope, a glitter of the early morning sunrise, emerging from beyond the horizon.

Chapter 2

Further west of the Atlantic, the early October sunset cast an orange-red glow on the surface of the water. The spherical shape of the sun, appearing halfway submerged into the deep of the distant horizon, displayed a magnificent gold-like emission engulfing the skies and the ocean below.

Emerging from the distant ocean-skylines was the Santa Amelia, a Portuguese vessel, slowly steering its course along the Malagueta Pepper coastline. Having sailed from the Guinean Coast of Kamsar, the vessel had been anchored off the coast of Cape Mount for the past four days.

It was an enormous merchant ship at least to an unsuspecting eye, but it was indeed a slave trading vessel. For the past several years it has been roaming these coastlines overtly trading in the pepper spice and other cash crops, but clandestinely seeking human cargo and shipping the lucrative commodity to Europe where slave trading agents secured their transit to the Americas.

The British and American Navies, in their quest to control the West African Coast by ridding it of slave trade, have searched this vessel many times and finding nothing, have awarded it the permit to sail without hindrance.

Business was bad at Cape Mount. Slave trading posts near the mouth of lake Piso, and the mountain overlooking the ocean to the left of the lake, were recently ransacked and razed by Gola Warriors led by Kponkay, a vicious warrior chief in a campaign to rescue their kinsmen whose villages and towns were raided by neighboring Vai tribesmen in the name of their powerful king, Jaingkai who was in partnership with the captain of the Santa Amelia.

The Portuguese Sea captain had sent two teams of 15 men each. One to secure the mountain at the left of the lake where they mounted their cannons and set up observation posts to scan the lake and far beyond for hostile tribal activities, while the other took on an expedition to locate a secret hideout of Jaingkai, to see whether he and his people were saved from the Gola raids.

The expedition team, armed with rifles and swords, and revolving machine guns mounted on the bows and sterns of three large boats rowed into the lake for two days in search of king Jaingkai and the remnants of his people, having found his town burned and deserted as smoke bellowed into the skies.

Half burned canoes, with some still glowing, lie on the shores of the lake including the charred and decaying corpses of Jaingkai men as the search team navigates through. Hatches and huts were all in arches as white smoke filled the air. The strong odorous smell of the mixture of burned fishes and human flesh fill the nostrils of the Portuguese sailors who struggled to come to terms with the level of destruction of the once bustling fishing town. The Gola raiders have spared nothing and no one.

With his town and surrounding villages pillaged and many of his warriors killed or captured, the once powerful king had been weakened, and it will be good to find him alive, hiding in one of his secret hideouts along the lake, which he had confided to his partner, the captain of the Santa Amelia when the king was once asked what plan he had in mind to escape, should his kingdom is attacked by his rivals and a new and emerging threat, the settlers from America, who for the past several years have been trooping at Cape Montserrado.

King Jaingkai, his family and his remaining men would be about 30 persons, according to details of his precautionary escape plan provided to his partner. They would be rescued, and protected, If the Portuguese found them alive. When they have fully recuperated, the king and his men would be armed to continue raiding the villages of his enemies for more slaves.

But what he did not know was he and his people were going to be lured into slavery, taken aboard and sold. This part of the arrangement the cunny and elusive Portuguese sea captain kept from his friend, the many years they had known each other, and did business together.

On the second day, finally figuring out its location with the aid of a sketch, Jose de Santos, a young Portuguese leading the purported rescue mission found the hiding place of king Jaingkai and his people. It was a small village overlooked by a mountain covered with a foggy dense forest, about a mile and a half inland, from the western side of the lake.

But the rescue team was late; the hideout had also been recently attacked, possibly prior to being sorted out by Gola trackers. As they walked through the village of tiny huts and white sand, the bodies of Jaingkai's family members and remnants of his men were lying about. Some, mainly the women, naked and strangled to death, were lying by a small creek that ran into the lake, with their fishing baskets by their side. The heads of others were stuck into the mud of the banks of the creek and died of suffocation.

Jose de Santos was standing over one of the corpses. It was a young woman, naked and butchered. She was lying on her back with eyes and mouth stretched open, conveying her shock at the way in which she was killed. He drew his sword, and tapped one of her breasts. The lifeless organ was still soft, meaning that the raid had occurred just a couple of hours ago, and the band of Gola worriers who had carried out this massacre may not be far.

The men were beheaded Jihadist style; their corpses were found in a kneeling position. Their hands were tied behind them with ropes made of woven palm thatches with their oozing headless necks resting on logs.

The body of the king was found in front of a hut. It was impaled on a wooden pole of about 12 feet long, inserted into its anus and protruding out of its throat. Its bearded head was chopped off, with both hands made to hold it from the beard like when holding the helmet of a Roman Soldier by its brush.

"*O nome do pai o filho o espírito santo,*" bewildered, and signing his cross, the soldier who discovered the corpse, recited the Holy Trinity in Portuguese.

It was soon surrounded by four other Portuguese sailors, including José de Santos. The leader of the expedition signaled to one of them. Immediately, the sailor stepped closer to the body and removed a tablet made of wood, hanging around the headless neck of King Jaingkai's corpse, and then handed it to Jose.

There were inscriptions etched on it in raw Arabic. The young and experienced Portuguese sea man, who learned a little of the language from his grandfather, who himself was a sea man roaming the Mediterranean coast during the last days of the Trans-Saharan Trade, tried to read and interpret the writing.

'So, shall it be for he who dwells in the evil trade,' the inscription read.

While pondering on this strange message, they all immediately became alerted to the cry of a baby, coming from the attic of an outside kitchen, made of sticks and palm thatches on the roof. One of the sailors, pointing his rifle in that direction, took careful steps as he moved towards the kitchen while the rest took up positions to provide cover for him.

Skipping over a log that barricaded the dirt floor of the kitchen, he entered and saw a body in a pool of blood. It was lying on the ground beside the fire hearth with a spear stuck in its back. Multiple stabs from the back of her neck down to the base of her vertebral column suggested that she was struck many times.

It may be the baby's mother, he thought. Looking above him, he saw the baby wrapped up in a brown country cloth stock between the sticks that made up the roof of the attic. He opened it and saw that it was a male, who had immediately stopped crying and was looking straight at him with its tiny hands clawing at the cloth at the same time stretching its legs. The sailor brought it out.

"It's the King's grandson," Jose said, holding the baby.

"So, what do we do with it?" asked one of the men.

"We take it to the captain," responded the head of the expedition. "I think it's time we get the hell out of here. The barbarians who did this might soon be back."

Back on board the ship, the captain, disappointed that King Jaingkai was dead, including all his best warriors, not for the purpose of losing a friend and partner, but for the intention of turning them into slaves, took the infant down the hull. Passing through a secret passage beneath a stair wall before entering the cargo hold, he entered a stretch of hall where there were more than twenty Africans captured from the coast around the upper gulf of Guinea.

They were bundled in chains, attached to wooden rails on the wall. He walked past them to the compartment where the women were chained. He searched amongst them, and then scooped over a frightened woman. She looked Mandingo, and was partially naked. Only a piece of cloth was tied around her waist, reaching mid-way between her curvy hips and her knees.

The captain laid the baby on the floor, and studied the woman who quickly covered her chest with her hands to prevent the Portuguese sea merchant from looking at her breasts. Initially resistant, she regarded him first, and then the poor baby on the floor, as he gently held her hands and slowly parted them. Then he held one of the woman's full and elongated breasts and gently squeezed it. Thick rich breastmilk flowed out of her dark and pointed nipple dotted with pimples forming a ring around it. She may have been snatched by native slave hunters while she was still breastfeeding.

A brass bracelet around her left ankle meant that she may be of aristocracy. Expressionless, he ordered one of his crew standing by to loosen, and take her to another compartment, a small and tight cabin with a mattress made of straw lying on the plank floor, and handed the baby to her.

"Tell her if the baby dies, I'll make sure they are both fed to the sharks," he told his crewman, who struggled to interpret this to the woman. "And make sure she's nourished a little more than the others.

After a day and a half from the coast of Cape Mount, the Santa Amelia was now anchored off shore, but far from view from the tip of Cape Montserrado which lay in the distance. Captain Edwardo Gomez, at the observation post, scanned the coastline at the right and left of the mouth of the Mesurado River.

The tall Portuguese slave merchant wore his hair in the style of a pony tail with a large W shape mustache. The beach ruffle shirt he was wearing was unbuttoned from the neck to his breastbone, exposing his hairy chest. The hem of the sky-blue trousers on him were flipped over the brown leather boots on his feet. A brown belt with a sword in its sheath hung around his waist.

Two British royal frigates were anchored a few knots at the bow and the stern. He assumed a third would be invincibly at his starboard, thus enveloping his vessel in a triangle. The British always use this maneuver to monitor vessels anchored within the territorial waters of Cape Montserrado.

In order to make it look like a merchant ship, Captain Edwardo Gomez, first reduced the size of his crew on the deck to 8, and ordered the rest into the secret cabins reserved for them, should in case his vessel was inspected and the British don't get alarm due to the huge presence of sailors, thus suspecting that the Santa Amelia was slave ship. Then he loaded three boats with merchandise to take them to shore at a stretch of land at the waterfront near Providence Island, where trading activities took place.

Early the next morning, the Portuguese, two in each of the three smaller boats, were rowing towards the estuary. On their way, they would occasionally wave to local fishermen, some of whom were young boys venturing out at sea in their two-man canoes, but at a safe distance away from the strangers.

They watched with amusement how two fishermen, both bearing resemblance with one of them looking older than the other, were throwing fish gills into the water as Seagulls circled overhead. The birds would dive and plunge into water and would fly away with the gills in their beaks as the younger one, presumably the son would swing his paddle to scare them away.

Throwing fish gills drenched in a special kind of substance into the sea was a ritual local fishermen practiced to attract more fish for a good catch.

Captain Gomez, now dressed like an ordinary Sea merchant, was at the lead boat with one foot over the gunwale. The rest of the crew with him were dressed in similar manner so as not to raise any suspicion. The boats landed at the wharfs, after an hour and a half row from the main vessel.

As usual, early morning commercial activities were springing up as buyers and sellers rushed to the docks where other boats or smaller ships were berthed to trade in the exotic goods in exchange for local ones.

Local Vai and Bassa chiefs and their subjects were bringing their locally produced merchandise. Settlers, who were free slaves from America, mostly dressed in attire reminiscent of the negro south were also at this commercial riverside, along with their local maids.

As the morning wore on, the cries of advertising in the local vernacular of Vai, Dei, and Basa filled the air. Gomez and his men were displaying their goods of mainly fine linen cloth, exotic gin and whisky, smoked fish, ornaments, and other attractive foreign goods.

The chiefs would stand by as their local subjects also displayed their products of mainly Malagueta spice, cassava and eddoes products and beautifully carved artifacts. Some of the locals would display live chickens and other species denizen to the surrounding mangrove swamps like the young of crocodiles, pythons and tortoises.

Militias, which were mostly settlers, organized by the American Colonization Society, on the lookout for suspicious activities such as trading in slaves, roamed about the water front with their raffles clung on their shoulders. Also, with them were the locals, which were mostly the men of the Bassa Chief, Bob Gray, who provided them to the settlers to be trained as militias. They were wearing khaki shirts and short pants, and were on the lookout, too, but without guns.

Far above, to the right of the waterfront was the land surrounding Cape Montserrado, called *Dubor* by the locals and renamed Monrovia by the settlers. At its immediate vicinity were Crown Hill and the highlands of Ashman Street and Sniper Hill, which were the administrative centers of the ACS.

"*Zimi nee-nay o, zimi nee-nay o*; fishes are here for sale," a group of Bassa men, and women displaying a variety of sizable species of cold water and sea fishes, advertised their produce in their dialect.

One of them, a slim man with small body, pop eyes, with a big head and long cheek had his eyes on a gold-plated pin, the size of a dime, stock at the forefront of the black visorless sailor hat captain Gomez was wearing, while he and one of his crewmen were making their way towards the group.

He was Garsuah Togar, a fisherman who mostly fished in the complex water channels surrounding Providence Island and the surrounding waters of Stockton Creek that made up Bushrod Island and beyond. He was good at catching the purple back fresh water crabs, and sold them to the settlers who extensively relished them.

He would attach fishing lines made of woven palm thatches to hooks carved out of wood, and attached fish gills, and other enticing parts of a fish to the hooks as bait and throw the lines into the river. After some time, he would first test the lines to detect whether a weight had been added, and if so, gently, he would begin to pull the lines. Huge marsh crabs, with their paws holding onto the bait, would be hauled out of the water. Garsuah would use the back of his cutlass to either break the paws or remove them from the bait and throw his catch into baskets made of Bamboo peelings. Sometimes, he would use his hands to remove the paws from the bait.

Recently, with the influx of the settlers from across the Atlantic, most of the areas where he caught his crabs were being occupied by new arrivals, especially around the northern Sinkor belt where an offshoot of the Mesurado River runs. Settler kids, whose parents lived at the edge of the swamps, were always fascinated to see Garsuah Togar catching crabs the way he did and they soon got accustomed to him. Sometimes he would give some of his catch to them to take to their parents.

One Saturday morning, when it had heavily rained all night, Jimmy, the 11 years old son of the Cox family who have recently moved near the swamp at the end of Chugbor, in Sinkor, wandered off into the marsh, which was a stone's throw from their backyard. He was accompanied by his sister, Madea, who was a year older than him. Imitating Garsuah, he tied some lead around a dead hen, which belonged to his mother, who was fond of raising chickens. Before going to bed, the night before, Sundayway, their local in-house maid may have forgotten to put the hen with the rest of the others in the coop, leaving it outside, which resulted in its death, due to the heavy downpour.

As his sister watched, Jimmy tied the tip of a robe around one of the legs of the dead hen. Holding the end of the rope, he threw it into the river. The dead chicken remained partially afloat for some time, and then it submerged. Remembering how Garsuah did it, the kids waited patiently. After a couple of minutes, Jimmy had gotten frustrated when he had not felt a weight on the line, which would mean a crab had not yet grabbed the bait. Suddenly there was a jerk.

The slim and feeble lad tried to pull what had jerked the line out of the water by hauling the rope, but instead, he was pulled. In the struggle, the line entangled his legs, causing him to fall down, and was being dragged into the water. Then, there was a splash and emerging out of the water was a huge dark brown Crocodile, with the dead chicken in its jaws. It spun on its back, exposing its beach and dotted belly and then back on its fore and hind legs at the same time swinging its neck violently.

As Jimmy fought to loosen his legs, the reptile was pulling the robes and dragging him into the mud. Soon he was into the murky edge of the banks. Madea, fearing for her little brother, screamed and ran to call their dad, Mr. Phillip Cox.

The animal had pulled the robes which dragged the kid some meters into the water. Just in time his parents arrived, and to their horror, saw what was happening. His mother, Martha Cox, a fair skinned settler, screamed when she saw the croc swimming towards her son. She threw herself to the ground, rolling in the mud and soiling her nightgown.

Fortunately, Garsuah Togar, who was paddling nearby, heard the screams and hurriedly paddled in that direction. Upon seeing the danger, he grabbed his cutlass and jumped into the water, attacked and killed the animal. The boy was then able to crawl out of the water and finally loosened the robes from around his legs.

Their neighbors, including other settler families, came rushing on the scene. They watched in awe as the slayer of the crocodile dragged the animal out of the water by its large and scaly tail. Everyone thanked him for his bravery in saving the boy. Some of the settlers went further to regard him as a true friend of the Pioneers, next to King Bob Gray and the Mandingo King.

"What's your name?" asked Mother Patricia Gardner, whose husband Rev. Jenkins Gardner ran the nearby Methodist Church.

"Garsuah Togar."

"Good name, but not good enough for a good and brave man like you," Mother Gardner breathed with excitement. "Because you saved the life of a boy, and prevented the loss of a father of a generation unborn, you will be called Abraham Garsuah."

From that day, the Bassa fisherman was known to the settler community as Abraham Garsuah.

Captain Gomez now stood before him, and Abraham Garsuah could not let his eyes off the pin on the hat, prompting the Portuguese sea captain to deduce that the crab seller before him was the secret contact of his partner on this side of the Malagueta Coast, King Sorteh Gbayou.

"How much for all these crabs?" Gomez asked in accented English, pointing at two baskets full of the aquatic creatures, foaming from their mouths, crawling on top of each other and pulling one another down as they scrambled to climb out of the baskets.

"Three American dollars for all."

"You take coins or notes."

"No coin. I'll take note."

That was the code. The fish and marsh crabs seller was the secret agent of King Sorteh Gbayou, a powerful ruler, one of few who were still engaged into slave trade along the Farmington River, made possible for its navigable features extending inland for up to six miles from the coast.

The captain removed his hat and looked inside. While taking out three dollars bills, he cleverly removed the pin and wrapped it in one of the dollar bills and gave it to the native slave trade agent. Without counting the money, he put it in a long sac hanging across his chest. After that he dumped the basket full of crabs into a large zinc bucket in Gomez's crewman hand.

"I am lucky today," he told Zeogar, a fellow fish seller who they both sold, side by side, when the Portuguese had left. "The white man has bought all my crabs, and so I am retiring for the day and won't be back for a couple of days."

"Three American dollars cannot keep you up for a month."

"I know. But I got a contract to plant a reef fence in the yard of a settler family who live somewhere in Sinkor to prevent crocodiles from lurking in the backyard. One almost killed their son," Abraham Garsuah responded at the same time looking in his sac, hauling out the dollar bills to count them.

"*Urh mon deh-keh*; What is it?" Zeogar suddenly asked in Bassa, when the gold-plated pin dropped on the ground while Garsuah was unfolding the note it was wrapped in.

He quickly picked it up and put it back in his sac as his friend looked on, frowning,

"*Urh say nee kpay-lo*: it's none of your business," he responded, then packed his things and left without telling his friend goodbye.

He climbed into his canoe which was parked far from the dock, and paddled into the larger Mesurado River. He had to be careful with which route to navigate to get to the slave trading Bassa King. The colonial authority was aware that King Gbayou and other native rulers were still engaged in the slave trade, because they were strong and powerful, and it was the source of their livelihood.

Their huge warrior armies had amongst them, slave hunting sects who were effective in sneaking in on isolated villages of other tribes snatching or raiding them. This was a new tactic they had developed since in fact raging full scale war on an entire territory would alarm the settlers authorities, which most times, with the help of British and American war ships anchored at sea, would intervene to rescue the besieged tribes.

Because of this, the authorities at Monrovia have organized and deployed their own spies, most of whom were friendly tribesmen from the territory of King Bob Gray. So, paddling along the coast would put him parallel to the beach of King Gray, the headquarter of the Bassa King, located a couple of miles east of Dubor.

Using that route would make his distance short to get to the mouth of the Du or Farmington Rivers, depending which one he Chooses. Unfortunately, it was going to be dangerous. Most of the fishermen along the beach were settlers' spies. The safest way was to take the three-day journey by connecting the complex waterways which bypassed the territory of King Gray.

He paddled northwards around Providence Island, took the offshoot at his right, where the highland of Crown Hill overlooked the river below. At his left, he entered into one of the complex channels that stretched towards the Bali Islands, which took him directly to the swamps of Chugbor. Garsuah Togar passed it at a distance, remaining obscured in the thick mangrove swamps, until he reached the dotted Islands, north of the tip of the settlement of Congo Town.

He continued all the way north east of the mangrove swamps until he reached dry ground. Then he hid his canoe, walked on foot, and passed through the territory of some Mamba Bassa people situated at the north of King Gray, north-northeast of the Du River.

These Mamba people would pose no threat to him because they were hostile to the settlers. They were a sec, who claimed that they were not treated fairly by their king and his ACS agents friends with the share of the proceeds when they all agreed to sell their land.

Nearly dark, he arrived at a remote part of the Du River, a couple of miles northeast of King Gray. He fetched and inspected his other canoe. Satisfied that it was still intact, he rested for the night. Early at dawn, he continued his journey navigating the course, making sure that he kept King Gray at his far right.

Within an hour and a half, he passed Duazon at its remote north, until he branched off into a small offshoot of the river which took him to the north of present day Harbel. In the late evening hours, he continued until he reached the territory of King Sorteh Gbayou, at a point where the offshoot enters into the Farmington River.

He spent the night at a small village. The next morning, he took the pin to the Bassa King. This was the message that in the next three days, Captain Gomez and his men would be sailing into the mid Farmington River to meet the king to buy all the slaves he had captured.

Chapter 3

The early morning tropical breeze blew Captain Summerville's face as he stood at the quarter deck watching his Boatswain coordinating the assessment of the damage done to the Freedom Star, which was now anchored in the middle of the Atlantic, after the heavy storm.

Lan Dole and some of the crewmen were up on the masts, inspecting the sails, and the railings that held them to the poles. The ones and the flying jib that were shredded were taken down and either replaced or repaired.

Owen Duffy and his team at the cargo hold were down the hull, inspecting the walls and the keel to make sure that there were no leakages, which could have been caused by the underwater rocks when the vessel squeezed through the twin sea mounts.

The passengers on board, still reeling out of the aftermath of the night, were in another shock to the news that Elijah Burgess was lost at sea, rescuing Daniel Roberts. The Baptist Licentiate, Charles Gooding III, upon hearing the news was making his rounds, visiting and praying for the families and their children who were playing baseball on the deck when the incident occurred.

He had attempted to visit Mrs. Angela Dripper Burgess, Elijah Burgess' widow to console her of her loss, but she refused to open her cabin door when he knocked on it several times. He only stopped when the steward boy told him that the captain said she should be left alone for now, as she was still in shock and mourning the loss of her husband.

On Deck, Jack Duval and some other crewmen were at the coxswain assembly getting into a rescue boat to be lower down into the water to go and retrieve the buoys they threw into the sea at the beginning of the storm to mark the spot Elijah Burgess drowned and retrieve his body which they assumed would be floating in the water.

Four crewmen were lowered down into the water and when the robes holding the boat were detached, they rowed off in the direction of the buoys, with the shark hunter, standing at the bow, his crossbar flung across his back, and with a compass in his hand. A wind vane was mounted at the stern to enable them to detect whenever there was another buildup so they should immediately turn back towards the ship.

"Are the lads in their right frame of mind to make these assertions?" asked Captain Summerville, sitting behind his desk at the captain's quarter. He was now dressed in his administrative outfit while in his office with his Boatswain, Jimmy Penhurst, the Licentiate Charles Gooding III, the ship's physician, Dr. Reid, and Benjamin Coffey, the steward boy.

"Yes, captain," breathed Charles Gooding III who informed the captain when he visited the families of the kids who were playing baseball on the deck. "You can speak to them yourself."

The captain nodded and signaled to Benjamin Coffey who went outside. Standing near the door were the Findley brothers and their mother, who was holding them by their hands, fuming with rage. He gestured to them to follow him into the office, and Mrs. Pricilla Findley, pulling her two sons behind her, dashed in, breathing heavily.

"Captain Summerville. My two sons are hell of the devil. But I don't think they have anything to do with Elijah Burgess' disappearance at sea!" she screamed.

"Certainly, Mrs. Findley. No one is accusing your sons, and I think they are good kids. But we just want to know what they told Mr. Gooding about our late CEO."

"What did you devils tell Mr. Gooding?!" she barked at Harold and Joel, who stood calmed, and not looking in her face.

"We will not be able to find out like that, Mrs. Findley," said the boatswain, Jimmy Penhurst. "As you may know, your sons may not be in their right frame of mind due to what they saw last evening when they were on the deck playing."

"How's that? Are you a psychiatrist?

"Sort of, Madam. And I am also a barrister."

"On whose side?"

"Remember he's the boatswain, who's in charge of the ship's crew and its important guests like Elijah Burgess," the captain answered, smiling at the same time. He was finding a way to assure and calm Mrs. Findley.

"Then my boys will need one as passengers."

"That's what we intend," Captain Summerville agreed. "That's why Dr. Reid is here."

"That is the law at sea," added Jimmy Penhurst. "The captain will serve as judge. We just want to know what happened to Mr. Burgess."

"So, are my boys helping in an investigation?"

"Right, mam," responded the captain. "We have already interviewed the crewmen who were trying to rescue him. They said something happened to him, and your boys may have seen that too, but from the point before he jumped into the water to save the Robert kid."

Still standing, foaming and holding the boys, she kept quiet and undecided. Tapping her right foot on the floor at the same time shaking her body, the big woman, still in her morning robe and her slippers that could not fit on her feet, because they were covered with thick stockings, looked at Harold, his brother, and then the captain.

"You're a good man, Captain Summerville. Thanks for saving our lives in that devil of a storm last night." When the Captain had nodded, she turned to the ship's barrister. "If you ever dare try to implicate my boys, I'll throw you in the bottom of the sea."

Mrs. Findley left the boys standing and took a seat, Benjamin Coffey had arranged for her, next to Dr. Reid. Penhurst led Joel Findley into the conference room, through a small door at the right of the captain's office. He was followed by Dr. Reid while Mrs. Findley, Harold, and Charles Gooding III remained with Captain Summerville in his office.

The boatswain sat at the tip of the long wooden desk shaped like an egg with his back turned toward the sea, that Dr. Reid and the kid could see through the plastic shield window, protected by wooden window bars, designed like a checkerboard. The ship's doctor and Harold sat at the other tip of the deck, facing Jimmy Penhurst.

"Can you tell this room what Mr. Burgess' state was when he suddenly appeared on the deck when you lads were playing baseball?" he asked, looking sternly at Harold Findley.

"Down to one out, the Saints were about to strike to finish their home runs, while we the Yankees were set to put the final out and prevent all their players on the bases from running home, and then it was going to be our time to bat," the kid began, very calmly.

"Wait a minute," interrupted Penhurst. "Saints? Yankees? How's that?"

"The Yankees is our team, made of us kids from the north while the Saints were the boys from down south," answered Harold.

"That sounds like you were a rival gang."

"No, Mr. Penhurst," rejected Dr. Reid. "As he said, they were two teams playing baseball. That's how kids do. And that's not the main issue we are holding this interview. Remember it's about what they say they noticed about Burgess, before the Robert kid fell overboard. Let's stick to that."

"Certainly, Doctor," agreed the Ship's barrister. Then he looked at Harold.

"Continue, son."

"My brother and I, as substitutes for the Yankees, were squatting at the port side. Just when Theodore Johnson was about to pitch the ball for the Saint's batter, Edwin Hayes, Mr. Burgess flung open the door to the deck. I saw him pulling his hair. It looked like he wanted to cry. And then we all turned our attention to Daniel, when Edwin struck. Next, I saw Mr. Burgess run towards the gunwale when Daniel, leaping for the ball, fell overboard."

"So, how did he look?"

"He looked scared. His eyes were red. It was like something was bothering him."

"But he wasn't scared to jump into the water after Daniel," offered the boatswain, making a face that the boy's account was conflicting.

Harold froze.

"That's not for the kid to say, Jimmy," Dr. Reid came in. "Our point of focus is at the point before the Johnson kid pitched the ball and when Edwin Hayes of the Saints struck it. So, I think Harold had said exactly what he and his brother told Gooding and his mom. It's enough for now. He's not going to say any more."

"Okay," sighed the barrister, reluctantly. "Then let him go. But I must speak to the other brother."

"You might hear nothing different, Mr. Penhurst," cautioned Dr. Reid.

"We have to hear his side, Doc. That's the procedure."

The doctor made a face like it didn't make sense to him. He shrugged his shoulders, and then led Harold out of the conference room. Benjamin Coffey, who was standing at the door following, opened it to let the doctor and Harold back into the captain's main office, signaling to Joel to enter the conference room.

Joel looked at his brother, who appeared calmed, and smiled at him. This meant Harold wasn't asked any question for giving their friend Benjamin Coffey their mother's sleeping rum, so he should not be afraid.

The interview with Joel Finely lasted for about 20 minutes, with the Barrister making several attempts to rephrase Harold's account to his brother to see whether both of them were making up the story to appease the captain to not be hard on them for giving his steward boy their mother's rum. As usual, Dr. Reid kept interjecting, when necessary to force the boatswain to stick to the intent of the interview.

"So, what did we get?" asked Cpt. Summerville, who entered the conference room after Joel was led out by Benjamin Coffey. Only he, Penhurst and Dr. Reid were in the room.

"It seems they are telling the truth," Informed the Barrister.

"They both told a similar story," Dr. Reid added.

"Similar story?" the captain raised his eyebrow.

"Just the regular kids' account of something they saw, with each trying to give his independent view," said the ship's physician.

"Howard Lustig thinks Burgess had a seizure," offered the captain.

"And his medical records didn't give a hint," pondered Dr. Reid.

"We should ask his wife if she's been observing anything unusual about him," suggested the boatswain.

"Not now," preferred the captain. "Let's concentrate on finding his body, first. And you both have to thoroughly analyze the accounts of Lustig and the kids so we can draw a concrete conclusion. And all interviews are suspended for now."

The three men came out of the conference room and entered the captain's main office, greeted with eager eyes. Captain Summerville looked at Mrs. Findley who also fired back with a stern and defiant look. She would vehemently reject anything against her boys. But the experienced seaman smiled, and gestured that all was okay with the boys.

"Thanks for your understanding, Mrs. Findley. Your boys' accounts would help us a lot," he said. "You can leave now. And I can assure you that they will not be called here again on this matter."

"Thanks, captain," Charles Gooding III stood up and extended his hand to the captain for a hand shake.

"Thank you too, Mr. Gooding for bringing this to our attention."

"Common Ben. Let's go check on the Flowers," Dr. Reid said, holding Benjamin Coffey by his hands and they both walked out of the captain's office.

At open sea, Jack Duval and team were employing every navigational means, using the compass, and plotting coordinates to determine the points they dropped the buoys and in which direction the storm may have forced the Freedom Star off course. This lasted for about 6 hours, before they finally located the buoys.

Initially, they surveyed the periphery, using the telescope. As they rowed closer, they circled the perimeters of where the buoys were floating.

This was the second day after the drowning. Within a few hours it would be day 3. This time the body would be floating and exposed to sea birds. Given the circulation of the current around the spot where Daniel Roberts was pulled back up on deck, they estimated that it would be the same spot where Elijah Burgess' corpse may be floating. But this proved futile.

Nevertheless, they continued to circle around the perimeters, covering every inch as they gradually closed in on the buoys. But still, they did not see the corpse, and their hope from the onset was dampened. It took them another two hours to reach the buoys, and briefly scanned the waters as daylight was fast expiring. Yet, they did not see the body of the Color Purpose CEO.

Jack Duval, with his face full of dismay, sat on the floor with his back against the bow, resting both hands on the gunwale. Pondering on his next move, he rubbed his face with his hands, and looked in his palm like he expected the answers to appear in them. Then he looked at the crewmen.

"Ready the tarpaulins, and anchor the boat. We will spend the night here, and continue the search in the first few hours at day break," he instructed.

"The anchor won't reach the depth," advised Lan Dole. "Neither the drag can stop us from drifting away from this spot."

"Tie the line to at least 2 buoys to add to the weight that will prevent us from drifting too far, before day breaks."

The seasoned British seaman nodded.

With the help of the other two, they rowed close to a buoy. Then one of the Crewmen formed a rope into a noose and threw it. It landed around the navigational instrument which tightened when he hauled the rope. The other crewman slowly released the anchor so that it must not plunge into the water with force to prevent the weight of the drag from leaning the boat sideways and capsize. After that, they readied the tarpaulins to cover the boat and protect them, in case it rains.

At night, Jack Duval fired a series of flares in the direction of the Freedom Star to inform the captain that the recovery team has not discovered the body and will be staying at the spot all night to continue the search early in the morning. He continued to fire the flares until he saw through his telescope, a faint glow in the sky from the direction of the vessel. It was the signal of acknowledgement, when Harry Reginald fired a flare towards their direction.

Chapter 4

East of Cape Montserrado stretches the coastal plain of thick mangrove swamps, dotted with water logs, many of which covered with acres of marshes, and manure prone alluvial soil. Lagoons are adoringly located between swaths of land and the sandy cream beaches.

This continues to the shoreline of Congo Town, with a high land of about 50 meters, a quarter of a mile from the coast. Another quarter of a mile further along the beach is a bay, extending about one and a half miles inland. After which are the coconut trees littered beaches of King Gray, where the headquarter of the Bassa King stretches into the Atlantic like an inlet. The coastal plain extends about 14 miles inland, reaching the fringes of the belt of rolling hills.

From King Gray, the beach continues eastwards, bedeck with canoes on its shores, and huge stockpiles of fishing nets lining the beaches, suggesting the existence of active fishing communities. From this point to Duazon, the sea is a host to canoes with fishermen far off near the horizon, throwing their nets into the water, while others, returning to shore, would brave the sometimes huge and rough waves with the mastery of plowing their water crafts through.

As they land on shore, their counterparts would hurry to help haul them further away from the landing waves. And scurrying to the canoes to negotiate for the fresh catches are women and children.

Few meters from the beaches are stretches of low bushes and scattered trees of mango and red palm, amongst which commences the beginning of the territory of the abundant Melegueta pepper spice. Towering above the plethora of red palm trees is a peculiar and sacred one; the palm tree with three heads, which stood about a 100 feet tall with its three heads pointing up the sky like a three-prong spear. Portuguese explorers or seamen like Petro Da Centa, and other early explorers, and now Captain Edwardo Gormez, anchoring at sea, always plotted their coordinates in locating the hot spots of the once lucrative pepper spice and where they were traded, by keeping their telescopes trimmed on this strange and gigantic palm tree.

This arable terrain continues to stretch along the coast, amidst the continuation of lagoons and the estuaries of offshoots of the Du and Junk Rivers. further eastwards, the main body of the Du enters into the Atlantic through the newly negotiated territory of Marshall.

Between Duazon to Marshall, canoes are highly seen on the shores or in the water. This part of the coastline is un-inhabited. It is extremely quiet, aside from the roaring waves dashing on the shores, ingesting tiny orange back sea crabs and the chirps of birds in the bushes beyond the beach. Anyone venturing here, risks being snatched and eventually sold into slavery.

A few miles east of Marshall is the estuary of the Farmington River. Around its mouth is a rocky beach and thick bush. From the coastal forest, huge cotton trees are occasionally situated along the river banks, with some extending inland.

High up in the top branches of one of the cotton trees, a particular one standing about 20 yards from the beach, a pair of thin and bony hands slowly parted the branches, revealing the tiny face of a man with bushy hair, sparkling pop eyes, long ears and cheek. His forehead was pointed and deformed. As he continued to slowly part the branches blocking his view of the mouth of the Farmington, and the ocean beyond, his entire frame was a bony figure, with long neck sticking out, bordered by collar bones, and a chest overtaken by a visible rib cage, like a sufferer of malnutrition caused by many years of famine.

Far off at sea the Santa Amelia was anchored. Captain Edwardo Gomez was standing at his observation post with his telescope focused on the ET looking man up the branches of the huge cotton tree. He was King Sorteh Gbayou most trusted scout, known to his people as Sinegar, interpreted in the Bassa language as spider man.

He was born out of stillbirth, during the many wars between the Kpelle and the Bassa tribes along the northern Farmington River. His mother, a distant relative of the King's father, was pregnant and in her 7th month when a large band of Kpelle warriors attacked a Bassa settlement, far into the hinterland, north of the Farmington River.

Sick and with a weak back, as traditional midwives and native doctors struggled to preserve the pregnancy, she, along with others survivors, fled on foot, passing through dangerous parts of the northern Bassa Forest, and crossing rivers on hurriedly assembled rafters. On many occasions, they were forced to climb high lands as the Kpelle warriors pursued.

Scurrying, and docking as they evaded Kpelle warrior scouts in the hunt for King Gbayou's father, a powerful warrior whose capture or death would demoralize the Bassa and eventually seize their fertile land, Sinegar's mother was no longer able to continue the journey. Many of the places they passed were tony bush that gashed their skins and ravines with sharp stones that pierced their feet.

Her husband, a close confidant of King Gbayou's father, was killed during the Kpelle raid. Unlike some of the women and children who got sick along the way, or warriors who were wounded, and left to die, he had vowed to save the wife and the unborn child of his friend.

He ordered some of his remaining men to build a stretcher of sticks and large wild leaves to carry her on it. While crossing a ravine, one of the men toting the stretcher on his shoulders slipped and fell when he had stepped on a slippery rock. Struggling to regain balance, the stretcher swayed, causing the woman to fall on her belly.

Early labor pain immediately grabbed her, and the few surviving traditional midwives were put to work with instruction to save the child or its mother. Her screams and whirls echoed into the forest and the highlands as she cried in pain, prompting the midwives to cover her mouth for fear that she may be heard by Kpelle warrior scouts, combing the forest, and this would eventually lead to their hideouts. After a struggle of about 4 hours, the child was finally delivered, but the mother died.

Wrapped in wide leaves, the baby was brought before the king's father. It was a male with a big head. Its body was tiny and frail with small hands and legs which made it look like a spider. It appeared like it was not going to live.

"He must be called Sinegar," announced the King's father, handing back the baby to the maid-wife who brought it to him.

After many days of wandering in the bush, they stumbled upon a village somewhere along the mid-St. John River, where they were relieved to meet their kinsmen, a small group of Bassa people who live by fishing, laying crawfish baskets and collecting an oyster known as *kiss-meat*, along the muddy banks.

But they seemed unaware of what was happening at the upper Farmington. The ambitious Kpelle king, Tokpa Gbowee, had put the Gola in the Todee region to check from the many wars with them, and had now thrusted deep into Bassa Land. With his enemies at his right flank now kowtowed, Tokpa Gbowee was determined to seize all the land east of Kakata to gain more space for shifting cultivation.

The aim of the warlike Kpelle king was to open that flank to the Sea so that he must be able to trade his farming products with the Portuguese. Karye Gbayou, King Sorteh Gbayou father, with the rest of his survivors settled in this village and others that were across the river. There, his son, now the king, was born.

Captain Gomez watched Sinegar crawl on a top branch like a chameleon, with his bare body painted from head to toe with a green dye, a camouflage to make him invincible on the branches in case the Portuguese were also scouting the area from their ship. The Portuguese slave merchant knew that it was the King's way of ensuring that he wasn't out for tricks as the business continued to face challenges as more American and British battleships were frequenting the coast on the lookout for slave ships.

On the other hand, the human cargo Sorteh Gbayou was selling on behalf of his aging father, has started to diminish. When he fled the Kpelle onslaught, Kaye Gbayou had successfully organized the people he met and eventually annexed all the other villages along the St. John, the Miclyn and the other rivers along the Bassa coast. Then, he formed a Chiefdom and was made Head Chief.

He established his headquarters along the Mid-Farmington, granting him access to the coast. During this time, he met the Portuguese sea captain and initially both traded in Malagueta pepper which lasted for many years. Now strong enough with a powerful army to wage war, Captain Gomez saw this as an opportunity to trade in slaves with the Bassa chief and supported his efforts to raid other clans that did not recognize his authority and sold the captives as slaves.

But agents in the business were receiving complaints from their clients that the slaves brought from the Malaguetta coast, east of Cape Montserrado were not strong enough, because they did not have in their DNA the traits of farming which was applicable for the large plantations slave owners own.

At a meeting of all the slave merchants that roamed that part of the Atlantic coast, it was discovered that the Kpelle who were situated further north into the hinterland from the coast were the best options for their skills in farming which was their way of life.

Fearing the expansion of the settlers at Monrovia, which would jeopardize his business, with massive support, Captain Gomez, lured Kaye Gbayou to wage a retaliatory war against King Gbowee with hopes to have him defeated and sell his people, now referred to as the gold dust of the slave trade.

Initially Kaye Gbayou seemed to be gaining the upper hand as he pillaged few of the Kpelle villages at the upper western Farmington in a surprise attack and captured a few of them. But the warlike and hawkish Kpelle king soon turned the tide and once again, the aging Bassa chief was on the run. Wounded, with a spear in his chest, his son, who was a commander in his army, managed to flee with him to safety. He was cured of his wound but later died of self-humiliation as Tokpa Gbowee was in reach of capturing him.

King Sorteh Gbayou, struggling to temporally slow the Kpelle advances, soon realized that out of a sudden, they were retreating. Relieved, he later learned from Sinegar, who for days, had been following the Kpelle's retreat from a safe distance from one tree top to the other, all the way to the surrounding bushes of Kakata, reported back that Tokpah Gbowee's sudden death was the cause for the Kpelle's retreat. And that they had blamed his death on one of his wives, Sando Karnley, the youngest daughter of the Gola king, Gbelley Karnley, who out of a peace deal, was betrothed to the Kpelle King. Out of instruction from her father, she had poisoned the King.

His only daughter, Lango Gbowee, succeeded him. She had sent word to the warriors pursuing the Bassa Chief to return for battle with the Gola, out of revenge for her father's death. Gbelley Karnley and his people were dealt with a sufficient blow by the King's daughter clearing them from as far as the area somewhere near which became the settlement of Careysburg. She later abandoned the vicious onslaught when it was later known that Sando did not poison her husband, and that Tokpa Gbowee may have died of natural causes. Furthermore, she was calmed down by the settlers authority at Monrovia who were negotiating with her to settle some of their people at Careysburg.

Learning of these developments, King Sorteh Gbayou, now assuming his father's role as head chief, loathed launching any direct reprisal attacks on the Kpelle. He rather re-organized his people, and expanded his territory all the way to the land east of the palm tree with three heads, subsequently transforming his territory into a Kingdom.

Suspecting that Lango Gbowee did not seem to harbor her late father's ambition to gain access to the coast through the Farmington River, he continued trading with the Portuguese captain in slaves, but through a subtle innovative means. Scouted by Sinegar he would launch small scaled raids on isolated Kpelle villages.

Since her ascendancy to the throne, and her friendliness with the settlers at Careysburg who were providing her with information about King Gbayou's activities, she had warned her people to be careful as they wander into the deep south of the regions around the Farmington, mindful that the Bassa king may launch raids to capture and sell them into slavery.

She was still recuperating from the battle with the Gola, and her army was weary of war and would not be strong enough to launch rescue missions to save them, if they were captured. But few of them, mainly former warriors of her father's army who had knowledge of the territory, were occupying these areas with their families setting up small clusters in the vicinity of the river.

It is these clusters that King Gbayou was launching these small raids, with his large and newly organized army which included the Nnin-gins or Water Genies, an occultic sect, specialized in underwater activities.

This sect, which he had militarized, had the ability to borrow under water for days, and at the right time, would sneak in on these isolated Kpelle villages. Another unit known as the Leopard Society sect, were specialized in combing the forests like green barrettes, to sniff out villages far from the river, and they were effective in snatching young men, women and children without any immediate notice.

With reconnaissance from Sinegar, King Gbayou would only order a raid, when the cluster had reached about 30 persons. Most times, he would be lucky to capture half of that number as the Kpelle would rather die fighting, then being captured alive.

Captain Edwardo Gomez, knowing all this, reasoned that the equally cunning Bassa king would take all precautionary measures as the trade was becoming more challenging as fewer people were captured alive. The Portuguese might be planning to turn on him, like he planned to do to king Jainkai.

That was the purpose for which the strange ET looking man was high up the branches in the cotton tree. Sinegar would communicate any sign of chicanery and Captain Gomez would lose his precious cargo.

Standing by Captain Gomez was Jose dos Santos, the young sailor who led the Lake Piso expedition to rescue King Jainkai, and another man, a local from Monrovia, who goes by the name, Witty Peter. His real name was Cho Vuyougar, a Bassa man, whose great grandparents were among the first that migrated from the mouth of the St. John River and settled along the shores of Cape Montserrado.

They established a bond with the Dei they probably met, and both tribes had since coexisted. His father served on the inter-tribal council of King Long Peter. It was during this period Cho Vuyugar was born and grew up in the quarter of old King Peter, one of the few Kings who were receptive and sympathetic to the early settlers. King Zulu Dumar, his real name, was the Dei King that granted Duzoah Island to them which they later renamed, Providence Island.

Vuyougar spoke clear English, Vai, Dei, and a little Portuguese, apart from Bassa, his native tongue. Because of such adroitness, and his proximity to the ailing Dei ruler, the settlers called him Witty Peter. Being in the employ of Captain Gomez as an interpreter, Vuyougar, pretending like a day boy hired to assist the sailors to ferry their goods back to their ship, got on board for the brief sail from Monrovia to the mouth of the Farmington.

"So, what do you think, Sir?" asked Jose dos Santos, his gaze focused on the mouth of the Farmington.

"We go in," responded the captain, taking his telescope from his eyes and folding it. "Lower the cargo boats with the king's merchandise, but each must be mounted with 2 of our machine guns, and five of our best trained sailors with their raffles properly concealed."

"Yes, sir," the young Portuguese turned to leave, but the captain held his right hand. "And be careful not to alarm the hominid I have been monitoring up that cotton tree." Then he turned to Witty Peter. "Are we expecting good cargo in return?"

"Yes, sir," responded the middle height man with a well-trimmed Afro hair, reflecting the style of America's negro south which was still kept by the settlers. He kept a long beard, dotted with traces of gray.

Sinegar watched as Gomez's men lowered the boats with merchandise and few men. Satisfied that he had seen enough, credit to his farsighted vision made possible by a Zoe, upon the request of the king's father, when Sinegar was about 5 years old. To do this, an herb made of potatoes, wild collard grains and red palm oil, drenched in a water used to wash the face of a kay-kay, a tiny mad-nourished looking hunting dog, was poured in his eyes.

The king's most trusted scout took a roll of what looked like the net of a goal post made of woven palm branches. He unrolled it from the top of the tree to the ground. In a few minutes, he was climbing down the net like a spider on its web. When he reached the ground, he quickly folded his climbing apparatus. Then, from a raffia bag hanging across his boney chest, he took out a small hand-crafted garden hoe and cleared the weeds from a spot between the roots of the tree. After that, he looked into the bag again, and got out a 12-inch-long dry coconut flower sheath with two smaller ones about 6 inches and sat the canoe-shape coverings on the ground.

Away from the rest, and positioned horizontally, he filled the 12 inch one with gravel he once gleaned from the grounds at a gravel field near Kakata. Next, he arranged the three 6-inch coconut flower sheaths vertically and in a straight line. In each, he put some dry sticks and five of the gravels. When he had finished, he first looked around, then collected the rest of his accessories, and put them back into the bag. Before disappearing into the thick bush, he picked some wide leaves and covered the sheaths.

About 5 minutes later, three warriors of the Leopard Society sect came crawling out of the bush from different directions. They were dressed in Leopard skin clothing, with their heads covered with masks made out of the big cat's face and teeth.

As the other two watched, one towards the direction of the sea while the other, the river, one of the warriors crept to where Sinegar left the canoe sheaths and studied how they were arranged. Then he signaled to the two, who immediately came crawling to him.

"*Kwee gar na gee?:* has the white man arrived?" one of them asked, speaking Bassa.

"Humm," with a deep grunt like a leopard, the warrior studying the arrangements of the sheaths on the ground, and what was contained in them, responded in the affirmative.

The 12 inch one lying horizontally with plenty of gravel inside, symbolized the 'Santa Amelia', anchored at sea, and the gravels inside represented the sailors. The three smaller ones were the boats, and their positions from the big one meant they were heading for the Farmington River. The small dry sticks and leaf stalks in them were the merchandise the white men were bringing, and the five gravels in each boat were the number of sailors accompanying them, thus adhering to the protocol and posing no danger.

After studying the arrangements of the sheaths, the warrior signaled to one of the men, who immediately stood up and removed his Leopard face mask, revealing a tall warrior with bushy hair and a long beard, bedecked with cowrie shells. He looked up at the clear blue sky, and cupped his hands around his mouth.

"*Singbay-doo-doo-doo-doo*," in a high pitch traveling through the forest, he imitated the call of the dodo bird.

Few miles up the river, where it was still possible to navigate, was a clearing, and that was where King Gbayou and his men set up the meeting point. Sitting on a platform made of sticks covered with palm thatches and banana leaves, surrounded by his warriors and elders, he heard the 'Singbay-doo-doo's' code and got the message. Captain Edwardo Gomez was on his way with his merchandise, and that he posed no threat, or else, it was going to be the irritating chirp of a Blue Jay.

Before the Portuguese could reach the mouth of the river, all the *Neen-gins* who were hiding in water holes in the shallow parts of the course, had swarmed away. If the Portuguese were out for something sinister, they were going to dive under the keels of the boats, and plant a substance made out of a liquid with adhesive properties extracted from a certain tree, which has the ability to eat into any hollow wood when coming into contact with water. This would eventually bore large holes into the keels, and cause the boats to sink very fast, downing the enemy, instantly.

Additionally, Leopard warriors hiding behind trees and under the thick scrubs at the high banks overlooking the river, including ordinary warriors with javelins made of long tiny poles whose pointed tips were soaked with the poison of black mambas, were ready to strike at the Portuguese. But they also abandoned their positions and disappeared into the bushes without any trace.

Gomez and his crew entered into the Farmington and were steadily navigating upstream. The bushes on both sides of the banks were quiet-only the chirps of birds could be heard up in the trees, and the sloughing of oaks and paddles through the water. Each of the sailors in the boat had their hands on the machine guns mounted on the gunwale in firing position. Covered with sacks full of flour, the weapons were properly concealed, even to an inquisitive eye.

The temperature was welcoming and the current was gentle. After 30 minutes of a steady thrust upstream without any hindrance, a faint beam ran across Captain Gomez's face. With assurance from Witty Peter, business was going to be good. The human cargo he was expecting to collect was not only plenty, but valuable. They were mostly Lango Gbowee's people, captured and raided from their isolated villages. Before the settlers exert their influence and authority in this part of the Malagueta Coast, he would have traded enough with the Basa King, and subsequently retire as a wealthy man.

At the same time about hundreds of nautical miles away, Jack Duval and his search and rescue team had covered the entire perimeter in and around the buoys from morning to the late evening hours, in search of the body of Elijah Burgess but to no avail. They rested at night, again firing flares into the skies in the direction of the Freedom Star, to inform Captain James Newton Summerville, and the rest of the crew that they needed at least another day to do the last search, but a little farther off from the immediate perimeters.

After several flares, Duval caught on his telescope, a faint glow far off into the distant sky signaling that it was the captain acknowledging them.

The next day, they continued for about five hours, extending the search areas north of their position, having detected the direction of the wind and the flow of the current which they assumed may have drifted the body in that direction. By noon they had abandoned the search, and used most of the afternoon to rest. In the evening hours they uploaded the buoys into the boat.

Because it took them lots of time to lift the heavy navigational aids out of the water, a very delicate thing to do, lest they crush the boat, they were exhausted by the time they finished. With the boat now heavy, and slowly plowing through the water, in the first few hours at night, they were only able to cover a few knots back towards the 'Freedom Star. They anchored and rested until dawn. Then they resumed while it was still dark.

Late in the afternoon, Captain Summerville was at his observation post with his telescope positioned at his right eye when he spotted Duval and his search team in the far distance coming toward the vessel from the portside.

"Ready the hooks at the coxswain assembly," he instructed Jimmy Penhurst, who was standing by him.

Immediately, the Boatswain climbed half way down the wooden ladder and shouted to the two crewmen standing near Allen Gables at the wheels. "Ready the assembly lines. The search crew is in sight."

It took the shark hunter and the search team another four hours before they reached the ship. The sun had set by the time they neared the ship. But it suddenly became windy as they got closer.

Fortunately, the wind was not strong enough to rock the boat because of the added weight due to the buoys and other navigational apparatus inside. In order to take a precautionary measure in case the wind gains speed, which will make it difficult to position the boat parallel to the ship and be lifted back up the deck, they maneuvered to the side of the stern, where the wind was less. Then they slowed down, and waited, studying the whining of the wind vane to determine when it would be appropriate to row to the starboard and get prepared for the lift.

It was getting dark. Duval was standing at the bow, and as usual, with his left feet on the gunwale looking up the quarter deck. Then he saw the window of a cabin slightly opened, with a tin glow of the dimmed orange light of a lamp flickering inside. A face, appearing white as snow, was peering out of the window, and looking down at them. As the wind blew, the long white hair was flipping and covering the face. Then the wind suddenly increased.

The shark hunter felt a sudden surge overtaking his body. He became stiff and numb. His head began to rise, and a strong wind blew his face, almost toppling him overboard, but the boat rocked and he fell backwards. He hit his back against one of the buoys, causing a pain on his spine.

"Duval, Duval," he heard someone shouting his name, and then he suddenly came to himself and saw Lan Dole standing over him.

"The wind has subsided. We row for the lift," said the seaman, studying Duval, who became shaky and struggling to control a fast-developing convulsion.

"He's gone, Jack," continued the Sea man, seeing that Duval was not responding. "Elijah Burgess is gone. You got to get over it. We are rowing now for the lift."

The French-American shark hunter, after he was tugged several times, came to himself and nodded. But his heart leapt, causing a pain in his chest, when he looked up at the window again, and saw that it was shut and the flickering orange light was further dimmed. The face he saw was gone.

They rowed towards the starboard where Penhurst and the three other sailors were at one part of the coxswain assembly, while Howard Lusting and two other sailors were at the other part, slowly letting down the robes from the lifting gear as Lan Dole, and the other three sailors in the search boat prepared themselves to receive them.

Duval was sitting in the middle of the boat, still trying to figure out what he saw at the window. The two giant size robes from the lifting gear reached the search team down in the boat in a few minutes, and Dole and one of the crew attached the clippers to hooks mounted at the bow while the other two crewmen did the same at the stern.

With the search boat positioned parallel to the Freedom Star, Penhurst and his men up on the deck first tested the robes, and were satisfied that they were strong enough to jack up the bow as Howard and his men did the same for the stern. Then they began to roll the gear. By gently tilting the bow and then the stern, the boat was lifted out of the water.

They continued in this sequence until it was pulled all the way up towards the deck as water from beneath the Keel poured back into the sea. It took about 30 minutes for the boat to reach the deck and a bit above the port side of the ship. Then Penhurst, Howard and their respective teams, shifted gear and the boat was slowly lowered down on the deck.

Weary and dismay that they did not find the body of the late Color Purpose CEO, the search and rescue team got out of the boat. The other members of the crew sharing similar emotion, wrung their heads in silence.

Captain Summerville was at the quarter deck, when Jack Duval, Len Dole, Jimmy Penhurst, and Howard Lusting approached him. Without asking the head of the search team any question, Duval looked up at the captain and sadly shook his head.

The decorated former Naval hero froze, his eyes suddenly becoming red. He removed his hat from his head, shoved it under his right arm, and walked close to his men. As he approached them, they all parted, giving way for him to pass. Then they followed behind him in silence, with those who held on their flat woolen sailors' hats, also taking them off and shoving them under their shoulders.

"Captain's on deck," announced the boatswain, immediately prompting the sailors who were on the main deck to abandon what they were doing when they saw him. They all followed suit, standing behind Captain Summerville.

They marched, continuing in the same silent sequence towards the port side, facing the sea. They remained standing, gazing at the vast blue body of waters in silent remembrance of their fellow compatriots, and humanitarians, who died at sea while in the service of humankind.

"I will expect a full report of your search," turning to Jack Duval, his eyes still red, the captain said.

They suddenly became distracted, abandoning their silent membrane when a group of the passengers on board rushed on the desk through the entrance door beneath the quarter deck.

"Captain," shouted Licentiate Charles Gooding III racing towards the sailors with a group of families, comprising the Roberts and their son, Daniel, the Philips, the Hayes, and their son Edwin, and Mrs. Findley and her two boys. "Have you men found Elijah Burgess?"

"No. They did not find his body. We believe he is dead," responded the captain who turned to facing them.

"No. This cannot happen!" cried Mr. Edmund Johnson, one of the passengers. "Who's going to give me the grant to do my business when we get to Cape Montserrado? Without that grant I am not going. I'd rather go back to America.

"Oh my God, Elijah!" Wailed Miss. Barbara Newland. "Who's gonna take care of us negroes."

More of the families were now pouring from the cabins on the deck when the news broke that they did not find the Body of Elijah Burgess. They were joined by Bishop Emilie Thompson, a huge, fair skinned man with dark curly hair, along with his wife, Olivia and their 15 years old daughter, Emily.

There were lots of cries on the deck, as if to say the passengers have just realized that the Color Purpose CEO was no more. Daniel Roberts turned to his parents, held them firmly and began to sob. The Hayes family were standing next to him. Then he caught the scornful eyes of their son, Edwin.

"You can never catch my hit," the main batter of the Saints whispered.

"No. But you saw what I did. I went for it and caught it-piece of cake."

"But it sent you overboard. Lucky for you the sharks were full."

"Hey you boys stop that crap," suddenly hissed Emily, interrupting the hash Gaze and whispers between the two rivals. "A decent man has died because of such foolish pride."

"Attention, please," Captain Summerville tried to calm down the increasingly anxious situation. Fortunately, the confusion on the crowded deck began to simmer down as the captain continued to call everyone to attention. "We all mourn the loss of Mr. Burgess, but rest assured, despite his death all of you on board will still be covered by Color Purpose. We will sail you through to Cape Montserrado, land will be purchased for you, and you all will be re-settled, with all the other necessary packages."

"Is it in the organizational law and the law at sea that when the CEO on board is incapacitated, the captain on deck resumes responsibilities of the company's activities overseas until he returns back to headquarters with a full report," added Jimmy Penhurst.

There was silence on deck for a while as the message was sinking in and beseeching the confusion and anxieties that earlier filled the deck. Then there was a sudden wail, from one of the women, followed by the others, but this time they were only weeping for the death of the man who has worked assiduously in the interest of the black race.

Then Barbara Newland raised the spiritual song, 'When the roll is Call up Yonder,' in a soul shaking alto, reminiscent of the negro Baptist south. After the James M. Black Chorus was sung for the second time, Bishop Emile Thompson raised his hands in the air.

"Unto you O God who is able to do exceedingly abundantly of all that we ask or think according to the power that works within us, grant the secret desires of our hearts as we make our common supplication unto thee. Bless and console the soul of our fallen brother, Elijah Burgess as he has departed this transitory world in the service of humanity," he offered a world of prayer, and told the people to say collectively, "Let the words of our mouths, and the meditation our hearts be acceptable in thy sight, O Lord our strength and our redeemer, Amen."

"There must be a memorial service in his honor, captain," suggested Licentiate Charles Gooding III.

Everyone remained quiet, awaiting Captain Summerville's response. The Naval veteran turned to his Boatswain and gave him the instructional look.

"We will arrange that," Penhurst said.

Not quite long, Benjamin Coffey announced. "It's time to get back to our respective cabins. The crew still has lots of work to do here on deck."

Chapter 5

Captain Edwardo Gomez and his crew had rowed into the Farmington. About an hour inland, they encountered some warriors, emerging from the bushes on both sides of the banks, appearing fearful and clad in sisal skirts made of woven palm threads, and fresh palm leaves tied around their heads, upper arms and around their knees.

Their faces were painted black, and their bodies were dotted with white chalk. From the way they held their spears, bow and arrows and machetes, they did not exhibit a warlike posture.

"*Mbay Guley, ay,*" Witty Peter, putting on a friendly face, recited the greetings befitting for the afternoon.

For a while, the Worriers were unresponsive until one of them nodded and waved at the strangers. Then, just as they appeared, they disappeared into the bushes.

The crew reached a part of the river where two canoes were at the left side of the banks. There stood a village of about four to five square-shaped huts, dubbed with mud, with palm thatched roofs. The frames of the structures were made of stakes, whose outlines were partially buried in the mud used to dab the huts.

At the front were scaffolds built of sticks, fitted on the top by bamboo splints, neatly tied together by ropes, extracted from the inside of tree trunks. Varieties of cold-water fishes, exposed to the sun to dry, were spread on top of the scaffolds. Behind the huts were banana and plantain orchards, on which hung the ripe and juicy fruits. Further beyond were stretches of cassava plots.

The sailors became alerted to sudden shrieks and squeals at the back of the huts. But they became calmed when some children, between the ages of 5 and 10, appeared from behind the huts, playing. Fascinated to see strange large boats carrying white men and merchandise, they ran towards the banks, after the boats as they rowed past the village.

"*Quee-blee, quee-blee, quee blee, White* men, white men, white men," completely or partially naked, they shouted.

They continued for some meters, scuffling for sweets thrown at them and expecting to get more. But they were soon intercepted, and shooed by some worriers who emerged out of the bushes, and then disappeared again.

From that point onwards, there was no sign of human activity. The bushes were denser. And shooting out, among the thick undergrowth were the stems of the malagueta pepper plants with their fresh green and semi-curbed leaves with the predominant red fruits visible on their stalks.

Further on, a number of streams and creeks, whose mouths were littered with rocks, ran into the river. This extended for about forty-five minutes before observing the presence of human activity. A group of women were at the banks washing their clothes. They were dipping them in the water and slapping them against the rocks with the smacking sound echoing across the forest.

Upon seeing the big boats carrying white men, the women felt uneasy. They hastily gathered their wet clothes, put them in large baskets made of bamboo, and helped each other to set the baskets on their heads. With the water from the wet clothes draining down their heads, they hurried away through a path that snaked into the bush.

It did not take long after this point, they were sailing in a part of the river where the banks were higher than the ones they passed earlier in the journey. They saw a group of girls, about eight in number. They were between the ages of 5 and 19 with no clothes on, except the sisal skirts they were wearing.

Their bodies, from head to toe, were painted with white clay. Their heads were covered with head ties made of country clothes. The ones whose breasts were full, were standing firm and alluring with rounded and pointed nipples. They dangled invitingly as the girls walked along the high banks in a straight line, with the older ones in front, looking down at the boats, rowing upstream.

"They are the 'Blunjue'; the Sande Society sect," informed Witty Peter, studying the other sailors who couldn't keep their eyes off them as they rowed past the girls. "According to our tradition, a male gets blind when he keeps staring."

"I am aware of a great deal of your culture, Mr. Peter," Captain Gomez responded, offering a gentle smile.

"*Fique de olho nos pedestres*," Jose dos Santos immediately called to his men in Portuguese, audible enough to be heard in the other boats, telling them to keep their eyes on the paddles.

One of the Blunjue, the one leading the possession, the biggest and tallest of them, stopped at the beginning of a path that led into the bush, allowing the others to pass. She looked back at the boats which were now about to enter into an elbow to the right, and her eyes caught Jose Dos Santos', who had decided to look back as a last-minute surety that the girls were out to nothing, but soon took his eyes off hers. She continued to watch, as the last boat bent the curve, and then she turned and hurried to join the other Sande bush school pupils.

It took the expedition a few minutes to get out of the elbow where the river looked narrower with branches of trees overlooking it from both sides of the banks. Then they entered into an area where it became wide with the banks cleared of bushes and trees on both sides, extending meters away from the river.

There were rapids ahead, indicating that they have reached the point where they could not navigate funrther.

Gomez and Witty Peter, who were on board the big boat, got into one of the smaller boats and along with the other small one, they rowed towards the shore while the big boat, with Jose Dos Santo and the other sailors inside, remained anchored in the middle of the river.

On shore, they were met by a group of elderly men, wearing sleeveless country clothes designed like vests which extended all the way to their knees along with the lappers of similar black and white colors as the vest-like shirts. Their hair and beard were all gray, and each held a staff with a brushy animal tail at its end.

"The king's elders," informed Witty Peter, turning to Captain Gomez. Then he turned to the elders. "Mbay gulay, ay," he offered the afternoon greetings.

"Ay na gee?" the elders responded in unison.

One of them stepped closer to the guests, briefly scanned them with his eyes and then gestured to them to follow him.

Flanked on both sides by the elders, the king's guests were led to an area under a big cotton tree. Immediately ahead of them was a platform made of logs. Sitting on a chair beautifully carved out of fine dark red wood in the form of a huge cotton tree with what looked like bats on the branches was King Sorteh Gbayou. Two young women, wearing country clothes, designed with Leopard stripes stood at his right and his left. In their hands were huge black feathers, about 18 inches long, they were using to gently fan the king.

Executing the proper rites, the elders greeted the king, through a brief speech by the lead elder. Then they all bowed in unison, including Cho Vuyougar and Captain Gomez who partially bowed. Then the guests were presented to the king.

"O Great King, the defender of the Bassa people and their land," Witty Peter stepped forward and spoke. "I, Cho Vuyougar, from the house of King Zulu Demour, the great king of Dubor, and ruler of the ocean, who the settlers call Long Peter, is proud to present to you your most valuable guests." Witty Peter bowed again and looked up to the king, who looked back at him, expressionless and turned to look at the Portuguese.

"I bring you greetings, O king, from the trade world," Captain Gomez began, as Vuyougar interpreted. "In continuation of the Partnership your father, the great chief and I have established and ran, I have come to fulfill my part to you, his son. First, I expressed sympathy for his loss, and it is in the spirit of the commitment we made, I have brought these goods as a symbol in furtherance of the partnership."

Upon hearing this, King Gbayou's face suddenly brightened, and then he nodded. He stretched his hands forward in an open arm, gesturing to the Portuguese slave merchant to display what he had brought.

Slightly bowing, Gomez also nodded. He turned and signaled to his men in the boats waiting on shore and to the ones anchored in the middle of the river. Immediately, a group of men were hauling the mechanize from the boats to the base of the platform. The others were in canoes, paddling back and forth, hauling the rest of the goods from the other boats in the middle of the river.

When the king had seen enough of the goods, and was satisfied, he gestured to Witty Peter and Captain Gomez to come on the platform and sit with him. The Portuguese saw that King Gbayou was of average height, dark brown in complexion, and muscular. His face was round and beefy, and he was wearing a black gown made of country clothes with black lining. Around his neck was a chain made of columns of ivory with a nugget carved like a Leopard's head.

When all the items were uploaded, the king signaled to his lead elder who ordered the group of men to follow him. They entered a thick bush at the edge of the clearing. Minutes later, the men came back toting the goods, meaning sacs of dried Malagueta Pepper seeds, and artifacts for the Portuguese.

Captain Gomez got up and went to inspect the goods. He made a face like he was satisfied and scooped over the mountains of goods he brought, took from a chest a case containing some bottles of Johnny Walker, and uncapped it. He poured some into the bottle top and took a sip. After a few seconds he brought it to the king.

"O great King," he said, again partially bowing as Witty Peter interpreted. "As a symbol of our continued partnership, I present to you these beverages."

King Gbayou signaled to one of the girls fanning him. She immediately came forward and took the bottle from the Portuguese hands, her eyes lit with excitement, for the first time being in close proximity to a white man. When she had handed the bottle of whisky to the King, Vuyougar and Captain Gomez went back to their seats.

The King got from under his country cloth gown a long cup carved out of the stem of a reef and poured some of the Johnny Walker whisky into it. After taking a long sip, he shut his eyes, shook his head, and uttered a deep grunt.

"*Or nummer gee, cha,*" he said, looking at Witty Peter. "The king says the liquor is very good," Cho Vuyougar interpreted.

Then Sorteh Gbayou leaned over to the other girl who was fanning him at his right and whispered to her. She nodded and left the platform for a small thatched kitchen at the back, and returned with four older women. Two of them were toting stools while the other two were bringing bowls made of calabash. Some of the bowls contained dumboy, a cooked and pounded cassava while the others contained pepper soup. The ones with the stool sat them before the guests, followed by the ones bringing the dumboy. Another pair brought theirs and set them before the king. They bowed and then left.

"You are welcome to join me in our principal meal," said the King, washing his hands as a maid poured water from a ghoul.

"O king. I appreciate the offer, but my health doesn't allow me to consume too much starch," responded the Portuguese, looking at the calabash bowl of the well pounded cooked cassava before him.

"Your refusal to eat with the king will be taken as an insult to his majesty and it's bad for business," hissed Vuyougar, and then turned to the King. "Our guest is more delighted to partake into this special meal with you, O King."

"The soup contains a whole rooster, and some succulent crawfish taken from marshes along the banks of the St. John River. More importantly is the pounded malagueta pepper spice, which has magical properties that enhance metabolism. It also strengthens the pounding of the heart, and the nerves," the king said when his Portuguese guest had taken in his first swallow of the dumboy by first using his bare hand to pluck out a portion and form it into a ball.

"I am aware of that O king and I must again thank you for this meal."

"Your precious cargo will soon be turned over to you," the King assured him.

The Portuguese face suddenly brightened.

"Business has been good," continued the King. "The Kpelle won't give up encroaching on our land due to their unquenchable lust for farming. So, we continue to raid their isolated villages. And, unlike her father, their new ruler is reluctant to retaliate."

"Which means Lango Gbowee possesses no threat, I guess. But there's a problem I see coming and will be bad for business. Like doves, the settlers from Cape Montserrado might eventually be advancing towards your territory. They have begun negotiation for the territory of Marshall.

Pretty soon, they will extend their influence and municipalize your kingdom. You will be reduced to a mere tribal chief, subjected to their rules like how they did to Long Peter and now Bob Gray."

"A group of ally chiefs and kings are working on a plan to ensure that that never happens. And for now, I can only tell you my part, which is to harass Lango, keeping her occupied and not letting her to interfere on the side of the settlers while the other chiefs and kings drive them into the sea. I will need your help here. I want you to supply me with firearms and to help me train my men how to use them."

"That will not be easy, O King," after a brief thought, the Portuguese responded. "There's a joint Naval blockade of American and British warships around the strip of Gibraltar. All vessels entering the West Atlantic coast are searched. They take stock of all our supplies including our weapons before we sail in and out of here. It will be alarming to see us carrying huge stockpiles of firearms and later returning without them.

The colonial authorities have informed them that certain merchants are supplying powerful African kings with weapons to wage war against one another for the sake of the business. And when they find out that I am also into that, I will be arrested and that will be bad for business."

"So, what other help can you give to successfully execute my part of the plan?" The king asked, studying the reaction of the Portuguese captain.

"We can help make you good weapons here on your own soil. You have an abundance of resources that we can use."

"That will be good," the king said, beaming at the white man.

Just in time, the maids who brought the food for the king and his guests suddenly appeared. They cleared the bowls and the stool, and immediately hurried out of the platform. All the women and the men who were hauling the goods that were brought for the Portuguese to the boats were also hurrying away.

The atmosphere suddenly became quiet. Then there was the sound of a horn, followed by the cry of warriors, coming from the bush. A group of them emerged into the clearing, parading with some people, blind folded with their hands tied behind them.

"Your Cargo," getting up, the King announced.

Edwardo Gomez, fascinated by the large number of men, women and children captured by King Sorteh Gbayou as they were paraded before the platform, heavily guarded, also got up, including Cho Vuyougar.

Capt. Gomez followed the king when he walked past them. The captives, about 30 in number with the men dominating, were brought before the platform. As king Gbayou descended, the warrior guards escorting the captives began to force them on their knees and bow their heads before the king. Some of them were refusing, but they were flogged with long and thick rattans.

The king descended the platform, with his guests following behind him closely. He pointed to one of his warriors who appeared to be the chief warrior guard and instructed that few of the men and women be brought closer to him. Then he rubbed the backs of each of the men with his hands.

"Do you see these marks?" He turned to the Portuguese and asked, pointing to long marks like pimples running in lines of twos from their necks all the way down to the spine and extending both sides to the lower rib cage. "These belong to the Poro Society, where young boys are taken and stayed for years to be groomed into productive manhood."

Scooping over to inspect the backs of the women, and seeing the patterns of marks around their waists, "The same with the women," he continued. The Sande bush school teaches these women effective household management. They will all thrive well in the plantations of your clients. They already have similar arts in their blood. So, your cargo is valuable."

Excited, the Portuguese slave merchant nodded to the king.

"Can I inspect them myself?" he asked.

"Yes. And after that, my men will accompany them to your boats," responded the King. "But here. Take this before I forget."

He took from underneath his gown, the pin that was given to him by Abraham Garsuah, and gave it back to the Portuguese. "I will be expecting this again, in a few months."

"With honor and pleasure, O King," Captain Edwardo Gomez responded, bowing before the king, this time properly and then tended to inspect his precious cargo.

He went to each one, studying the face, especially around the lips to see whether there were blisters at the corners which would mean the presence of fever, the eyes, whether they were yellow, to suggest yellow fever or Jaundice.

The male captives, with some of them refusing, were bent over so that the captain could look into their anuses for traces of liquid feces. As the stubborn ones were subdued and restrained, he saw none, meaning that they were in good health.

"We made sure that they are kept in good health," interpreted Witty Peter when the King spoke. "Apart from most of the herbs we administered to them, we also included in their diet, the meat and bones of Cassava snakes to prevent or fight off Jaundice and yellow fever."

"Certainly. As I can see, the Gaboon Viper is very good against Jaundice," admitted the Portuguese slave merchant. "I am ready to load my Cargo, O king," he turned to King Gbayou and bowed again. Then he turned to his crewmen in the small boats waiting on the banks of the river. "Bring the shackles."

Thinking they were just captives in a raid so as to force their leader, Lango Gbowee into negotiation to prevent her people from encroaching on Bassa land, and then they will be turned over and swear to never return to where they were captured, they were appalled to see their captors, with some white men fastening collar bracelets attached together with long chains, around their necks, their hands and feet.

The women and children in the group began to cry as they were bundled and led into the boats. One of the men, a huge and bearded one, sensing that they were sold to the white men as slaves and will be taken from their land to a faraway country, managed to free himself when the robes binding his hands and feet, were ripped off just in time before they were replaced by the shackles.

The man raised across the clearing and was about to enter into the bush, on the north side but some of King Gbayou's men were upon him, pouncing, and wrestling him to the ground. 10 of the Bassa warriors guards were on top of him, fighting to restrain him. Three of them were stepping on his head, pressing his face to the ground causing him to groan and snout dust out of his nostrils.

"*Ele está sufocando! Tenha cuidado antes de perdê-lo*!" two of Captain Gomez 'men raised towards the scene, shouting, "He's suffocating! Be careful or we will lose him.!"

"Kpakolo," suddenly screamed at one of the women, seeing how the man was treated, and threw herself on the ground. The weight from the chain on which the iron collar around her neck was attached, pulled the others with her to the extent that the rings around their necks were choking them.

The king shouted at his men to ensure that the cargo were safe, as the warrior guards and the Portuguese struggled to bring the situation under control.

"O King!" Captain Gomez said, breathing heavily. "Next time please allow me to bring more of my crew. They have the expertise to handle such delicate cargo or else we will one day experience huge losses due to unexpected fatalities!"

"*Chen-or gbo, nye say wuon :* Tell him I disagree," King Gbayou said to Witty Peter.

"The king says he would rather prefer the same number of men you are allowed to accompany you to train his men since they themselves are experts in handling the cargo," the shrewd interpreter conveyed to the Portuguese slave trader, instead.

Subdued, humiliated and broken, the slaves, once proud men and women whose quest for pursuing the subsistence and economic wellbeing of their progenies, for which purpose they had ventured deep into fertile Bassa land, were arrayed in a long queue with shackles around their necks, hands and feet.

Guarded by King Gbayou's warrior guards they were led to the boats, and were bundled five in each of the small boats. After two trips back and forth to the main boat, King Gbayou and his men watched as the three boats rowed downstream, heading for the mouth of the Farmington and then onward into the Atlantic Ocean where the Santa Amelia was waiting.

Guarded by King Gbayou's warrior guards they were led to the boats, and were bundled five in each of the small boats. After two trips back and forth to the main boat, King Gbayou and his men watched as the three boats rowed downstream, heading for the mouth of the Farmington and then onward into the Atlantic Ocean where the Santa Amelia was waiting.

"Please repeat these words after me," thousands of nautical miles away Bishop Emile Thompson said to the licentiate Reverend Charles Gooding, III.

He was dressed in his white Alb, partially reaching his torso with a black chasuble designed in flowery gold colors, and a black scarf worn across his chest. On his head was his black Biretta, with the symbol of a cross designed in gold. His daughter, Emily Thompson, dressed in her altar gale garments befitting the occasion, was standing behind him, holding the gold crozier staff of a bishop.

This was the memorial service of the fallen Color Purpose CEO, held on the main deck of the ship. But it began with the ordination ceremony of the Baptist Licentiate on general consensus of the passengers on board for the power of his exhortations, and his faithful prayers during the night of the storm. And that he must be the one to preach at the memorial service.

A few feet from an elevated platform, some members of the family of the passengers were seated in rows of benches arranged by the ship's crew. To the right of the platform sat a group of ten persons comprising six females, with Sister Barbara Newland among them at the forefront and 4 men wearing choir garments. The left of the platform were also seated by eight persons comprising deacons and deaconesses from the Presbyterian, Baptist and Methodist denominations. Captain Summerville and his Boatswain, Jimmy Penhurst were seated at the far back of the platform, facing the congregation.

The weather was good, and the tide was calmed as the tropical breeze blew across the main deck. A group of women were seated in the middle row. They were all dressed in their expensive Victoria era funeral dresses, and their veiled covered colonial Williamsburg hats, stretching their necks in an effort to glance at the widow, Mrs. Angela Draper Burgess, seated alone at the end on a bench at the front row.

Since they boarded the ship, all the passengers were interviewed by Mr. Burgess, but they only heard he had a wife. Only a few families, like Bishop Thompson's, the referee James Cooper's parents, saw her on one or two occasions. But they hardly knew the beautiful widow of the late CEO.

Also seated at the front rows along with their parents, were the kids who were playing baseball on deck. Among them was the ship's steward boy, Benjamin Coffey, making sure that the lads behave themselves as they harshly whispered to each other on which team was going to prove better than the other, if Daniel Roberts had not fallen overboard.

Few of the crewmen on deck including Jack Duval, Lan Dole, Howard Lusting stood around the starboard and the port side, keeping an eye on the sails and flying jib.

"I reaffirm my belief in one God the Father Almighty, the maker of heaven and earth," continued the Bishop as Licentiate Gooding III repeated after him.

"I reaffirm my belief in the birth, the death and resurrection of his only begotten son, our Lord and Savior Jesus Christ, whose death has washed away the sins of the world.

I reaffirm my belief in the holy trinity that God is the Father, the Son and the Holy Ghost.

I reaffirm my belief in the mystery of faith, that Christ has died, Christ has risen, and Christ will come again.

Upon these values I reiterate my commitment to preach the gospel to the poor to all parts of the earth, including the Malagueta Coast.

Upon these values I will continue to be the Good Shepherd, tendering to his flocks, which I will take as my very own, void of prejudice, and the influence of earthly authority."

After the bishop and the Licentiate went on with the long order of affirmation, he ended and was repeated by Gooding, "So help me God."

"Can you please kneel before heaven and earth," Bishop Thompson then instructed.

Licentiate Gooding knelt down. A lad, seated on a stool right next to the chair reserved for the bishop, also attired in his altar guild robes, came forward and took the Golden Crozier from Emily. Then she hurried to a table on the right of the chair reserved for the bishop, a silver aspergillum, and unscrewed the bottom. She also took a vial from the table and filled the instrument with water and screwed the top. Then she brought it to the bishop, and stood by him, with her hands across her torso. The bishop held it and raised his voice.

"With the spirit of the Lord upon me, to bear me witness to the reaffirmation of your faith in our Lord and Savior Jesus Christ by the rejection of sin and the proclamation of the gospel to the poor and to tender to His flocks, I hereby present to Thee O God, Licentiate Charles Gooding III as Reverend Charles Gooding III. Upon this duty, as I consecrate him, he shall continue to practice righteousness in all his undertakings in the name of the Father, the Son and the Holy Spirit," Bishop Emile Thompson then sprinkled the holy water on the head of the Licentiate by shaking the aspergillum. And when he had handed the staff back to his daughter, who remained standing, he laid his hands on the head of Charles Gooding and declared. "Licentiate Charles Gooding III with the power vested in me as a Messenger of God, I Bishop Emile Thompson of the southern Conference of the Negro United Methodist Church hereby ordain you as Reverend Charles Gooding III."

Just as the congregation said "Amen," in unison, Sister Barbara Newland raised the song 'When Jesus Call Me, I'll Answer', followed by singing, dancing and jubilation.

Eugene Tubman, a tall man dressed in a black coat and brown trousers sat behind a wooden piano, and was displaying melodies of soul music and a drummer, a young dark-skinned man named Nathaniel Giddings was seated behind the drums, beating the instrument, southern Baptist Negro style. As the newly ordained reverend was still kneeling, the Choir, along with the deacons and deaconesses danced around him, while the congregation was also singing and dancing.

After some time, Reverend Charles Gooding III with tears of joy in his eyes, as he reflected on the many challenges before becoming a reverend, a profession he inherited from his late grandfather, the Right Reverend Charles Gooding, rose up, accompanied the bishop to his seat, and then waited as two of the ship's crewmen toted a podium almost at the edge of the front of the platform.

The newly ordained Baptist Minister danced towards the podium when the crewmen set it properly and left as the singing, dancing, and the music got more frenzied. This continued for some minutes. Some of the women in the congregation, especially those whose sons were playing baseball on the deck and were rescued from the storm, were jumping around and shouting 'Alleluia'.

The reverend then held both hands in the air to quiet down his congregation and the singing and dancing and the music gradually slowed down. Then it stopped amid loud cries of 'amens' and 'alleluias' mixed with occasional holy spirit filled wailings.

"Let the congregation say amen," Reverend Gooding said, and the entire congregation responded.

"I would like to extend my many thanks and appreciation to Captain Summerville and crew for allowing this noble occasion. And to Bishop Emile Thompson for performing another task on a servant of God. And to you the congregation for your support.

One thing I must tell you Christian brothers and sisters, when God sanctions anyone to do good, everywhere that person goes, he will do good. When our heavenly father sent our Lord and Savior Jesus Christ into this world, everywhere he went, he was doing good. He raised the dead, healed the Leper, and when the cripple saw him, they started walking.

And because he touched Elijah Burgess, everywhere he went he was doing good. And it is the good of Elijah Burgess that brought us thus far and is going to take us to the land of our ancestors. O my Christian brothers and sister, it is the land where absolute freedom will reign.

Now let us stand and sing the old song that says 'Everywhere He went, He was doing good.'"

Barbara Newland raised the song, followed by Eugene Tubman's brief testing of the keys to determine the tone, and when he had picked up the melody of the song, he then expertly converted it into a full-grown music when Nathaniel Giddings hit the drums.

Emily Thompson shot disdainful and warning eyes at the boys at the front bench, especially the Findley brothers who were giggling and laughing at Mr. Giddings, for the way he was furiously beating the drums like an animal. She knew they were laughing at the way he kept his bushy hair and long beard, and the way he stretched his eyes.

"Everywhere He went, He was doing good," Reverend Gooding re-echoed the title of the song, when the singing and dancing had stopped. "But you know what? Many people don't do good, because there is always an ultimate sacrifice associated with it. Christ was the ultimate sacrifice for the good He did by watching our sins away. Elijah Burgess was lost at sea because of the good he did to rescue the kid, Daniel Roberts. Let the congregation say Amen."

He scooped slightly to open a small door at the back of the pulpit and took out his big black King James Bible. He placed it on the book stand, opened the Bible and began to flip through the pages.

"Nevertheless, there is also a divine duty associated with doing good. And I want you all to open your bibles to Mathew 5:16," resumed the newly ordained Baptist prelate, and paused as he lifted his head and gazed at the congregation to the sound of the flipping of pages with little mummering in the congregation.

Mrs. Findley, sitting between her two boys was flipping through hers and was getting frustrated as it appeared she did not know where to begin to find the book of Mathew. She paused and hesitated, shot her two boys a 'I dare you to giggle' look, and then handed the Book over to Ben, who was sitting right next to Harold Findley when he gestured to lend a hand.

"If you are there, say Amen," continued Reverend Gooding, followed, one after the other by shouts of amen. "'Let your light so shine before men that they may see your good works and glorify your Father who is in heaven,'" he read the scripture and continued. "This is the message I have for you, Christian brothers and sisters. Let Your Light So Shine. Elijah Burgess has shone his light. How many of us are ready to shine ours'?

We are returning to the land of our ancestors that is considered the dark continent. And one thing we don't know about ourselves is that we are special people endowed with the ability to lighten the land of our forefathers. But the lights that are in some of us are getting dim by the day, and the danger is, we will not be able to see our way into this dark land of our ancestors with the dim lights within us. So, we need to rekindle our lights so that it can shine to see our way through. Let the congregation say amen."

There was a loud amen after this statement.

"To rekindle the dim lights within us, we must first forget the past that we were former slaves or the children of former slaves. Even though the slave trade is evil, but a good thing we got out of this predicament is that we are all Christians with the ability to follow the examples of our Lord and Savior Jesus Christ so that others, like the descendance of our ancestors who are living in the dark can see the light and follow. Remember the scripture says, 'Let your light so shine before men that they shall see your good works and glorify your father in heaven.' Let the Congregation say amen."

Reverend Gooding then descended the platform and went walking between the center rows.

"But how can we rekindle this light like the late Elijah Burgess' when there's a deep-rooted segregation amongst us?" He resumed. "The fair skin color among us feel that they are better than the black skin color while the black skin color feel that they are going to own more rights to the land of their ancestors because they are pure black with no traces of white blood in them. And dangerously of all, they harbor the view that if the new land of liberty is established, the leadership will be entitled to them. Let the congregation say amen."

This time the amen was faint, as the congregation remained largely silent, though with low mummering from the middle and the back rows.

"I know I have struck a core, and so I cannot get a loud and sincere amen," the Reverend, seeing this, chuckled.

Then he raised his voice, "Let me get a loud amen if I am telling the truth."

The amen became loud and clear.

"O yes, my Christian brothers and sisters. Elijah Burgess was born and raised in a white home to a white father. He was never treated or seen as a slave or the son of a black woman. He never did the work that we former slaves or our grandparents and parents did. He was well educated like his white half brothers and sister, but he chose to shine the light in him by identifying with black and colored people. That's why he established the Color Purpose Organization. And we all can bear witness to his good works.

And so, it is now time to shine our lights like the fallen CEO. But how can we do so when the dim lights within us have been passed on to our children? The incident on this deck about a fortnight ago was a clear manifestation of how our kids are inheriting the dim light of segregation from us, their parents.

Forming two baseball teams, one, the Yankees, comprising only fair skinned colored kids while the saints, comprising of dark-skinned kids with one eager to show dominance over the other while the other was poised to reject that, even in the mid of a storm, led us to having a memorial service of one of the finest persons the negro race can boast of.

How can we shine our lights on the shores of our forefathers, the dark lands of our ancestors when right here amongst us I have heard kids ask their parents, 'Why do children and their parents live in trees, over there? Is it true that they worship the ocean, rivers and mountains? Why do their kids not wear clothes or are often partially naked? Do they turn to big birds and fly at night to harm kids like us? And all I hear parents say, yes, they do because they are savages. While there, stay away from them. Don't let them into our homes. There are other kids and families who got there before us. They are just like us from America. You can play with them as our family will only mingle with their family.'"

"Preach on, reverend," shouted Mrs. Henrietta Jackson, one of the deaconesses.

"You can shine the light in you and pass them to your kids by telling them if they see an indigenous kid sleeping in a tree, calmly call that kid down and teach him or her how to live in a shelter. Tell them to clothe those without clothes, teach those who worship places about a one and true living God. Make your kids understand that there are also stories of witches that fly by night on broom sticks on the plantations and they can be redeemed by the blood of his only begotten Son, our Lord and Savior Jesus Christ. And that is how you are going to shine the light in you, your kids, and others living in the dark will follow."

"Tell us, reverend," A tall man by the name of Author Brown, seated in the middle of the congregation, suddenly jumped to his feet and shouted. "Many of us need to hear this."

Reverend Gooding paused for a while and suddenly became serious and winced.

"O My fellow Christian brothers and sisters, if these things and many others are not done, I can see us losing the glorious opportunity as touch bearers of our Lord and Savior Jesus Christ, enlightening the dark world of our ancestors.

That was why my grandfather always preached that we must accept our fate as slaves as God was using it to prepare us to one day return to the land of our forefathers to shine the light in us to its darkest parts. And as many of us understood, he was vilified for such preaching, and now here we are on the journey as the touch bearers he envisioned.

Oh yes, I can see that if we don't stop this segregation amongst us and our native brothers and sisters, this glorious land of liberty we all envisage will be in turmoil from generations to generations. And if we don't begin to shine the light in us, posterity will surely be our judge."

Reverend Gooding went on preaching other related issues and ended his sermon with this statement: "I don't know about you, but this little light that is in me, I am going to let it shine."

Sister Barbara Newland then raised the song 'This little light of mine, I am going to let it shine' followed by the music and then everyone was singing and dancing. After some time, he raised his hands to quiet the group, and the singing and dancing gradually subsided.

"Let the kids who were rescued from the deck when the storm began, come before the platform," he ordered, and when they had assembled, he turned to Bishop Emile Thompson and announced, "We will now call on Bishop Thompson to pray for these young men in whose hands bear the touch light of enlightenment, righteousness, and leadership. God has a purpose for them as they enter into the land of their forefathers. I believe that was why he saved them or, they all could have been swept away in the storm."

The bishop got up, and walked to the end of the platform with the aspergillum in his hands as the lad holding the crozier walked behind him.

"Let the Lord continue to guide and protect you, as you grow in wisdom and righteousness," the bishop said, as he walked from the left to right, sprinkling water on their heads.

After that they were all ordered back to their seats. Then the Bishop announced that it was time to pay tributes to the late fallen CEO of Color Purpose, Elijah Burgess.

After the sermon, two crewmen brought a frame wrapped with old newspapers and set it right next to the pulpit. They removed the paper, revealing a portrait of the fallen CEO. It was a magnificent piece of aesthetic quality by the artist Nathaniel Brownell, a son of a former slave, on board the Freedom Star.

The visual effects presented Elijah Burgess in his navy-blue satin frock coat with a white ruffle shirt, and golden cravat, seated, legs crossed, on a golden chair with a fireplace in the background. In his right hand was a fountain pen slightly above an inkwell he held in his left hand. It appears like he was about to dip the pen into the inkwell to write something on a scroll lying on his lap.

The colors were vivid, portraying the Abolitionist as a fair skin individual who could more easily pass for a pure white man, except for his dark brown eyes and his mostly brown and curly hair. But Brownell was keen to show that any one viewing the portrait could see that Elijah Burgess was a black man.

Even though the CEO fiscal expression displayed a smiling and hopeful character, the general interpretation of the painting unveiled a dedicated humanitarian reflecting deeply on propagating and upholding the dignity of the negro race to the rest of the world.

The two crewmen unfolded two long wooden stands from the sides of the portrait so that it could stand by itself. When the painting was unveiled, most of the women and some men in the congregation started weeping again. Suddenly, there was total silence when a woman, dressed in black sleeveless dress, walked to the portrait, sobbing and convulsing occasionally.

Her hands were covered from her fingers to her shoulders with a pair of black neon opera gloves. She held on a black skeleton vintage hat with a black fishnet veil covering her face. Through the veal, peering eyes struggled to recognize the face of a fair skinned woman with Latino eyes and nose. To everyone's guess, she was Mrs. Angela Draper Burgess.

She stood in front of the portrait of her late husband, weeping and shaking. Bishop Emile Thompson got up and hurried down the platform. When he reached her, he wrapped his arms around her shoulders at the same time, padding her on her back.

"Your husband was a good man," he whispered. "We will forever remember his good works. The angels in heaven are rejoicing to receive his soul. And may it rest in peace."

Mrs. Burgess convulsed for some time and bowed her head in a deep reflection of how she and Elijah Burgess met.

It was at Continental Inn, overlooking the James River at Rockettes, where he frequented whenever he was visiting his birth place, in Richmond. The owner, Alexander Gerald, was a close friend of his father, who did not hesitate to stand as the young Burgess' God Son at the time of his baptism.

"Hi there," he greeted and made his way over to her when he saw this beautiful woman, dressed in a white Victoria dress, seated at the bar.

She turned to see who was entering the inn and their eyes met and locked for a few seconds, and then she turned to the bartender. She looked aristocratic, and appeared like she was waiting or more probably looking for someone.

"Can I buy you a drink?" he asked, taking a stool, adjusting it close to her and sitting on it.

She looked sideways and didn't respond.

"Unfortunately, pretty lady. I don't take no for an answer, and so I would take your non-response for a yes," mused the young Color Purpose CEO, and looked up at old Bill Hayes, the negro bartender who was wiping glasses and putting them into a tray. "A Tignanello for us, please."

"Sure, sir," the negro bartender responded and reached for the dark purple bottle of the Antinori's brand, set it on the counter and gently place two glasses Infront of his two customers.

"It must be an irresistible charm of yours to compel me to accept your offer," she spoke for the first time smiling, after taking a light sip, when Elijah Burgess had filled her glass and his, with the refreshing Italian wine.

Burgess smiled too, and then raised his glass and took a sip. "I wouldn't call it a charm, pretty face. I would say It's a long dead craving that has awakened the moment I saw you."

The brief reflection of her husband was interrupted when she felt the bishop's hands around her shoulders padding her on her back. She continued to quiver and sop. And when it was obvious that she wasn't going to say a word, Bishop Thompson led her to a seat right next to his wife, Mrs. Olivia Thompson.

"Tributes can now begin," he announced when he appeared In Front of the congregation again.

At the pulpit, Reverend Charles Gooding III held in his hands a list of persons who were to pay tributes to the fallen Humanitarian.

"We also share your loss, Madam Burgess, for your husband was a great soldier in the fight to unveil the true dignity of the colored and the negro race. And we remain forever grateful to him, Captain Summerville and his crew, and the Color Purpose Organization for committing to the vision of Elijah Burgess to ensure that we are properly re-settled when we arrive at the land of our ancestors. We owe the life of our son, Daniel to him, and we promise that one of our grandchildren will be named after him," Mr. Jason Roberts, Daniel Robert's father, like the other families who had paid their tributes, concluded, after recounting all the good things Elijah Burgess did. Standing behind him was his wife, Mary Antoinette Roberts, and their son, Daniel.

"May the Soul and the souls of all the faithful departed rest in perfect peace. In the name of the Father and the Son and the Holy Ghost," he ended his tribute at the same time signing his cross. He and his family took their seats, while the choir along with the congregation sang the song 'On the Day of Resurrection'.

Two days after the memorial service, Captain Summerville was seated in his office, reviewing the draft report, submitted to him, of the incident on the deck that led to the drowning of Elijah Burgess. Also in his office was Dr. Reid, Jimmy Penhurst, the Boatswain, Jack Duval and Howard Lusting, all seated opposite the captain's desk.

"So, Elijah Burgess may have had a seizure which paralyzed him just before the inflatable tube was thrown in the water to pull him up. And, because he was unable to move his hands and legs, it caused him to drown."

"Certainly, Captain," responded Jack Duval who still looked pale and worried.

"Now, we know that. And we also know, before that, he came on deck, looking devastated, according to the Findley boys, which does not suggest that the devastation on his face was because he saw a group of lads playing baseball on the deck when a storm was developing. But what we don't know is what made him spooked before getting on the deck."

"Yes, Captain. We hope his wife can tell us what she observed about him during the time they were together," suggested Dr. Reid. "Something that could suggest a prior medical condition."

"And with her permission, we could also search among his belongings to see whether we can find any prescription he may have been taking," added Jimmy Penhurst.

"I think it was something like an evil spell cast on him," interjected Jack Duval. "When I saw what I saw up the cabin window, I was spooked, I could not move my hands and legs. It was like an evil spell was cast on me."

"He believes something like an apparition is on board this ship, Captain," added Howard Lusting.

"There is nothing scientific to suggest so," objected the ship's physician. "You and crew were two days out at sea, after a massive overnight storm, searching for a corpse with pain-taken efforts. That may have an effect on you."

"So, what do you suggest, Doc.?" asked the captain.

"Exhaustion, anxiety or an unexplained medical condition caused by the search at open sea. But I need to run a test on Duval and his search party."

"I have been on the open sea all my life as a kid with my dad fishing at Cape Cod Bay, and over 20 years at sea as an adult, hunting sharks. I have never experienced what happened to me when I saw what I saw," insisted Jack.

"Describe again what you saw?" asked Dr. Reid as Captain Summerville looked at the Doctor and then Jack, at the same time making a face that he was getting weary of Jack and the ship's physician going back and forth on the matter.

"A dim light flickering through a cabin window at the main deck drew my attention, when we were about to receive the robes from the lifting gear. Then I saw a face peering through that same window. It was white like snow with dark eyes which sometimes turned scarlet. Then the eyes turned dark blue like the universe and started revolving like two heavenly bodies with tiny stars emitting splashes of lights. It was then that I was spooked; motionless; paralyzed."

"A face white as snow with dark eyes which turned red? It's a description of a ghost," Dr. Reid came in. "Like I said, it's not scientific. Running a psycho-analytical test on you will determine probable cause of what you consider an evil spell. Your years at the open sea doesn't suggest that all that time, a condition has not been developing in you."

"Oh, come on, Doc." Duvall Flare up, becoming agitated. "After we got the Daniel boy out of the water, I looked into Burgess' eyes when I sent the inflatable tube down to him. He suddenly stretched his eyes while looking up. Like he saw something. Then he became motionless, and next he went down. I don't think it was the seizure that got him spooked. I experienced the same thing when I saw what I just described. it was an evil spell."

"Why only you? Little Benjamin Coffey roams this vessel every day and night. But he has never seen, and reported anything strange."

"Have we asked him?" asked Jack, looking at the ship Physician and then Captain Summerville, who was flipping through the pages of the report.

"Okay. That's enough," said the captain, looking at Dr. Reid and Jack Duval. "We need to run the test, Jack. From your report of the search mission, humidity was extremely high, the tide was still rough, after a stormy night, and the fog was thick, thus blurring your visions, and at the same time you and team were taking strenuous effort searching for a corpse in such a condition. We want to know the effect it had on you all. That's all for now. The doc and I will speak to Mrs. Burgess."

They all, except Dr. Reid, left the captain's office. It did not take long for Mrs. Angela Draper Burgess, accompanied by Bishop Emile Thompson, to enter. The Widow of the fallen CEO was dressed in a gray sleeveless dress with similar design like the black one she wore at the memorial service, except that the neon opera gloves she was wearing was also gray.

Captain Summerville and Dr. Reid could make out her face covered by the black fishnet veil, cascading from the colonial gray hat on her head. The captain gestured to a seat which she sat in, legs crossed, exposing the black seek knee high booties she was wearing. Bishop Thompson sat next to her.

"We are again sorry for the loss of your husband, Mrs. Burgess," the captain began, studying the beautiful face behind the veil, but showing no expression that the wife of his fallen CEO was extremely beautiful. "Our investigation shows that he had a seizure which paralyzed him while he was in the water."

"That caused him to drown because he was unable to move his hands and legs to keep him afloat when our crew threw the inflatable tube to him," added Dr. Reid.

"The ship's physician and I want to know whether you observed any strange behavior about him from the day you both met."

"I have known my husband to be very excited about us, from the day we met. We loved each other, and it was difficult to tell whether he was having some internal issues. The only time I saw him thoughtful was when he was at his study, working."

"Had he mentioned any condition he had been experiencing from childhood?" Asked the ship's Physician, after listening to Mrs. Burgess who spoke in a calm and nice voice.

"No."

"Did you discover any medical prescription in his coat pockets or anywhere else?"

"No, Captain."

"Can you reflect on the many moments you shared?" Dr. Reid asked.

"Hope this is not an interrogation of a widow who had just lost her husband," stated Bishop Thompson, becoming alarmed as he nervously adjusted the white clavate he wore under the collar of his black shirt.

"No, Bishop. We are trying to find out what happened to Burgess. We are not looking for suspects," assured Dr. Reid.

Mrs. Burgess convulsed and after sobbing for a while, she took a white handkerchief and dabbed her teary eyes. Then she wrung her head, folded her arms, and uncrossed her legs. She leaned forward, gazing at the nose of the sleek booties on her feet.

The captain and the ship's physician watched patiently as Mrs. Burgess mentally navigated her way into another deep reflection of the time she and her late husband spent together.

"So, tell me," Elijah Burgess had asked her, after draining the second glass of the Tignanello. "What a beautiful woman doing here in Richmond, all by yourself?"

"Just a free colored girl from Montgomery in the quest for an adventure."

"Oh! What a coincidence! I am Elijah Burgess. People call me Mr. Adventure. In couple of days, I'll be sailing across the Atlantic Ocean taking with me free negros like me to a place called Cape Montserrado, or Monrovia."

"Coincidence seems to be nice to you, then," laughed the then Miss. Draper, the dimples on her face taking the man before her by storm. "And if you won't mind, I would like to be on this adventure of yours," she paused, studying the young and handsome man, spellbound, as he could still not believe his eyes to be in a company with such a beautiful woman. "Hello," she said in a harmonious tone at the same time stroking her glass with her fingernail, snapping the young CEO to attention. "I am Miss. Angela Draper. My late father was a sea merchant who left me with a lot of inheritance."

"Year I thought so. Some white dads, like mine, are the nicest persons on earth. I am certainly impressed. A toss to that," he mused, raising his glass.

She did likewise and after a toss, both took a long drink. And when they both sat their glasses back on the counter, almost simultaneously, the ferry beauty looked back towards the entrance of the inn to a black coach waiting outside.

"Yours?"

"Hired."

Elijah Burgess nodded. He emptied the remaining Tignanello down his throat and gently sat the glass back on the counter.

"Just a second," he said and excused himself from Miss Draper.

He strode over to the inn manager, a white man sitting behind a desk at the far right of the counter and said something to him. The man nodded. Then Burgess fished into the inner pocket of his coat, took out a piece of paper and a pen and wrote something on it. He signed and handed the paper to the man. In exchange, the man handled what looked like a key holder to the Color Purpose CEO.

"Hey Todd," the inn manager called outside to a black man sitting at the door. "Get the luggage from the coach waiting outside, would you?"

"Right away, Alex," Todd responded. He and another black man got up and went to the coach.

Elijah Burgess watched as Todd got to the front of the coach and said something to the coachman, an old white man with a spotty face dressed in a black coat and wearing a black Top Hat. He got down and both went to the back. Then the CEO turned to Alex and said, smiling, "I will anticipate an elaborate accommodation for my guest."

"Heard you, son," Alex responded, his attention on Miss Draper, who looked back at the two men, returned a pleasant smile and then fished into a black purse she took from under her arm. "Never seen you so excited," observed the inn manager.

"Yeah, You're right, Alex. And it's quite alluring when a man inadvertently bumped into an attractive and extremely beautiful woman and right away both realize that both were the long-sought soul mates."

Both men laughed, and then Elijah Burgess went back to join Miss Draper at the counter.

"I got an abrupt adventure in mind, pretty face," he said, taking the stool next to her right instead of the one he was earlier sitting on at her left.

"I will be obliged to embark on that. What is it?"

"Be my guest as long as you are in Richmond," The Color Purpose CEO offered, taking the key holder from his pocket and swinging it before her eyes. "There's a suit upstairs reserved for you."

"You are so generous and kind, Mr. Burgess," she said smiling. "Are you going to show me this suit or what?" She then asked as she gently held his hand and folded it with the key inside.

Immediately Burgess was on his feet and ready to take Miss Draper to the suite. They both took a stair to their right, when they entered into a lobby and went to the 3rd floor which was the last floor. At room 13, they met Todd at the door standing with the luggage. Mr. Burgess opened the door to the suite and demonstrated the welcome gesture by slightly bowing before her, swinging his right hand in the direction of the open door for Miss Draper to enter.

She smiled, in appreciation of the politeness exhibited by the colored aristocrat, and then entered the suite with Todd following behind with the luggage. Elijah Burgess was the last to enter, as his guest admired the elegance of the place; its beautifully decorated plank wall made of dark wood, vanished orange-yellow, on which hang the portraits of President Monroe, and governor Thomas Mann Randolph Jr.

"Magnificent," she mused, looking at the beautifully set up Winterthur Dining room with the arrangement of chairs made of red wood around a table of similar design.

"Thanks to old Alex," admitted the Colored Purpose CEO, observing as she could not keep her eyes off the chandeliers designed like clover leaves. "We're done here, Todd," he then said to the inn attendant who stood, lost in a gaze.

"I am sorry, sir," Todd said and left, shutting the door behind him.

Miss Draper continued to survey the room, as Elijah Burgess looked on. "Let me give you a little space to familiarize yourself with the suit while I go see my dad, just a few clicks from here," he offered, smiled and turned to leave.

"Not after some more refreshment with wine," she preferred, striding to the liquor cabinet on the wall across the dining room.

"Certainly," he agreed and took one of the wooden chairs with a spongy sky-blue flowery seat in the sitting area near the fireplace.

The beauty queen uncorked a bottle of Chateau Margaux and poured the vintage wine into two glasses. She brought them to the fireplace, enjoying the warmth when Elijah lit it, and handed one to him. Sitting close to him, she offered a toss. When they did, they took light sips.

Pretty close to 2 hours, they charted, laughed and geekled. Then Elijah got up to leave.

"See you at the bar in three hours," he told his guest.

"I can handle that, provided I wouldn't be made to wait too long."

"You wouldn't," he assured her while at the door, and then gently took her hands and kissed them. In return she kissed him on his jaw and closed the door behind him when he gleefully stepped out.

At the entrance of the Inn, Todd brought Jumbo, Elijah's horse, a huge dark-brown Fleuve given to him by his father. He told him that its mother was native to Africa, from around the river Gambia region. It was a gift from an old African King who was his trading partner during his days as a slave trader, along the West African Coast.

"So, have you given it a thought, the migration plan I discussed with you? In two months, the company will be sailing a number of free men like you across the Atlantic," he said to Todd, when he mounted the horse.

"I did, sir," responded the Inn attendant. "But I am ok right here." Expecting Todd to explain further, Elijah Burgess did not say a word as he steadied Jumbo who seemed eager to gallop with its master. "Like you said, I am a free man. I got a job to take care of my wife and kids. And Alex needs me here. He's a good man. A good white man like your dad."

"Fair enough, Todd. And don't forget to watch over my guest," Elijah Burgess said and then with a nudge on its sides, Jumbo suddenly neighed, kicked off, raising his forelegs in the air, and galloped with his master, towards Williamsburg.

CHAPTER 6

Along the upper Farmington that forms the northwestern frontier of Bassa and Kpelle Lands, where the low coastal plains, stretching from the coast meet the highlands, the river forms splinters of water falls as torrents of cascading flows crash into the rapids prone plunge pool bellow.

On this particular sunny day, it was the dry season where the torrential flow had subsided as the water level reduced at this time of the year. Along the base are huge rocks which are not visible during the height of the rainy season. At such times, the surface of the river is littered with dead woods and the leaves of the predominant semi-deciduous trees that stretched along the banks. Animals trot at the edge to drink.

A large meaty bushbuck, chewing its cud, suddenly emerged from the bush, hopping over a dead tree that was lying in its path. It first raised its head, stopped chewing its cud, at the same time swinging its long ears back and forth, as its instinctive faculty worked to pick up and process any sound of danger.

Satisfied that there was none, it resumed chewing its cud and cautiously strode towards the banks. Soon followed by a herd of other deer and black barked duikers.

As they bowed their heads over the surface of the running water, drinking, the sound of the crack of a dry stem suddenly alerted them. Almost in unison, they raised their heads to attention, waiting for another crack which would mean danger was around, and time was up. Drinking for the day was over, and to immediately take the flight, dashing back into the bushes.

A few meters north, Yallah Kolliemenni, a young hunter was about to emerge from the bush but trampled on a dry stick that cracked under his feet. He hissed his teeth and swiftly ducked for cover behind a large tree when the alerted bushbuck looked his way.

Pissed with himself for not following a simple hunting rule to always look where to step when stalking an animal, especially in the dry season to avoid tramping on a dry stick and alert the quarry, he stood frozen. He held his hunting spear close to his chest and repeatedly tapped the diamond shaped pointed edge on his fore-head, telling himself that he ought to have known better.

The former warrior who once served in the army of Tokpa Gbowee and his daughter, Lango Gbowee, during the campaign against King Sorteh Gbayou as one of the youngest members of the units of spearmen, used his spear to slowly part the branches of a low bush blocking his view. He saw that the buck was still looking his way, now transfixed and extremely alerted. Any moment it was going to signal danger and there would be an avalanche of flights.

Kolliemenni was aware that in such a situation, it's best to charge immediately for an aim, if it was not throwing his spear at a particular animal. But as a well-schooled and experienced hunter his age, this could be a callous attempt for it was the practice of rookie hunters who many times got into trouble when a female or a nursing animal was killed.

This was an adage against the rule of hunting, to kill a female animal, which were preserved to keep the supply chain steady, except it was absolutely necessary. His target was the large bushbuck that was looking straight at him waiting for the information from its stimuli, to tell it within milliseconds the extent of the danger, and its best escape options.

This put the young warrior hunter in a delicate and pressing moment where he had to charge immediately at the herd within the milliseconds it would take the gigantic stag to transmit the alertness of danger to actual danger and dash out of there in one leap.

Before he came out of his concealment, never caring to trample on dry sticks on the ground as time was not in his favor, the animals were now fully informed of the danger, hence the expected avalanche of flight in all directions.

Yallah Kolliemenni, in full adrenaline mode, with his spear in lancing position, was sprinting towards the herds as each animal, young and old, nursing mother and its young, made for the run in a frenzy. Such a charge, with a specific target in mind, can be extremely difficult. Only the best hunters are successful.

For such hunters, their antics are almost supernatural; their eyes must be swinging in all directions to look out for large trees standing in their way, lest they bump into them and get smashed. They must also watch out for a termite hill to swiftly dodge or jump over, depending on the height and distance, or, on the ground for sharp stamps that would pierce their legs and get stock, at the same time keeping an eye on the game.

Despite his impressive speed, Kolliemenni was far away from the fleeing herds. His distance from the animals could have been short, if he was going to be sprinting on the rocks that littered the flow downstream. But he opted not to do so, because he was aware that he was within the vicinity of Bassa territory, where some of the rocks are indeed traps set up by King Sorteh Gbayou's *neengene*.

A rock would suddenly give way, when stepping on the wrong one, and land a person right into a waterhole. This local traditional Navy SEAL sect had a way of making rocks appear to be protruding out of relatively stagnant water with a large water hole underneath, waiting to entrap the unsuspecting enemy. During the war, Tokpa Gbowee's men, pursuing retreating Bassa warriors making their way across the flow by sprinting across the river rapids, disappeared without trace under such rocks.

Nevertheless, Yallah Kolliemenni, with full confidence in his marathon skills, as it was the prerequisite of becoming a spearman which recruits were only town criers or conscripts with the gift of a town crier in their DNAs, continued sprinting and sometimes jumping over rocks along the banks where he assumed it was safe until he managed to gain some distances with the Stag now in sight. The next moment he was dodging his way around some of the animals he had caught up with in the fray.

At one point he jumped over a nursing doe standing over a rock at the edge of the rapids, trying to save its young that got stuck between two other rocks beneath it. Even though the Stag was still far ahead, he was satisfied with the distance he had gained.

The animal had now sensed that it was the targeted prey and was making some long springs covering large distances of about a quarter of a mile per leap. But the son of a former town crier and hunter had managed to maintain a considerable distance.

Kolliemenni suddenly leapt, with both of his legs stretched wide apart, over another animal whose pointed horns missed his scrotum an inch. The horns would have ripped it open, had he not leapt higher when the large wild goat that had apparently gotten confused in the disarray had turned his way. He landed, almost tumbling, but managed to balance himself and continued after the Stag. But the animal, taking advantage of this, had increased the gap between them, and had crossed the rocky banks at his far right. It was heading straight for the bush.

The former spearman had again increased his pace, this time sprinting over two to three rocks per leap to regain the distance he had lost. As he anticipated, the next leap taken by the deer would land it right into the bush, and it would be impossible to chase it under the dense undergrowth, thus slowing down his speed. And that would be the end, a fruitless end.

Fortunately, he was at the distance he wanted, providing him the exact range to throw his spear for the instinct kill. Now all he had to do was to continue to maintain that distance or increase it and at the same time to create an angle that would lock the neck region of the Stag into his striking range.

As a spearman who uses both his left and right hands to strike, and with the position of the deer slightly at his left, he was relieved. But it was time for the lead rein deer to take a leap into the bush and disappear.

Yallah Kolliemenni leapt very high in the air, flipping his spear from his left hand to his right, just as the stag leapt for the bush. While still in the air, and at the same time arching his back to exert the requisite force to lance his weapon, he threw the spear, yelling, landing and tumbling.

Like a javelin fired from a missile system, the spear tore into the air, forming an arc, and landed right into a spot between the base of the deer's head and the neck, piercing through the animal's throat with almost half of the object coming out on the other side. The stag landed on the ground on its left side with its hind and fore legs stretched.

Rolling several times on the ground, Koillemenni finally stopped, resting on his right knee and his left foot. He gently hauled out his long hunting knife from a sheath made of goat skin hanging across this dirt littered back, and watched the deer grunting at the same time kicking its legs. It got up after several kicks, but fell back to the ground.

Its eyes were stretched in bewilderment and its tongue was lolling sideways out of its mouth as it tried to lift up its head. The young hunter got up, dusting the dirt and dry leaves that covered his body. With his hunting knife pointed forward, he began to take careful steps toward his prey.

Getting close to the dying stag, he circled around it from the back to avoid being kicked and probably get severely injured. As an eleven years old kid, he was once given a massive back kick by a large deer his late father had pinned with his spear, while both were out hunting in the forest of Bolola, northeast of Kakata. Before he was instructed how to proceed, the excited Bolola juvenile hunter had rushed to the dying beast from the side of its belly around the hindlimbs with his small hunting knife to slit the animal's throat to finish his father's kill.

But he was severely struck. The blow from the lower limbs of the animal sent him smashing on the bark of a big tree, seriously damaging his vertebrae column. For almost a year his body from the upper arms to his pelvis was wrapped in splinters and at some point, it was thought that he wasn't going to walk again.

His worried parents were however grateful to the healing powers of an old herbalist who warned that the child will be able to walk again if he himself exerted the effort to do so as the traditional herbal therapy was being administered to him. On the very day he eventually began to walk again, his father became proud of him.

"Now I know I have had no regret for naming you, 'Yallah', a Lion," he confided to his son. "For you are strong like a Lion."

Now about 5 '11" tall, a well-built physique, bright in complexion-reminiscent of the meaning of his surname, he stood over his kill, looking around to make sure no one was watching him. Satisfied, he rummaged in a small hunting bag slung across his hairy chest and took out a bundle of robes made of the inside of tree bark. Squatting, he took the hindlimbs as the kicking and jerking were gradually subsiding, and carefully tied them. Then he went over to the forelimbs and did the same.

He reached for the head, sat on its pair of longhorns and pulled it by jolting the nostrils slightly upwards to expose the throat. Using his hunting knife, he slit it by running the blade across the neck. The buck convulsed, and kicked, stretching its tied hind and forelimbs, as the blade tore through its flesh. It ingested several pellets of faces as blood gushed out of its slit jugular vein, with some splattering on Kolliemenni's face and his hairy chest. He held onto the head as the blood continued to drain out until the convulsing subsided including occasional undulation of bodily spasms. Next, the beast lay lifeless.

Kolliemenni stood up again. Stepping on the animal's slit neck, he pulled the spear, looking at the blade as a sheen of pride covered his face. He was suddenly drenched with a sense of exhilaration, a triumph he had once experienced after his first successful human kill as a spearman.

It was several years ago, during the hay-day of the war with the Bassa, a group of Kpelle warriors were amassing a huge army to pursue Sorteh Gbayou, when an enemy spy was spotted, hiding behind a large tree several kilometers from where the general muster was taking place. Having noticed that he was spotted, the lanky enemy spy took off with an impressive speed. Supported by his lame body, he was sprinting down a steep valley, taking one giant leap, covering a distance of about 30 ft, per leap.

A group of spear-men, with Yallah Kolliemenni among them, were alerted and put up the chase after him. The enemy spy had significantly increased the distance between him and his pursuers, many of whom were slowing down due to exhaustion. But Kolliemenni continued with the chase, surpassing his compatriots and gaining distance as he sprinted like a cheetah after its prey.

It was a matter of moments before he gained the distance he wanted. Just as the enemy spy had thought he had outrun his pursuers, the rookie spearman took a decisive leap over a termite hill that stood about 10 ft tall in his path, landing on the top at the same time lancing his spear. From a distance of approximately a quarter of a mile away, the enemy spy was struck from the back.

The spear bored through and thrust out of his stomach to the extent that the pointed edge pierced the ground.

Startled, the man uttered a loud cry. He struggled to pull the spear, keeping him pinned almost halfway to the ground, causing blood to ooze from his mouth. After several futile attempts, he raised his head and saw Yallah Kolliemenni standing before him.

Next, a machete was at his throat and soon the other spear men came trooping on the scene, jubilating. Before his death, a great deal of information was extracted from the warrior spy, and it played a significant role in King Tokpa Gbowee's campaign against King Sorteh Gbayou.

Kolliemenni wiped the bloody stain from the pointed edge of his spear. Reminding himself that he was probably in enemy territory, or, possibly in 'No Man's Land' where the enemy sometimes ventured, he looked around, scanning the perimeters around him and the distant periphery ensuring that he wasn't watched. Satisfied, he chopped off some branches and covered the dead animal with it. Then he went into the bush, and was back at the spot toting some young palm branches on his shoulder.

He squatted next to his kill, and started to make a Kinjah out of the palm branches and some small sticks to accommodate his kill, which will take him two and a half days to tote to his little farming village, west of the river. After half an hour, the Kinjah, large enough to store his meat, was ready.

Then he chopped a log out of a tree branch and laid the dead stag's neck on it. With one swing of his hunting knife, he chopped off the dead animal's head, then chopped the limbs and the body into four segments and placed them in the wicker basket he had made.

The former warrior spearman briefly inspected his *Kinjah*. The meat in the basket was well arranged; the animal's head was inserted in such a way that the horns jutted out of the neatly plaited fresh palm thatched wicker basket.

Pleased, he pulled it from the ground by two sets of robes attached to the left and right side of the top and the bottom of the Kinjah to weigh it. Then he knelt, and turned his back to the basket. He put his hands between the robes until they reached his shoulders, got up with the *Kinjah* now on his back like a back pad, and collected his spear. He strode towards the banks of the river where some of the water between the rocks form water logs.

At a certain spot, he gently removed the Kinjah from his back, sat it on the ground, and squatted on top of a rock when he had made sure it was not a water hole trap. He cupped water to wash the blood stains from his face and chest, but stopped when he looked slightly to his right at a tree several meters down the banks of the flow.

Something like a giant chameleon in the ever-green tree, the few that grew along the banks, caught his attention. Chameleons don't grow that big, he thought. It might be a large ants nest covered with leaves.

Convinced, Yallah Kolliemenni continued to wash his face and his chest. When he had finished, he took a few steps away from the spot for an area where the water was running and got out a small calabash ghoul attached to his wrist. He uncapped and filled it with water, and fastened it around his wrist.

He suddenly froze to the sound of splashes in the water a few meters into the flow. They were coming from behind a huge rock, ahead of him. With his adrenaline pumping up, in one dash, he raced for his spear, lying by the Kinjah.

He looked to the tree where he saw the chameleon or the aunt's nest, but none was there, and the splashes in the water still continued, audible above the sound of the flow. It might be a *neengene*, and luckily for him, it did not know someone was around as it continued to splash the water so loudly.

Capturing one alive will be good. For fear of them, many of his kinsmen loathed venturing into the lands across the river where the ground was more fertile for farming. Extracting vital information from this one to learn the secrets of the *neengene* will be a breakthrough to the advances of Kpelle settlements across the upper Farmington.

His heartbeat began to rise. His eyes were sharp and flickering in all directions. With his muscles pumped, he began to take careful steps on top of the rocks leading to the direction of the splashes. His spear was pointed in the aiming position. A decisive strike to the middle of the vertebral column will instantly paralyze this enemy.

After several careful steps, and leaps on the rocks, docking, and waiting, he finally sprinted to the one beyond which the splashes were coming from. He was about to strike, but froze.

It was a young girl bathing in the water. She was naked and her back was turned to him. From the curvature nature of her rear, especially from her wrist down, she possessed an incredibly attractive and enticing body. When the girl bowed down to cup water to waste on her back, a sensational chill ran down his spine to the extent that it tickled his groin.

She suddenly stopped, apparently seeing from the reflection in the water that a man was standing on top of the rock above her. Surprised, she suddenly gasped and turned.

Yallah Kolliemenni was transfixed, staring at the girl facing him. She was extremely beautiful, and looked in her late teens. She was dark in complexion, with thick black afro hair. Her eyes were dark/brown, with thick black and bushy eye-brows. She had a smooth and semi-elongated face and a sharp nose. A pair of medium-size and long breasts, standing out of her chest dangled before his eyes as she took deep breaths to control herself.

Kolliemenni, with his spear still in his hands, remained mesmerized. The girl standing before him may be the princess of the *neengene*, and his indecisiveness to strike the pretty, innocent face and alluring morphology, had him trapped.

Their eyes caught and locked, trading an uneasy admiration for each other, even in the mist of the volume of suspicion clouding their minds. And then the man standing before her lowered his spear and moved his eyes away when she suddenly covered her breasts with her hands, and sloughed her way partially behind a rock, occasionally peering at him to see whether he was still there.

This convinced Kolliemenni that the girl was innocent and not harmful, at the same time marveling at what a beautiful girl was doing in this part of the bush all by herself. Sensing that she wanted him to leave so she could get out of the water, the young spearman hopped back to the spot where he left his Kinjah. Not quite long, the girl came slouching out of the water, partially docking, with her hands still covering her breasts to conceal her nakedness.

For precaution, Kolliemenni looked her way. Confident that she still did not pose a threat, he struggled to take his eyes off her as another dose of sensational chill traveled through his body; her triangular pubic was visible as he could make up strains of curly hair extending from her navel, down her belly.

Completely out of the water, the girl made her way to a spot, a couple of meters at Kolliemenni's right, where she kept her clothes. She docked behind a big rock, put on her clothes, and oiled her skin with burnt palm kernel oil mixed with spices with a pleasant aroma.

Yallah Kolliemenni watched, squatting and at the same time sharpening his hunting knife, by rubbing the pointed edge against a stone, as the girl came from behind the rock wearing a piece of white tie-dye lapper designed with the black paintings of a village around her waist, reaching slightly above her knees. The same cloth was tied around her breasts and knitted at her back. Also, around her hips and her neck were a mixture of dark brown and black beads.

He immediately stopped sharpening the machetes, slid it back into the goat skin sheath and stood, still watching. The girl was dragging a bucket-size neatly plaited bamboo basket towards him. 4 ft away, she stopped to rest, looking at him with her hands akimbo. Judging from her countenance, the young spearman observed that she did not seem bothered that he did not land her a hand.

Kolliemenni felt a sense of guilt, but he quickly brushed that away. Although she was beautiful and appeared innocent, he wasn't too sure that she did not present any danger. He remembered the words of old man Flomo Zawolo, the instructor at the school where they trained spearmen.

The former town crier always reminded his conscripts that Bassa women possess an implacable beauty, powerful enough to beseech the best and more precocious warriors. They are at times used as spies or subterfuge due to their alluring and bold advances to men and they can be extremely deadly when their covers are about to be blown.

His heart leapt, reaching for his hunting knife, attempting to pull it from its sheath when the girl left the basket and walked closer to him, her eyes sparking with delight as they roved all over his body. Kolliemenni knew that the charm of this girl had bewitched him when she had gotten within a foot from him and he could not still pull his machetes. Old man Flomo Zawolo had been right.

"*Deh guy or nor mon gee*!" she mused in her Bassa dialect saying to herself 'What a handsome man!' She was touching his face and then his hairy chest. "*Ne yen neh mon Saydah,*" she continued, repeatedly pointing to herself, telling him that her name was Saydah.

"*Hein-naa waa Kolliemenni,*" he answered with a deep voice, after a long thought, saying his name was Kolliemenni in Kpelle. But his hand still remained on his hunting knife. "Yallah Kolliemenni."

Saydah laughed at the way he spoke, thinking that the big voice in which he also introduced himself was meant to scare her. But Kolliemenni was still expressionless, his eyes now reverted on the basket she left behind. She followed his eyes and looked behind her.

Sensing his curiosity, she took his hands, the one on the machetes and gently pulled him behind her as she walked towards the basket. When they reached it, she put her hand inside and got out a fresh crawfish the size of a mango and pointed it to him. "*Or mon Chunnah,*" she said, telling him that it was a crawfish.

She offered a board smile, exposing her pink gum and her fine white front teeth when he slightly nodded.

"I live in a small family village about a day and a half walk down the river. This is my first time coming this way to lay my fishing baskets. The sun was extremely hot and I felt the need to bathe in the water. It was refreshing," she explained.

Then she trimmed her eyes on the Kinjah lying to where Kolliemenni was sharpening his cutlass. The now unsuspicious spearman also following them walked towards his Kinjah and just as he expected, Saydah followed him.

"*Or mon daylay*!: 'Its deer meat!'" she exclaimed, cupping her mouth with her hand and stretching her eyes, when she saw the dead buck's horn sticking out of the Kinjah. "*Or vlen, cha*!" she continued with the pleasantries, saying, ``It's a very large one! This part of the forest hosts large animals, like this deer and the crawfish I caught."

Then she eagerly hurried to her basket full of crawfish and took a small one the size of the can of paint and dipped it into the basket. She filled another one and brought and laid them at Kolliemenni's feet.

"Take them," she gestured.

The young hunter again nodded, this time less slightly. Then he squatted, shoving his right hand into the Kinjah and felt a limb of the dead animal and gently pulled it out. He gave it to her.

"*Ah! ne zuo o!*" she gasped, telling him thanks, as she received the dead stag's hindlimb. "*A mua batou o*; 'We are friends now,'" she declared, putting the meat on the ground and first touching her breast and then his chest. "*Batou,*" she emphasized the word 'Friends' at the same time displaying a friendly gesture.

"Humm," Yallah Kolliemenni grunted in the affirmative, but rather pretentiously reluctant.

Saydah again uttered another laughter to the sound of Kolliemenni's grunt, making the warrior hunter to again wonder what a strange girl who every word he uttered sounds funny to her. Then she picked up the meat and gestured that she wanted him to help her put her basket on her head. He followed her to the basket still full of crawfish.

In order to help reduce the weight on her head, he gestured that she should wait. Surveying nearby, he saw a young palm plant growing at the edge of the bush, hurried to it, and chopped off a few branches. He folded them into a ring, a *katter* to serve as a bridge between her head and the base of the basket.

She received and set it on her head, revealing her armpit hair, which scant emitted an erotic fragrance. This prompted Kolliemnni to think that Saydah was mature, and had reached the age of coupling, but he quickly expelled that thought out of his mind. Getting closer to her, about half a foot, he bent over for the basket and lifted the heavy load with ease, and gently set it on her head. "*Ne zo, o*: 'Thank You'," she said.

He nodded, and she smiled.

"*Ne mooe o*," she said, meaning she was going, and then turned to leave, skipping on top of the rocks. When she had reached the edge of the bush, she stopped, turned and waved him goodbye. She laughed again when Kolliemenni slightly lifted his spear in the air to return her goodbye.

The former spearman continued to watch as Saydah made her way into the bush, south of the edge of the flow, looking around again to make sure the whole episode was not a distraction, and that he wasn't being watched. He took a deep breath, got his *kinjah* from the ground, and mounted it on his back. He made his way northwest of the river, in a cautious fashion, ensuring that he wasn't being tailed.

A few minutes later, a sudden rustle in the branches of the tree where Kolliemenni thought he saw a giant chameleon or a large ants' nests startled a flock of birds resting on the branches, causing them to fly away. Among the branches was Sinegar, his body painted with green dye. He quickly descended and crawled his way to where Saydah and Kolliemenni were.

Exasperated, he clenched his teeth scanning around him. A daughter of the Bassa people had made friends with the enemy, and had bartered with him. The same enemy he blames for the death of his parents, more especially his mother who gave birth to him in forced labor while fleeing from Kpelle warriors. Then a sudden glee appeared on his face; a Kpelle settlement may not be far away, and it will eventually be good for business.

He opted to tail the fool to lead him to this settlement so that it can subsequently be raided, and its inhabitants taken down to the coast to be sold as slaves. But he decided against that; the man seems no fool, after all. He was quick and alert and had almost made him up in the tree. Thanks to his camouflaged dye.

So, tailing him will be for another day. When he has gained the confidence of the disobedient Saydah, the extreme caution and alertness he has noticed will desert him. And that will be the best time to tail him all the way to this Kpelle settlement.

Still infuriated, and shutting his eyes, at the same time shaking his head to demonstrate his desire to undo what he had just witnessed, he followed the trail in which Saydah had taken and disappeared into the thick undergrowth.

Chapter 7

Percy Mac-Adams has been a coachman all his life. In his late teens, he was among thousands of Scottish immigrants that trooped to southwest Virginia to work in the coal mines. He made his living by hauling coal deposits on wagons driven by horses, transporting them to storage sites. Though he was not a quaker, he once lived with a family of the protestant sect, while transiting in Pennsylvania from New York before migrating to Virginia, and has always kept its values.

He was a quiet man. People who knew him during his days at the Monongah site said he was active in advocating for better safety regulations for fellow coal miners and even helped organize the Monongah Miners' Union.

After working for many years at the Monongah County site, he left following many unheeded warnings of a disaster he predicted in the future, due to poor safety regulations.

He then moved to Virginia where he established a self-transport service. And with his vast knowledge of the network of routes of coal mines throughout the state, he transported persons and hauled cargo from all parts of the Virginian country-side to Richmond.

He was briefly active in the American Revolution, but not in active combat. As his contribution to the freedom cause, he transported wounded Continental soldiers and sometimes British soldiers on his horse driven wagon thus, saving hundreds of lives on both sides. He once rejected receiving the Patriot Award, offered by a Washington based political organization that recognized people it termed as Patriots in the service of humanity, run by a Continental Army colonel whose life he saved. He said his reason for his role in the war was only meant to serve his conscience.

The Scottish American further defended this, stating that it was predicated on a deep-seated pity he had for potential young American lads, who had bright futures ahead of them in pursuit of manifesting their own destiny. But instead, branding themselves as local militias, they sadly chose to wrestle with the well-equipped British Army in the name of total freedom from the crown.

Few weeks ago, he received a request to transport a lady from Fairflax, who was lodging at Charles Inn. As per the requirement, the transport service request only identified the person as a lady, traveling unchaperoned, through the county from Nashville, and seeking to be transported to Richmond. There she will board a vessel for New York. That was all Mr. Mac-Adams needed to know and so he rendered the service.

He had dropped her off at Continental Inn. And, as per the service arrangement, waited outside the inn until she met a man, Elijah Burgess who agreed to accommodate her for some time until she eventually headed for New York.

The former coal miner did not need further questioning; Elijah Burgess runs a shipping company and the affluence looking mistress could be an associate or a prospective business partner. After his service was over, he first rode to his private service office at Sydney, outside of Richmond to collect a stack of papers from his mailbox. After that, he rode almost the whole night to his small ranch at deep creek, Norfolk County.

As a habit, before going to bed, he would always go through the stacks of papers to get himself abreast with the Virginian weather forecast. But his main interest was glancing through the announcements columns to know when the former coal mining company will begin paying debts it owed to former workers or contractors like him. He sat behind his desk with piles of newspapers illuminated by the glow of a flickering table lamp. A bottle and a half-filled glass of Jim Beam bourbon sat right next to the lamp.

"The Virginia Cardinal?" he suddenly asked himself, flipping through a newspaper, after a sip of the Kentucky whisky. "Never heard of this one," he made a face and decided to toss it away but reluctantly opted to go through the pages.

He suddenly drew the newspaper closer to his face when a headline at the center page caught his attention; '**Mass Murder at the Cottonwoods, near Gunston Hill: Plantation Razed. Owners and Several Others, Including Slaves Feared Dead. By Oliver Price.**'

This headline looked interesting, he thought, but he wanted to see who was the editor of this strange paper. Usually, he always reasoned that the best way to value a newspaper's story or article is to find out who is the editor, and so he hurried to the editorial column and saw the name Jim Wolfe.

"I thought so," he muttered, holding the paper with a hand while the other reached for the glass of bourbon.

The name Jim Wolfe rang a belt. The editor was once a Public Relation Officer of a coal mining company. He was forced to resign because it did not treat black workers fairly. He went on to write articles for other papers denouncing slavery, more especially when it was abolished by the federal government.

But resentment from powerful slave owners forced these editors to let him go. At one point he was hunted by men who rode at night on horse backs, with their faces covered with white hoods. Wolfe had since remained in hiding for fear of his life where he secretly published articles, and now this newspaper, 'The Virginia Cardinal'.

Mac-Adams flipped back to the center page and began to read the full story.

'Barely a week after the severe flogging and brutal hanging of a slave, Robert "Bob-bob' Douglass for attempting to run away, a fire mysteriously gutted the Cottonwood tobacco plantation near Gunston Hill in Fairfax County. All occupants, except a negro woman survived the fire. But the slave plantation community in the county is grappled with fear that a woman believed to be the half-sister of Mary-Ann Cottonwood, wife of Perry Cottonwood, the man who took over the Plantation from his aging father is yet to be found and feared kidnapped by the mysterious perpetuator of this fire.

Many believe that the razing of the plantation and the kidnaping of this woman is due to avenge for the hanging of Robert 'Bob-bob' Douglass who many of his fellow negroes believe that his attempted escape to freedom was a set-up by the overseers who loathed the faithful slave earning his freedom when he had requested for it and was promised by his slave master.

"Oh my God!" Suddenly gasped the old coachman.

He immediately stumbled to his feet, rattling the chair he was sitting on, at the same time rocking the table and almost knocking off the table lamp. He was looking at the sketch of the missing woman. The illustrator was good; the woman looked just like the passenger he had ferried to Richmond earlier in the day. His heart began to race, and he began to sweat profusely.

The woman he dropped at Continental Inn doesn't look like someone who had been kidnapped. But he now realized that she did look like someone who was getting away. No doubt she might be the perpetrator. She appeared like she was not running away from someone or something, but was indeed running away because of something she did, so chief constable Richard Arlington at Richmond must know about this. He took his pocket watch from the small side pocket of the vest he was wearing and studied the time. It was after midnight. He could make it back to Richmond.

The next moment he shoved the Virginia Cardinal under his left arm, grabbed his coat and his hat hanging on the door and hurried out of his small wooden cabin to his stable, a few yards across his picket fenced yard.

The retired coal miner rushed into his stable, and grabbed a lantern hanging on the wooden wall. And when he had lit it, he hurried to his coach. This was not the one in which he transported the woman, but this one was a small four-wheeled single carriage which can be driven by at least two horses. The wheels were in good shape; he recently had the spokes changed by the Watkins brothers.

Percy Mac-Adams then hurried to the compartment where he kept his horses. Out of the seven of them, he had used four on the bigger four-wheeled double Carriage, and so he needed to use two of the remaining three that were not used. He needed to get to Richmond fast, and the single carriage coach driven by the two fresh horses will do. At least they have rested a lot and he had made sure he fed them with enough oats and corn to boost their speed and endurance.

All was now set for the 30 miles journey back to Richmond. The former coal miner was on his way to alert the chief constable of a mass murderer lingering in his city. He was optimistic that he would arrive at the city, either at, or, before dawn. Seated at the driver's seat, holding the reins with both hands, at the same time cueing and lashing the horses, the animals galloped with speed as their hoofs tore through the dirt of the dark Deep Creek trail, brightened by two lamps at his right and left.

Next to him was his loaded rifle in its sheath, and fastened beneath the seat rail. Carrying a loaded weapon was absolutely necessary as run-away slaves were becoming rampant and he had just read that they had resulted in burning plantations to the ground. It is more likely that he could bump into a group of them and he will have to defend himself, if they mistook him for a slave master or simply see him as another white man who would report their whereabouts.

About 15 minutes on the trail, half way within Deep Creek vicinity, just before reaching the Great Dismal Swamp, a barrage of thoughts filled his mind. What was he going to achieve after all, when he had alerted constable Arlington and the woman was arrested? Was it going to be justice for the Cottonwoods or for the slaves who also lost their lives in the incident? Or, for both?

Sometimes old Mac-Adams wondered whether he abhors slavery or welcomes the inhumane act. These were questions that always lingered in his mind, and the answers also triggered a guilt that made him afraid of himself.

During the revolution, he never cared to ask why he was always given only the white wounded Continental soldiers to transport to their medics posts, as there were almost equal numbers of the black ones on the front lines who were getting wounded as well. But it has since experienced a gilt that it was inhumane, transporting only the white ones while their black comrades who chose to fight for America's freedom, a path way to gaining theirs, lay wounded and in anguish, watching him with appealing and dying eyes, ferrying their white wounded comrades to safety. It made him appear to concur with this kind of discrimination, and that was the guilt that made him afraid of himself.

Nevertheless, it was an incident that finally took the years of guilt away. It was once, on one of his many trips hauling cargo from the banks of the Potomac to some parts of northern Virginia, he bumped into a runaway family of four, hiding in the woods along a track he often used from Fauquier to Loudon counties. It was a man, Andy Carson, his wife, Mae, their 10 years old son, Earl and their 6-month-old baby, Annie-mae. They were heading for an isolated area along the Potomac River where they would meet an underground railroad agent, a Quaker only identified as the Bushmaster. He will take them to a waterman to ferry them across the river to Maryland.

The fugitive family had lost their way and found themselves trapped in the woods west of Leesburg. They wildered in the mash littered woods for days, almost depleting their ration and were hesitant to enter into a town whose inhabitants might apprehend and turn them over.

Andy and Mae's feet were sore and swollen. It was excruciating as they walked. One day, after trekking in circles for several hours, the parents could no longer make it, as under their feet began to split, and watered. So, they sat by a large Red Maple tree to rest.

"You are a man now, Earl," Mrs. Carson said to her son, with tears rolling down her eyes. "I am leaving you in charge of your baby sister. Your dad and I can no longer make it. Take her with what is left of our ration. Use it wisely and head northeast until you reach the river. You will meet the Bushmaster. He will take you and your sister to the waterman to ferry you across to Maryland."

The lad, with tears also running down his cheek, looked at his dying father who could barely speak, but kept muttering, "No. Mai. Go along with them. Just leave me here."

Without hesitation the kid grabbed his baby sister and the ration and continued the journey. As he trekked along, he would point his hand in the northeastern direction just how his mother taught him. While on the track, the kid suddenly leaped into the bush when he heard the sound of a wagon approaching ahead of him. He hid behind a tree, with his sister clung to his chest.

Percy Mac-Adams, who happened to be riding the wagon spotted the kid and pretended like he did not notice him and passed. But he rode several meters and then parked along the track. Startled to see a kid and a baby all alone by themselves, he got down and hauled out his rifle. Circling around them from the rear, he made his way back on foot to where little Carson was hiding.

"What are you doing with a baby all by yourself in such a place?" he asked when he jumped from behind a tree facing them, and pointing his gun.

"Are you the Bushmaster?" startled, Earl asked, his voice quivering. "Are you going to take us to the waterman to ferry us across the Potomac to Maryland?"

"Oh my God!" exclaimed the old miner, lowering his rifle. And as if he had just realized that this may be a ploy by some runaway slaves hiding nearby to have him distracted to steal his wagon, he again raised his rifle, pointing it at the boy and his baby sister.

"Are you alone? Where are your parents?"

"We left them to die, somewhere in the woods not far from here. They sent us on our way to the Bushmaster," Little Carson explained, his eyes on the nuzzle of Mac-Adam's Henry rifle pointing at him as tears profusely ran down his cheeks.

"Did you see them die before leaving?" asked the old coal miner, overwhelmed with a sudden gush of emotion as he struggled to hide the thrilled voice in which he spoke.

"No. But they were about to die when they sent us on our way."

"Are you sure about this?"

The kid did not answer immediately, but kept staring at the gun pointing at him at the same time rocking his baby sister who was stretching her hands and legs and was about to cry.

"Yeah, quite sure," Earl managed to say. "Are you going to shoot me and the baby?"

"Nah. You take me to where you left your parents. And If I find them still alive, maybe I'll shoot them instead," the old miner grumbled.

He was irritated. Why would these parents leave their two kids in the woods to fend for themselves?

At the Red Maple tree further into the woods, they met the Carsons lying against the tree partially covered by the red foliage. Mae Carson was seated upright, her back against the tree trunk, humming the hymn 'What a Friend We Have in Jesus' as her husband lay unconscious on her lap.

"Mom!" Earl called as he ran to them with Mac-Adams walking behind. "We met the Bushmaster. He's here to help us."

Mrs. Carson lazily brushed the leaves from her face with her faint hands when she heard her son's voice and the cry of her baby. She was startled to see a white man walking behind them with a rifle slung on his shoulder.

"No Earl," she said, startled-her voice barely audible. "He's not the Bushmaster. That man is here to kill us and take you and your sister away and be sold."

"No mam," said Mac-Adams. "I am here to help you and your family, though I intend to shoot you for leaving your kids all by themselves in the woods."

Mrs. Carson was weak and could not understand what the man with the rifle was saying. She was about to be unconscious.

"Please don't harm my children," she kept muttering.

"I will be back," Percy Mac-Adams told the kid and hurried off when he had felt the purse of his father and it was still beating.

In no time he was back riding one of his horses with another one behind him. With efforts the Carsons were lifted on the back of the horses and as Earl walked behind him, still holding his baby sister, the old coal miner led them to where he left his wagon and laid them among the cargo he was transporting, including Little Earl who sat near his parents. On the way they were given food and water as Mae Carson, gaining a little strength and looking at her son with disbelief, stretched her hands for her baby.

After an hour's ride, Mac-Adams reached a little cabin in the middle of the woods. It was made of logs. At the back was a barn in which he stored his goods, whenever he was contracted to hauled cargo from the Potomac, and then transported them to their final designations. This private transport point was situated beneath the foot of a mounting. And at the front was a wide field with two ponies tied to a tree that stood a few yards from the cabin.

He disembarked the driver's seat and hurried to the back. He looked around to make sure there were no runaway slave scouts watching him. Satisfied, he rolled the thick curtain half-way up and climbed at the back. The Carsons, including Andy who had also gained little strength were all seated up, their faces masked with uncertainty.

"I am going to lodge you and your family here until you recuperate and are strong enough to be on your way, but I must first be sure of certain things," he told them.

"We are running away to Canada," Mr. Carson informed him.

"Did you kill anyone to get here?"

"No sir," answered Mr. Carson. "We are faithful Christians who have never harbored any malice for our owners, despite our treatment, but we just want a bright future for our kids. We have been praying for this for years."

"We are followers of the Right Reverend Charles Gooding, Sr. If you ever heard the old man preach, he never encourages revenge. But we just need a bright future for our kids, as my husband said," Mrs. Carson added.

The Right Reverend Charles Gooding, Sr was a Baptist Preacher well known throughout slave communities in the south, but much detested for his stance on revenge, and killing of slave owners. Owing to the Biblical story of Joseph, his message was peace with the slave master and embracing the inhumane treatment as a blessing in disguise that can be acquired as the mastery of the white man's ordinary business of life. And that such treatment can later be used as the apprentice for a profession, more especially in the plantation business. He became more vocal when the Federal Government abolished slavery and when he heard of the American Colonization Society that was repatriating free men to Africa, the land where this blessing acquired from plantation life can be beneficial for these free men.

He had a son, Charles Gooding, Jr, who in his late twenties impregnated a slave girl. The Reverend, a free man, took care of the slave girl, with arrangement with her owners who were relatives of his former owners, until she gave birth to a boy. When their son was five years old, the two young couples ran off, leaving their son with his grandfather, because the girl wasn't free and Young Charles thought it was the best way to grant his love her freedom.

They were never seen or heard of again. Until one day, while on his pulpit preaching, the old man collapsed and died, when there was news that the young couple died in a blizzard in the woods on the edges of Buffalo, New York while on their way to Canada. His grandson, Charles Gooding III was 12 years old and had since followed in his grandfather's shoes.

The old coal miner said nothing else, but pretended to believe them. He gestured that they remained in the Wagon until night, and when he had prepared a place for them in the barn, he provided them more food, water and attended to their wounds.

One morning a group of runaway Scouts came galloping at the edge of the yard, close to the turnpike. Mac-Adam was at the stable near the barn, tending to his two ponies. As Andy watched through a tiny space between the planks that formed the wall of the barn, three of them rode into the yard towards the coachman. He immediately stopped what he was doing, got his rifle leaning against the wall of the stable and waited as they approached him.

"We are in search of a runaway family we believe are hiding in these woods," said Austin, a young man, who appeared to be the head of the gang.

"Did they kill anyone?" asked Mac-Adams, instead, swinging his rifle across his left shoulder in a drill formation fashion.

Austin studied the old man standing before him wearing a long-sleeved shirt, and dungaree pants stripped with a suspender.

"What if they didn't?" he asked.

Percy Mac-Adam sighed with relief, careful not to hint to the group that he was harboring fugitives.

"If I find them, I will turn them over to their owners, provided of course, they display proper ownership documentation."

Austin then threw a cloth bearing the sketch of Andy and his wife, at the old miner's feet. "There's a price tag of a thousand bucks. You wouldn't want to miss that, old man."

"I didn't ask for a bounty, son."

Suddenly James Travers, a twin of the Travers brothers in the group galloped towards the old coal miner, advancing his rifle. "What if I just shoot you right now, Quaker," said the trigger hungry juvenile.

"Come on, dick head," snarled Austin, tapping James Travers at the back of his head, almost toppling his hat. "He's Percy Mac-Adams, a hero of the revolution. Without him, you and your brother wouldn't have had a dad and a mom wiping your snotty nose." Then he galloped around Mac-Adam. "Remember, old man. It's a thousand-dollar bounty." The rest of the gang circled around the old man for some time and then rode off.

Percy Mac-Adams watched as the gang disappeared down the road, and waited for some time until he was satisfied that they had gotten far enough. In the barn he met the Carsons. Andy knelt down before his host, urging his wife to do the same, showing lots of gratitude.

"We told you we didn't kill anybody," he said.

The coachman nodded. "You and your family are safe here for now," he assured them, and then pointed at a wooden slap on the floor behind them. "That's a basement door. It leads to the foot of the mountain. There's also a trail that leads to a shaft up the peak. You can use that to observe scout parties from a distance whenever you hear them coming. Never leave this place until I tell you to."

The Carsons remained hiding in the barn until the next fall where there weren't many search parties. One day, he told them it was safe to leave, and accompanied them to the trail that led to the isolated parts of the Potomac. There, they met the Bushmaster who took them to the waterman and were ferried to safety. Years later, he received a postcard from Hamilton, Canada. It was signed with the abbreviation, E.C, with a handwriting of a youth, thanking and referring to him as the Bushmaster.

That was when the guilt he had harbored for many years left him. He had saved the life of a family, and had preserved the existence of a generation. At least that can compensate for the many black Patriotic soldiers that lay, wounded and vanquished, as he passed them transporting white wounded ones. Now there was a dangerous woman on the loose and she was capable of wreaking havoc in Richmond.

As he rode on, he was overwhelmed with a sudden fear. Elijah Burgess was in danger. He did not know the young abolitionist, but many years ago, he once interacted with his father Roger Monroe Burgess to transport a coffin to a cemetery somewhere in Maryland. His instruction was to take it to a certain undertaker who would ask him no question.

He also knew Samuel Burgess, the oldest white son of the former slave merchant. Samuel was the lawyer who helped him secure his lawful rights to the land he used as transit points throughout Virginia. He even helped him secure the ranch he owned at Deep Creek, including the office space at Sidney. Roger Monroe Burgess, like him, had overcome the guilt he too harbored as a former slave merchant when he made the bold decision to denounce the trade, and granted the few he owned their freedom.

He had reached a bridge that ran across the murky part of the dismal swamp, when the horses suddenly neighed in a frightened manner. A fireball like the planet Jupiter appeared in the sky. It was spinning very fast, like the earth on its axis and was getting large as it glided his way. As it got closer, his head started to swing when he looked at it. And the horses' neigh got louder to the extent that it was extremely deafening.

"What the hell!" Percy Mac-Adams whined, and reached for his rifle attached to the seat rail. In the fireball was the woman, naked, holding a doll that looked exactly like Elijah Burgess. She had a knife to the doll's throat.

The old coal miner immediately cocked his gun and fired at the ball. It burst and scattered into hot red droplets raining down on the wooden bridge, and setting them ablaze. Some of them were dropping into the water below, turning the surface into steaming red hot bubbles. Like molten, others landed on the horse's back, melting its skin and flesh at the same time revealing both vertebral columns and ribs charred by the lava flowing down its sides. The next moment, the horse's entire body was consumed, turning it into molten. It also melted the plank floor of the bridge and flowed into the murky creek below.

The other horse continued to neigh at the same time swinging its head violently. Its eyes were suddenly scarlet, and then changed into the color of the universe with what looked like tiny stars sparkling like a galaxy. The animal became wild and galloped, its two forelimbs in the air and jumped from what was left of the bridge, down the creek, pulling the carriage with it. Percy Mac-Adams attempted to jump from the driver seat, but the reins mysteriously coiled around his wrist and down his legs, keeping him tied to the seat like it was bewitched.

Now screaming, calling for help as the carriage went down with him into the steaming creek, he reached for his knife attached to his belt around his waist to cut the reins to set himself free, but it was difficult to pull it from the leather sheath. The bewitched reins strapped around his waist was squeezing the sheath, making it difficult for him to pull the knife. This woman was a witch, the thought ran into his mind, increasing his fear. She was responsible for what was happening to him.

The horse plunged into the creek, the molten steam peeling its skin and scalding its flesh. Before it drowned into the boiling murky water, its entire body became a skeleton. Next, the carriage started to sink very fast, as Mac-Adams was frantically making an effort to pull his knife from its sheath. After several unsuccessful attempts, It was then that the coachmen saw the sting of death. The two front wheels of the carriage were now submerged, and the steaming hot water was reaching the footrest beneath the driver's seat.

For fear of drowning and being scalded by boiling murky water, the only option that ran to the old coal miner's mind was to turn his raffle on himself. But he lost it in the frenzy while trying to reach for his knife. Seeing that death was now upon him as the heat from the boiling creek began to tear his skin and face causing huge blister that burst open, Percy Mac-Adams reached for the Virginia

Cardinal folded in the inside pocket of the black cloak he was wearing, which too was getting torn up by the excruciating heat.

The coachman made an effort to shove the newspaper through a space between the mental rail under the seat until it dropped inside the box that made the driver's seat. Then, shutting his eyes, and screaming, he covered his head with his cloak as the entire carriage sank and disappeared with him under the water.

Chapter 8

Jumbo was sniffing, and swinging its head in all directions, a thing he did as a sign of excitement whenever he recognized a familiar terrain when Elijah Burgess reached the vicinity of the Burgess Estate at White Oaks. The colored aristocrat himself was feeling the same way; he hasn't been back home in three years.

As they approached the main entrance gate of his father's estate, he slowed down and cued the horse to trotting. The afternoon was just beginning and the autumn weather seemed nice, riding on a path through the coniferous woods.

He reached the gate and stopped, looking at an arc above it with the inscription, **'Welcome to the Burgess' Estate'**. The excitement of the horse began to increase when Elijah tamed it to a halt. Instead, it was digging its hoofs in the ground and kicking out dirt as its master stared at the vine covered garden gate, his face brightened with the re-emergence of his childhood memory.

"Welcome back home, buddy," he said, leaning over at Jumbo's right ears, and padding the horse on its neck. "Comm on, let's go for the jump." He nudged the horse on its sides with the back of the heel of his booth and the animal galloped towards the right side of the gate, riding along the 15 feet high white painted picket fence.

Down a slope where the fence seemed about 3 feet lower, Elijah stopped the horse, turned to his right and rode a few feet away from it. Then, he swung the animal back towards the fence.

He kicked Jumbo into speed and they both headed for the fence. Upon reaching it, Jumbo jumped over it, with his fore and hindlimbs about 4 inches above the pointed edge, and landed in the yard.

"Wow! Buddy. You are far better than Lord Ranelagh's 'The Wonder,'" cheered the Color Purpose CEO, praising Jumbo for the magnificent jump, and comparing him to the horse that won the first English National Horse Jumping back in 1826.

Due to his lust for jumps racing, he never rode through the entrance gate, as jumping over this part of the fence always excited him. He once broke his legs when he was 14 years old when Jumbo was just a little horse and was still learning how to jump.

He galloped up the hill passing through the apple orchard. Next, he was into the lawn planted with an interval of beautiful flower trees. He was riding on the brick path that led to the family house, a two-storey mansion with extensions at its left and right elevations. At the front, bedecked by a turnabout surrounding an artificial fountain bordered on all sizes with beautiful flower garden, he was met by Lennox, the gardener who was an old negro, one of the many former slaves whose freedom

Roger Monroe Burgess had granted and who had since volunteered to be in the employ of the former slave merchant.

Lennox held on to the reins as his employer's son climbed down from the horse and greeted him with excitement.

"Happy to be back home and to see you looking so good, Lennox," he said. "How's dad.?"

"Me, too, Eli," responded the old gardener, referring to how Elijah was called by his father and his siblings. "The old man is out in the glade with Richard and Joey, hunting. They may be back by now."

"And Meredith?"

"Always home and abandoned," snickered a woman, standing hands folded by the veranda in the middle of a suite of the extension of the Mansion. "Looking good while your sister is weary and drained," she said when Elijah looked behind.

"Oh, comm on, Meredith. Not again," said Eli, briefly forging a disappointed face, but again offering a smile and stretching his arms to embrace her, as he walked to his oldest sister, whom he had spent most of his life with.

He embraced and held her firmly but she refused to wrap her arms around him. Watching this, Lennox shook his head in pity and went walking with Jumbo at the back of the house. When he removed the straddle from the horse's back, and was about to usher it into the family stable, the animal looked down towards the field, and seeing other horses grazing in the distance, it neighed, and then happily galloped towards them.

As the two siblings stood looking at each other without a word, Elijah Burgess observed that his sister looked older than the last time he left her. She was in her late thirties, but now looked in her mid-fifties. She had not been herself for a little over a decade, since her husband, Joey McAllen, a former associate of her father, abandoned her and their two boys who were now in their early teens. "Your entire family has gone nuts," he wrote in a letter to her, referring to Roger Monroe Burgess' denouncing of slavery.

"Uncle Eli is here!" suddenly chipped two boys on horse backs, galloping side by side like they were racing. From the back of the mansion, they were making their way to them, between an alleyway that separated the flats that made up the extension at the left elevation of the mansion.

"Richard and Joey. Happy to see you guys in one piece. I was told you and dad went out hunting."

"And we did get some good kills, too," Richard McAllen, the older brother said, disembarking his horse and running to his uncle.

"Poor turkeys have over populated lately with lots of smelly poos, polluting the sweet fragrance of the foliage," added Joey McAllen, also jumping down from his horse, and running to his uncle.

"Granddad said we are on a mission to reduce them a little," Richard said, adjusting his hunting rifle on his shoulder.

"They never seem to reduce," laughed their uncle. "Dad used to take your uncles and I for hunting when we were kids just like you."

"You see this one. It was shot at 200 yards. But Richard says it wasn't good enough an aim," Joey reached for one of the dead birds attached to a string lying on the horse back and showed it to his uncle.

"I shot this one at 240 yards. Farther than yours," argued Richard, also reaching for his kill and showing it to uncle Eli.

"And I did this big one also at 240 yards. What's the big deal?" shuddered Joey, displaying that one too.

"Okay guys. That's enough. You did good. At your ages, your uncles and I have never aimed from that distance," mused Eli.

"Why don't you guys take them to the kitchen? Will be with you soon to help prepare some barbecue," urged their mother.

"And I will join you for the barbecue when I have met dad," added Eli, watching his two nephews hurrying to the back of the flat.

Meredith reached for a bottle of whiskey and a glass sitting on a drink table on the porch. She poured some of the liquor into the glass. Eli watched her take a sip, and made a face as if he had just realized that his sister was not looking good.

The former daddy's girl was looking so dejected. She was old enough when her father brought Eli into the home when he was two years old. It didn't take long when Mrs. Burgess died, and Meredith was the one who took care of him.

"I suggest that you cut down a little on that, Meredith," Eli told his sister.

"Why?" she smirked, taking another sip. "Will you also cut down roaming the seas saving souls to satisfy dad's old guilt while no one gives a damn about me anymore?"

"Saving souls is where the new man in dad lies. It appeases him for turning away from the old man he was. So, we got to support him here, Meredith."

"I have been supporting dad all my life, and you know that, Eli. From the time he had you and brought you in, he didn't want to hurt mom, and so I took you in. And when mom died, I stood in the gap for your wellbeing, supporting him. But now, he doesn't even care how I feel after McAllen walked out of my life. Dad had never been supportive as to how I am still coping with losing the man I love. And you are following in his shoes, Eli."

Eli remembered this very well. His father brought him when he was just learning how to talk. Because Roger Monroe Burgess didn't want to hurt his wife for having an affair with a negro and having a child out of wed-lock, his beloved daughter took the kid in.

He was five years old when Mrs. Burgess died, and it didn't take long Meredith got married to Joey McAllen, a promising young attorney who was an associate partner to his aging dad, the veteran lawyer Vince McAllen who, for many years, was a close friend and family lawyer.

Samuel and Monroe Burgess, Roger Monroe Burgess' two white sons, apprenticed under the McAllen law firm until both went on to New York to advance themselves. Samuel became a Washington lobbyist working between firms and congressmen as a constitutional liaison, seeking business legislation on behalf of the former, while Monroe Burgess landed as a New York Stock Broker.

When their father denounced slavery, Vince McAllen also supported him, and this caused the firm to lose its wealthy slave owners' clients and so it went bankrupt, leading to the old lawyer's death. With the young McAllen now in charge of the struggling firm, he was forced to dis-associate himself from the Burgess. He moved to Mississippi with the daughter of a wealthy slave owner, where he established the McAllen Law firm working with state congressmen fighting against the abolition of slavery.

Eli also remembered how he was often mis-treated with racial indifference while living with the McAllens. The young lawyer hated him a lot, especially when Joey and Richard were born. But Eli kept this to himself because he did not want this to cause a stir between his sister and her husband.

As a kid who knew that the young lawyer would eventually abandon his sister, he made sure that it was not going to be for the ill-treatment he received and so he did not even mention this to his father.

"If anyone is to be blamed for that, it will be me. Not dad," he told his sister, and began to cry. "I should have had the courage to tell you that Joey was going to run off. He hated Dad and I so much, after Dad's denouncement against slavery, and when his father subsequently died.

He did bad things to me, and I did not want to tell you and Dad. I was afraid of what was going to happen to you like it is happening now. I was even afraid of how my nephews were going to take it, Meredith. I have now realized that if I had told you or dad, sooner, it would have been better than now. I'm so sorry."

With tears now flooding her eyes, she reached out to her little brother and received him in her arms. Both of them were now sobbing hysterically as Eli buried his head in his sister's chest, holding onto her firmly.

"I am also sorry, Eli," she mourned, also holding her brother firmly. "Didn't know this had been happening to you."

Suddenly, she eased herself from his grip, and pulled him slightly away from her. She held both his shoulders like she used to do to him as a troublesome kid who was always running around the flower garden, tramping on the flowers and breaking the flower pots, chasing Nightingales and Wrens.

"Now listen to me, Eli," she said. "You are a man now, and a very brave one. But you need to be a complete man, too. You must face dad and ask him about your mother. Don't let him continue to hide that part of you away from you. You got to do this. Let him tell you who she is, or was."

"Don't you think you will be using me to hurt dad because you think he doesn't care for your feelings? He has had enough guilt, then to add this one."

"Don't you think he should be like John Newton singing 'Amazing Grace' and moving past his faults?"

Elijah Burgess remained thoughtful for a while. Then he took his pocket watch from his vest and looked at the time. It was approaching 6pm, and he remembered that he had a date at Continental Inn. Putting the watch back in his vest pocket, he looked up at his dad's flat, and saw someone slightly pull the curtains, and recognized the shadow behind the draper in the midst of the glowing lamp.

"I think dad is waiting for me," he turned to his sister. "I will be back for the barbecue."

In rapid strides, Eli was before the main entrance of the mansion. He was met at the door by Mr. Archer, a white man dressed in dark trousers, a white shirt and a black vest who opened the door for him. He greeted his father's long-time butler enthusiastically, and then entered. Someone was playing a familiar song on a piano upstairs at the back veranda. He knew right away who it was, and smiled.

He then hurried up the stairs, passed his father's study and entered the flower decorated veranda. A slim old man in morning robes was seated at the piano at the far left with a hymn book opened in the middle before him. He would bring his face close to the pages, then he would look up at the ceiling like he had memorized the notes, at the same time swaying his body in a circular motion as his fingers glided over the keys.

"…..And through the truth that comes from God,

Mankind shall then be truly free….

Faith of our fathers, holy faith,

We will be true to thee till death."

Elijah Burgess ended the last stanza of the third verse of the hymn 'Faith of our Fathers Living Still' and sang the chorus in a sensational tenor as the man behind the piano ended the notes in an ecstatic mood.

"Lyrics by Frederick Faber (1814-)," Elijah stated, beaming as he walked to the man.

"Music composed in C Major by Henri Hemy (1818-)", added the man behind the piano, as if he was responding to a password or a code. Turning away from the instrument, he got up to meet Elijah.

"Until all of mankind is truly free irrespective of race, no man is totally free of his own conscience. Good to see you, son."

"Good to see you, too, dad."

Both embraced firmly for a while.

"Blessed is he who toils to restore the dignity of others. Thanks, son, for your hard work."

"And may the glory of God shine on he who is in the vanguard for such a noble cause. Thanks, Dad, for the opportunity."

Roger Monroe Burgess slightly drew himself away from his son, and held him by his shoulders.

"So, in a couple of days you will sail for the Malagueta Coast," he said. "What a success that will be, Eli. I have read all your reports. We're even in good standing with the figures."

"Yes, Dad," Elijah sighed. "The Freedom Star is well capacitated to ferry 101 passengers, comprising 45 women, 30 men and 26 kids, all free people across the West Atlantic along with over 10 crew, the best trained." He then held his father's shoulders, and the old slave owner did likewise. "And speaking of success, I fear that in the coming months, the number will swell, and we will not be able to cope with the rise in repatriation packages, and this will cause a strain on the family's fortune."

"A fortune built on the toil of the worst human denigration, ever? There's no more room for storing such treasure. It is my conviction that on this principle, God will make a way, son."

"There is a way, father. It was mentioned in my last report when the idea to sail to the West African Coast came up."

"Really? Maybe I missed that one," said the older Burgess, dropping his hands from his son's shoulders and gesturing to follow him in his study. "Here is it," he confirmed his son's claim, when he searched among the stacks of papers on his desk and in his drawer.

"There's an abundance of Acacia trees growing on the fringes of the south western Sahara that produce enough latex to meet the growing demands of the ever-increasing chewing gum industries here in the United States and Europe. The safest and shortest route to reach it is by the Guinea Coast where it would take a caravan a week to reach the Milo River, a tributary of the Niger River at Kankan. The river is navigable hundreds of miles into the northern fringes of the Malian desert where the wild crop can be cultivated and transformed into a mechanized plantation and the latex can be extracted and imported into the United States. The huge profit from this can pay for our repatriation cost and save our family fortune. This is legitimate business, Dad. Labor will be paid for, but not forcibly extracted out of unwilling men who are perceived less inferior."

"I am seeing the sketch of the map. How did you get this?"

"An old English explorer gave this to Captain Summerville a long time ago. He's suggesting that it's time we check it up."

"That part of West Africa is French territory and further north is probably Portuguese. What is the United States standing with these two European countries? If it is not cordial, then it will pose a hindrance," cautioned the formal slave merchant.

"These are American allies, Dad. And, our interests are different; we will be seeking business ventures on an endeavor less known while they occupy themselves with colonizing the entire continent."

"Okay. It looks promising. I'll take my time to go through the details. If the prospects convince me further, I will host a meeting with you, the captain and your brothers, upon your return."

"What about Meredith?" Elijah asked. "She's your daughter and like the mother I have never known," the last sentence, he said in his heart, careful not to wear the old man down on another guilt and risk stalling his approval of the proposed southern Sahara venture.

"Oh yes. I almost forgot that," said Mr. Burgess, robbing his face and his white hair. "But your sister needs to put herself together and stop thinking about that moron. You see how Joey and Richard are doing? Those boys will never be a fool like their dad."

"I will make sure that she's okay. And be daddy's girl once again."

"Will be counting on you, Eli," his father said. "And I want you to take a look at this," he continued, when it occurred to him that he wanted to show something to his son. "It's the Virginia Cardinal," he said, flipping a newspaper across the desk to Elijah. "I know the Editor, Jim Wolfe, an abolitionist. We need to support his paper. I am told there are less than 10 copies published every month. So, we need to start thinking about how Color Purpose can support him in his endeavors."

Without glancing through the pages, Elijah folded the paper and shoved it under his arm. "I guess you mean upon my return from the Malagueta Coast," he said. Then he took his watch from his vest pocket and looked at it. "Got a date, Dad," he mused. "Will be sailing along with the most beautiful woman I have ever met."

"Got you, son," said the older Burgess. "It's all work and a little play. Let me see this woman upon your return. Would you?"

"Of course, Dad," responded Elijah, as his father looked at him, beaming.

The Turkey Barbecued at Meredith's was nice. Since his youth, Elijah liked how she prepared and served it with roasted potatoes, green beans, tomatoes, and cherry wine. After dinner, he spent a little time with Richard and Joey at the veranda explaining and sometimes answering a barrage of questions as he told them about his voyages in the Caribbean. And they were fascinated to hear the stories about rescuing slaves and repatriating them to the United States and Canada.

"Can a crocodile really ferry people across the river on its back," Richard had asked, bewildered, mid-way of an experience his uncle was sharing with them while once on an expedition to rescue a group of slaves, somewhere in the Caribbean as Meredith quietly listened from behind the curtains.

"The Slaves were trapped on an Island deep in the Jungle," Elijah explained. "The water surrounding this island was murky and infested with large crocs, the size of lifeboats. Our lead exhibitionists' boats were smashed by these huge reptiles and they devoured most of them, with the lucky ones managing to swim to shore. And the crocodiles were now more aggressive to the taste of human blood"

"Were you also in one of the boats?" interjected Joey, his mouth opened and full with the dessert of the goat cheese salad he was chewing.

"Nah," Eli responded. "The rest of the team and I remained on shore. We have not entered into our boats, yet; the lead team and some Arawak Indian tribes men who were in the boats, volunteered to test a myth that the crocs were bewitched by some Igneri, another Indian tribe hired by Spanish slave merchants holding the slaves on the island. Their intent was to ensure that no rescue boats were to cross that river safely.

So, when the myth proved true, following the smashing of the boats, a sect of the Arawak men with us suggested an antidote to the bewitched crocodiles. And that was when the heads of wild dogs were slid, and attached to hooks and were used as bait to entice and hypnotize the crocs.

Each of these Arawak men first drew the animals out of the water by hanging the wild dogs head over it as blood from the dogs' heads dripped into the water. Then they climbed on the crocs' backs and crooned them to turn towards the Island. They urged 15 men each on the backs of each croc, controlled by the tribe's men."

"Why wild dogs?" Richard McAllen asked, increasingly mesmerized.

"They say crocs like to feast on dogs," answered his brother, his eyes on his uncle for confirmation.

"Sure, they do, and that was the reason," admitted Eli. "Each tribe's men stood close to the back of the crocs' head, at the same time, steadily holding the sticks attached to the hooks with the dogs' heads slightly above the heads of the crocs. Hypnotized, the reptiles became drawn to the appetizing dogs' head, and they remained afloat and swarmed with us on their backs across the river. We all landed on the island unharmed."

"Did you let the crocs go after that?" Joey wanted to know.

"Yes. And they were fed with the dogs' heads. We found the slaves, captured the merchants and some of the Igneri tribesmen. 150 slaves, including men, women and children were rescued that day."

"Were you all ferried back across the river on the crocs' backs?" Inquired Richard.

"No. We were shown another route by some of the free slaves and the Igneri men we captured," answered Elijah Burgess. Then he suddenly got up, when he sensed more questions from his nephews. "Got to go," he said, looking at his pocket watch. "Got a date tonight."

"A date?!" From behind the curtains, Meredith came out through the door and asked. "You got a date?!"

"Yeah. She's a beautiful woman just like you."

"Did you tell Dad?!"

"I did. And he approved before I could finish telling him."

"And you didn't ask him what I told you?"

"No. I didn't. At least not yet, Meredith."

"Uncle Eli needs to get ready for his date, Mommy," said Richard, just in time she was about to throw another question at her brother.

"Sure," she struggled to say, forging a smile to mask her disappointed face.

"Okay guys. Will see you early in the morning," Uncle Eli said and went to his flat.

After a few minutes he came out, adorned in a dinner outfit, riding on Jumbo's back. He trotted past his sister's flat as his nephews who were still at the veranda waved. He did likewise by taking his hat off his head and slightly bowing. Meredith watched her brother as he approached the main entrance gate of the Burgess mansion. He met Lennox at the gate who opened it for him.

"He's a happy man," mused Roger Monroe Burgess, who had come down to his daughter's flat and quietly watched his son gallop out of the yard.

"Dad?!" surprised, Meredith suddenly turned and asked.

"I guessed you left some of the turkey barbecue for me," the old man said, as his daughter stared at him in dis-belief.

Mrs. Angela Draper Burgess called for a glass of water. Dr. Reid reached for a jog sitting on Captain Summerville's desk and poured some into a wooden cup and handed it to her. As the ship physician, Bishop Thompson and the captain patiently watched, the widow took a sip and handed the cup back to the bishop. Then she dabbed her red teary eyes with the back of her palm.

"I first saw a successful and happy man, the night I met my husband," she said, sobbing. "But later that same night I realized that he had been hovering a deep emotional pain in him for years. And because he loved me, I was the only one he revealed such pain to."

"And what was that?" Dr. Reid asked.

Mrs. Burgess again folded her arms and gazed at her booties. As she gently rocked her body, she resumed reflecting on the night at Continental Inn.

From his family mansion at Williamsburg, the Color Purpose CEO arrived at the inn late that evening. At the bar, he ordered Bushmills with little coke added, and took a long drink. The lobby was crowded with customers as he surveyed the crowd to see where his date was sitting, waiting for him.

"She's at her suite, waiting," Old Bill Hayes the negro bar tender leaned over to him and whispered.

"Thanks, Bill," Elijah Burgess responded and smiled. Then he hurried upstairs.

"Come in, Elijah," he heard her voice from within, just before he was about to knock on the door.

"How did you know it was me?" he asked, rather amused, than startled, when he opened the door and entered.

"I know your footsteps," answered Angela, standing close to him, dressed in a white flora gown and holding a glass half full of Bushmills mixed with coke.

"Impressive. And by the way, my apologies for showing up late."

"Never mine," she said, handing him the glass. "My mother always told me that waiting too long for a date can be emotionally relieving when the date finally arrives, unlike being terribly disappointed and stressed when the date didn't show up at all."

"She must have installed into you such exquisite and understandable qualities to commensurate with the pretty woman you are," Elijah again mused, and took a sip of the drink, but made a face like he was surprised that it was the same Irish whiskey with little coke added, he ordered at the bar. "Did you see your mother?" he asked, after brushing aside the thought of how possible such a coincidence could be.

"Yes, I did and remembered her quite well. I was 12 years old when she died. Did you see yours?"

"No." Elijah answered and suddenly felt a strong feeling when he thought about what Meredith told him. He took another sip of the Bushmills, walked past Angela without saying a word and sat in the chair next to the fireplace. "I am always hesitant to ask my dad how she looks. He brought me to his house when I was two years old," he finally spoke when she came over to him and sat on the arm of the chair.

"Why?" she asked, massaging the back of his neck.

"I am afraid of multiplying his guilt for not letting me know about my mother all these years. I believe he assumes I am wise enough to give him time to monster the courage to tell me one day. And, I suspect he would. Maybe it would be the usual way people facing such circumstances do. That is, on his deathbed. But my sister thinks it is now the time to ask him."

"I think it's appropriate to wait for such a time. You are doing just the right thing."

She got up and knelt before him, smiling as the Color Purpose CEO eyes brightened – he had found someone who agreed with him on the subject of how he should approach his father about telling him who his mother was or is. He wasn't sure his brothers, Samuel and Monroe were going to support him here. She leaned over to him and kissed him.

"But if you want, I can make you remember your mother," she said, after they kissed again.

"How can you do that?" Elijah asked, trying to control his breath, due to the high rhythm of his heart beat, after another round of intensive and passionate kisses.

"It's a massage therapy I inherited from my mother. You just need to trust me while we demonstrate it together."

Elijah pulled her to him after a long thought and soon they were kissing again. This time it was more sensual.

"We can do this, so long it will not hurt me," he agreed, breath-takingly.

They kissed again. After that she got up, walked to her bed and took from under the pillow a small bottle with a red liquid inside. Then she gingerly made her way to the liquor cabinet. Angela reached for a bottle of Chateau Lafite, and used her teeth to pull the cock. Then, some of the fancy red wine was poured into a glass until it was half full. She waited for some time and added the red liquid into it.

"Take a sip," she said when she brought the wine potion to Elijah Burgess, after she had taken a sip, herself.

"Tastes good," mused the Colored Purposed CEO, after he had taken a sip, and soon realized that he was overtaken by a sudden urge for a pleasant relaxation.

"The portion in the wine has special relaxation powers, "she explained, aware of the sensational mood he was in.

Then she leaned over and took his hands, and gestured that he follow her into the bathroom. Inside, she loosened the lace at the back of her flowery gown. It slid down to the floor, exposing her naked and enticing body. Bemused and eroticized, he stood, watching the beautiful woman undressing him.

When they were both naked, she held his hands and stepped into the bathtub. While both were now in, she loosen the faucet and it was filled with a streak of warm water. Then she poured some of the red liquid into the water and it began to foam.

"We got to do this together, Elijah," she whispered at the same time, gently massaging the region around his neck, and urging him to lie down in the tub, now covered with red foam.

With both her hands gently massaging his temples, they kissed for a while, and then she gently inched further up so that her naples should touch his quivering lips.

"Imagine my nipples as your mother's at the time you were breastfed, Elijah," she whispered in a husky and seductive voice.

He held her breasts. In a kind of frenzy, he repeatedly sucked one after the other, at the same time uttering soft groans. This lasted for some time, and then his groans became louder when she slid down to her original position, reaching under his cheeks with her lips, drawing and sucking the flesh around them.

His groans intensified when she slid her lips down his neck, his Adam Apple, the middle of his hairy chest, his stomach, and finally beneath his naval, burying her head into the warm foamy water. With her head now between his spread legs, his solid hard erection was in her mouth and then she was slowly easing her head up and down.

Elijah Burgess, with his eyes shot, continued to experience a pleasant sensation as he held firmly unto the sides of the tub, convulsing with uncontrollable bodily spasms of unimaginable pleasure. This continued, causing him to utter a mixture of deep grunts and soft moans until it reached an apex. Then he screamed out loud, climaxing in her mouth, and then suddenly released himself like he had fainted from an overwhelming elation.

Angela eased her head from between his legs and laid on top of him, resting her head sideways on his chest. She stretched both hands reaching for his temples and began to gently massage them.

"I never felt like this before," he whispered, lazily.

"I have never given a man such pleasure," she also whispered, in a like manner. "Now I want you to listen and count your heartbeat."

The young Abolitionist counted to 10, and then dozed off. He suddenly appeared in a dream. There was an Inn, and there were young men sitting at tables drinking, with some of them playing cards. This seemed many years ago. At one of the tables sat two young men, also drinking. One was older than the other, but they looked like the working-class.

Elijah Burgess gasped in astonishment; the younger one looked like his father in his mid-twenties. Then he recognized the older one. He was the veteran lawyer and his father's longtime friend, Vince McAllen.

While both men sat, drinking and smoking as they conversed, the young Roger Monroe Burgess' attention was suddenly drawn to a negro woman who was serving drinks to the customers at the other end. She was light in complexion, tall with broad shoulders and beautiful. Receiving glasses full of drinks from a huge and beefy white man behind the counter, she stepped like a model, moving back and forth between the counter and the customers at the tables. The man behind the counter was Jerry Cullen, the owner of the inn, and a reputable dual specialist.

Then their eyes met, and locked. The young Burgess was full of admiration as his friend, Vince McAllen, observed suspiciously. Another time, while both men were sitting at the same spot, the beautiful bartender modeled her way to their table and served them. Again, the then young ship builder could not take his eyes off her, this time exploring her physique. She was about to leave when he held her hand and asked for her name.

"Mabel," she whispered, after hesitating and nervously looking back at Jerry Cullen at the counter, and at the same time gently pulling her hand.

Another time. The inn was emptied. It seemed like the late evening hours and many customers had left, except two or three of them with their faces bowed on the table, snoring heavily as their breaths reeked with still liquor.

Mabel was at the table where the two young regular customers sat. She had just served them their drinks and was being interviewed by Burgess, why his friend sat impatiently and occasionally studying his pocket watch. Suddenly there was a roar when Cullen came over, grabbed Mabel by her hair and dragged her back to the counter, hitting tables and chairs as emptied bottles and glasses fell and crashed on the floor.

She was screaming. It was deafening, horrific and awful. The then young Burgess could not bear this. With rage, he slammed the table with his palms, stormed to his feet and raced towards the counter as Vince reluctantly followed.

"What the hell is wrong with you Cullen?!" We were just talking!" bawled Roger Monroe Burgess.

"Now you get this straight, son. She's not your whore. She's my slave and I can do whatever I want to her and then get rid of the bitch. You stay away from my business and never bring your ass back here again."

"Then let me buy her," Burgess offered, which sounded like a demand, startling his friend.

"Find something better to do with old Monroe Burgess' wealth."

"What about my bullet in your head or yours in mine. We can make a deal with that. I die you take my old man's shipping yard and you die I take her, only her."

"Oh, comm on, Roger. That's crazy!" cried Vince McAllen. "You want a duel with Cullen? You know he never loses."

"You stay with me on this, or you stay out of this, Vince," Burgess turned to his friend and said, as Mabel looked on, horrified.

"I'll be glad with a nice one in your stupid head, son," Cullen said, as his face broadened with a grin. "It's quite amazing if you want to die for this negro bitch," he ended, then coughed out a nasty glut and spat it on Mabel's face.

Burgess stood, fuming with rage. He attempted to charge at Cullen but he was stopped by his friend.

"At the dual, mud brain," mocked Cullen, offering an ominous smile as he formed his left hand like a pistol.

As Vincent hauled his friend out of the inn, the inn owner demonstrated the sign of shooting Burgess in the head.

The next moment was what appeared like a clearing in the woods. The young Burgess and Jerry Cullen stood about 25 feet from each other both wearing black suits. Around their waists were belts with revolvers in their holsters. Burgess' was brown while Cullen's was black. Standing behind Burgess was Vince, representing him as his second, while no one, except Mabel, stood behind her master with her hands folded beneath a white apron covering the front of the dress she was wearing.

Also sitting next to her was Spike, Cullen's huge guard dog. Like he did in all his duels, the Inn owner did not need a second. A man who looked like Constable Richard Arlington stood in the middle at the far right of both men. The parties agreed that he should be the umpire.

Richard Arlington, was holding a white handkerchief in his hand. He looked at both men and then raised it in the air for a moment and dropped it. Quickly, Jerry Cullen and the then young Roger Monroe Burgess reached for their pistols. In no time the rivals pulled their revolvers from their respective holsters, and released the ejector rod to drop the cylinder.

Tensed, and in a frenzy, each man hastily fished into his breast pockets of their respective coats for a bullet, but carefully inserted it into the chamber. Then they slammed the cylinder back into its frame in one swing, cocked and pointed their guns at each other to shoot.

Unfortunately, Burgess' pistol jammed when he squeezed the trigger.

"Oh my God!" terrified, Vince McAllen cried out loud. His buddy was about to get killed as Jerry Cullen gently squeezed his trigger, and the hammer slightly lifted.

"I will not shoot you in the head, you little stupid fuck," snarled Cullen, lowering his gun from the then Young Burgess' head, to his chest. "Why not I just shoot you in your right atrium and make you watch while you die slowly as I let my dog have the bitch and then rip her into pieces."

"No, you sick son of a bitch," suddenly screamed Mabel, and then pulled her hands from under her apron, revealing a long knife. She charged at her master, repeatedly stabbing him on his right jugular vein, spilling out blood.

The Inn owner and dual specialist, gasped, reeling with bewilderment and turned to Mabel with his gun still in his hand and made an attempt to shoot her, but she stabbed him in his chest, several times. Cullen staggered backwards, dropping his pistol and holding the side of his neck and his chest. Then he fell to his knees as the empire, Burgess, and McAllen, all watched in horror.

Mabel was shocked, and confused, watching her master die. With her hands and dress covered with Cullen's blood, she dropped the bloody knife and covered her face in disbelief of what she had done.

"Get her, Spike," the dying man groaned.

The vicious black brown bloodhound snarled and barked, and charged at Mabel who screamed as it knocked her to the ground, tearing her dress, as she fought to prevent it from mauling her to death. Just then, Burgess and his friend raced to the scene. The young ship builder, whose life was saved by the negro woman, held the dog by the collar around its neck and wrestled it to the ground, while Vince McAllen helped the woman up.

After that, what looked like an argument between the umpire, Richard Arlington and the two friends lasted for some time as Mabel sat on the ground looking transfixed and watching with uncertainty. And then what appeared like an agreement was reached. Roger Monroe Burgess examined his pistol and walked over to Cullen who was now lying on the ground fighting for his life. He pointed it at the severely brutalized man and shot him in the head as Richard Arlington, took a piece of notepad and wrote something.

Thereafter, Elijah Burgess saw what looked like an isolated cabin in the woods near a creek. Then, there was a sound of hoofs on the leaves littered dirt road. Instantaneously, a man on a horse came riding towards the front of the cabin. He got down, tied the stallion on a hitching post not far from the cabin and strode to the door. He removed his hat from his head and held it under his arm after he knocked on the door twice, and waited. Elijah saw that it was his father.

A few seconds later, a woman opened the door. She was Mabel. Her complexion had gotten lighter. Her shoulders were broader and her fine black hair was braided in a flat twist double notch pigtails. Like couples who had not seen each other for a while, they embraced. Then Roger Monroe Burgess entered the cabin. He came out after what appeared like three hours later, adjusting his coat and putting his hat back on.

Then another time he was at the cabin. As usual, Mabel opened the door for him. She looked bigger than the last time. Her face was a little puffy. Her once slim and long neck looked stuffed up with what appeared like wrangles around it. More especially, her stomach was bulging. They embraced, but this time it was gentle to avoid the ship builder pressing against her swollen belly. He gently rubbed it and then both entered.

This time It was a cold, wheezy and frosty winter night. There were sounds of huffs and neighs. Men, about ten in number, were riding on horseback, with their faces covered with white hoods. They were holding touches in their hands galloping towards the cabin.

One of them, the only one dressed in an orange garment, got down from his horse. Having planted a pole in the form of a cross, and set it ablaze, the rest of them threw their touches on the cabin as they rode around the tiny house. Then they all got into a straight-line formation and watched the cabin burn to the ground. After that they rode away.

Early the next morning in the mist of the fog, Roger Monroe Burgess and his friend Vince McAllen were riding in a coach heading to the cabin in the woods. When they arrived, they first saw the burning cross, then the cabin in ashes. Vince looked terrified but Roger remained calmed. He tapped his friend on his shoulders and walked among the rubble.

At the far end of where the kitchen was, he took a pair of gloves from his coat pocket, wore them, and then pulled couples of debris away from a particular spot, thus exposing what looked like a mental door. With some effort he pulled the handle and it opened. Then he descended a stair that led down to the basement. In a few minutes, he came out with Mabel and a little boy who looked two years old.

As Vince looked astonished, his friend nodded, with an expression on his face that he knew the kind of person Jerry Cullen was. He was a meticulous personality who could accomplish his unfinished business, even after he was long dead. He suspected that he was not only an Inn owner who never refuses a duel, but a member of the white supremacy group that had been taking roots in Virginia. He was also aware that the Klan was never going to believe that someone like Roger Monroe Burgess could kill their member in a duel.

The ship builder had been right; Samuel Koresh, the local arm store dealer, from whom Burgess bought his pistol for the duel, was also a member of the Klan, which explained why his pistol jammed. Aware of all of this, the young ship builder had prepared how he was going to protect Mabel.

While the four of them waited in the coach, with Vince unaware of why they were waiting as he nervously adjusted himself on his seat, soon arrived another couch, ridden by a man dressed in a black coat, wearing a top hat.

The coachman had a spotty face. Elijah Burgess thought he also recognized him as the coachman who was earlier parked In front of the Continental Inn, except that the one in his dream was young. Roger Monroe Burgess disembarked from his coach, and walked over to the coachman. After they exchanged a word or two, the Coachman walked the ship builder to the back and pulled what looked like a black coffin. The father of the young abolitionist nodded, fished into the inner breast pocket of his coat, took out a brown envelope, and handed it to the coachman.

"You got to trust me with this, Mabel," he brought his mouth closed to her ears and whispered after they had embraced for a long time, as the two years old kid peered while he and Vince sat in the coach. "I got to do this to save you and our boy."

With tears rolling down her eyes, Mabel grabbed Burgess and they both hugged and kissed for a while. Then he took a small handkerchief from his pocket and held it unto Mabel's nose until she dozed off. After that he and the coachman laid her in the coffin.

"Eli," Mr. Burgess called, and the two years old boy with the help of Vince descended the coach.

His eyes suddenly turned red with tears when he looked at his son. The kid's eyes were on the white handkerchief in his father's hand. He looked innocent and unconcerned. Now fully weeping, he opened his arms and the boy ran to him. The ship builder knelt as he and his son embraced for a while. He was now shaking hysterically.

"I'll keep him," he said, barely audible as he could no longer control his emotions.

The coachman closed the lid of the coffin, and slid it back into the cargo compartment after a nod from Roger Monroe Burgess. Then the transporter mounted his coach and rode off. The ship builder watched, at the same time robbing his mulatto son's hair as the coach disappeared into the mist of the early dawn.

Elijah Burgess then saw what looked like a cemetery in the backyard of a deserted church. But he recognized that the topography was different. This wasn't the state of Virginia. It was in the middle of the foggy night; the coachman was riding on a deserted wooded two-lane road. A gray squirrel, its crispy fur reflecting in the moonlight, sprinted across the road as the coachman turned right, and headed on a single lane road for some time and then stopped at an entrance gate at the back of the cemetery.

An elderly man, a negro, dressed in black winter coat was waiting at the entrance gate. He opened it as the coachman rode in the yard. The man mounted the coach and directed as the coachman rode to a certain house and stopped. Both got down and hauled the coffin into a small chapel at the side of the house.

Mabel, still unconscious, was taken from the chapel and laid on a small bed in a small room on the east side of the chapel. Both men then brought the emptied coffin outside and laid it in an emptied grave and sealed the top. Then the coachman rode off, towards Virginia after he and the negro in the winter coast exchange few words and shook hands.

Hours later, in the small room, the negro was sating in a rocking chair by the small bed in which Mabel was lying, looking at the window when suddenly she coughed and opened her eyes.

"Where am I?" she asked, in a hoarse whisper.

"You're somewhere safe now." The man replied, assuredly. "You must be hungry. There is food on the table. Follow me."

"And the boy?" she inquired, now sitting on the bed and looking around, when the man got up to usher her into the small house.

"The coachman says he's not coming."

"Oh my God! Eli!" she suddenly started to weep as she buried her face in her hand.

Elijah Burgess also awoke, crying too. He eased himself from the bathtub, angling his knees upright, buried his face between them and continued to cry. Then he felt a sense of joy; repelling the thought out of his mind that it was just a dream, he entertained the surety that his mother was alive. He had seen and felt her, and had remembered her well. She saved his father's life, and he did likewise.

Elijah Burgess had discovered a new meaning of himself. The circumstances surrounding his birth were extraordinary, and there's a purpose for which he was brought into this world, and he must fulfill it.

He got out of the bathtub, reached for a morning robe hanging on a hook behind the door, and slipped into it. From the bathroom, he stepped into the living area, wrapping the velvet wool housecoat around him and tying the belt, roman style.

Angela was at the dresser with her back turned to him, brushing her hair. She was wearing a white fur bathrobe with its lapel half way sliding down her back. Like a mermaid's, her long and fine dark brown hair fell over her shoulders and spread over her armpits, whenever she shook her head.

"Was she beautiful?" she asked, with her back still turned while she continued to brush her hair.

"Just like you, Angela," he answered. Now getting close and playing with her hair. "My father wouldn't mind dying for her."

She turned to him smiling, her robe sliding down her body and falling on the floor, exposing her naked body again.

"Will you be with me forever?" once more mesmerized by her amazing beauty and enticingly appetizing body, he asked her.

Angela Draper smiled. She took his hands and placed them on her breasts, urging the young Color Purpose CEO to play with them while she responded, squirming and swaying her body in a snake dance fashion. Then she leaped on him, wrapping her legs around his waist as they kissed. Still kissing and rubbing each other all over their bodies, he carried her to the bed and laid her down. Soon they were rolling from one part of the bed to another moaning and groaning.

"Oh yes, Elijah. I will be with you forever," climaxing, she screamed out loud, her body language, urging him to thrust harder.

Mrs. Angela Draper Burgess opened her eyes and wiped the tears rolling down her cheeks. Her expression and body language showed that she could no longer bear the retrospection and continue the memory of the wonderful and short times she and her late husband had spent together. Bishop Emile Thompson shot Captain Summerville a look, urging the naval decorated hero to cut off the interview. They had heard enough.

"So, what do you think, Doc?" asked the steerer of the Freedom Star.

"You heard it. Long and deep-rooted emotional pain can cause stressful hypertension which can lead to paralysis. And I think that was what happened to Elijah Burgess."

"We need that to be included in the report, stating all the necessary medical conditions caused by this emotional pain; yearning for his father to tell him who his mother was, and at the same time pressured by his sister, but worried that by asking, it might hurt his father. And that this predicament may have possibly developed the medical condition that caused Elijah Burgess to drown. It should include the circumstances at the time; the boy he went to save in the water in the midst of a vicious storm," the captain instructed Dr. Reid after the bishop and Mrs. Burgess left the office.

He was alone in his office pondering over the shape of the report when his boatswain entered.

"Sir. The Cape Verde Islands are in sight," Penhurst informed.

"Good. We dock at the Port of Praia to repair and resupply. Make sure all passengers remain on the ship. These islands are still host to privateers and pirates. The men should be on the alert. In two days, we sailed southwards along the West African Coast. Send a telegram to Monrovia."

"Aye Captain," the boatswain said and left Captain Summerville's office.

Later that day, as the Freedom Star gradually sailed towards the archipelago, Captain Summerville was at his observation post observing the once prosperous island. The harbor was bustling and full of commercial activities during the hay days of the Trans-Atlantic Slave Trade.

In the early days of enforcing the abolition, he was once involved in a deadly Naval Battle with pirates and slave merchants. It was so severe that the harbor was damaged. It lasted for several days until the slave merchants were overwhelmed when reinforcement from the British Navy arrived.

Once a host to Portuguese explorer Vasco Da Gama who anchored at the harbor in 1497 before setting sail to India, it had experienced many wars including the Anglo-French episode. In the early 18th century, it was the first port where Charles Darwin anchored with his HMS Beagle. As Captain Summerville observed, the port of Praia was gradually regaining its commercial status due to its ideal locations for the repairing and re-supplying of vessels.

A commotion suddenly erupted between the passengers and the crewmen who were preventing them from overcrowding the deck, when the vessel was nearing the harbor. The excited returnees were eager to see and to show their kids the port where their forefathers, captured from their ancestors land, were transited before being taken to America and sold as slaves. But the crewmen wanted it in an orderly fashion. The captain had to hurry down from his observation post to calm everyone, urging the uncontrollable and enthusiastic returnees to allow the crewmen to do their job.

At the far side of the quarter deck, Dr. Reid and Jack Duval were standing, monitoring the activities. Then he turned to the shark hunter. He still looked pale since his encounter with what he believed was an apparition.

"You'll be good, Duval," the ship's physician tried to cheer him up.

"There is evil on board this vessel, Doc," he reiterated. "And I am going to find out."

"Maybe you need to do something more meaningful than that, son," sighed Dr. Reid, tapping Duval on his shoulders. "You need to do a little shark hunting to put you back in the right frame of mind you seem to have lost lately."

For a while, Duval stared at the doctor with a considerate expression on his face. Then he looked towards the famous bay of sharks in the far distance to his right. His face was soon lightening. He must find a way to cool off, he told himself, before commencing his own investigation.

CHAPTER 9

The Colonial Administrative office, upper Front Street, Monrovia Town, Cape Montserrado. On a bright Monday morning, the gate at the front of the courtyard of the Settlers-Indigenous Affairs Section (SIAS) on the ground floor of the three-storey building was crowded, mainly with the Indigenous seeking redress of various complains of settlers mistreatment and encroachment of land not part of the Land Purchased Agreement signed by their rulers and colonial agents.

This SIAS had undergone some reforms, following the ascendancy of Deputy Agent, Rev. Dr. Lott Carey as Acting Governor. His first task was changing its name from Native-Settlers Relations Section to the Indigenous-Settlers Affairs Section or the SIAS. Since then it has become very active, with its staff, consisting of settlers and some indigenous.

As Part of his reforms, the Baptist Clergyman, Physician and Missionary made it a routine, by listening to the complaints and grievances brought before him for hours, before entering his office to begin work for the day. Then he would instruct Director Charles Deshields, the head of the section to carry out the requisite actions to address these concerns.

Director Deshields was a dark-skinned settler who was in his early 40s. He was fat and popular amongst the indigenous people. He loved their dishes and liked wearing their attires, especially the Vai shirts made of country and tar-dye cloth. He was noted for always munching on something, either at work or at home. He lived somewhere at the corner of Broad and Roberts Streets, and liked to walk to work and back home every morning and evening.

This morning, the crowd was full of anxiety and agitation as Charles Deshields had not yet come to work, including Governor Lott Carey. Many of the people who brought their complaints during the previous week were contending that some settlers were not adhering to Governor Carey's intervention on their behalf. These settlers were arrogantly refusing to comply with the decisions taken to address their grievances, wherever legitimate.

"Since the death of King Zulu, the colonial authorities have stopped paying attention to our complaints. These people are looking for war," brawled Dazoe Varney, a Dei landowner who claimed his land along the eastern side of the mouth of the St. Paul River had been encroached by the Newberry family who were building a fishing pier. "And we are not afraid of wasting their blood."

"They don't understand that Zulu is no longer alive to be talking for them. The only thing they can understand now is our cutlasses chopping off their heads, and their wives' and children's. For me, if I don't hear anything good about my case today, I will leave for the interior and start mobilizing my people for war," whined Paye Garmugar, an elder who belonged to a sec of the Mamba tribe whose disenchantment began when they felt cheated when king Gray sold the land at Mamba Point which according to them for a little of nothing to compensate for their relocation.

Since then, he and these Mamba people had been hostile to the King, denouncing him and pledging their allegiance to King Garmondeh, his fellow kinsmen who controlled a territory around what is now Mount Barclay.

Recently, when Governor Carey took over, following the death of the ACS Agent at the time the land was purchased, the sec named Garmugar as their spokesman. He started by constructively engaging the authorities prompting the missionary governor to agree to compensate them in the interest of peace. But for a while now, the administration has held back with the payment.

"Yes, mehn. We are tired of this thing here. Just because we gave them our land, they are now taking advantage of us. I think that war can solve this problem now," shouted a woman, removing her head-tie from her head and tying it around her waist, while exhibiting a posture that she was ready anytime for war.

"For me I will blame Deshields," snarled Kawah Tombikai, an influential elder from the Vai tribe who organized some of his kinsmen, including his five children to grow cassava for the Wilsons, a fair color settler family who ran a small industry, processing the crop into flour and exported them. "Because he takes money and food from his people, he is not able to carry out Governor Carey's decision. Then he comes and laughs and jokes with us as if to say he's in the native people's interests. If war ever breaks up, he will be surprised that he will be the first we will deal with."

Business had been bad for Mr. Kenneth Wilson whose wife and three sons assisted him to run the industry. Because of this, they had not paid their workers for months. When Mr. Kawah as he was commonly called, complained to them that his people was pressuring him for their pay since in fact he was the one that hired them on behalf of the Wilsons, the proprietor, in his frustration for incurring lots of debts from a British merchant, who was threatening to seize the plant, if his debts were not paid, first tried to appeal to the Vai Labor Broker for a little more time to be able to find the money to pay the workers.

But when Mr. Kawah vehemently refused stating that his people were accusing him of eating their money, Mr. Wilson asked Mr. Kawah to get the hell out of his Bushrod Island compound and threatened to shoot him with his musket, if he returned.

Just then a group of men ran to help a girl who suddenly collapsed before the main gate of the courtyard. Weak, mal-nourished and pregnant, she looked to be in her mid-twenties. There were sore corners (angular cheilitis) at both ends of her mouth. Her feet were swollen. On them were a pair of rubber slippers, worn-out at the heels. Clung across her chest was a bundle of a few old lappers and blouses.

"I want to drink," she whispered in Vai, when the men attempted to help her sit on the side of the road.

When they suspected that she was hungry and may have not eaten since morning, a man bought her two pieces of doughnuts covered with lots of sugar from a little boy who sold them in a wooden box with` glass veil at the front and back. He also ordered a cup of Kool-Aid from the same boy who held it in a white rubber bucket, and gave it to the girl. She gulped them and shyly gestured for more. The man asked how much each cost, and paid for two more when he was told both Kool-Aid and doughnut cost a red penny.

Ouch my back! take it easy please," wincing with pain, she complained when the men saw that she had gained a little strength and tried to help her on her feet.

When they finally sat her up, the man who bought her the doughnuts saw fresh stains of bruises and lacerations on the old red silk blouse she was wearing, indicating that her back was bruised and sore with deep laceration. She had been flogged, and the wound had not been properly treated.

"Who did this to you?!" he demanded.

"Estella Carter; the woman I am living with in Sinkor. She wanted to kill me, but I ran away from there and I came to see my uncle who works here."

"What did you do?" asked a woman who came by.

"I will explain it to my uncle who works here. His name is Mr. Kamara. He works in Mr. Deshields office," the girl answered and said nothing else as she remained sitting on the side of the road, holding her stomach and continued wincing in pain.

Mr. Foday Kamara was sitting on one of the big granite rocks at the backyard of the building overlooking Water Street. After chewing half of a red kola nut, he was smoking his second wrapper, his every morning habit.

He had just finished cleaning and preparing his boss' office when he was approached by the security guard, an indigenous man who looked to be in his early 20s, wearing a khaki shirt and short trousers with a pair of brown rubber sanders and a thick red kit hose almost at his knees.

The Security guard told him that he was informed by some of the people at the gate that a girl who said her name was Bendu wanted to urgently see him. She said she's a relative, and is pregnant. She also looks very sick, and has been flogged by the people she's living with.

Mr. Kamara immediately rose to his feet and ran towards the front gate with the security guard following.

"Bendu!" he shouted, almost weeping as he forced his way through a group of people who had gathered around the girl. "What happened?!"

"The people want to kill me," she said and began to cry when she saw her uncle.

Suddenly, the crowd started running up Front Street, when someone among them shouted that Mr. Deshields was coming.

"Okay," breathed Mr. Kamara, the tobacco scent from the wrapper he was smoking filling his niece's nostrils causing her to frown with discomfort. "I have to go and help my *bossman* with his bag. Let me take you to the office and rush back to meet him. Please help me, Dayzar."

Both Kamara and Dayzar, the security guard, held Bendu by both hands and gently carried her into the building. Inside, she was ushered into an empty room used as a lodge for the office boys and the yard cleaners located at the back of the main building, near the lavatory. They ease her on a wooden arm chair. After telling his niece he was going to return shortly and listen to her, Foday Kamara and Dayzar hurried to the gate to meet Mr. Deshields.

By now the head of the Indigenous-Settlers Affairs Section was almost approaching the gate, but was barricaded by the crowd which had now increased by some street sellers who had followed him from all the way to upper Broad Street at the same time displaying varieties of food products and urging him to buy from them.

As usual he was wearing a white and black country cloth woven in the form of a vest with a huge pocket in front of it with a black trousers and a pair of locally produced leather slippers made of animal hide, which the setters called African Slippers.

"*I say my people your wait small, na,*" in local colloquial English, he shouted above his voice, meaning that the crowd should calm down and address him one at a time. "For those of you who came to the office today to see me or the governor, please go and wait in the Courtyard. Let me finish dealing with the people who brought their market to sell." Then he turned to the security. "Dayzar. Please lead the people who came to see me in the yard."

"Papa," crooned a woman who forced her way through the group of peddlers. She set a basket she was toting at the feet of the colonial administrator, after the group who had brought their grievances had followed Dayzar into the courtyard. "I am the one, Siatta, your Custo-woman who can bring fresh corn all the from Careysburg. I bought some today."

"Oh yes. I missed them," said Mr. Deshields, his eyes on the basket full of fresh corn which he loved to eat, boiled with little salt, and sometimes along with the juicy husks. "*Aan see you for a long time: I* haven't seen you for a long time."

'Yes, o. I was in the interior taking care of my new baby. He's walking now."

"Oh! you got a boy child?" surprised, asked Mr. Deshields. The corn seller's absence for more than a year was because she was pregnant, had had, and was nursing a new baby boy. "Can you bring him when he gets a little bigger so he can stay with me?"

"Ah. Let me ask his father first," Siatta said, giving her regular customer the assurance look.

"Okay. Then, let me see the corn you brought today." Having briefly inspected them, he called the office boy when he saw him coming. "Over here, Kamara. Take my bag and open the side pocket. Take 25 cents and pay the woman for all her corn." Then he addressed the other street peddlers, after buying a few items from a number of them. "Okay my people. I am alright now. I gotta go talk to the other people waiting for me. Tomorrow I will buy from all of you. Where's the boiled ground pea woman? I didn't see her today."

After looking among the group for the woman who always sold boiled groundnuts to him, which he also enjoyed munching more especially when boiled with a little salt and lime, he resumed walking towards the gate of the Colonial Office, followed by Foday Kamara with his boss' bag hanging on his shoulder.

Apparently not yet convinced that their regular customer was done with them for the day, the sellers were also walking behind him, displaying their produce, some directly in his face, forcing him to brush them off to see ahead of him.

Upon reaching the gate, he caught a glimpse of couples of the employees, some of whom were his own staff, making their way to the back of the fence to avoid the indigenous crowd waiting In Front of the courtyard. Lines of disappointment ran across his face at the irony that SIAS staff would shy away from a key part of their responsibility; mingling with the natives.

He sighed, telling himself that there's lots of work to be done in this regard, and then entered the yard when Dayzar opened the gate for him. Kamara and the woman with the basket full of corn also entered the yard.

The group of complainers gathered around him when he reached the main entrance door of the building. He gestured to Dayzar to take the corn basket, and the other items he bought from Siatta. The security guard did and after emptying the basket, he brought it back to her. Next, she was escorted out of the fence.

Director Deshields then walked to the elevated concrete stairs that bordered the square where the flagpole that hoisted the colonial flag was planted, to address the group.

"Where is Cho Vuyougar," he asked, looking around for the interpreter, Witty Peter. "I told him to be here early this morning."

"I'm here, Director Deshields," announced the interpreter appearing from among the crowd. He had been recently hired to work as an interpreter for the SIAS section.

"Okay come and stand by me so that your people can clearly understand what I am about to tell them."

Annoyed that Director Deshields was not going to tell them anything without Willy Peter to interpret, the group started grumbling. But they became quiet and attentive when he appeared and stood right next to the director.

"Good morning, my People," he began, followed by deep grunts of returned greetings from the crowd. "I am sorry to say that the governor will not come to the office until late this evening. He has gone to attend the re-naming ceremony of a new territory the colony has acquired. Quite recently, as you may be aware, the Bassa King, Gbessagee, agreed to join the colony and has turned his territory over to the Administration. This would have started a long time, but was halted, following the death of Long Peter. And the new settlement will be called New Georgia. But he instructed me to give you this message:

Firstly, he said to tell you that all your concerns are legitimate. And he is doing everything possible to ensure that the people who wronged you abide by the measures he has taken to address them," he paused to allow Witty Peter to interpret, in Bassa, Vai, and Dei.

Shores of our Forefathers

"For some of you who support the colony and are having issues with some of the settlers, they are now acknowledging they have wronged you, and have offered some proposals that the governor is keen on presenting to you for discussion by the time he gets to his office, tomorrow morning,"

Deshields resumed when Vuyougar had finished interpreting his first comments.

"Mr. Dazoe Varney. The Newberry family has proposed an amount for the piece of land they encroached on to build their fishing pier. The governor has added some good things besides the money that they have agreed to pay you. And tomorrow morning, at 10, he will host both of you.

As for you, Mr. Tombikai, Kenneth Wilson has offered to pay some of the money owed to the workers. The governor will discuss the payment plan with you both, after tomorrow at 10 in the morning.

And for you, Musu Kandakai, the land dispute between you and the Moore family will be heard by the governor on Wednesday morning at 10. Both parties must be present and on time."

"But Hestor Moore and her husband say I have no right to the land, because I was not married to Kandakai. So, I should not be in the meeting. They can only allow my late husband's brothers because they have bribed them," said the woman who was agitating about war and how she was ready for it.

"Don't worry about that," Mr. Deshields assured Musu. "We have in our possession, statements made by your tribal chief confirming that you are the legitimate wife of the late Molly Kandakai. So, you will be part of that meeting."

"But woman na geh right to own land, here!" interrupted Mr. Tombakai, saying that a woman does not have a right to own land. "Da bad law y'all bringing here so, o. And you, Musu. You know our tradition. Don't let this people's church business you have jumped into make you go against our culture."

Soon there were heated exchanges between Mr. Tombakai and Musu. But Mr. Deshields made several attempts to quiet both of them, which they heeded to.

Then he resumed.

"The land issue with Musu Kandakai and the Moore family happened within colonial territory, and also the chiefs and elders have agreed that she must have a say in it.

And for you, Paye Garmugar, the reason the administration will not settle you now is because we are investigating claims that you are involved with slavery on colonial territory. If it is established that you did, then it means you have broken a clause in the Land Purchase Agreement which says, 'you are not to engage into slavery on any territory the colonial authority has acquired, either by forfeit or by purchase'. So, you and the people who reported your doings will see the governor on Friday morning at 10."

"But it's King Gray's people who are the ones accusing me. They are not happy because I refused to apologize to the King, and Governor Carey has agreed to settle me. For these reasons they have lied on my name," barked Mr. Garmugar. "You people really want war now. I will not submit to any investigation with people who are already against me. Governor Carey must be prepared to settle me as he promised, or else, all the settlers footing on that land will not be in peace. I mean it." He said and then stormed out of the gathering, talking to himself.

The director took his time to listen to other complaints of land issues and took note of all of them. He rescheduled a couple of them for the following week while others were the week after. It was now approaching 11 am when he had listened to all the complaints relating to land.

"For today we have done listening to all the land issues. Those of you whose complaints we did not record will have to wait after two weeks, "he again addressed the group before him after the ones with land issues had left. "As you can see the complaints are many and the governor will take his time to listen to all.

Now. It has been brought to our attention that there are complaints of settlers' mis-treatment to some of your children and relatives, including those who are living with them. And even they have wounded and injured some of them.

I am told there's a boy who, along with his friends, went to pick almonds and cracked them in one Mrs. Gertrude Digs' yard somewhere near Congo Town. And that he was caught and after she made him sweep the entire yard of the almond dirt, not satisfied, Mrs. Digs forced a hot red charcoal in the boy's hand, folded and squeezed it for him to really feel the pain. Still not satisfied, she slammed his bare back with her fire spoon she took from the coal pot, as a warning that he and the other kids must never sneak into her yard to pick almond and dirty it again. Is the kid here?"

"Yes. We brought him," cried a woman who appeared from among the group with a 10 years old boy. His left hand was rubbed with a black herbal paste. It was swollen and the skin around the inside of his palm and the back, including some of his fingers, were peeled as brownish-red sore-water oozed from the wound. The affected arm, akimbo, was placed in a red head-tie, tied around his neck. The boy looked mal-nourished and weary due to constant and severe pain from the wound.

"He is my son. His name is Eastmond Baryogar. His father is a fisherman. Three days ago, he went to Gberzon by sea for the burial of his relative," the boy's mother explained in Bassa, her attention on Witty Peter as he interpreted. She sounded hoarse and her eyes were red due to prolonged crying. "I don't know what to tell my husband when he returns," she burst up into tears. "Just for picking almonds in her yard, this woman did this to my son?"

"*Kpagon hay:* I am so sorry," patting her on her back, Mr. Deshields consoled the woman in Bassa. "Kamara," then he called his office boy and instructed, "Take this woman and her son to the clinic. Explain as you heard to Mrs. Gibson, and tell her to treat it as an emergency." Now to the boy's mother, he assured, "Do not worry. The governor will look at the boy's hand when he comes to the office later today. Then tomorrow, after 12 O' clock, you and the Diggs will be here, okay? We have invited her and her son, the Militia man who discharged his firearm when the people gathered in their yard, to protest the inhumane treatment done to your son."

Mr. Kamara led the woman and her son to a white house, adjacent to the administrative building, whose front door was painted green, safe for the painting of a white cross in the middle.

When they left, the head of the Indigenous-Settlers Affairs Section continued to listen to similar complaints including an incident with a young girl who was flogged at a school owned by a settler missionary.

Because she was caught peering through the window and watching the other kids her age learning how to read and write, Isaac Coker, the principal of the all-settlers Center of Primary Learning and Care, located on Broad Street, grabbed and gave her 25 lashes on her bare buttocks with some of the strokes landing on her back and causing deep cuts and blisters.

The Proprietress, Mrs. Grace Johnson Morris had traveled to the United States for school supplies. Mr. Coker justified his action that the little girl was caught behaving unusually strange, like a witch, at the opened window of the 2nd grade class which startled the kids, causing some of them to faint.

After flogging her, he forced her to confess that she was a witch and was sent on a mission to hypnotize and kidnap some of the students for ritualistic purposes. The girl's parents and the rest of their family claimed that Coker, a dark-skinned settler from Sierra Leone had falsely accused their innocent daughter, and so they have brought his complaint to the governor's office.

"The governor will hear your case today, when he comes," he told the family when the girl was brought before him and was shown the extent to which the child was lashed. "And we will also attend to her." He assured them. "Mr. Kamara will take you and your daughter to the clinic."

It was now past noon. Mr. Deshields had listened to all the cases. Soon he felt a pinch in his stomach and thought about his boiled corn and wondered whether Mapue, a woman who worked in the building as a yard cleaner, had finished preparing them for him.

That will be his lunch for the day. When he finally entered his office, he told his secretary, Miss Henrietta Wilson, an old slim, fair skinned woman, that he would be in his office, and would not like to be disturbed, until the governor came to work. And that she should only knock on his office when Mapue brings his boil corn.

A queue of black and brown horses were galloping in two straight lines parallel to each other, from the direction of Water Street. On them were settlers' militia men adorned in their colonial military attire with swords attached to their waists and muskets, pointed up, in their hands. Behind each flank, were two lines of indigenous militia walking on foot. They were wearing short sleeve shirts and khaki trousers, holding batons on their right shoulders brandishing them like firearms.

Immediately after the first group of the procession, was a four wheeled open top couch driven by two white horses. Also behind it were another two lines of horses ridden by settler militia while further behind them, also trekking on foot, were the Khaki attired indigenous militia.

As they rode on, to the amusement of people who were standing on both sides of the road, among whom were shop owners and street peddlers, they would greet and wave at a man sitting in the coach. He was wearing a black suit, white ruffle shirt with white cravat knot bow tie. Sitting next to him was a woman, dressed in a white Victorian dress, southern United States negro style.

"Good afternoon, Mr. and Madam Governor," they would shout, and the bearded Governor, wearing an immaculate haircut with a line at the left, would nod and wave back at the onlookers.

Governor Carey, his wife and entire entourage were returning from the re-naming ceremony of the newly acquired territory handed to the colony by the Bassa King, Gbessagee. They have crossed the Mesurado River from the west in specially made water crafts, and had briefly stopped at Providence Island whose name was recently changed from the local name Duzoah, to check on some settlers brought from Sherbo Island.

They had been quarantined on the Island to undergo malaria treatment which they contracted from the island. When their conditions improved, they would later be relocated to the mainland of Monrovia.

The procession turned right, and entered Mechlin Street. It then proceeded up the dirt road, with more onlookers, dominated by indigenous street peddlers on both sides of the road following behind. At the middle of the intersection of Front and Mechlin Streets, Captain Ashford Capehart, leading the convoy as the head of the governor's security detail, suddenly halted, hauled out his sword from his right side and pointed it in the air. The procession also came to an immediate halt.

The huge and bearded settler militia, dressed like a Black American continental soldier at the time of the American Revolutionary War, expertly spun the sword and pointed it to the right. He gently jolted his horse. The animal tilted its head and kicked dust. Then it turned in the direction of Snapper Hill to the cheering of the crowd.

"Attention, attention, the governor arrives," announced Capt. Capehart when the convoy reached the gate of the colonial head office.

Two of the militia on horseback galloped towards the entrance gate and waited on either side as Dayzar and another security guard in Khaki uniforms opened it. Capt. Capehart and the others formed two straight lines on either side of the gate and saluted as soon as the governor's coach rode into the yard.

The former Virginia slave from Charles City County took the right hand of his wife and kissed it. After that he disembarked and walked to the double wooden entrance door of the building. At the stairs, he stood and watched the coach drive his wife to the front of a building adjacent to the main one. Before entering the building, he waved to the crowd outside of the gate, with many of them cheering and waving back.

As soon as he entered his office on the 3rd floor, he made a face like he was weary of his official dress code, which seemed to go contrary to his missionary lifestyle. He immediately took off his coat and hung it on a wooden hook at the back of the door. With his expression now portraying success for his latest achievement, acquiring and securing more land for the colony, he walked to the wooden window behind his desk, opened it, drew the beautifully designed linen curtain apart, and stared at the distant mouth of the Mesurado River and the Atlantic Ocean to his far left. His brief reverie of rowing into these historic waters as one of the early pioneers was interrupted by a knock on his office door.

"Come in," he responded in his familiar Baptist preacher man voice, while still looking out his window, his gaze now fixed towards the Atlantic, beyond which horizon lies many free men of color, free men only by acclamation. Men who are yearning to make the perilous journey to the shores of absolute freedom.

"Good afternoon, Governor," entering his office, Ebenezer Butler, his Deputy Governor for administration greeted.

Governor Carey turned away from the window, nodded and gestured to the tall man with brown skin and brown hair to take a seat In Front of his desk.

"We received a cable from the Freedom Star, a vessel currently berthing at the Cape Verde Islands and is due to arrive in the colony within a week with 101 former slaves comprising 45 women, 30 men, and 26 children," informed Deputy Governor Butler, handing his boss a sheet of paper.

"Good news. But the ACS is not scheduled to ferry new arrivals across the Atlantic, anytime soon," said the governor, reading the cable Deputy Governor Butler handed to him. "Color Purpose? This must be the private Humanitarian Organization, I once heard of, which now seems to be imitating the ACS."

"It is based in New York, too," added Butler.

"Yes, but with its roots in Richmond," agreed the governor. His eyes suddenly brightened. "It's owned by Roger Monroe Burgess, a former Virginia slave owner, and run by one of his sons, Elijah Burgess. The colored one."

Deputy Governor Butler raised his eyebrows in astonishment.

"His grandfather, Monroe Burgess, owned a large ship building yard on the James River. When he died, his son Roger Monroe Burgess took over and ran the yard. Before I came here, I learned that they were operating in the Caribbean, recapturing and repatriating free men to the US and Canada. I interacted with Roger once when I ran a tobacco warehouse for my former slave master."

"The company is requesting the purchase of land for the arrivals," informed Deputy Governor Butler, amazed by his boss' knowledge of the Burgess family.

"Just in time the colony is rapidly expanding, and King Gbessagee was generous enough to turn over all his territory to us. That's enough space to offer to the new arrivals. And there would be more if other local kings follow. At least they are realizing that they need our protection from other hostile kings who are bent on pillaging their territories, in their diabolical quest to capture and sell them into slavery."

"It is my prayer that this latest arrival does not further exacerbate the hostilities of the kings that oppose us. They don't wish to see more of us arriving, at least not with search frequency."

"And speaking of frequency, new arrivals by the ACS are expected in about 6 months which will further alarm them. Next, they would launch an attack on the colony for fear that we are plotting to take over their entire land," Governor Carey concurred with his deputy, and continued after taking a deep breath. "But we can't stop the arrivals. More especially people wishing to return to their ancestors' land."

"Enough reason to turn Bob Gray and Golajor against us. The successor of Long Peter is already reluctant to turn over Banjor to us."

"Yeah sure," nodded the governor. "What we need to do is to convene a meeting with Golajor and King Gray, so they shouldn't be taken by surprise by the new arrivals and think we are ought for something sinister."

Deputy Governor Butler said nothing, and was waiting to hear what his boss would suggest how they would prevent the attack he mentioned. Governor Carey shot him a look, the continence of the missionary and clergy man depicting weariness and hate of what he was about to tell his Deputy Governor.

"We should now start increasing the volume of the ammunition we are making, should incase."

"Elijah Johnson thinks we have enough arms and ammunition. I am afraid he's ignoring the fact that the natives are getting bolder and they are no longer intimidated by the discharge of firearms," warned the Deputy Governor.

Resting his forehead in his right palm like he was having a headache, and at the same time taking a deep breath, the governor shook his head, and offered a faint smile.

"The decorated hero in the war of 1812 needs to understand that on these shores, it's a different, delicate and difficult matter. He has to be enlightened to this."

Both remained silent for a while as they digested the harsh reality of preparing for war. The hostility between the settlers and the natives was growing by the day and it never seemed to abate. Moreover, the uncompromising Elijah Johnson, left in charge with the Colonial Militia by the Late Governor Judi Ashmun, did not regard the hostile and powerful native kings as a threat, and most often downplayed their constant threat of war.

However, upon his ascendency as Acting Governor, Lott Carey's strategy to ease down the tension between the native and the settlers was by employing diplomatic humanitarianism. With the Indigenous-Settler Affairs Section fully functioning, he had suggested first warning settler families who continued to take advantage of the natives, and then finally expelling them from the Colony, if they did not heed to these warnings.

"Expel our people to where? Back to Sherbro Island for the mosquito to drain the blood out of our veins, or, to the hinterland so our people shall be the food chain for these hateful native cannibals?" shouting above his voice, protested Samuel Brisbane, a fair skinned influential Colonial Council member, representing a swath of territory at the southeastern tip of the St. Paul River.

It was at a meeting with the new Governor, a few weeks after he assumed office and reformed the Setters-Indigenous Affairs Section and was overwhelmed with the numerous complaints brought against the pioneers.

"Oh, my Goodness, Brisbane! That's a dangerous lie," said Mrs. Irene Wilmot Dennis, one of three women on the council from Mount Barclay Territory.

"Never heard of cannibalism in the hinterland. Benjamin J.K. Anderson can attest to that."

"Ben hasn't even gone beyond the fringes of the Gibi Highlands. How will he know for sure that the people beyond that point are not cannibals?" asked another council member, Clarence Horton, representing Central Monrovia. "Anderson has only so far explored a fraction of Kpelle land, and their ruler Lango Gbowee is not hostile to us."

"And it is my understanding that she advised him not to travel beyond that point, either," interjected Councilman Benedict Russel, from the territory of Caldwell.

"All these are malicious fabrications, advertised beyond proportion," denounced Councilwoman Irene Wilmot Dennis, storming to her feet in disbelief.

"Okay. Let's table the issue of expulsion," Trying to simmer down the heated argument, Governor Carey reconsidered his suggestion. "But we need to find a way to make our people see reason to coexist with the indigenous people."

Despite his efforts to calm down the argument, and bring sanctity to the essentially crucial meeting, it continued for a while with Mrs. Dennis, Deputy Governor Butler and another Councilwoman, Esther Haywood Dunn who ran a small convent of indigenous girls, teaching them the Bible and home economics, siding with the governor but not necessarily defending the idea of expulsion.

They were proffering a more rational and robust setters' reprimand. Their voices in these debates could have increased to three powerful women if councilwoman Comfort Dixon Wallace, a tough talking fair color settler, had not traveled to the United States to attend to her ailing husband, Joshua. Recently, the governor received a cable informing him that she would have to stay a little longer as Joshua Wallace's health hasn't improved.

Councilman Brisbane and Russel, vehemently rejecting the idea of setters' expulsion were contending that while it's still early, with the native still blind, it's best to claim all the land and one such person to effectively execute that task. given his military experience, was Commander Elijah Johnson.

"Any attempt to enlighten the natives will have an adverse effect on our very survival," cautioned councilman George Smallwood, representing the settlement of Oldest Congo Town. He had been neutral all along but suddenly took side with Councilman and fellow family friend, Benedict Russel.

Reflecting on all of these, the Governor and his Deputy talked about other pressing matters. It was concluded that they began engaging King Gbessagee and other friendly rulers for more land to provide more areas for the new arrivals to be re-settled.

Time was not in their favor as the Freedom Star is expected to arrive within a week. After the hour-long meeting, he saw Deputy Governor Butler out of his office. Governor Carey then went down to the Indigenous-Settlers Affairs Section.

Charles Deshields was seated behind his desk. He had finished eating his boiled corn and was reviewing all the complaints he had prepared in a report for the governor, when suddenly his secretary, Henrietta Wilson rushed in and announced Lott Carey. Before he could get up from behind his desk to meet Governor Carey at the door, the missionary had already entered. He had folded his shirt sleeves and a pair of stethoscopes was hanging around his neck.

"I was waiting to be summoned, Governor."

"Never mind, Director Deshields. Your job is getting more important by the day. You need all the time. By the way, how was the volume of complaints today?"

"Around 85, in terms of new cases. All seem legitimate. Our people think that being citizens of the colony automatically gives them a special kind of privilege over native lands."

"Humm," grunted the governor. "And the ones we are about to resolve. How did the complainants take it?"

"Kawah Tombikai, and Darzoe Varney, seem eager to listen to what's contained in the proposals the accused are offering, but the Mamba, Paye Garmugar is still demanding the balanced money for his land and is threatening war, if he doesn't get it. I don't think he is interested in the investigation of the slave trade allegation against him."

"That's good with Tombikai and Varney. But we will still conduct the investigation with the Mamba, and if he's innocent, we give him his balanced money, but if he's not, we won't. And, if he likes, he can bring the entire band of Mamba warriors, if he doesn't feel good about it. Commander Elijah Johnson and his forces will be waiting for them. Our friendly indigenous rulers will support us because it is their children and relatives that Garmugar is snatching and secretly selling as slaves. So, what kind of new cases do we have on our hands?"

"Land and of course, settlers' mistreatment. We got two serious ones, sir. Corporal Victor Digs, a militia guard, and the son of Gertrude Digs fired his weapon at a crowd of protesting natives, sending them heather scatter and injuring scores of them. The crowd had gathered at the Digs' demanding explanation why Mrs. Digs put a hot red charcoal in a little boy's palm, forced him to hold unto it until his palm burned, and then steamed his bare back with her hot fire spoon, only because the child picked her almonds and dirty her yard.

And next," breathed Deshields. "A daughter of the hostile Vai King, Gbanjah Kiatamba was severely flogged and almost killed by Estella Carter. She was living with them. The more troubling part is that she's pregnant, and according to Mrs. Gibson, our head nurse, it's a seven months old pregnancy."

"Who is responsible for the pregnancy?" asked Governor Carey, becoming emotional.

"Tom has something to do with it. But Bindu Kiatamba, this girl could not disclose his name when Estella noticed that she was pregnant. It was then that she started flogging her. Now here is the worrying part, Governor. After listening to her, I sent her to the clinic, so that you will take a look at her condition, but she fled as soon as you arrived."

"Jesus," whispered the governor. "Kiatamba already wants war. That's enough alibi to make a case for one."

"How did you confirm that she's Kiatamba's daughter?"

"She's also a relative of my office boy, Foday Kamara. She was found lying in the street, outside the colonial office, sick and hungry and at the point of death. She told the people who rescued her, and provided her something to eat, that she came to see Kamara. And he confirmed it."

"Okay," the governor signed. "Let me speak with this Kamara, later. "As for the Carters, let me speak to them early tomorrow. Also, I will have Secretary Smith do a letter requesting Commander Elijah Johnson to suspend Corporal Victor Digs for a month without pay for discharging firearms amongst innocent people causing them to flee and get injured. Let me also speak with Mrs. Digs tomorrow. Put her in the afternoon."

"Yes sir."

"And by the way you got more work on your head," said Governor Carey when he was about to leave Deshields' office. "We are expecting new arrivals within days. This is not the ACS. It's a private organization initiative. So, you need to start working on an integration program. I think it might help reduce some of the misunderstanding we are experiencing on all sides."

"Yes, governor," responded the head of the Indigenous-Settlers Affairs Section, after a brief thought.

"I am at the clinic for the rest of the evening."

"Yes, governor, but before I forget, there's a complaint brought by the parents of a little girl who was accused of witchcraft activity at Grace Johnson Morris Center of Primary Learning and Care. Mr. Isaac Cooker, the principal, had her flogged and forced her to confess, performing strangely before his 2nd graders, and causing the pupils to faint."

"Really?" mused the governor. "Mrs. Morris is returning in three weeks. We will have to ask her to send Coker back to Freetown, so he can hunt and flog people's children and say they are witches."

When Governor Carey left his office, Charles Deshields remained sitting behind his desk and went through some papers for a while. After that he called his secretary Miss Wilson to come along with some sheets of papers and a fountain pen. She entered, and took her seat opposite his desk. With her legs crossed and laying the sheets of papers on her lap, she used the top of the fountain pen to scratch her partially gray and well pressed hair, as she waited for our boss' instruction.

Mr. Deshields got from behind his desk and walked to a portrait of the settlers landing on Providence Island, hanging on the wall. Part of it showed Agent Eli Ares, Capt. Robert Stockton and others in the background, negotiating with indigenous rulers for the purchase of their land.

"Write this down as the heading," he instructed his secretary. "'Settlers' Integration Program."

CHAPTER 10

She was born in the hinterlands in the deep west of the Po River region, a couple of kilometers west of the St. Paul River. Her father Gbanjah Kiatamba was a Powerful Vai King who conquered most of Dei lands west of the Banjor Forest. He had many wives and her mother was one of them. As one of several children of the Vai ruler, Bendu Kiatamba loved visiting *Ducur* along with her mother, who sold farina, a grain manufactured in the interior from cassava crop, which was widely consumed by the settlers.

She admired the dress code of the pioneers and marveled at how some people who looked like or almost like her would dress, walk, speak and eat differently. What fascinated her more was how the ladies braided their hair, and how the little girls wore ribbon bows of different colors in their hair.

At the market sites near the water front of the Mesurado River, she would accompany the settlers throughout the market toting their purchases, whenever all her mother's farina was sold. One of few settler families she frequented with were the Carters, mainly because of their seven years old daughter, Agnes who most often accompanied her mother to the market. She took to liking Agnes, and would never cease admiring her long hair.

Whenever Mrs. Carter or she and her husband, Thomas Carter, along with their daughter come to the waterfront to shop for local food stuff, Bendu will be with them, until they are finished buying all the things they wanted. This continued until she was 15 years old, and then her mother became ill.

And when her condition became critical, and thought that she was not going to live, to the king's dislike, she handed Bendu over to the Carters who agreed to take her in. The girl lived with the family until she was 20 years old at which time, becoming like a handbag to Mrs. Carter. She would mind Agnes, go to the market, cook, serve their food, wash, clean the house and run errands.

Bendu became more useful and dependable when Estella Carter found a job as a bookkeeper for an American company that exported camwood. Two years later, she left the company when she was appointed as an Assistant Governor at the Colonial Bureau of Commerce. She went to work early in the morning at the Bureau's Bushrod Island office, and came late in the evening hours. Mrs. Carter was very hard working and tough. Many people feared her for the vigor she exhibited in her line of duty, assisting the Deputy Governor for Trade & commerce, the old and ailing Anthony Greenfield, to oversee the commercial activities of the colony.

Her husband, Mr. Thomas Carter was a construction worker who was exceptional at building the plank frame houses, famous at the time. He was light in complexion and very tall. He had a birthmark at the right side of his nose, which was clearly visible. The Carters also had a son, Jeremy Carter who was about Bendu's age. He attended the United Methodist Church school located somewhere on

Ashman Street while Agnes went to Mrs. Grace Willson Morris Center of Primary Learning and Care.

Every morning Mrs. Carter took her children to school before going to work. And because she often came home late from work, Jeremy or his father would bring Agnes home, after school.

When little Miss Carter turned 8, Estella began to experience a stomach ache, especially during menstruation. She sought medical attention and treatment. The cramps subsided for a while but resumed after a few months, and even extended beyond menstruation.

This continued for a while but again stopped. Strangely though, it only hurts, with the cramps becoming unbearable whenever her husband slept with her. And when she could no longer bear it, she stopped sleeping with him completely. Every attempt to arrange for her travel abroad for medical attention was fruitless; the workaholic became more addicted to her job, rather than seeing after her own health.

For a year, Thomas Carter did not bed his wife, and he dared cheat on her for fear of the way she would handle it, if caught. Moreover, no woman risked sleeping with Estella Carter's husband knowing of the perpetual disgrace and torment she would get. People saw how she treated Caroline Appleton, a young woman in her mid-twenties and fellow church member who she suspected of sleeping with her husband when her stomach condition first started.

Persistent denials of having an affair with Thomas Carter, even when other church members testified on Caroline's behalf could not convince Mrs. Carter, but rather aggravated her more. Caroline was beautiful and attractive and worked with her husband on the churches' Remodeling Committee as secretary, and Mr. Carter was the chairman. To further de-escalate the altercation between her and Estella Carter, Caroline wasn't only forced to resign as secretary on the committee but withdrew her membership.

"Young lady. You think you will deceive me by pretending to avoid my husband?" She had raged at Caroline, on one Easter Sunday, after service, stirring up a heated confrontation between her and the young woman. "Why the eye contact between you both, during the entire service? Is it because of the fact that you have slept with him and such feelings remain indelible as is the pain of always thinking about it?"

To everyone's surprise, the easy-going Caroline Appleton became furious to the extent that she vehemently rejected Mrs. Carter's allegation. Engaged, and hysterical, she could not imagine why Estella Carter could still harbor such a notion of having an affair with her husband, having done all that she could to avoid him.

She fell off, and when rushed to the health center, she was diagnosed of having a heart condition that was long developing. From that day she became frail and slow in her movements. She was advised not to attend service anymore. Few months later she suffered a stroke, and when rushed to the health center, she was pronounced dead of high blood pressure.

A year after that incident, Mr. Carter had refrained from associating with other women. For nights, he lay beside his wife, his erection prolonged and extremely hard until dawn. This caused him back pain and a strain around his waist, including mental anguish.

Sometimes he would suddenly feel an erection in his pants, causing in front of his trousers to bulge while walking in the streets. He would be embarrassed when curious passersby trimmed their eyes on the awkward appearance of the front of his trousers.

"My man. You got to find a nice and young woman to ease your mental tension," his friend, Mr. Cornelius Caesar, a fellow construction mate, and partner, told him. "You just got to be discreet, that's all."

"Discreet?!" gasped Thomas Carter, laying a plank on the side of a house he and his friend were working on, and giving him a look as if to say Cornelius Caesar has forgotten the kind of person his wife, Estella is. "You know what Estella will do to that woman when she finds out. It's like you have forgotten what she did to that poor girl, Caroline from our church. Just imagine she was someone I had nothing to do with."

Caesar Jovially laughed at his friend upon hearing this. "That's the point I am making, Tom," he then said. "You had nothing to do with the late Caroline so you did not need to be discreet. But Estella will never notice when you are having a secret affair, unless you want her to know."

Thomas Carter said nothing, but kept looking at his friend as he maintained the expression that he had really forgotten who Estella is and that he was just listening to him so that the work they were doing should go on smoothly.

"Look, Thomas. It's up to you to decide. But let me tell you this. Most educated and ambitious women don't really border on sex when they have had a prolonged marriage and with kids, too. What they concentrate on is their professional career and watching their kids or sometimes their grandkids grow. This gets worse when they pass 55, and more often at such times, we husbands look like brothers to them. What most of us do is to just find some young girl from whom to get that portion of lost happiness."

While holding a timber between his legs as Cornelius Caesar chiseled the edge, the construction man shot an eye at his partner, and suddenly got attentive, rather than just listening.

"So, if you like, given your wife's condition, you can continue to embrace the predicament of not sleeping with her and live the rest of your life with that kind of mental torture, or, you can take my advice to find a companion as the only remedy and be discreet about it," seeing that he had gotten his partner's attention, Caesar presented the options.

"If it comes to that, it will not be any of these young women out there that Estella can easily detect," Thomas Carter stuttered, suddenly becoming embarrassed for hearing himself concur with Caesar.

"Why look out there to attract suspicion when you can find one under your feet," chuckled Caesar at the same time, and then paused. Chiseling the timber, he continued, "That little indigenous girl, Bendu, is growing fresh under your roof while you are talking about looking out there. Estella will least expect you to have any affair with her. And don't think that Bendu will not be out for it. Remember she's indigenous and she's from a polygamous setting. I think it's time that you start nurturing that *country chicken* or else some tribal chief will notice her and one day come knocking on your doors for her hand in marriage.

You don't have to be surprised, my friend. This is what we the men of our sect do. We nurture the ones under our roof and send them out at the appropriate time. You need to learn this, Carter. Only one key thing you must do. Make sure she doesn't get pregnant."

From that day Thomas Carter began to look at Bendu Kiatamba differently. He had now realized that the indigenous girl did look good for grooming in the way Cornelius Caesar described, and blamed himself for not noticing this ever since. Bendu had gotten big in size, and her breasts were full and inviting.

He first started giving her money secretly and bringing things for her, warning that his wife and children must know nothing about it. This went on for some time and when he was confident that she had kept their little secret, he started stroking her breasts and knocking her increasingly enlarging buttocks, and she seemed to be okay with it.

Late on one Saturday evening, Estella was out with the children, visiting a relative for his 70th birthday celebration. Mr. Carter came home late from work and met only Bendu at home. She had finished her work for the evening and was taking her bath in the outside bathroom. Immediately he knocked on the bathroom door.

"Who is it?" she asked and stopped splashing water on her body to remain attentive.

"It's me," whispered Mr. Carter in a seductive tone.

Bendu first hesitated and then responded. "Mama and the children went to the party. She said to meet them there when you come."

"I know," he said. "Just let me in."

For a while, there was silence. Thomas Carter became nervous; his indigenous maid could be shocked with disbelief. But that didn't last when he heard her footsteps approaching the bathroom door, and the unbolting of the latch. The door slowly opened.

Bendu stood before him, with soap foam covering her face and arms. A lapper, with some portions wet, was wrapped criss-cross around her body with the tip tied around her neck.

"Bendu. Let what I am about to do be another secret between us, okay?" he pleaded, his voice quivering.

Bendu stood and said nothing. She shyly bowed her head, gazing at the gravel floor of the bath room. Mr. Carter stepped closer to her. He held her breasts with both hands and gently squeezed them. He could feel the fullness as they wobbled in his palms. His heart beat began to rise and his breathing increased. Then he held her by her shoulders and gently turned her around.

A wave of feverish sensation ran through his body causing his fingers to tremble as he loosened the knot of the tip of the lapper tied around her neck. It slid down her body and fell to her feet, exposing her nakedness from the rear. For some time, he rubbed, squeezed and massaged Bendu's large and firm bums. Then he gently bent her over.

"Where's the soap you were bathing with?" he asked. Bendu stretched her hand to a soap lying on a cement brick a few inches away from her right foot and gave it to him. "Draw the bucket closer," he urged.

Still bending over with both hands holding her knees, the young house maid spread her legs when Thomas Carter gently pulled them apart. From the bucket, he splashed some water between them and rubbed her organ with the soap, his urging triggered to the rough and thickness of puberty. A number of times, he added more water and then asked her to balance herself properly by holding the rim of the bucket.

"*Da my first-time o*," whimpered Bendu, her legs trembling, telling him it was going to be her first time.

"I know. That's why I will take my time and it will not be long," Mr. Carter said, unzipping his pants and pushing them down his legs.

After several trials, and finally easing his penis into her, Thomas Carter deflowered his maid. As he gently stroked her from behind, he began to groan with pleasure, while Bendu whimpered with both sensual gratification and pain.

Careful to not explode prematurely, and ruin the pleasure he had missed for years, he struggled to compose himself and control his rhythm. Unfortunately, his arousal reached its apex, causing him to lose control. He shut his eyes and raised his face in the air.

Thrusting harder, Bendu fumbled over the bucket, almost knocking it over, but Thomas Carter continued, uttering deep groans. By now, her whimpers had increased and had turned into a full cry. At orgasm, the builder's legs suddenly trembled, and his knees almost buckled as his body ejected arousing spams. It was finally over.

"Here. Take this, and be careful how you buy some things for yourself, before your mother asks who is giving you money," he said, giving her some dollar bills when he put his trousers back on.

He hurried out of the bath room-relief but still erected, due to the length of time he had not sex.

The next few weeks no one noticed anything. The housemaid did not show any sign of the loss of virginity. She was well and healthy and her behavior did not change. Every time, when the opportunity came, they had fun. It became regular until Bendu suddenly started becoming overweight. She also became forgetful, and sluggish, and always found sleeping when she was supposed to be doing her daily chores.

"Mama. Bendu almost burned my skull with the pressing comb," Agnes informed her mother, early one Sunday morning while the family was getting ready for church.

"Bendu! Why are you sleeping, time like this?! What happened to you?! I have noticed you don't look well these few days!" inquired Mrs. Carter when she went into the house maid's room to ask why she had delayed ironing the dress Agnes was wearing to church and met her sleeping with the clothes in her hands.

"Humm! Ma Esthella," said Musu, Mrs. Carter's traditional midwife who she always invited from across the Mesurado River at Vai Town, to check on Bendu whenever she was sick. "Die *trouble o*!" she lamented, emphasizing that there's a problem in the Carters' house. "Bendu is pregnant for seven months."

Immediately the housemaid was asked who impregnated her, but she said nothing. Mrs. Carter sent for her mother to tell her about her daughter's pregnancy, but the messenger was told by the people in her village that her mother was still ill. Her condition had worsened and was taken somewhere further deep into the Gola Forest to a traditional healer.

"You were a fool to have gotten that girl pregnant, Carter," growled Cornelius Caesar, when his partner broke the news to him. "Now you see what your wife is doing, ordering the arrests of the indigenous boys she claimed were fending around Bendu. What are you going to do about it? The people will soon start gathering at your house protesting the release of their sons. Remember your wife has a bad reputation among the natives."

"My man, for the length of time I had not had sex, it was difficult to control myself," cried Mr. Carter. "Bendu will not call my name or lie on anyone's name. I told her to keep quiet, until I find a way to send her into the interior to a native family I know and remain there, until she gives birth."

"Why not send her back to her mother and be secretly sending support?"

"She doesn't want that."

"Why?"

"She wouldn't say."

"How long will it take for the people you are talking to come to town? That girl cannot continue to be in your house, before your wife does something to her," warned Cornelius Caesar.

"Well, yes," breathed Thomas Carter. "There is going to be a problem if that girl continues to live in my house with that condition."

"Okay then. Let me talk to my former maid about it and see whether Bendu can be with her until the people from the interior you are talking about can come."

"I will appreciate that," said Mr. Carter. "I will really appreciate that."

"And what are you going to do about the two boys currently held in detention at the police station? Your wife is going mad. And the family of the boys are complaining. The Bassa people will soon gather at your house to demand the release of their sons."

"I have already talked to commandant Ezekiel Dempster to release the boys. He told me the boys have repeatedly denied knowing anything about the pregnancy. And he is convinced; native boys just don't deny pregnancy when it's theirs."

Estella Carter was furious to learn that the boys were released later that week. She attempted persuading Commander Elijah Johnson to re-arrest them, but she was strongly advised by her husband to refrain from that before she ignited a Native-Settler commotion. And that the girl must simply be sent away.

"Bendu will tell me who impregnated her," she avowed. "I need to know the fool that came into our house and impregnated that poor girl. And if nothing is done. Who knows? Our daughter, Agnes, might be the next before she turns sixteen."

When Bendu still could not disclose the name of the person, Mrs. Carter could no longer put up with it, and began to flog her almost every day, and at times making her stand on her feet all night until morning, repeatedly asking her to confess. One time she almost strangled her housemaid to death, causing her to faint. That night Mr. Carter had to resuscitate the maid by sprinkling alcohol in her nose.

After that incident, Estella Carter gave her two days to confess the person's name or else she would send her to jail. The next day Mr. Carter gave Bendu some money and asked her to go to Monconjay, Carter's former house maid, and be there until the people from the interior can come for her. And that she should rest assured that he will be sending her support.

Early on the morning of the second day, Bendu fled the house. Monconjay, who she also knew, agreed to host her. She was an older woman who lived in a little Bassa village along the beach somewhere south of Sinkor. While with the Caesars, she was also molested. But because she had gotten married, and was afraid that her husband might one day detect what was going on between her and Cornelius Caesar, she was forced to abandon her job.

After much urging, she recommended his current housemaid, a relative of hers. Sometimes Monconjay would meet Caesar at a place where he often went to buy raw wood for the timber to be used for his construction work. She would ask her former boss for little assistance which he sometimes did.

Bendu stayed with her older friend and her husband for some time. Every month, Monconjay received support through Mr. Caesar.

Gaye Geesay, Monconjay 's husband was a canoe maker, and the wrestling champion in all of King Gray. He had fine dark skin and was stocky and extremely muscular. He earned his championship when he defeated the former champion, Juenawei Gaye, in the last wrestling competition.

At the final of the bi-annual traditional wrestling festival held on the beach, fearing to destroy his relative fame, Gaye Geesay was reluctant to wrestle with him. He had forfeited the match by refusing to fight, but was compelled to reconsider his decision when the champ who kept on provoking him and making remarks that the fight was necessary to dispel the widely held notion that he was indeed afraid of the younger Gaye.

Less than ten seconds in the fight, when both men held onto each other and were locked into a tussle, the champion was raised about six feet into the air and slammed to the ground. As was the rule, enough beach sand was stuffed into the champ's mouth until he called off the fight and shamefully accepted his defeat.

For the way he was disgracefully whipped by his junior, Juenawei Gaye was forced to leave the settlement for Gberzon. Moreover, Monconjay, who had earlier agreed to marry him, married Gaye, instead. The night after the fight, the new champion won her heart.

Gaye was against the idea of his wife allowing a pregnant girl to stay with them. To make matters worse, since the arrival of Bendu in their house, he had never seen any man visiting her, which meant the pregnancy had no owner. Even if someone was responsible for the pregnancy, that was hiding and was secretly supporting it, evidence of the extra his wife sometimes brought home.

This was confirmed when one day, Mr. Carter had gone to purchase some raw wood at the raw wood trading site, somewhere in the bush near the settlement of King Gray, to process them into timbers, for his construction work. He was negotiating with some of the local men to hire them to haul the products to his construction site.

He met Monconjay, who had followed her husband to this site. He was part of the group of men that fell trees. But for him, the trees he fell were used to make the canoes he sold. She had gone to see a native doctor who lived in a village not far from the site for some herbs for the wound on Bendu's back. Since her flogging, the housemaid had not fully recovered from the wound caused by the whip Estella Carter had used.

Gaye Geesay was carving a canoe paddle out of wood when a man came over and whispered to him that his wife was talking to a strange man. Grabbing his cutlass, he hurried to where this was happening.

"Who is this man you are talking to," he demanded.

"A friend of the people I was working for," she answered, calmly.

"I am Thomas Carter. I work with her former boss, Caesar, who often comes here to buy raw wood."

"I know this man!" one of the locals suddenly shouted. "He is the husband of that wicked woman who often brings people here to disturb us for collecting fees."

"Who?!" choked Thomas Carter, very astonished.

"Estella Carter. That woman who collects money from people. She says we must pay for all the trees we cut here because it's on the colonial authority land."

"We were first cutting our trees behind Chugbor, but she kept harassing us to pay fees claiming that it was the administration land until we were forced to leave that area and find this place," another local explained. "Not satisfied, she brought her commerce fees collectors here the other day demanding fees or we move from here, because King Gray has turned this place over to the colony."

"I suggest you leave this place now. And I don't want to see you around my wife again," warned Gaye Geesay, pointing his cutlass at Thomas Carter.

Seeing that more of the locals were gathering around him, and were becoming agitated as some among them narrated many stories about his wife, he got afraid and abandoned the raw wood he had purchased and then hurried out of there.

Later that night, Gaye Geesay pressed his wife until she told him that Mr. Carter was the man who impregnated Bendu, and that she was living in their house.

"We cannot continue to keep your friend here," he told his wife. "The Canoe makers are now afraid that Estella Carter will soon find out about this place and bring her people here to collect fees. And we will not be able to do anything about it, because our King is working with the colony."

Every night, whenever he came home and saw Bendu, Gaye would quarrel with his wife for still not letting her friend leave his house. Pretending to be asleep, Bendu would listen to them.

"The girl is still sick. Let's wait until she gets well," she often pleaded.

"No. I don't want the people to blame us for keeping this girl here. When Estella Carter gets to know that she's here, she will come looking for her, and when she finds out that we sell canoes here, she will send her people to collect fees," he would argue. "It's better we send her on her way now and we are saved from that woman."

Early the following morning, Monconjay had gone to the beach to buy some fish to cook pepper soup. When she returned, Bendu was gone. She left a message that she was going to see her uncle Foday Kamara, and there was no point in avoiding him while he will be able to take her in, without problem.

At the health center, she explained all that had happened. She refused, when asked whether she wanted to go back to the interior. Her father was already mad at her for refusing to return home when her mother sent her to live with a setter filmily. Also angry with her mother for this, he abandoned her when she became sick.

Deshields told her he was going to inform the governor about this when he comes to the office, and that the Carters will be invited to hear their side of the story. Also, since going back to her father was out of the gestion, her uncle suggested that she should live with him, and Mr. Carter can continue with his support.

Aware of the unfortunate incident with Caroline Appleton, Bendu had a second thought. Now that she has disclosed Mr. Carter's name, and remembering how vicious and threatening his wife had been, wanting to know who was responsible for the pregnancy, Mr. Kamara's suggestion made no sense.

Moreover, imagining how she would react to her husband's admittance to the pregnancy, the woman will find and continue to torment her. she didn't think Thomas Carter would be prepared to protect her. With her condition, and fearing for her life and her unborn baby, she wasn't prepared to handle any more stress.

She was eventually admitted, and was put on the list of patients Dr. Carey would see urgently. While waiting, she asked for the restroom which was located at the back. Instead, she fled the clinic, descending the rocky slope for Water Street.

She reached the market at the waterfront where she met Momo Shafia, a tight man she knew at the time she and her mother used to visit *Dubor* to sell. Though small and with a frail body, he appeared energetic. Bendu remembered him to keep a small and sharp beard. He was afraid of trouble but was argumentative, always at the center of some discourse propounding his view, especially when it came to defending the coming of the settlers.

"Before the coming of these people, selling each other into slavery was rampant," he would say. "Now look at how this is saving our generation from being sold and taken overseas?"

Bendu liked him for these views, but he would tease and frighten her that he would one day pay her dowry and send her into the interior and have his kids and never return to *Dubour*. She would cry when her mother pretended to agree.

But she later grew fond of him when she realized that he had always been kidding. Living with the Carters, she always stopped by his selling place whenever she came to the market.

"Your father will definitely go to war with the settlers when he learns about this," Momo Shiafa had said, looking at Bendu's condition when she had explained her ordeal to him. "And the war will spoil everything; we will not be able to sell our products which we are making our living out of. There will be no chance for our children to learn the *kwee* book, which the settlers promised us. And people will die."

Bendu began to cry as if she had just realized what was going to happen if her father found out. she wondered in horror, whether she would be able to live with it, if war breaks up. How would she face the fact that the *Dubor* and its settlers inhabitants she admired so much would be annihilated for her sake?

"Okay. Don't cry," Momo Shiafa, reading her thoughts, began to pacify her. "I know just what to do. I will take you to my place and hide you there until you get well and have your baby. But we must pray that your father does not find out and have me executed."

He ushered Bendu into his thatch hut tent, where he kept his products when he came to town to sell. He made sure she was not seen until it was late in the evening when the marketers had all left. Then, Momo Shiafa helped Bendu into his canoe, and peddled across the Mesurado River. Then he joined Stockton Creek to the west, navigating between the thick mangrove bushes, all the way to his village.

Chapter 11

Captain Summerville, dressed in his full attire, descended the staircase that extended from the quarter deck to the main deck. It was in the afternoon. The weather was a bit foggy, and the sea breeze was gentle. The Freedom Star had maintained a steady course for the past 8 days from the Cape Verdes islands and was slowly sailing at a certain part of the ocean where the sea breeze emitted a salty scent that burned one nostrils when inhaling.

Waiting for him on the main deck were the boatswain, Jimmy Penhurst and some of the crewmen. Also on deck were a number of passengers including Bishop Thompson, his wife, and their daughter Emily. Reverend Charles Gooding III, Sister Newland, Mrs. Findley and her boys, the Roberts, the Flowers and other families were also on deck. The weariness in their faces were clearly visible as they were still reeling out of another unfortunate incident that occurred at Cape Verde.

Jack Duvall, accompanied by Howard Lustig and Lien Dole, was severely bitten by a shark while shark hunting at the Bay of Sharks. He was lying in wait against the top of the bow of the rowboat in aiming position when unexpectedly a large shark suddenly emerged out of the clear and calm blue waters, and went for his head. Had Lustig not pulled his legs in time, the fish was going to chew off his entire head. But it took half of his jaw with it and splashed back into the water.

"I am sure I know who possesses great evil on board the Freedom Star," he had told Lien and Howard, just before rowing into the bay. "I am just waiting to catch it right-handed, and they will believe me."

"Is it a person or a phantom?" Howard had asked.

"It's both. And, it's certainly responsible for Burgess' death, and made an attempt on mine, too," he had responded, and by now they had reached the area frequented by sharks, but not as big as the large gray one that attacked him.

He had remained posted, pointing his spear gun east of his direction, waiting to spot a shark. For a while he saw none. They would be further off in the bay, he thought.

He had turned to Lustig and Dole to further explain his claim about the evil on board the Freedom Star, when he saw in the corner of his eyes a dorsal fin emerging and was fast approaching the boat. Taken unaware, he swiftly turned and attempted to shoot when it was within range but suddenly froze. The shark had leapt out of the water, and opened its mouth. In it was a spinning bulb in the form of a globe bearing the universe with heavenly bodies emitting sparkles of light that are hypnotizing to the human eyes.

Howard Lustig, who was sitting directly behind him, saw the danger and charged, pulling the shark hunter out of harm's way. The big fish, with sea water falling from its body into the boat like heavy droplets flew over the boat from the bow to the stern. Lian Dole, sitting on the stern seat, rowing, dodged when it flew over him and landed back into the ocean.

Bleeding profusely with his gum and molars exposed from the vicious bite of the shark, Duval lay unconscious in the inundated floor of the boat. Howard Lustig laid his head on the stern, so that he wouldn't drown. Racing against time, he struggled to pull water out, to prevent the boat from sinking, as Lien Dole exerted great efforts to row them back to shore.

The severely wounded shark hunter was taken to a hospital run by a French missionary, where he was stabilized. Days later he was taken on board an American warship heading back to the United States.

"I am pleased to inform you that we received cable that Jack Duval continues to respond to treatment," Captain Summerville informed the group standing before him, followed by an air of relief gushing out of every one's breath. "But we are sorry to say that he may not be able to talk again, because his jaw is severely damaged."

There was total silence on deck as he allowed that to sink in.

"Captain," suddenly called Allan Gables, the coxswain, standing at the wooden rail of the quarter deck. He nodded when the captain looked up at him.

Then he took from his waist pocket a small compass, made some adjustments on it and studied the device for a while. After that he nodded back to Gables. Then he fixed his eyes on his eager onlookers, both crew and passengers alike.

"We have been sailing south of the Gulf of Guinea for the past 16 hours. And I am pleased to announce that we are now at a bearing that will place us in the next few hours, parallel to the mouth of the Mesurado River," Captain Summerville finally broke the news. "We are in the territorial confines of the Malagueta Coast. Welcome to the land of your forefathers."

Like a wildfire, the entire deck erupted with jubilation. Soon the rest of the passengers and crew in the cabins got the news and started singing and dancing. Sister Barbara Newland leading a group of men and women were dancing in circles and clapping their hands.

"Over in the glory land, where the mighty ocean stands;

over in the glory land.

I saw flesh came creeping over Ezekiel bone,

over in the glory land..."

They sang as they formed a long queue marching on the deck and into the ship and back on deck, with men, women and children joining them. For every crew member they would meet, they would triumphantly lift him up in the air. Dr. Reid was lifted in the air several times, rolling as he bounced from one group to another, almost toppling him overboard.

"Was definitely going to be another disaster," putting his hand on the left side of his chest, and resting his back against the portside, the old physician breathed with relief.

In the middle of the celebration, Rev. Charles Gooding III called the group together after much effort. By now the Freedom Star had sailed out of the foggy weather into the clear gray sea. Captain Summerville was at his observation post, looking towards the shorelines.

"Behold the land of your forefathers," he announced, stretching his left hand at a lush of vegetation outlining the distant beaches, as they sailed past the coastline of the Banjor forest.

This time the Jubilation erupted like a volcano, seeing the curvy white beaches dotted with lagoons and water logs, and the mouths of small rivers and streams emptying into the Atlantic Ocean. Everyone was elated as far as the eyes could see, the waves dashing, sometimes on the coastal rocks along the shores.

"This meets the description of where my grandfather told me his father was whisked," suddenly overwhelmed with tears of joy, crooned Nathaniel Giddings, the drummer. "Oh yes I can feel it in my bones," he began to cry when it was announced that they were sailing past the mouth of the St. Paul River, known in a local dialect as '*Dey*'.

Reminiscing the narrative handed down to him by his grandfather, his great grandfather was a brave warrior drummer boy who roamed the mouth of '*Dey*', a big river with rough current, bordered on both sides by lush mangrove vegetation.

The river was frequented by early Portuguese traders. As a teen, one day, he and other boys were taken on board one of the Portuguese ships and were given a strong rum which put them to sleep. When he woke up, he found himself in the hull of the ship, bonded in chains.

"Today, as we celebrate the safe return to these shores, and listen to the song we are singing, I am reminded of the prophet Ezekiel and the valley of dry bones," Rev. Charles Gooding III, holding a Bible in his hand, addressed the crowd. "The danger we faced along the way in the midst of vicious storms that plagued us, the dreaded circumstances surrounding Elijah Burgess' death and the shark's attack on Sailor Jack Duval while on this journey, have ended. Those were the valleys of the dry bones we have triumphed over."

"Oh, my goodness," shouted a woman, Mrs. Olive Craigwell, rejoicing and hugging her husband Wilmont Craigwell. "Yes, we made it through."

"There was a time when the children of Israel were forced into captivity and were longing to return to the land of their forefathers," continued the reverend, flipping through the pages of the Holy Bible. "Ezekiel Chapter 37 verses 1 through 14 tells us that while in their destitutions, the Lord, in a vision, took the prophet to a certain valley filled with dry bones and asked him. 'Can these bones come alive?' 'Only thou knoweth,' was the prophet's response. Then the Lord told Ezekiel to prophesy to the bones to come alive.

Elijah heeded the Lord's command and prophesized. Behold! Flesh came creeping over the dry bones and the entire valley became an army of living souls. As we rejoice upon seeing glimpses of our ancestors' land, the dry bones within us have been filled by the spirit of God. We must always remember to thank him for keeping our hope alive. The hope that brought us safely on these shores.

We must also remember the great sacrifices of those that labored for our freedom, and the Color Purpose Organization that is standing in the vanguard of our repatriation and resettlement, the courageous and hard working crew on this vessel, and most important of all the bold step we took to embark on this journey.

Oh yes Christian brothers and sisters, I can see the bones of Elijah Burgess rejoicing, and for sure, soon and very soon, flesh will once more creep over his bones. And on that fateful day, where soul and body will meet again, there will be eternal life and everlasting joy."

The passengers continued to rejoice after the brief exhortation by the young Baptist prelate. Some family members were preparing food and serving them. Mrs. Findley was serving ale and rum. At the far corner of the starboard, Mary Antoinette Roberts held her son, Daniel Roberts in her arms weeping and at the same time thanking God for saving his life, when Sister Barbara Newland raised the song, '*We have come a long way, O Lord. The mighty long way.*' Directly behind her were the young couples, Derrick Hart and Henrietta Patmore huddled up in each other's arms, and joining the chorus.

The Findley boys were standing at the spot where Daniel Roberts fell overboard, and describing the entire episode. They were joined by Gabriel Philips, David, and his brother Albert Coleman, buttressing Joel and his brother. Soon there was an argument of which team was going to win had Daniel Roberts not fallen overboard, when Prince Royce, Hebert Tolbert, and Lawrence Freeman of the saints joined them.

"Have you boys not learned your lessons?" Emily Thompson stopped and asked while walking past them. "You are supposed to join other kids that are rejoicing for our safe arrival."

"That shouldn't be a problem to you, altar girl," Albert Coleman snorted, looking at the Bishop's daughter with disgust.

"What's there to rejoice? All I see is a crooked coastline beyond which extends a smoky dense forest," sconed Henrique Cassel, also joining the group.

"Let God have mercy on your souls, "also showing lots of disgust, Emily said and then walked away to join the celebration.

It was now late in the afternoon, and the jubilations seemed unabated. The Freedom Star had drifted away from the coast line, which was now highly seen. After some time, the anchor was released. Not quite long, it was joined by an American war ship sailing towards the east of its direction. As it got closer, the sailors on board waved at the passengers amid cheers.

"We are now parallel to the mouth of the Mesurado River," the captain announced, again. "The colonial authority will receive us at dawn."

The next morning the vessel, accompanied by the American warship, was once more within sight of the glimpses of the coastline of Cape Montserrado. Then it anchored at a certain point, where the distant mist of trees at Providence Island was partially visible.

The life boats, cramped with passengers along with their belongings, were lowered from the ship down into the water. Within 45 minutes, Cape Montserrado was the first feature visible to their right and then beyond was the forested land where they were going to spend the rest of their lives.

The land they were eager to return to, but to their sudden apprehension, bore no resemblance to the United States where they were born and knew all their lives. There were no postal service, no mailman, and no alleys connecting neighborhoods. The food would be different, so was the environment to cultivate their crops. Even the climate may not be conducive to them and the seeds they brought along. The jubilant mood of the night had changed to one of hope, and determination, feud by the plethora of uncertainties they had no clue of, awaiting them.

"The Lord will provide; the Lord will provide.

In some way or the other, the Lord will provide."

Henrietta Patmore, clung on Derrick Hart's chest, raised this soul inspiring chorus written by Mrs. Martha A. W. Cook, the wife of a puritan preacher in Boston. When asked where did she learn such a faith reviving song, she said she learned it from a friend of her late mother, who was a maid for the Cooks. The new arrival joined her to sing as they rowed past Cape Montserrado for Providence Island. Triggered by the song, their faith was soon strengthened to deal with what awaits. Their courage was soon revived to adapt to the new environment, the health condition, the food and the way of life of its inhabitants.

The new arrival joined her to sing as they continued to row past Cape Montserrado and were heading towards Providence Island. Triggered by the song, their faith was soon strengthened to deal with what awaits. Their courage was soon revived to adapt to the new environment, the health condition, the food and the way of life of its inhabitants.

To most of them this was a new beginning. And to others, they were yet to determine whether they will be greeted with the same segregation they experienced in the United States. A cultural clash between them and the indigenous looms. The next moment they were rowing into the Mesurado River.

Captain Summerville and some of his crew, including Jimmy Penhurst, and Dr. Reid, were in the lead boat, filled with lots of merchandise. In their minds they anticipated that they were going to spend a few days negotiating with the colonial authorities and native kings for land for the new arrivals.

The merchandise were a sign of appreciation to the native rulers who would agree to sell their land. Referring to a map in his hands, the retired decorated Navy hero pointed towards the island as soon as it was within perfect view.

At the southern tip were Governor Lott Carey with high-ranking colonial officials waiting to receive the new arrivals.

Also waiting were kings Bob Gray, Golajor the successor of King Long Peter, and Gbessagee along with their entourage. Standing far behind the group were the colonial militia and the local ones. Commander Elijah Johnson and Captain Ashford Capehart stood side by side, talking. They were joined by Major Rudolf Crayton, a slim and fair colored man. He was Elijah Johnson's deputy for recruitment and intelligence.

"Occasion like this, seems to be a perfect alibi for hostile native clandestine activities," said Commander Johnson, facing his deputy.

"Most likely Kiatamba is expected to call for a general muster. We've posted our local spies to monitor the waterways of the Stockton Creek and other surrounding creeks to detect any unusual canoe movements from the east heading westwards towards the upper St. Paul. But so far nothing sinister has been detected, except an alarm from a fisherman claiming a sighting of schools of crocodiles lurking in the deep swamps of the southern fringes of Caldwell," informed Major Crayton.

"Crocodiles?" asked Captain Ashford Capehart. "And how are you going to treat that?"

"Well," sighed the colonial intelligence chief. "Unless we learn something else about the sighting, we have ruled that the mangrove swamps are infested with these dark brown species."

"Obviously, but such movement is going to take place, only after this occasion," proffered Captain Ashford Capehart.

"And we expect Sorteh Gbayou to attend that meeting, where he would formally pledge his allegiance to the Vai king," added Major Crayton. "And if he did, we might intercept some of his men upon their return, and use them to identify some of the Bassa king's moles planted among us."

"The sooner the better. The governor is perplexed about the disappearance of one of Kiatamba's daughters who was living with Estalla Cater, our Asst. Trade and Commerce Chief. It is our understanding that she's seven months pregnant and very ill. Taking care of her will be a good gesture that will compel him to delay going to war. Governor Carey believes it might even change the Vai king's mind," stressed Captain Ashford Capehart.

"Certainly, we are doing everything we can to find her. Our local guys are on the watch for where she might be," said Major Rudolf Crayton.

The three men were silent for a while as they observed both sides of the river. There were crowds of people watching as the boats got closer. Some of them, mainly the indigenous were pointing their fingers at the boats, trying to count the number of new arrivals.

Among the sea of faces of onlookers at the edges of the river, with some watching with keen interest as the new arrival rowed towards the island, It was obvious that spies of hostile native kings were in the crowd, thought the head of the colonial militia.

"Well," sighed Commander Elijah Johnson. "Your mole might be right in that crowd, Major."

Major Crayton nodded, his face full of contemplation and then watched as Captain Summerville's boat finally touched the shadow waters. Two sailors jumped down and helped hauled it on the edge of the island. The captain waited until the rest landed. Then he got down, followed by Jimmy Penhurst and Dr. Reid. The three men stepped forward towards the group waiting for them. The American battle ship was anchored on shore with its commander at his observation post monitoring the events.

"Greetings," the captain spoke, extending his hand.

"Greetings," responded Rev. Dr. Carey, stepping forward and also extending his hand.

"Captain James Newton Summerville. Captain of the Freedom Star, a vessel owned by the company, Color Purpose. I bring on your beautiful shores free men longing to make this place their new home, and a new life free from segregation. On these shores they crave for a renewed human dignity in the aspiration of peace and prosperity that had been denied them for so many years," the captain, shaking hands with Governor Carey, introduced himself and stated the purpose of their arrival.

"I am Reverend Doctor Lott Carey, a former slave from Virginia, and acting Governor of the American Colonization Society, the ACS. On behalf of the ACS, we welcome you and crew on these shores, and extend our many thanks and appreciation for bringing back to the land of their forefathers, our brothers and sisters. In the coming days we will begin and hope to conclude with our indigenous counterparts on the acquisition of the land you so desire for them."

The governor then introduced his entourage, and then the tribal rulers. King Golajor nodded to King Bob Gray who stepped forward, with King Gbessagee joining him. King Gray then signaled. Soon a group of indigenous brought large calabashes filled with pure white rice with a mixture of red and white Kola nuts and laid them at the feet of the captain. Then the King took a piece of the kola and bit it. He also took a portion of the pure white rice and tasted it.

"As our tradition depicts in welcoming strangers, we the true owners of these lands present to you these items. The pure white rice is a symbol of the clearness of our hearts as we embarked on negotiating the return of the children of our forefathers who were snatched from these shores. The red kola nuts symbolize a reminder of the toil, and the misery of human degradation our forefathers experienced as slaves.

But these white kola nuts are a sign of the everlasting peace and prosperity these new arrivals will expect while here with us," The king spoke, and after Witty Peter had interpreted, he presented the small calabash to Captain Summerville.

"As we receive these gifts wholeheartedly, we also present ours to you," responded the retired US Navy veteran who then signaled to his crew in the boat to get the mechanize out.

The three native rulers watched as Owen Duffy, John Macalister and Terry Pipes, the crewmen from the cargo hold of the Freedom Star, hauled the goods from the boat which included bundles of fine cloths, stacks of tobacco, perfumes and ornaments, cases of smoke fish and other exotic goods. As the men deposited the gifts, the king's men toted them away.

The governor, Captain Summerville along with the tribal rulers walked towards the boats to meet the arrivals. As each family descended, the captain would introduce the ones he could recognize to the governor and the three kings. The Roberts and other families were introduced including Bishop Emile Thompson, and his family. Then the Tolbert family, the Colemans and the introduction continued as the boats shuffled to and from the Freedom Star, ferrying the arrivals.

"Rev. Charles Gooding, Sr was my grandfather," answered Reverend Charles Gooding III when he was introduced to the governor.

"Oh really!" exclaimed the governor. "I used to listen to his sermons. They lured me into becoming a Baptist, I would say. I am glad to know that you are his grandson."

"I am glad to be stepping on these shores, run by someone who knew of him, Governor. I am already feeling at home."

"And we both got lots of work to do," the governor said. "Will be needing someone like you to help me carry on my missionary work as my current portfolio is not allowing me to do that now."

After the formalities of introduction and handshakes, the arrivals were ushered to another part of the island prepared to host a welcoming ceremony in their honor. A group of settlers girls dressed in African lapper suits led them to rows of benches made of planks.

The governor along with Ebenezer Butler and Charles Deshields led Captain Summerville and his crew to a platform and took their seats. Other platform guests already seated were the vice governor for Commercial Affairs, the old and ailing Anthony Greenfield, and his energetic assistant, Estella Carter.

Colonial Council members also at the occasion were Samuel Brisbane of Western St. Paul Territory, Clarence Hutton of Central Monrovia, Benedict Russel of Caldwell, Irene Wilmot Dennis of Mount Barclay territory and Esther Haywood Dunn of north eastern Sinkor.

Councilman Brisbane looked excited. Studying the faces of the new arrivals, he suddenly called councilman Hutton's attention.

"I can smell more professionals, among them with fresh ideas of how we will expand this colony, rather than missionaries with their far-fetched integrationist ideas," he whispered.

"I hope so, Sam," responded Councilman Hutton, also whispering and shifting his heavy torso to lean over to councilman Brisbane. "And a cause for concern; old King Gray said that they are the true owners of the land."

"A complete disregard for our ancestors who were sold and taken away from these shores," grunted Brisbane.

"And a complete disregard for the sanctity of this occasion for you both to be harboring such ill-fitted notion," interrupted Councilwoman Esther Haywood Dunn who eavesdropped on her two fellow councilmen while entering the platform from the back stage where she had been conducting a last-minute rehearsal with some of the indigenous girls of her convent of a home economics demonstration they will be performing for the guests.

Both men, with Samuel Brisbane extremely annoyed, said nothing as they wished to avoid a scene, and watched Mrs. Dunn walked past them and took her seat, a row behind Governor Carey. Samuel Brisbane called his colleague's attention again, and was about to say something but paused when the Master of the Ceremony, Charles Deshields announced that the program was about to start.

It began with a Rev. Dr. Lott Carey ascending the podium.

"We are excited today to receive on these shores, some of our brothers and sisters who embarked on the perilous journey in pursuit of human dignity and freedom," he began. "From the bondage of slavery to the misery of racial segregation you chose this journey in pursuit of a new beginning and a more dignified way of life. A way of life free from all sorts of oppressions, dominations and degradations.

We can assure you and the Color Purpose Organization that as the essence of your journey lies on these shores, you will experience the abundance of liberty. On these shores, the ethos of the universal right that all men are born equal in the sight of God is paramount. Hence, you can rest assured that you have stepped on a land where all black men are born free. A land that inhibits coexistence with those we met here, early arrivals and indigenous alike.

My fellow brothers and sisters, we have all stepped on a solid ground; a ground so solid to uphold the principles of Christianity in adherence to propagating the Gospel as we embarked on another journey to enlighten the land of our forefathers by illuminating the path of serving the one and only true God.

And with the righteousness we seek to permeate throughout this land, we will endeavor to abolish slavery, or, prevent it from happening while we are on these shores. That, we can assure you will be fought with our sweat, tears and blood. May God help us all."

The people were clapping and cheering, as the governor descended the podium in a rousing standing ovation. The rest of the occasion was followed by more cultural dance, a drama performed by a mixture of settlers and indigenous, depicting the discovery of providence Island and the insuring negotiations for the purchase of land by ACS agents and the native rulers they met.

Other items on the program included stories told by the new arrivals represented by Bishop Emilie Thompson on the many encounters they experienced while in the United States, and the journey on the Freedom Star.

Councilwoman Esther Haywood Dunn could not stop cheering for her girls as they performed some of the home economics they learned at the Convent. King Bob Gray, King GolaJor and King Gbessagee watched with amusement as the indigenous read portions of the Holy Bible and recited some verses.

"As we receive the descendance of our forefathers who were taken from here and sold into slavery, we are encouraging our parents to embrace them for the many good things they have brought with them and are imparting into us, evidence of what we are demonstrating here today. With this, we will be witnesses to the establishment of a great nation, the first in the history of Africa." Having everyone jumping to their feet, clapping and cheering, Henfore Gbah, a five years old girl of the convert recited.

Chapter 12

Somewhere deep in the smoky and dense Gola Forest, the sound of drums echoed through the branches of trees, and reverberated around the surrounding highlands. Among the kinds of drums were the Sankpahs, the lead drums with their high melodious pitch. And then the thunderous sound of the Djun Djun, the base drums. The mood of the music occasioned an ultimate call to duty; a call all warriors must obey.

At the eastern side of the clearing, lined up several dozens of drummers attired in their traditional drummer costumes demonstrating the mastery of drum beating. They were divided into groups of different drummers identified by different costumes. The Sankpah drummers wore yellowish brown sisal skirts with dark brown waistbands made of animal hide, designed into hula lapels, bedecked with cowrie shells worn around the skirts. The Djun Djun drummers also wore sisal skirts, but the white ones. And worn around the skirts were black hula styled waist bands.

The upper parts of the bodies of the drummers in both categories were painted with white chalk. The ones playing the Djun-Djun were huge and muscular than the sankpah players. Their muscles trembled to every beat of the instrument they were playing.

A group of Gola and Vai tribesmen, appearing from multiple directions in the jungle, marched towards a large clearing of pasture, following the sound of the drums. They were fully clad in their warrior outfits, shouting the battle cry and displaying different kinds of weapons.

They were brandishing spears, machetes, catapults, and bow and arrows. Within a few minutes the clearing was full of warriors with some displaying mystic powers with different kinds of capabilities. Some of them were doing the war dance as the sound of the drums raged.

With their faces painted black, and around their eyes and lips painted red, the fearful looking warriors would convulse in an animated fashion like an evil spell had possessed them and they would occasionally shout in a dreadful and eerie manner that scared away birds in the nearby trees.

Tondo, a huge and muscular warrior of the Gola band displayed his mystic powers when he wrapped his arms around a tree of about 20 feet tall with a diameter of approximately 16 feet and up rooted it. Zinnah, another one, repeatedly walked over logs of blazing fire, unharmed. An awfully looking warrior stood in a defiant manner, bracing himself and urging his colleague to strike him with any weapon. He would laugh mockingly at the vicious strikes of spears, machetes, or bow and arrows as each did not penetrate his muscular body.

The sounds of the drums immediately came to a halt. The warriors also ceased displaying their mystical gymnastics and began to fall in formation in an orderly fashion by tribe, clan, and fraternity.

The forest became silent. Suddenly, there was a roar sounding like a lion. Then, filtering in the air beyond a hill in the nearby bush, west of the clearing, was the melodious ringing of a belt, followed by the sound of a Kono, a wooden drum made with a two-inch elongated slit whose front and back was not covered with animal pelt.

Within that moment, a Nafai, with an elaborate mask whose head pointed in the air like the horn of a unicorn, ran down the hill towards the clearing of warriors with two men following behind it. known as the frisky devil, the masquerader demonstrated a series of magical acrobatic performances as it neared the warriors.

Having demonstrated several performances for some time, and inspected the warriors, the devil danced its way towards the drummers. It moved to the left flank and sat on the ground. The two men following it stood by, fixing the straw of the raffia outfit it was wearing.

Then, there were two Gbetus, each appearing from the left and the right side of the hill, followed by men playing the kono. The masqueraders also performed as each would suddenly become tall and then short as they made their way towards the warriors. The Gbetus also inspected the warriors, and then proceeded towards the Nafai, and sat near it.

Suddenly, a horse neighed with a high pitch deafening sound. Again, there was silence. Two men emerged from a distance not far from the hill with dammas, or talking drums hanging In Front of them. Then another two followed them. Between their right arms and front-upper shoulders were two large tortoise shells. With a six-inch stick, the men were stroking the shells, in coordinated rhythms.

After another neigh, a white horse, dotted with brown spots on its forehead, extending all the way under its neck and its fore and hind limbs trotted from the right side of the hill. Layers of tiny beads, fitted together with robes, were attached above its hoofs like shackles. Riding on its back was the Vai-Gola ruler Gbanjah Kiatamba.

A number of well-armed warriors, barricading the horse on both sides, provided a protective corridor for the king. The procession matched in a sequence to the rhythm of the tortoise shells, and the dammas. And most incredibly, they were marching in accordance with the sound of the shackles-like beads above the horse's hoof, whenever the animal took a step.

The physically built and huge king was adorned in his warrior outfit which included a fur-like vest with puffed up shoulder pads all made out of the skin of a gorilla he once killed. On both of his hands were the same fur-like texture designed into wristbands. He was wearing a cone shaped hat with bird feathers stock at the foreface. In his hands was a staff made out of the arm of the gorilla with its hand in a clenched fist.

It is said that a certain gorilla once roamed the forest surrounding the kingdom, destroying farms and sometimes killing people it would meet in the forest. Because of this, people were afraid to venture into the bush to farm, and even to streams and creeks to fish, when the bodies of some women were found. A number of brave warriors trying to arrest the situation to save their people from starvation were killed. It was Gbanjah Kiatama, then a boy, who mustered the courage and killed the beast.

Shores of our Forefathers

As old King Kiatamba pondered over the thought of how to announce Gbanjah Kiattamba as his successor over his two older brothers in a way to avoid the issue of right to the throne which was by tradition ascribed to the first born, his two elder brothers mysteriously disappeared from the kingdom and were never seen again.

Though the old king grieved for his sons, and suspected that his brave young son may have had a hand in their disappearances, nonetheless, he maintained in his heart that it was best to the interest of the kingdom, as Gbanjah was best suited to succeed him.

Gbanjah Kiatamba always wore this outfit, and carried the staff made of the gorilla arm as a symbol of his prowess and bravery. Since he became king, he fought and won many battles and extended the Gola-Vai kingdom.

He rode between his warriors as he inspected his fighting forces. For every warrior he would meet, he would tap his clenched fist staff on that warrior's forehead twice and the warrior would jerk and convulse like a fresh dose of power has been injected into him. When he was finished, the king galloped towards the masquerades.

First it was the Nafai, then the two Gbetus. They sprinted from where they were sitting, danced and performed In front of the king for some time. The Gbetus suddenly stretched and became about 50 feet tall. Then, they split themselves into several smaller Gbetus, and again came together as the two original ones.

Satisfied with the performances, the king raised his staff in the air in triumph and then trotted towards a platform made of huge logs with its roof, covered with fresh palm thatches to provide a perfect shade. At the front edge, he descended his horse, with some of his warriors falling to the ground on their bellies so that the king's feet must not touch the ground.

At the platform, he stepped, majestically, with opened arms, toward a throne made of mahogany wood, carved in the shape of a gorilla. On both sides of the throne were two human skulls, resting on wooden poles. They were the skulls of two powerful kings he defeated and beheaded, during his campaign to extend his kingdom. Had it not been for a truce made between him and King Dumar, the Dei king, his kingdom would have extended from the Lofa River to the St. Paul.

"Brave sons of Vai-Gola land," King Kiatamba addressed his warriors. "As we recognized your call to duty in the interest of our father land, we now await the arrival of our guests."

A few clicks away was a dark green offshoot of the Po River. Further down, it flows into a swamp, partially surrounded by a piassava groove. The swamp was quiet, except for occasional ripples caused by the verities of fishes swimming close to the surface.

A kingfisher swooped from its perch and hovered over the dark green surface scanning beneath it for its prey. It soared and flew further towards the edge and made a dive for a catch. Just before plunging into the water, the bird suddenly screamed and flew away.

Two large green menacing eyes popped out of the water, and then the head of a crocodile emerged above the surface. The reptile swarmed to the edge and landed on the muddy banks. Then, it opened its mouth.

A man, wearing a sisal skirt and a small raffia bag hanging across his chest, crept out of the crocodile's mouth. He stood up and looked around him. Surveying the terrain, his attention was suddenly drawn to a piece of cassava peel about 3 inches long, lying, with its inner part visible, between the roots of a piassava tree.

With precaution, the man walked to the tree and studied the pealing; its four edges were pierced with small bamboo sticks to hold it to the ground. The visibility of the white inner part meant no danger or else, it would have been the pink part.

To make sure his readings were accurate and the source of the intel was reliable, he looked up a nearby tree. The branches suddenly shook just when he spotted Sinegar leaping for the lines of trees in the direction of the clearing, where King Kiatamba and his warriors were waiting.

Relieved, he immediately hurried back to the edge of the swamp, and took a few steps into the water, until it reached his wrist. He took out segmented pieces of reefs from the raffia bag and fitted them together, until they formed a 24 inches long stick flute. He curled his lips around the mouthpiece and put the end into the water. Then he began to blow into the tube. Bubbles began to form around the end.

As he continued, scores of crocodile heads began to emerge from the water, one after the other, and soon the fully grown reptiles swarmed towards the edge of the swamp. As they landed and opened their mouths, men, dressed just like him, crept out. Soon the edge of the swamp was full of a band of warriors.

A gigantic one landed and opened its mouth. Three warriors crept out, and then the Bassa king, Sorteh Gbayou. He stood staring at his neengin warriors to ensure that all of them were accounted for.

He was a little distracted when another two enormous crocodiles landed, and opened their mouths. Three neengins ran to them and started hauling out warriors' outfits and weapons, and were distributed amongst the others.

Some of the king's men dressed him into his royal outfit while others quickly assembled a king carrier made of fine wood with the interior upholstered with animal hide made of leopard skin. When it was ready, the king climbed in and sat on a throne like a seat. Immediately, four huge warriors lifted the four edges of the carrier and set them on their shoulders. The other group of warriors formed two straight lines barricading the king, and a procession began.

Ahead of the entourage, the warrior who first landed at the edge of the swamp, was taking the lead, studying other pieces of cassava peelings on the ground, carefully planted by sinegar to direct them to the clearing where King Gbanjah Kiatamba and his men were waiting.

A horn sounded from the right side of the clearing. In that moment, the procession of the Bassa king, comprising 150 warriors, with 75 each, flanking the king on both sides, appeared from that direction, and matched towards the platform. King Kiatamba stood up to receive his guest when the Bassa king and his entourage reached the edge of the platform.

The four warriors toting the king's carrier on their shoulders immediately dropped to their right knees and the carrier was lower to allow the king to get down. As King Gbayou ascended the platform, the host king took a few steps forward towards his guest.

"O, you great ruler and son of the east, where the mighty rivers flow. You are welcome. Many thanks and appreciation for honoring my call," greeted the Vai King, interpreted by witty Peter who was also at the meeting. "Please sit with my right hand."

"I am most gracious to have honored your invitation for the common purpose of regaining our land, O you great King of the West, and a slayer of beasts."

As king Gbayou moved towards the right side of his host throne, his men detached his throne from his carrier and hurriedly set it a few meters next to it. King Kiatamba gestured for his guest to take his seat.

"Today we have with us a great ruler from the east," standing at the edge of the platform, king Gbanjah Kiatamba addressed the group of warriors and the masquerades. "An uncompromising ruler in protecting and preserving our heritage, against the strangers from across the ocean.

He has come to join forces with us to dispose of these land hungry grabbing people, the heritage destroying pests that are ravaging our land to erase our identity forever, an unforgivable evil my own daughter has fallen prey to. I therefore present to you King Sorteh Gbayou."

After the announcement amid a sudden uproar of war cries, and the dancing of the masqueraders, the Bassa king got up and made his way beside his counterpart waving his staff towards the huge assembly of warriors.

"Warriors of our land, and brave sons of our forefathers. Your king has said it all. But let me end with this. Your presence here today is a manifestation of the most honorable response to duty and responsibility. Seeing how you are ready to take on the most noble task of defending our values, the land on which we practice them, we your rulers can assure you that we will lead you in these battles and give you total victory. A victory that will untangle our kids from the dragnet that is erasing our identity. A victory our children and their children will enjoy forever."

After the Bassa king spoke, the uproar of battle cries increased as the warriors demonstrated, in a frenzied manner, their willingness to fight to the death

"We will inspect our forces together," King Kiatamba told his guest, and both rulers descended the platform and walked amongst the warriors. First it was Sorteh Gbayou's men, and then the Vai, Gola and Dei Warriors.

After the inspection, both kings retired to the platform and sat on their respective thrones. Their faces were Gleaming with delight, as they watched the warriors continue to perform the war-like dance with incredible acrobatic display.

"King Garmondeh sends his greetings and reiterates his support to our cause," King Gbayou informed King Kiatamba. "He could not come; the settlers authorities' eyes are on him."

"I feel sorry for him. Most of the land adjacent to his territory is now under settlers' control. And they are now right under his nose, allowing them the opportunity to monitor his activities."

"I partly blame King Gbessagee for this," stated King Gbayou. "Had he not cowardly given his territory to them, they would not have gotten so close to King Garmondeh. Anyway, we are resolved to get all his land back."

"I will blame Golajor for his leaning towards the settlers' side, which gave Gbessagee the confidence to follow suit. How prepared are you, King Gbayou? As you can see, I have been preparing my warriors for months, now."

"O King," breathed the Bassa ruler. "I am fully prepared.

"Lango Gbowee is at your north and at your immediate west is King Gray. These two rulers are friends of the settlers. I beg your indulgence to enlighten me on how you are prepared to attack the settlers to the west without going through King Gray and at the same time preventing the Kpelle princess from pestering you from the north."

King Gbayou offered a smile. Even though he and the Vai king are now trusted allies, he will not disclose all his strategies. He was aware that not all that were displayed before him were the actual fighting sizes and capability of his counterpart.

"We have devised a way to prevent Lango Gbowee from launching any attack. Or, if she does, we have devised measures to prevent her from crossing the Farmington to infiltrate into my territory while I am engaging the settlers, or, the Du River to her south which she might use to send her warriors to help them."

King Kiatamba was silent, his continence urging his guest for more details.

Sensing this, the Bassa king replied, "O king and my brother to our cause. I cannot say much as the strategy is not matured. I admonish you to accept what I have explained, for now."

"Humm. The strategy addresses dealing only with the Kpelle Princess. But how about King Gray?"

"Though he supports the settlers, he has repeatedly said he will not go to war with his kinsmen. And at the same time, no one will use his territory to attack them. So, we have also found a way to launch the attack on Dubor without marching through his territory, or at least, detected."

"Then care must be taken as to how we plan and execute our attacks," cautioned the Vai King.

"So, what are you considering from your end?" King Sorteh Gbayou asked.

"I will march with my forces from here all the way to Banjor and dethrone King Golajor, who can no longer be trusted; he has been secretly negotiating with the settlers to relinquish the territory just before crossing the St. Paul. I will have him executed and replaced with Jahtono.

During my father's reign, I have had an eye on Banjor and have always wanted to cease it. But the old king had always refused, because he had a certain weak spot for King Zulu. So, I have been waiting patiently to succeed him. Now I have, and it is now time that I weed Banjor out of the influence of King Zulu."

After I capture Banjor, Kandakai Goyah, my chief warrior, will lead the first assault on Ducor. He will seize a little Vai Town along the way, secure it and wait for you and Garmondeh forces to thrust in from the north. With a buildup of our huge forces, we will march on Ducor. When the settlers are weakened, I and one of my sons will march with our forces and pillage the colony."

"Which means some of your offensives will be launched out of Gbanjor?"

"That's correct."

The two rulers were silent, pondering and considering the merit of their strategies. Suddenly, there was a loud sound coming from the jungle at the north of the platform. Trees were cracking and falling. For every minute, the sound grew larger as the cracking and falling of the trees got closer to the clearing.

Then it was followed by a brief and heavy storm that swayed the heads of trees, which immediately prompted the warriors to form battlefield formations.

To provide the first line of defense, a large group of the spearmen, chanting battle cries raced towards the edge of the jungle, where the disturbances were coming from. The other group, including the Gbetus and the Nafais, and Sorteh Gbayou's men, raced towards the platform and formed a protective circle around it.

A few meters behind the spearmen, all the drummers were lined up, beating the war drum, its tempo, surreal and enigmatic, depicting the readiness for battle. Immediately behind the drummers were the archers. With their bow and arrows drawn, they were ready to shoot anything that will come out of the jungle. At their far right, stretched and ready to aim, were the warriors with the catapults.

The cracking and falling of trees have reached the edge of the jungle just before the clearing and then stopped. Anticipating an attack at any moment, the spearmen raised their weapons.

About 10 minutes afterwards, no one or nothing came out of the bush charging at the spearman. Then Kandakai Goyah, Kiatamba's chief warrior, climbed the platform and knelt before his king.

"We await your orders to charge at whatsoever that is bringing the disturbance our way, O King."

Before the king could give his orders, there was a loud sound of a trumpet. It was the sound of an elephant. Immediately, a large gray one emerged out of the bush tossing a large tree it had uprooted from its path. Then it raised its trunk in the air and trumpeted again, this time longer than the first.

"Let the horn men do the assembly call," instructed King Kiatamba, and then turning to his counterpart who all the time sat calmly, "We have an unexpected guest and an ally," he informed.

A group of warriors holding cattle's horns under their right shoulders immediately raced to the center of the clearing when the order was given. They formed a straight-line formation and began to blow their horns. Upon hearing this, the warriors began to fall back to their previous formations.

Then the drummers changed into a non-war tempo as they marched back to their original positions. In less than ten minutes, all the warriors were re-assembled. The king got from his throne. He walked to the edge of the platform and looked across the field where the large elephant stood.

The beast trumpeted again and walked towards the clearing. Four slim old ladies with their entire bodies dotted with white chalk and wearing white sisal skirts, marched behind the elephant in a straight line. There was a large winnowing fan made of bamboo peels on the head of the last elderly woman.

After the old ladies was another gigantic gray elephant. Riding on top of it was a middle-aged woman, dressed like the four old ladies and holding a white fluffy staff in her hands.

"She is Jebbeh *Kar-mar-bai;* the mother of elephants," the Vai king informed his counterpart as the woman on the elephant drew nearer.

"Mother of the elephants?" asked the Bassa King.

"Yes," replied King Kiatamba, his eyes still on the procession of elephants as they neared the platform. "We go back many years. I first encountered her when I was a young hunter roaming the forest. I thought she was from a strange land and was lost. So, I invited her to leave the jungle and come and live in our kingdom, but she refused. Later, my father, the old king, told me that just before I was born, some unknown raiders plundered her village and her parents were killed. She was very little when she fled into the forest and has since lived amongst elephants."

"No wonder why she commands them."

"Yes, my friend and brother, the king. And she possesses many powers. Years ago, she predicted that I was going to kill a terrible beast and be made king of our land."

Jebbeh, *Kar-mar-bai* has reached the platform. The four old ladies hurried to the elephant she was riding, and hissed at the animal. It instantly went down on its belly. Before the priestess could descend, the last lady took the winnowing fan from her head, sat it on the ground, and the priestess stepped inside.

"O great priestess of the forest," hailed the Vai king. "What a surprise."

"The whispers of the branches are my ears and the birds of the air are my eyes," she replied, standing like a statue with her staff laying across her hands as she fixed her gaze up at the sky. "Preoccupied with your current endeavors, I am not surprised that you have forgotten this."

"I knew you would be listening no matter how far you were, but I didn't expect you to show yourself to our guests who have come from afar."

"Which means I am here on an urgent matter," Jebbeh said, her eyes now fixed on King Kiatamba. "It is important that you know that the strategy you and your guest are planning may have some weeds on its path that need to be cleared before you tread them."

"Except there are aspects my colleague, King Gbayou and I have overlooked, we are so far planning our strategies well."

"One aspect is Kponkay. He will attack you from behind and disrupt your focus if you attack Ducor. Remember, months ago, he destroyed Jaingkai's Kingdom and beheaded him in the most vicious manner unimaginable for his dealings in the evil trade. And your partner here is into that kind of trade. Kponkay will not hesitate to come in defense of the settlers who he believes, like him, abhors such trade."

"He won't survive if he dares cross the path of the slayer of beasts. He's a bandit and has no organized army."

"Gbanjah. Believe me. Kponkay has gotten strong. Within a twinkle of an eye, he routed the forces of Jaingkai, as powerful as he was, and slew his entire generation. He may not do that to you, but he is capable of causing a severe setback to your campaign."

"So," the Vai King exhaled after a long thought. "It will be good to first hunt the bandit down and execute him before turning my attention to my more pressing initiative."

"No," rejected the Priestess.

Kiatamba's countenance certainly turned into a frown.

"Doing so will not negate the fact that there is another aspect you will still have to address. The Mandingo King from the northwest is friends with the settlers. Just a few months ago, he traveled to Ducor and beheaded two kings for causing problems for them."

"The Mandingo king is faraway. Before he reached Ducor, my allies and I would have completely captured it and rid it of the settlers. And it will be a grievous mistake if he still wants to pick a fight in a territory he's not familiar with."

"He will swiftly respond in the event of an attack on Ducor. But I have a plan for both Kponkay and the Mandingo King. For the many favors I have rendered Kponkay, only one in return he has agreed to render. I have asked him to attack the Mandingo King to keep him occupied while you and your allies attack Ducor."

Surprised, the Vai King asked, "Why attack the Mandingo King?"

"He also beheaded a relative of mine who was an aid to one of the Kings he beheaded. He was the last known family member I have traced a few days before he was beheaded," for the first time in a trailed voice, said the mother of elephants. "I thought all my relatives died when my village was raided many years ago until I tracked him. He may have fled and roamed the bushes along the coast until he was found by this ruler who took care of him."

"We will follow your council O Jebbeh. And I am sorry to hear this."

The priestess nodded. She was about to say something, but stopped when the elephant trumpeted.

"I must leave now," she said, after she looked back at the beast. "But one last thing you must do. Do not launch your attack from Gbanjour. To do so, you will have to cross the Dei where It borders the ocean from the south. You will be spotted from the white man's ships anchoring parallel to the mouth of the river.

Remember they are the ones who are bringing the settlers to our shores. To protect them, they will pound you so that you must not cross the river to attack their protégé."

"You are suggesting another crossing, then. One that will be far from their view."

"Yes, Gbanjah," admitted Jebbeh. "I will be waiting at the elephant crossing, the day you are ready to ferry your troops across the river."

"I will do that. And I will use the Gbanjor crossing as a ploy."

"Excellent," the priestess said, and mounted the elephant.

For a while, King Gbanjah Kiatamba watched the priestess leave before joining his counterpart. Throughout the remainder of the evening, they re-visited their strategies. Very late afterwards, the Bassa King departed.

Chapter 13

The Afro masker, a Bassa dancing devil usually performed at festivals. When Christianity was introduced, upon the arrival of the settlers, it began to perform during the Thanksgiving Day celebrations and the Christmas season. Many settlers and their kids enjoyed watching it dance to the beautiful traditional music by a group of men who sang and beat drums behind it. Fascinated, onlookers would cheer and throw money on the ground as the Afro danced.

Garkpwee was one of those who used to perform as an Afro masker. But because of his short height and small body and the way he walked, even after performing, people often recognized and identified him to be the one who was portrayed as the Afro masker. This did not draw much excitement when people recognized the person in the mask.

To remedy this, he later trained Sundaygar, his friend who was from the former territory of King Gbasaygee to replace him. Now assuming his new role as one of the men who sang and beat the drums, Garkpwee was satisfied that his average height and well-built friend proved to be his perfect replacement when people could no longer identify who it was, in the Afro costumes.

He was also responsible for the costumes and the face mask the Afro masker wore. The original one looked fearful and often frightened the settlers' children and so whenever it came out to perform, the kids would run away from it and their parents would be angry. Because of this, there would be no money thrown on the ground. Garkpwee managed to design his face masks similar to the blue diamond type, he saw on a sailor of a European vessel that was berthed at the waterfront where he once worked as a cargo loader. He made it more adorable for children to like, and soon he and his crew started making money again whenever they performed.

"O mama gee nor nay, a yah lay-lay, lay lay o.

A yah lay-lay, lay-lay o.

Papa gee nor nay, ayah lay-lay, lay-lay o.

A yah lay-lay, lay-lay o."

One sunny afternoon, while walking in the forest of the northern fringes of King Gbasaygee's territory, northwest of Monrovia, Garkpwee was singing a favorite song they sang behind the Afro Masker whenever they brought the devil out to perform. As his favorite song, he himself liked to dance it when he was an Afro masker.

He was on his way to a location where certain softwoods used for calving face marks out of them, grew. Thanksgiving Day and Christmas were around the corner and so he needed to get his crew ready for the festivals.

It was rumored that the new arrival had brought enough money with them, and they and their children would be excited to spend their first thanksgiving and Christmas season at their new homes, watching the Afro masker dance in front of them.

After repeating the chorus several times, he began to whistle the melody of the song at the same time, clearing the weeds overlapping the foot path he was walking on with his machetes. A swarm of fleas suddenly hovered and buzzed around him when he chopped off an overlapping branch, they were perching on.

"*A kay nay*," In Bassa, he uttered a generally idiomatic expression of shock, and hurriedly took off the sleeveless African Vai shirt he was wearing to fend off the insects.

He ran from the sport with the insects chasing him. But at a certain distance they abandoned their chase, and flew up the high branches on both sides of the path.

After brushing his body, Garkpwee flung his Vai shirt around his neck and continued walking at the same time blowing his nose, and picking the corner of his eyes to remove some of the bugs that got in.

He reached a creek, and found his canoe from a nearby under-growth. With little effort, he dragged it into the water. He got in and paddled further up until he crossed to the other side. Then he continued his journey along a footpath at the edge of the creek.

"Ah!" he uttered when he had gotten to the area where the trees grew; someone had chopped down most of them.

With his hands akimbo, he stood, his countenance masked with disbelief. He was the only mask maker who knew where the soft wood grew. How in God's name did someone discover this, he wondered. Then he heard low voices in the bush, followed by something being hauled from the bush to the edge of the water.

"It must be slave hunters," he gasped, and quickly leapt from the path into the undergrowth and hid himself.

He managed to creep to a safe spot where he could clearly see what was going on. Garkpwee could not believe his eyes. A group of five men, apparently the ones who have been cutting down the softwood, were sitting on the ground calving one of the pine wood in the form of a crocodile. They have completed four and it was the last one they were working on.

He was about to come out and walk to them to ask whether they were sculptors, but he suddenly froze and became horrified when another five men emerged from the creek toting a large crocodile squirming in their hands. Its mouth was tied with ropes made of wild vines.

Garkpwee watched how the men threw the animal on the ground and turned it on its back. As the other four men firmly held onto it, one of them butchered its stomach with a long knife and skillfully removed the intestine, the flesh and the bones including the ones on the hand and forelimbs.

They measured one of the sculptures lying on the ground with the skin of the reptile and it fitted neatly. After that, they brought a wild leaf folded into a bulb and opened it. Then they got from the leaf a black paste that looked like a tar and began to rub it on the surface of the sculpture. When they were finished, they carefully inserted the sculpture into the animal skin, beginning with the tail.

To Garkpwee disbelief, the sculptor looked exactly like a living crocodile. The men brought additional crocodiles one after the other and butchered them like they did the first one. They dug holes and buried the intestine, the bones, and other organs of the crocodiles and carefully concealed the spot.

One of the men sat on the back of the sculptor, closed to the neck and opened its mouth. Two men crept in one after the other. This continued until all of them entered the crocodile sculptors in pairs. The Afro mask maker observed how they moved on the ground like real crocs and then dashed into the water.

Guypkwee waited for about thirty minutes. When he was sure that the strange men had left, he dashed out of his hiding place and raised down the path for his canoe. He hurriedly paddled across the creek, disembarked and ran for about 45 minutes. He only stopped to look back when he had reached the vicinity of a nearby village.

"*Mbay gee oo. Mbay gee deh-lo gyane oo*; Come everyone. Come and see what I just saw,'" cried Garpkwee.

A man, sitting by one of the few huts, chopping a palm head to separate the palm nuts from the chaffs, suddenly left what he was doing and ran towards Garkpwee.

"What happened?!" he asked, helping the former Afro mask dancer up, who upon seeing the man, threw himself on the ground, holding his chest to catch his breath.

"In the forest beside the creek, I saw some men turning into crocodiles," wailed Garkpwee.

"*De hen chen keh,*: What are you saying," shouted the man at the same time, shaking Garkpwee.

"At the place where I often go to cut my stick to fix my false face, I saw strange men cutting down the trees and calving them into crocodiles. Then they caught the big live ones and butchered them, and used the animals skins to cover the sculptor which made them look like real crocodiles. Next, I saw them entering the sculptors through the mouth and plunged into the water. I think they were witches."

"King Gbayssaygee must hear this," the man said.

After giving Garkpwee some water to drink. The man called two other men and they immediately hurried with the mask maker, who could barely walk, to see the king at the bigger town a few kilometers from the village.

Three weeks after their arrival, Governor Lott Carey and some officials of the colonial administration watched the last boat leave Providence Island to join the Freedom Star anchored at sea. From the 101 former slaves, 71 remained at Cape Montserrado. 30 family members were setting sail for Bassa Cove, east of Monrovia.

Made possible by the Montserrado colonial authority, and Bassa Cove, some families, like the Findley, the Harmon, the Johnson, the Dennis, the Duns, the Smith, etc. were able to trace some of their family members who came earlier, and settled at Bassa Cove.

During the course of the three weeks, the authority and Captain Summerville worked tirelessly to negotiate with the local rulers to purchase land for the new arrivals that remained at Cape Montserrado, at the expense of Color Purpose.

The days following that, Charles Deshields had been busy conducting classes with the new arrivals and some indigenous, especially the ones who sold their land to them, on the new Settlers-Indigenous Integration Policy, he was mandated to develop and approved by Governor Carey.

"I would like to thank everyone for the job well done in these past three weeks. I am unable to resist the over joy that the repatriation process of the new arrivals went smoothly," Governor Carey addressed his staff, and some members of the colonial council, later that afternoon, in a meeting in a conference room at the colonial head office. "Many thanks and appreciation to King Gray, King Golajor and King Gbasegee for their continual cooperation.

Besides that, we are still trying to see how we can convince and incorporate the local kings who are still hostile to us. We have a situation on hand that we need to address quickly. King Kiatamba's daughter hasn't been found, yet. And it will be to our mutual interests that we find her and ensure that she's treated well. This I believe will be the first step to getting the Vai ruler on our side. So, Commander Johnson. What have we got so far?"

"My Deputy, Major Crayton has some information to provide," responded Commander Elijah Johnson, and turned to his left. "Major?"

The deputy commander for recruitment and intelligence nodded and opened a folder containing stacks of papers before him. Then he adjusted his seat and spread his arms around the folder on the conference table. After studying the faces trimmed on him, he hunched over and looked down at the folder.

"Mr. Governor and staff and members of the colonial council, I have reasons to believe that while we were busy integrating our new arrivals and their families, King Sorteh Gbayou of the Farmington River Territory paid King Kiatamba a visit. The meeting was to consummate an alliance and to plan an attack on the colony. What we don't know is how soon they will attack us. But what we do know is that, fearing that Golajor will turn over his territory to us and embarrass his crossing of the St. Paul to attack us, Kiatamba is preparing to cease Banjor.

And what is more troubling is that the Bassa King traveled with about 150 men. And they passed right under our nose unnoticed. Had we known we would have averted his passage and made it difficult for him to meet the Vai King.

The meeting was held probably deep in the Gola Forest. And here is how we believe Sorteh Gbayou met with the Vai King. Few days before the new arrivals came, a local fisherman was alarmed over his sighting of schools of crocodiles lurking in the mangrove swamps at an offshoot of Stockton Creek, south of Caldwell.

Just three days ago, Garkpwee, a local mask maker spotted a group of men calving wood into crocodile sculptures around a creek at the northern fringes of King Gbasegee's territory. The interesting part of his discovery is, the men killed crocodiles and used their skins to cover the sculptures. Then they crept into the sculptures through the mouth and went into the water like real crocs.

We believe that was how King Gbayou, transported his men to the meeting with the Vai king. They cleverly used the complex water systems of the mangrove swamps around us to get there.

"So, it is through these waterways Gbayou will attack us. Most possibly while we are at sleep," added Commander Elijah Johnson.

"There you have it, Governor," snared Councilman Samuel Brisbane. "While we are wasting our time on a setter-indigenous integration policy, the natives are using theirs wisely to devise means to penetrate the colony and take us by surprise."

"We are not wasting our time, Councilman Brisbane. The policy is leading more indigenous to our side and may increase our numbers to defend ourselves if this conflict further deteriorates. They are now embracing the education we are giving their children along with the civilization it brings," spoke Charles Deshields.

"The civilization you speak of is an illusion while our enemy seems to be craftier by inventing a submersible watercraft to invade us, I must admit," stated Councilman Benedict Russel, his expression full of scorn.

"Are you councilmen saying that we are that dumb to only focus on fostering peace with the indigenous that could win the hostile ones over to us and at the same time not finding means to defend ourselves?" asked Councilwoman Irene Wilmot Dennis. "I am afraid to admit that xenophobia has blinded Councilman Russel and Brisbane."

"Certainly. That's the folly and thought of the first victim. Councilwoman Dennis will soon realize that she had been wrong, but only when painted face savages have burned down her house, butchered poor old Alfred Dennis, and dragged her and her daughters into the bush."

"How dare you say that, Councilman Brisbane?" scoffed Councilwoman Esther Haywood Dunn, coming in defense of her fellow councilwoman "Indeed, xenophobia can turn honorable men into morons."

"Obviously, like birds of the same feathers. I can see that your affliction might even be worse when the native warriors apprehend you and your family."

"Quite correct, Councilman Brisbane," said Councilman Clearance Horton. "Flocking together like rice birds, they will land right in the farmer's net."

"That's enough. I don't think Major Rudolf Crayton has finished his briefing. "Let's listen to him," the governor came in, and after some effort, everyone calmed down and turned to the intelligence officer again.

"Let me demonstrate on the map of the colony pointing to the areas where King Gbayou may have ferried his men," Major Crayton said, taking a map from under the conference table and unwrapping it.

He got up and walked to the wall where everyone could see and hung the map.

"This is the territory of King Gbayou, and here is the Farmington River," the major resumed, pointing to the locations he was describing on the map with a ruler. "An offshoot of the Junk River empties into the Farmington at this point.

We believe that King Gbayou used it to connect to the northern part of the Du River where it connects by an elbow south of the remote village of Kongba thereby bypassing King Gray settlement at the north. Then he joins the Mesurado River through the complex waterways of the mangrove swamps north of Monrovia.

He continued into the mangrove swamps through Stockton Creek and carefully followed it all the way into the upper part of the St. Paul River, north east of Caldwell and then crossed by an offshoot that connects to the Po River in Dei land."

"So, the most appropriate strategy the natives will deploy is to put us in an arc at our north and pushed us towards the Atlantic," added Commander Elijah Johnson, as Major Rudolf Crayton drew an imaginary arc with the ruler, partially circling the mangrove swamps and complex waterways at the north and using the Atlantic coastline as the chord.

"And it is with these submergible crocodile sculptors they will use to pile up their warriors on the dry grounds of the swamps using the mangrove branches as their cover," the major said.

"Will Kiatamba ferry his men in like manner?" asked Councilman Benedict Russel, shifting nervously in his seat.

"That's a possibility, sir," replied Major Crayton. "Since he and King Gbayou are now allies, they will definitely share their battlefield secrets and strategies."

"Why has Golajor not turned over his territory to the colony?" asked councilwoman Dennis. "Doing so might prevent Kiatamba from using Banjor as the crossing point to attack us, as you have said."

"I hope there's an answer for that," replied Deshields. "But I suspect that he does not fully trust us. At least not yet."

"If I was in Golajor's position, I would do the same. The attitudes of Brisbane and like-minded will be a factor," opined Councilwoman Dunn.

"Maybe we can deploy our boys along the swamps to plant dynamites to kill any crocodile that will be lurking in our water channels." Councilman Horton cut in before Brisbane could respond to the councilwoman.

"That will be very dangerous, Horton. We will risk killing local fishermen and annihilating these freshwater crocodile species and eventually denying the generations after us substantial research," rejected Councilwoman Esther Haywood Dunn.

"So, what do you think we must do?" roared Councilman Brisbane "To sit idle while you and your partner of doom lead us to our destruction?"

"Jesus! God forbid!" crooned Councilman Russel.

"No. But to simply avert the catastrophe you and your likes believe is the only way out of this crisis by destroying our natural habitat, and not doing the wise thing to listen to Commander Johnson and Major Crayton who are the experts on matters of security," replied Councilwoman Dunn.

"How did Gbayou and Kiatamba manage to understand each other in the first place?" asked Councilwoman Irene Wilmot Dennis.

"They were using interpreters," replied Major Crayton, watching the councilwoman nodding and making a facial expression indicating that was just what she thought.

"Which would likely be someone who speaks Bassa, Gola, Vai and Dei," buttressed Charles Deshields. "The colony has one in its employ."

"Let me speak to Commander Johnson and Major Crayton in private," Governor Carey Spoke, breaking the over 10 minutes of silence in the room. "Ebenezer and Deshields can join us in my office.

The Colonial Militia commander and his deputy followed the governor and his two trusted lieutenants to his office. They remained there for about 30 minutes discussing and then they re-joined the others in the conference room.

"Ladies and Gentlemen," Commander Johnson addressed the group as he stood at the right side of the map on the wall. "After much deliberation with the governor presenting our strategy to prevent any surprise attack by our hostile neighbors, the governor has accepted that we execute the following: we will deploy our boys with King Gray's men along the banks of the Junk and Du Rivers to monitor movements in the water and along the banks. We will plant some of them deep into these remote villages north and east of Duazon to be our eyes and ears. Some will also be deployed at the northern fringes of King Gbasegee's territory especially where these soft wood pines species grow."

"These will be our preventive measures for now, since these attacks won't happen until these hostile rulers receive signals from each other. And these signals are delivered by their spies who would most likely use these trails," added the major.

"There will be enough time to deploy our people since Kiatamba will not be attacking us anytime soon unless he finds his daughter," Governor Carey said.

"And we believe she hasn't gone home to her father, yet," informed the Major.

"That is our preventive measure for now. We think that the defensive part, if we are attacked, will be left with us," said Commander Johnson.

"So, we urge all of you to increase your personal security around your homes. And never forget to monitor the indigenous ones, no matter how they are loyal," Deputy Governor Ebenezer Butler spoke for the first time.

"Mr. Deshields. You spoke about the colony having an interpreter in its employ. Who is it?" Asked Major Rudolf Crayton.

"Well, I think most of you know Witty Peter," Mr. Deshields replied. "His real name is Cho Vuyougar. He is Bassa, but was raised in King Long Peter's quarters. He is one of few indigenous who is able to speak Portuguese, English, Vai, Gola, Dei, and some Mandingo."

"We need to summon him right now and ask him to show us others like him in the colony," suggested Deputy Governor Butler. "We might have a mode among them"

"Is he at work today?" Asked Governor Carey.

"No, Governor. About three weeks ago he asked for an excuse to attend the burial of a relative who, according to him, lived in the interior," responded the director of Settlers-Indigenous Affairs, and suddenly gasped, "Oh my God!"

"And when exactly was that?"

"The day after the arrival of the new setters, Major."

"I'll be damned! He's the mole!" declared Councilman Brisbane. "All this time you were having a traitor in our employ, Charles?!"

"I only hired an interpreter. He was the only qualified one recommended by Long Peter, before he died," Charles Deshields explained.

"But your unconditional attachments to these natives finally got you a traitor," insisted Councilman Brisbane.

"How could I have known? In fact, you are jumping into conclusions now. We have not investigated him yet."

"Deshields is right," interjected the governor. "Upon Vuyougar's return, we will investigate him only when we are able to establish that he visited Kiatamba's territory the same time we believe the meeting with King Gbayou was held." Then he turned to Mrs. Estella Carter, the Assistant Governor for Trade and Commerce. "What the state of the economy looks like, Mrs. Carter?"

"As it looks, our collections of fees and fines seem to be good," she began, as she stood up, looking down at stacks of papers before her. "But I am afraid that we might experience a deficit due to continuous requests for funds to purchase the ingredients used to make ammunition.

Just the last three months, we collected about $15,000.00 in trade including exports of raw material. But up to date, we have spent about 75% of that amount on the manufacturing of ammunition."

"What would it cost, if we simply input the ammunition?" asked Councilman Benedict Russel.

"It would cost almost all of the $15,000.00 we raise per quarter."

"That's correct," said Commander Johnson. "Taking into consideration the long time a vessel will arrive with the ammunition, it reduces the risk, given our current crisis, as Cheeseman and his boys are manufacturing the bullets in time, and at a far cheaper cost."

"We need to raise our collection to adequately meet this urgent demand."

"Agreed, governor," Mrs. Carter admitted. "But we do have plans to step up agriculture to produce more yields for exports. For the past two years, production from the hinterland has dropped due to constant snatching of farmers bringing their produce to the coast and the middlemen along the trails by slave hunters. The alluvial soil along our estuaries are fertile enough to produce the quantity we need to augment our collection in exports.

Secondly, recent expansion of our jurisdiction has incorporated more natural resources within our Jurisdiction. As we all know, King Gray has extended his territory further north of Duazon, a region with the abundance of wild palm whose price has recently quadrupled in Europe and America. Also, is the additional camwood that will be accrued from the territory of Gbassegee. Our projection puts us at about $50,000.00 in exports as soon as these virgin lands are tapped into. Had it not been for the refusal of some British merchants to pay the required fees at our Wharf, that amount could have been about $70,000.00."

"We need to complain about this to the Americans," suggested Brisbane.

"We already did, through the ACS board in America," Governor Carey responded.

"But we gotta keep reminding them about this."

"Certainly Councilman Brisbane. "But we have to be careful about this. The British navy is assisting us to ensure that the slave trade is eradicated from these shores. Sometimes they respond quicker than the US navy."

"This is why the governor is proceeding cautiously," added Commander Johnson. "The British Navy is also protecting their commercial vessels."

"We are not paying for their efforts in fighting the slave trade and so it's a tacit understanding that they expect that we don't collect or enforce the collection of fees from these commercial vessels. If we can identify more alluvial soil along our estuaries, the expected yields from the crops can offset the loss we are discussing here," Governor Carey further explained.

The meeting was finally adjourned after much discussion on the matter with the behavior of the British merchants and other issues with Councilmen Samuel Brisbane, Benedict Russel, and Clarence Horton occasionally deviating and throwing jabs at Charles Deshields. The director of Settler-Indigenous Affairs would either dismiss their allegations or paid no attention to them.

"Mrs. Carter. I would like to see you in my office for a brief discussion," Governor Carey told Mrs. Estella Carter when the Assistant Governor for Commerce had just finished arranging her stacks of papers, after her presentation, and was about to leave the conference room. "Ebenezer and Charles. I will be needing you both, as well."

Mrs. Carter and Mr. Butler waited in the governor's office while he stood outside the door, which was left open, chatting with Council women Dunn and Dennis, and Charles Deshields. After what appeared like a brief talk on effective monitoring of indigenous staff and interpreters at the colonial office, both men entered the office when the two council women had left. Then the governor took his seat behind his desk.

"Mrs. Carter," he said, looking into a folder lying on his desk. "I once again commend you for your splendid presentation on our business outlook. And, as you may be aware, Deputy Governor Greenfield is aging and can no longer handle our Trade & Commerce Bureau. He has tendered his resignation and has recommended you as head of the bureau. So, I am here by appointing you as Acting Deputy Governor for Trade & Commerce. This is your appointment letter."

"Congratulations, Governor Carter," Deputy Governor Ebenezer Butler said, as Mrs. Carter, who could not hold back her astonishment, received the letter from Governor Carey.

"In our next meeting with the colonial council, you will be confirmed as full Deputy Governor through a vote. Trust me, all of them will vote for you, due to your hard work in effectively handling the commercial section of the Bureau. The ACS board oversee will be duly notified afterwards. Congratulations."

"I am highly honored, Governor," chirped the now acting Deputy Governor. "Tom will love this."

"He's waiting at the door," Governor Cary informed her.

"I trust that you will serve in that position well," Charles Deshields said to Mrs. Carter. Then he got up and went walking to the door. Deputy Governor Butler nodded when Governor Carey winkled at him. Then he also got up and followed Deshields.

The SIAS director opened the door. Immediately Thomas Carter stepped in. As soon as Deshields shot the door behind him, with excitement, Estella Carter jumped from her seat. She ran to her husband and gave him a huge hug.

"I have just been promoted as acting Deputy Governor," she announced.

"Congratulations, Estella," he responded in a cold tone, stunning her.

"Can you two please have your seats? And what I am about to tell must be between us."

"I wonder what is it," Mrs. Carter pondered, looking at her husband and then, her boss, the elation of a just appointed Acting Deputy Governor suddenly disappearing.

"Tom. You can tell your wife what you told me when the issue of Bendu Kiatamba was brought to my attention."

Mr. Carter nodded, and then faced his wife.

"I know this is our family's personal affairs, but as you may have heard in your meeting, the issue with Bendu is now a matter of the security of the colony. The pregnancy she is carrying is mine. That's why she has been refusing to reveal the owner."

"When she ran away from you, she came here to a relative who works in Deshields's office, and that was how we got to know," added Governor Carey, his face full of remorse. "Then we invited Tom to ask him about the claim and he admitted."

"Was this appointment meant to calm me down and to stop pursuing her before she goes to her father who will use her ill-treatment as an alibi to attack us?" Inquired Mrs. Carter, looking at her husband with rage.

"There's no other person in this colony more qualified for that position than you. As the tension between us and the hostile Kings keep deteriorating, we need every resource to defend ourselves if this leads to war, and you are the only person who can accomplish that as our Deputy Governor for Trade and Commerce."

"I understand, Governor," cried Estella Carter, her voice quivering with hurt and rage. "Tom has once again proven that he's not only a pig, but a dirty one."

"There are circumstances that you and I know that led to my action, though how despicable it was. I beg your forgiveness, Estella."

"Now that I know who did it, I will no longer be interested in what will become of her," said Mrs. Carter. "I will now concentrate on my new role."

She suddenly got up to leave and then turned to her husband, still surprised that his face was full of remorse, but not in the cowering way it was when she accused him of the affair with the late Caroline Appleton.

"I am taking the children with me to their grandparents. We will be there for a while, as I find a piece of mind to perform my new role. That doesn't mean there won't be consequences on your part, Thomas," she said, her eyes red, and full of tears.

Governor Carey watched her storm out of his office, feeling bad that his newly appointed and able Deputy Governor was hurt, but was forced to swallow her vengeful attitude in the new portfolio she now held and cherished.

Chapter 14

Aiden and Deon Watkins hated that they were sons of a brave patriot who fought in the American Revolutionary War. Their father, Captain Denver Watkins was part of a Virginia regiment that took part in the battles of Yorktown, and Great Bridge, two crucial battles that led to the defeat of the British.

The young and decorated Captain met Heather McGlown, the boys' mother, a dietitian in the cafeteria at fort Hammington, where he was assigned. He engaged the beautiful blonde, just before he was promoted to the rank of Major and sent off to replace a continental army Major who was killed at the battle of Great Bridge. They married soon after he returned from the war, a hero.

Three years in the marriage Aiden was born, and a year later, Deon. In these times, Virginia was in an economic turmoil, due to the destruction caused by the retreating British Army. There was hardship throughout the state.

In addition, Washington had scaled down federal support for the states that were still engaged in slavery. The situation with Virginia got worse, and the poverty that ensued hit the Watkins family very hard.

Adding to their troubles, the veteran major refused to join a group comprising the state's rich and powerful who were keen on challenging Washington and opting for seceding from the Union.

"It will be a total disregard for the blood that was spilled to drive the Redcoats and upheld the Union," he said in a meeting with the group when he was invited and was offered to organize and head its military wing. "There are better ways to engage Washington than to adopt a violent approach," he spoke and walked out of the meeting.

From that day, he lost honor and respect for his constant refusal to join the group. Every effort he made to regain his honor as a battlefield hero, an added advantage for noble recognition in seeking employment was fruitless as it seemed the powerful men whose offer he refused were the ones influencing all the decisions against him.

Alienated, but not deterred, he eked out a living by establishing his steel workshop to produce and repair the wheels of carriages. The family struggle had its toll on Heather. She became sick and never recovered until she died.

The Town's coroner ruled that it was due to depression and the loss of will to live. The boys were in their teens when this happened. This caused a devastating blow to Major Denver Watkins when it happened unexpectedly and at a time the family had made the decision to move to New York.

"I just need a little time to remember where I hid a map of a trove of treasure buried somewhere underneath Deep Creek. We can sell some and use the fortune to build ourselves a big steel factory in New York," he once told his family over dinner. "There's a map I confiscated from a Redcoat officer I captured during the war. I hid it somewhere in our home. Will definitely remember where exactly I hid it and locate the treasure."

On her first death anniversary, Major Watkins wept bitterly at her grave. Recovering from Heather's death had proven difficult.

"Only if you had just held on a little, Heather," he sobbed. "We all would have been long gone from this God forsaken place. Now I am taking the boys to New York without you."

Unfortunately, a few days after he told them he was going to embark on finding the treasure map, the boys were shocked that their father began to experience memory loss. Days later, the war hero's condition further deteriorated. Like his wife, he eventually died of similar circumstance, leaving Aiden and Deon devastated and confused and without any clue as to where their father hid the map.

The coroner ruled that amongst other conditions like stress and depression, a kind of dementia was the result of his acute memory loss which possibly resulted in his death.

The only thing they knew was his brief narration about how he got the map. The British soldier he captured confessed that a group of Mohawk Indians, fighting alongside them, offered to take him, their commander, to where a huge pile of gold was hidden, in exchange for their family's escape to England when it seemed the Americans were winning the war.

The Redcoat officer agreed. In the heat of the battle, the Indians took him to a place at Deep Creek where they hauled from under the water several canoes with stock piles of gold.

While trying to upload the gold from the canoe to a wagon, they could hear the roar of American cannons fast approaching. And there was no time to get all of the stock piles of gold into the wagon. So, the British officer told them to bury the canoe back into the water.

When the last one was buried, he ordered his men to kill the Indians. Then he killed his own men. After that, he hastily drew a map of the place and while escaping to return some day, when the war was over, he was captured.

"Had you remembered where you hid that map and found the gold, mom would not have died and we would not have been in this shit, dad," snarled Aiden, one day standing over his father's grave. "Deon and I are going to sell the family home and get the hell out of here."

Later that evening Deon was sitting in the hammock at the back of their house leisurely swinging the stitched red cloth couch, a thing he always did whenever something was on his mind when his brother came to him. With his blonde hair, he looked just like their mother, Aiden observed.

"Hey, check this out," Aiden said, dropping a newspaper on his brother's lap. "That's our way out of here," he added, when he saw Deon's face brightened and assumed that he had just read a portion about an advertisement to hire steel workers who have experience working with iron by a new steel company in New York. "We are going to use all the skills daddy taught us to earn ourselves a big job. It's now time to get out of here."

The following day, they hung the 'House for Sale' sign at the pike gate In Front of their house. Next, they were getting rid of all the junk in it, and a small barn at the back of the yard.

"Oh my God!" exclaimed Aiden, on the afternoon of the third day when he found and opened a cloth map neatly shoved into the hollow at the foot of the sculpture of a continental soldier, lying between the logs that made up the foundation of the barn.

He immediately believed it was his father's lost treasure map, when he unfolded it and read the handwriting at the top, *'Map of the Mohawk Indians Gold'.* **Location:** *At the bottom of Shallow Stream about 15 meters* **away** *from the Bridge at Deep Creek.* There were more details dotted under the legend.

"Deon," he called, sitting on the ground weeping with joy. "You gotta see this."

Deon came and when he saw that it was the treasure map, he sank to his knees and began to cry. That evening after supper, they studied every detail on the map. Then, the brothers made plans to find the gold. They decided to suspend the sale of the family house for a while to focus on locating the treasure.

"You need to apologize to dad," Deon demanded, looking his older brother straight in the face. "It was because of the devastating blow of mom's poor health and death, and the dementia the coroner mentioned in Daddy's death report that caused him not to remember where he hid this map."

"What was the reason for dementia?"

Deon studied his brother for a while, relieved that the question meant Aiden had also believed. "It was probably due to years of being under heavy bombardment from the British."

"Okay," he sighed. "I'll visit the cemetery and do as you have demanded. Then we will go and take a look at the creek."

Two weeks later, driven by four horses, the boys were riding a large open wagon towards Deep Creek. In it was a rowboat. Attached to the stern was a large wooden dredge in the form of a comb. From the map, they traced the exact spot where the treasure was submerged, about 15 meters from the bridge.

They rowed at this spot a week ago to measure the average depth of the water which information they used to build the dredge including an estimation of how far the underwater current may have dragged the gold-filled Mohawk canoes from their original spot over the years to give them an ideal where to begin the search. To be sure, they added an additional 15 meters beyond the original spot.

"This is it," said Aiden, when they reached an area along the banks at the right side of the creek.

The boys halted the wagon, and got down. With a little effort, they detached the dredge from the boat. After that they got the boat out of the wagon and dragged it to the edge of the water. When they rowed a few meters into the water, they went for the dredge and attached it at the stern.

"You can detach the horses and carry them across the stream, now," Aiden ordered.

Deon watched as Aiden tied the nose of the bow with a long robe and threw a large potion to him. He held onto the robes, and rode along with the three horses all the way over the bridge and crossed the stream at the other side.

"Are you ready?" he cupped his hands around his mouth and called to his brother sitting in the row boat, a few meters from the edge of the water.

"Yeah, make sure you pull the horses gently or else the boat will flip over. You hear me?"

"Yeah."

Deon attached the robes to two of the horses and gently stroked them. As the animals moved, so was the row boat, pulling the dredge. Anything under the water will be dragged to the edge with the help of the horses. After some time, the boat was almost at the edge of the water, with nothing in the dredge.

"Okay, Deon. We need to cover 30 meters from here under the bridge and beyond until the dredge pick up something,"

Deon waited until his brother turned the boat to face the right side of the banks before he drove the horses back across the bridge. Again, he stroked the horses. They moved and gently continued, followed by the row boat with the dredge plowing the water bed.

For a couple of hours, they rotated and repeated this process until they were almost under the bridge. Then the horses stopped and so the boat. This time it was facing the left side of the banks.

They had covered about 23 meters moving back and forth when the boat stopped moving.

"I think we got something!" shouted Aiden, his voice full of excitement.

"The horses are not moving, either!"

"There's a lot of weight. Add the other horse to increase the power," instructed Aiden.

Deon did, and the boat began to move, but this time slowly. Aiden could feel that something was caught in the dredge. Most likely one of the Mohawk canoes with the stock pile of gold.

The horses managed to pull the row boat close to the edge. As the dredge became visible above the water surface, Aiden's excitement began to diminish; he was expecting the dredge to pick up a canoe, but it had dragged out a coach.

Caught between the teeth was the right wheel at the back. This time Deon stroked the horses harder to increase the pace. About half of the coach, full of mud, lying on its left side was now above the surface.

"What the hell?!" Aiden exclaimed, when the entire coach, which appeared half burned, was now out of the water, with the skeletons of its horses still attached to the harnesses.

"Oh my God!" wailed Deon who had stopped the horses and rushed to the edge of the water to see what they had pulled from underneath.

"It's the coachman's," his brother told him, pointing to the rim. "Look at this. We changed these spokes about three months ago."

"Jesus. How did it get here?"

Aiden did not reply, but rather waited until most of the water drained out. The mud was also sliding down, exposing the frame of the coach. The boys were spooked when the sliding mud formed something like a mummy covering the steel box at the seat rest.

"It's a cadaver!" cried Deon.

"It's Percy Mac-Adams'," said Aiden. "No one, but only him, rides his coaches."

"Something terrible happened here."

"Maybe something made him slip off the bridge."

"Maybe something like a fire may have started and forced the horses to leave the bridge and jumped into the water, taking old Percy and the coach with them," Aiden added, his eyes on the skeletons of the horses strapped to the half-burned harness and the muddy coat on the corpse. "Take one of the horses and ride to town to inform the sheriff. I will wait here."

Immediately Deon ran to the wagon, almost stumbling. He got out the saddle, ran to where he left the horses, and saddled one of them. In one kick, he was galloping towards town.

Aiden Watkins watched his brother galloping in the distance, as he sat on the banks of the river, dismayed. The discovery of Percy Mac-Adams' coach, instead of finding the stock pile of gold, has stalled their efforts.

But his face suddenly brightened; their dredge did prove effective, and the method they were using to find the stock piles of gold, buried underwater with the Mohawks' canoes, would work. They will resume when the matter surrounding the discovery of the dead coachman is over.

Roger Monroe Burgess was at his piano, playing the hymn 'Rock of Ages'. His eyes were full of tears as he mourned his son, Elijah Burgess. He received the news of Eli's death about a week after Captain Summerville returned to the United States.

The family had been mourning since then, but with a sense of elation that the Color Purpose CEO drowned at rough sea, trying to rescue a little boy who fell overboard. This was easy to accept; the boy was saved, and Elijah's death, though unfortunate and painful, was heroic.

But a week ago, Constable Richard Arlington thought otherwise when he received the news and went to verify the discovery of the dead coachman dredged from the bottom of a stream in the Deep Creek region in Norfolk, by two brothers who did not say what they were looking for, according to the town's sheriff.

The findings of his preliminary investigations ended with a suspicion that the day before Percy Mac-Adams disappeared, he transported someone to Continental Inn, and that person met with Elijah

Burgess, which Todd, the baggage man at the inn, old Bill Hayes, the bartender and even Alexander Gerald, the manager and owner of the inn, confirmed.

It was a discovery, while examining the corpse and wreckage, that prompted the old constable to inform Roger Monroe Burges, that Eli's death may not have been an accident.

Learning of this new development, the mood of mourning Elijah Burgess has changed. He was murdered. And so, the owner of Color Purpose invited Captain Summerville to inform him of Arlington's discovery so that the pieces of evidence can be put together to identify the person who murdered his son.

Sitting behind him were his two sons, Samuel and Monroe, and their sister, Meredith, all in tears. At his left and his right, sitting on the piano bench, were his two grandsons, Joey and Richard McAllen.

The door to the family living room suddenly opened, and Mr. Archer, the butler peed in and nodded to Samuel Burgess who caught his eyes. The Washington base lawyer got up and walked to the door.

"Captain Summerville, and Constable Arlington along with a man are waiting," he hissed, and then stepped aside to allow Samuel Burgess to see the men.

He looked and saw the captain and the constable, and another man, a well-dressed negro, sating on the couch in the hall way. Captain Summerville and constable Arlington followed, except the well-dressed negro, when he gestured for them to come in. As the butler ushered, both men sat adjacent to each other.

"Captain Summerville and Constable Arlington are here, Granddad," receiving a signal from his mother who slightly nodded, Joey whispered in his grandfather's ears.

"Not the labors of my hands can fulfill thy law's demands;

Could my zeal no respite know, could my tears forever flow,

All for sin could not atone; Though must save, and thou alone," as if he didn't hear Joey, Roger Monroe Burgess sang the second stanza of the hymn, as he violently glided his fingers over the keys.

"Lyrics by Augustus Montague Toblady, 1763, music composed in D Major by Thomas Hastings, 1831," the old man, after playing, turned and spoke, forcing a smile and wiping his tears. "Just what Eli would have announced, if he was right here in this room."

"And he would have ended the last verse in his usual awe-inspiring tenor," slurred Meredith, suddenly bursting into tears.

Her two brothers held her at the same time patting her on her back. But soon they both joined their sister, crying.

"It's okay now," their father, along with Joey and Richard came over and consoled them. "Your brother is with the lord, now." They all held on to each other for a while. Then Roger Monroe Burgess turned to his guess. "Shall we do this?"

Mr. Archer led the men into Roger Monroe Burgess' office and offered them seats while the old man went into his room to change from his morning robes. Samuel and Monroe later came into the office when they had accompanied Meredith to her living quarters.

"Having read the report from the Freedom Star, everything suggested that Eli's death was an accident. A part of the report, quoting Jack Duval's thoughts, could not have been considered until Constable Arlington's latest discovery," the owner of Color Purpose spoke in a calmed voice when he entered his office and sat behind his desk.

"Percy Mac-Adman's corpse was clinched to the mental rail of the driver's seat like he was protecting something inside when the coach plunged into the water in flames. This got my attention and so when I opened the box, I saw this newspaper intact. It is the Virginia Cardinal. It carried the story of a fire incident and a mass murder at Cottonwood Plantation somewhere near Gunston Hill.

The paper reported that there was one person uncounted for. And the illustration matches the description of the person the coachman transported to Continental Inn. She's the woman that met with Eli, "explained constable Richard Arlington, displaying the newspaper covered with mud stains.

"I gave a copy to my son, the last time he was here. That night he told me he had a date waiting at the inn, and Alex had confirmed that the illustration is the woman he was with."

"Before his departure, my brother sent me a note telling me that he has just gotten married to Angela Draper, a free woman from Montgomery," informed Monroe Burgess, Eli's lobbyist brother in New York. "I was appalled that he was about to get married without informing dad, or any of us."

"Angela Draper told us during the investigation that Elijah had been worrying about how to ask his dad about his mother. That was what may have led to the sudden seizure while he was in the water," said Captain Summerville, looking at the illustration. "This is exactly Angela."

"Gentleman it's time I invite Dean Goldman who's been aiding me with the investigation," Constable Arlington said. "He's been working with me investigating crimes in black communities."

"Let him in," instructed Mr. Burgess and Mr. Archer opened the door of the office and went out.

He re-entered with the well-dressed negro, who looked in his fifties and smoking an Apple tobacco pipe with gold band around the shank.

"Excuse me," he said, taking the dark brown egged pipe from his mouth and shoving it in his vest pocket, when he observed the eyes on him.

"Can you give us what you got?" asked constable Arlington.

"Sure," replied Dean Goldman, removing his hat from his head. "I think it is getting clear that the woman whose illustration is in the Virginia Cardinal may not be who your son thought she was, Mr. Burgess. Now this is what we know.

Records from Montgomery, dating 5 years back bear no free colored woman name Angela Draper. Interestingly, the same person registered at Charles Inn in Fair Flask County as Theresa Blackwell. The inn keeper also confirmed the illustration.

He said he felt a strange surge of what he described as a paralyzing reluctance when he looked in her eyes to ask where she was from.

Now what is of concern is that two days after the fire incident at Cottonwood, this woman checked in at Charles Inn."

"A rummage of stacks of papers in Mac-Adams' private office found a request to transport a woman from Charles Inn to Richmond a week after the arson," Added Constable Arlington.

"A timing, we believe, was not of coincidence but a well concocted plan," Dean Goldman averred.

"Wait a minute. Are you saying that this missing person may be the same woman who my son dated?"

"What Constable Arlington and I are saying is that the sequence of occurrences surrounding this missing woman is leading us to suggest that she was escaping the United States and had used your son as the conduit, Mr. Burgess," replied Dean Goldman. "A fire destroyed the entire plantation and did not only wipe out the Cottonwood family, but their slaves as well."

"Which meant that someone wanted to get out of there without a trace," added Constable Arlington. "We believe that the coachman saw the Virginia Cardinal amongst his stacks. He may have read Jim Wolf's story, recognized the person whose illustration was the missing woman, and while on his way to Richmond to report that it was the same woman he dropped off at Continental Inn, he got killed."

"According to sheriff Chamberlain, Norfolk experienced a sudden thunderstorm and lightning the night of September 8. The next morning it was discovered that the bridge over Shallow Stream was gutted with fire, which burned down a huge portion, "explained Dean Goldman.

"That was the only part of Deep Creek that got burned. The bridge was rehabilitated afterwards. And months later, the Watkins brothers discovered Mac-Adams' corpse half-burnt under that very bridge," buttressed Arlington. "His horses, still harnessed were also burned to their skeletons,"

"Sounds like the coachman was targeted," admitted Samuel Burgess.

"These were strange occurrences," conceded Captain Summerville. "The paralyzing reluctance described by the Charles Inn keeper is similar to what Jack Duval had been describing, since Elijah's death." The captain froze after he said this. His expression suggested that he had remembered something. "Two of my sailors said Jack Duval told them that he was nearing to finding the person who cast the evil spell on Elijah that made him paralyze in the water, when suddenly he was attacked by a shark while shark hunting at the bay of sharks at Cape Verde. Jesus! All the pieces of evidence that we could not see are now coming together."

"So, this Angela Draper woman or Theresa Blackwell could be the same person my son dated and married."

"We think so, Mr. Burgess," replied Dean Goldman. "Only with a visit to Gunston Hill will we be able to authenticate all of this."

"Hold on a second," interjected Monroe Burges, flipping through the pages of the Virginia Cardinal. "Who are you going to talk to over there, when according to the article, no one survived that fire except the half-sister of Mary-Ann Cottonwood. And if you are saying that she may be this Angela Draper, Theresa Blackwell or whatever, she's gone, hiding in some place along the West African Coast."

"Sure. But it is obvious that Oliver Price, the reporter of the story, had a source who is most likely a survivor, who was unnoticed," offered Dean Goldman." I can find that source and get more details."

"I think you need to do that, Mr. Goldman and report back to us in a week," admonished Mr. Burgess. "Finding this woman and bringing her to me will compensate for Eli not having a grave today." Then he looked towards the door where Mr. Archer stood. "Can you get us some drinks?"

A few meters west of Gunston Hill, at the edge of the field of what was left of the Cottonwood Tobacco Plantation, Elaine Mason came out of her wooden cabin with a small garden hoe in her hand, prepared to go to work in her garden where she grew collard greens, cabbage, potatoes, beans, field peas, and a few corn.

Since the day of the fire, she had not been herself. She could not understand how it happened. But it started when the whole plantation was asleep. She was the only one up that night. The head house-maid, once with a big body, had gotten frail. The toil of gardening has affected her greatly. She was only used to, not just supervising, but cooking, cleaning, and doing the laundry. While inspecting her field peas, she heard a horse neighed. She looked, and saw a man galloping down the hill on a brown horse.

The man rode towards what was left of the tobacco field. He got down from the horse, and walked through the rows of dry tobacco leaves, holding the reins as the horse trotted behind him.

He was well dressed in an all-black suit, black tailcoat, a pair of black gloves and black booths. He bent over and plugged a dry tobacco leaf, folded and rubbed it in his palms to form a ball. He took his pipe from his vest pocket and inserted the tobacco ball into the chamber.

After striking a match, he put the glowing flames into the chamber and took his first few draws, letting out smoke through his nostrils as he closed his eyes and enjoyed the taste. With the pipe still in his mouth, he took off his hat, stuffed it under his right arm, and continued walking towards Miss Mason.

Her eyes suddenly brightened with astonishment. He was a black man. As he got closer, she could see that he looked somewhat around her age.

"A nigger amusing himself with raw tobacco planted with the sweat and blood of fellow niggers. Lord have mercy!"

"Miss Mason?"

"Who's asking?"

"Dean Goldman. A free man from Richmond. I investigate crimes in black communities," he introduced himself, as Miss Mason watched the pipe dangling in the corner of his mouth as he spoke. "No disrespect. Kindly excuse my addiction to tobacco."

"Like I told Price when he come here inquiring about the fire, I don't think this was done by a nigger. The fire just started."

"I am not here to ask you about that, Mam. I am here to learn about the missing woman."

"I don't know what happened to her, either."

"But you know her. You were the head house-maid, right? You served the old master, then, his son. You also served this woman. The half-sister of Mary Ann. A fortunate colored girl you must have liked and missed, too."

"Why are you interested in all this?"

"Because I think she's alive," Goldman replied, taking the Virginal Cardinal from the side pocket of his tail coat. "Here. Take a look at this. It's her right?"

Miss Mason flinched when she saw the illustration. Dean Goldman caught that, and struggled to suppress the glee appearing on his face.

"I have some cornbread and Kool Aid," she said, her tone suddenly inviting. "You have been riding for hours, I guess."

"That'll be good," the free black investigator accepted, and followed Miss Mason to her cabin.

Dean Goldman was offered a seat on the porch, and then Miss Mason brought some corn bread and a jar of Kool Aid. She sat in a chair, her eyes on her guest, as he took a bite of the bread and a sip of the Kool Aid.

"Bob-bob enjoyed eating the corn bread and drinking the Kool Aid I made," she said. "But he got hanged for messing around her."

"Messing around who?" Goldman stopped chewing.

"The woman for whose business you are here."

"Who she really is?" The free black investigator asked, pretending like he wasn't eager for a response as he continued munching on the cornbread.

"Let me show you something in which I believe lies the answers you seek," Miss Mason said, after staring at her guest for a while and then got up and went into her cabin.

After sometime, she came out, cradling with a chest, compressed against her torso. Dean Goldman had finished with the bread and was occasionally sipping the Kool Aid.

"This was entrusted to me a long time ago when I served the old master and Mrs. Cottonwood," she said, laying the chest at his feet. "He told me to never show it to anyone. Now he's dead, and it seems meaningless to me now."

In no time the Black slave community investigator opened the lid and rummaged through its contents. He saw some portraits at the bottom and one after the other he began to unfold them.

First, it was the portrait of a man dressed in a Navy uniform. Before he could guess it, an inscription at the bottom right read: Admiral James Chrystal Eagleman; 1790.

"Mary Ann's father," he muttered, and then picked and unfolded the next one which was a portrait of James Crystal Eagleman and another Admiral. Inscribed at the bottom right was: Admirals James Crystal Eagleman and Charles Norman Drake; 1811.

"Keep searching," Miss Mason urged when he lifted his head and looked at her.

He continued searching among the stash of portraits and unfolding each until he suddenly froze when he unfolded a particular one. It was Admiral Drake and a little girl of impeccable beauty. Charles Norman Drake was dressed in a business suit. He was standing behind the little girl wearing a Blue English Silk dress. She was sitting in a chair.

"With my beloved…," he struggled to read the inscription and then paused, his heart rising. "So, this is her name; Rebecca Drake, Marry Ann's half-sister," he crooned, comparing the illustration on the Virginia Cardinal to the little girl in the portrait with Admiral Drake.

"We called her Ann," said Miss Mason. "She was a little girl when she was brought to the plantation. Bob-bob, loved by master Perry and his dad, was her chaperon until she grew up into a very attractive woman. But he got hanged for flirting with her and trying to run away."

"Flirting with the master's in-law and trying to run away? Niggers get hanged for that."

"It was not like Bob-Bob to flirt with anyone. Even, it was not like Master Perry to flog and watch someone he loved, hanged," Miss Mason began to cry. "In a fight, Bob-bob once broke the arm of James Burk, one of the overseers, for lashing Thomas, a slave. The kid did not show up in the field early, only because he was not well. But Burk couldn't reason.

'You were lucky Bob-bob didn't kill you, James,' was Master Perry's exact words."

"And Bob-bob was not punished?"

"That's what I am saying. He just laughed at it and patted Bob-bob on his back," she replied, wiping her tears. "Come let me show you around."

For the next few hours, Dean Goldman followed Elaine Mason through the abandoned tobacco field.

"They say a family is going to buy this place and continue with the plantation," she informed him.

"I pray that your new masters will be good."

"A free man from the city. At least you don't have anything to worry about," she said. "That's what Bob-bob wanted. He wanted to be a free man."

In silence, they continued to walk through the field. Then she led him to a part of the plantation where stood a dilapidated two-storey house. Walking between a row of walnut trees, they reached what was the entrance of the house.

"This was the Cottonwood main house. You see that part," she said pointing to a portion of the ground floor. "That was the kitchen. I was mixing dough that night. And, I have just finished applying some yeast on the flour and covered it with a baking tray. I came out and sat on the stairs right here to catch some fresh air. While waiting for the dough to rise, suddenly, I heard a wheezing sound.

Next, the house was on fire. Then, with an unusual rapidity, the entire plantation was gutted in split seconds. Everyone was screaming and calling for help. The slaves and overseers' quarters were consumed completely.

'Perry. Where are you? I can't see anything. Too much smoke. I am suffocating,' I heard Marry Ann screaming. I rushed to the main entrance door, but a force from the heat flung me to the ground a few meters from the burning front door."

"And you could remember nothing, afterwards," offered Dean Goldman, sounding remorseful, but with a little concern. "Where was the Oven?"

Goldman assumed maybe the oven was overheating and burst into flames.

"You see that structure over there," she said, pointing at a dilapidated frame which looked like an outside kitchen. "That was where the oven used to be. And it did not burn."

Quivering with uneasiness, Dean Goldman struggled to swallow that one. Obviously enigmatic, he thought. The source of the fire did not come from the oven.

"I remained lying on the ground, unconscious, until morning when the town's sheriff, with a group of people who came to put off the fire, arrived," continued Miss Mason. "The only thing I could remember, roasted bodies were pulled from the rubble. Gary Jackson, an eleven years old kid was found alive in the rubble in the slave quarter. His entire body was covered with soot. Only the white of his eyes shone through the dark as dawn approached."

They were now passing by the slave quarter. Dean Goldman felt a cold sensation running through his body looking at a row of about 10 brick cabins, half burned down from the chimneys while others completely razed to the ground. The battered and soot covered ruins could tell how devastating the fire was.

"This was the laundry, and that other one was the loom house," Elaine Mason explained, as they toured this part of the plantation. "That spot over there was the carriage house, completely burned down."

"Quite strange. The fire made sure it destroyed the transportation sector," wondered the free black community investigator, appalled by the vicious devastation of the house. "Someone or something was sure that he/she or it was the only one to survive and get away, and disappear."

"Here's the stable," said Miss Mason, now sobbing hysterically. "Half of it was gutted. A few feet to the right were the gallows on which they hanged Bob-bob Douglass." Now she fell to her knees, weeping. "It was like Master Perry was paralyzed with a strange reluctance to forgive the slave he so loved and spoiled." Overwhelmed with grief, her voice wheezy and barely heard, "They were both born and grew up together on this plantation. His mother died when he was young and so Master Perry's mother made sure he was okay," she lamented.

Dean Goldman patted the old housemaid on her back, his eyes sorrowful and red with tears, as she was still on her knees, weeping.

But something instantly registered into his mind; Elijah Burgess was suddenly paralyzed with a seizure, and Jack Duval, according to captain Summerville, felt a strange paralyzing feeling taking hold of him. The Innkeeper at Charles Inn also recounted a strange paralyzing reluctance, and now Miss Mason has just revealed a sense of strange paralyzing reluctance on Master Perry's part, the day Bob-bob Douglass was hanged.

The free black investigator's heart suddenly leapt when he thought he felt the same, when it occurred to him that these sequence of occurrences had a common factor. The strange paralysis occurred when the victims, one way or another, interacted with this Angela Draper who he now discovered to be Rebecca Drake.

"Who's over there?!" he suddenly shouted when he heard what sounded like someone was knocking on a wood.

Elaine Mason heard it too. But with her arms folded, she was still on her knees, gently rocking herself in solace.

Receiving no response, Goldman pulled out his pistol from the inner pocket of his coat wrapped in a cloth. He unwrapped the revolver, given to him by Constable Arlington, and began to take careful steps towards the direction of the sound.

Then, he saw that the sound was coming from behind a large tree, a few feet at the back of the partially burned stable. It appeared like someone was calving on the tree trunk. It continued for a while and then it suddenly stopped.

"Whosoever you are, get the hell from behind that tree right now," pointing his pistol, Goldman, called out.

A boy immediately stepped from behind the tree with a carving knife in one hand and a chisel in the other. He was wearing torn-up trousers reaching his knees with a shirt that looked big for him. A gouge was in the right corner of his shirt pocket. On his feet was a pair of sandals with the sole carved out of wood.

"Who are you and what were you doing behind that tree, son?!" lowering his pistol, and putting it back in his coat, Dean Goldman asked, panting.

"He's Gary. The one who was found in the rubble," Miss Mason spoke, standing behind Dean Goldman. "His father, James Jackson was the plantation craftsman. His mother worked in the laundry. They both left in the fire that night. He lives with me now."

"What were you carving on that tree?"

The boy did not answer but ran to Miss Mason and embraced her, his eyes on the black man with a gun. Out of curiosity Dean Goldman walked to the tree and went behind it to take a look.

"Are you kidding me!" marveled the black community investigator.

Carved on the tree trunk was a scene depicting the plantation stable as it was, before it got burned. There was a gallows at its right. It portrayed a slave standing on the platform with his hands tied behind him. Hanging from the crossbeam, the noose of a robe was looped around his neck. Fastened on the level was a robe also attached to the harness of a horse.

The carving also pictured about 15 persons gathered at the gallows to watch the execution. Among the group, a woman who looked like Miss Mason was weeping at the edge of the scaffold. A man stood between two women in the group. He looked like Master Perry. The other woman looked like Mary Ann's sister in-law, Dean Goldman quickly recognized from the portrait.

Mary Ann's sister was holding Master Perry Cottonwood's hands leaning her head on his right shoulder. The carving revealed an ominous grin on her face. But her eyes were transfixed at the condemned slave. A cone shaped optical prism ran from her eyes to Bob-bob Douglass'.

Appearing weary and sympathetic, the other woman, standing on the other side of Master Perry Cottonwood was not holding his hands. They were folded.

Dean Goldman suddenly gaped when he discovered that part. To him, the way Master Perry and his sister in-law held each other's hands, as she laid her head on his shoulder, meant that there was intimacy between the two. He assumed that the other woman with the weary and sympathetic face was Mary Ann.

Then, he noticed the carving of a toddler who he immediately recognized at the far right of the scene, standing with a wooden tablet and a small paint brush in his hand. It looked like he was painting the entire episode.

He suddenly felt a strange feeling. His head was rising and he could not move his hands. He was breathing heavily and tried to step away from the tree, but he couldn't move his legs.

"Help!" he struggled to cry out.

"What is it?" Miss Mason rushed to him. She grabbed, shook and pulling him from behind the tree.

"I don't know," he replied, breathing heavily when he came to himself; his eyes, dim and awful, were on Gary, but they finally sparkled with relief.

"Did you do this?" asked Miss Mason, looking at Gary and then at the carving.

The kid nodded nervously, as Dean leaned forward holding his chest and wincing, like he was experiencing some pain.

"He was there when they hanged Bob-bob, "she told the investigator. "It's enough for today now. You must be tired," She turned to Gary. "We have a stranger staying over for the night. We got to clean your room."

The next morning Dean Goldman was galloping towards the other fields of the plantation with Gary sitting behind him. He looked energized and determined, following the brief eerie encounter he had while looking at the lad's carvings. Thanks to Miss Mason hot corn bread and tea he had that morning.

During the night, as he lay in bed, reminiscing on what he had gathered so far, all began to make sense to him now. Robert 'Bob-bob' Douglass flirted with Rebecca Drake and got hanged. Master Perry Cottonwood had an intimate relationship with his sister-in-law and then the plantation was gutted with fire, killing everyone, except Miss Mason and Gary.

Elijah Burgess married Angela Draper who is Rebecca Drake and drowned at sea while they were on their honeymoon. The facts were now steering at him. This was seduction and manipulation.

Nonetheless, something that was not clear, baffled him. And he was determined to make sense of it, too.

"What happened to the horses in the stable?" he asked Gary Jackson early that morning. "Did they also get burned in the fire?"

"They ran off," answered the kid.

"How did you know?"

"I see them often in the fields."

"How many did Master Perry have on the plantation?"

The kid paused for a while, and then responded. "11."

"Can you take me to the fields?"

As Gary directed, they rode some acres west of the plantation and then they reached an opened field.

"There they are," Gary Pointed to a number of quarter horses in the distance. "They are scared," he warned when the animals suddenly became uneasy, kicking dirt and neighing when Goldman attempted to get closer to them. "They've been like that, since the fire."

"There are 10 of them," The free black investigator stated, after counting the number of horses, twice. "Can you count?"

The kid did not respond, but kept staring at the horses. "We had 11 horses. After the fire, only these 10, I always see. The spotty brown stallion is missing."

"The spotty brown stallion?"

"Yeah, it's a Gypsy Vanner breed with large white spots, " I heard Bob-bob say. Ann rode it sometimes."

This is it, Dean Goldman taught. His notion that someone wanted to get away without a trace was now confirmed. Rebecca Drake got away on horseback. And it was her horse; the spotty brown Gypsy Vanner.

He took his pipe from his coat pocket and put it in his mouth. Having lit it and took a couple of draws, he turned sideways and shot Gary a look in such a manner that he hoped that the kid was correct.

"I learned how to carve on the trees behind the stable," Gary said, when he caught Goldman's eyes. "I carved happenings I witnessed on the plantation."

"So, you were frequent around the stable. That's how you knew the horses."

The kid nodded. Goldman waited, anticipating that Gary was going to explain more of his experiences on the plantation so he could pick up more details, but the kid remained silent.

Satisfied with what he had accomplished so far, Goldman spun his horse around. "I think lunch is ready," he said, and then they rode back to the cabin.

Back in Richmond, a few weeks after his visit at Cottonwood plantation he and Constable Arlington were able to work out more details on the background of Rebecca Drake. With luck, it was the discovery of the Georgia Gazette and an interesting article by Elijah Poe, the paper editor that finally hammered the murder of Elijah Burgess on Angela Draper's head.

"She bewitched and killed my son," cried Roger Monroe Burgess when it was revealed to him.

Four days later, the free black investigator was in a boat off the shores of Cape Cod Bay. He was being ferried to a nearby Island about 3 nautical miles off Herring cove beach, where Captain Summerville told him Jack Duval would be.

The row boat landed at a pier on the Island and Dean Goldman got down while the black man who rowed him, waited. He met a group of fishermen, mostly black men loading a large catch of lobsters in wooden crates while they were being supervised.

"Howdy," he greeted the supervisor, an old white man. "Dean Goldman. I am in search of Jack Duval." The man looked at him, expecting more explanation. "Captain Summerville sent me," Goldman added.

"Few clicks down this way, if you will be lucky to see him," the supervisor replied, pointing to a trail, at his left, looping up a sand dune, covered with beachgrass. "He doesn't venture on the beach these days."

"Ever met him?" asked the supervisor when Goldman was about to leave. He shook his head, no. "Look up for the loner with the mummy head."

Goldman followed the direction and ascended the sand dune. There, the shark hunter was. He was standing at the flattened tip, facing the breezy beach below. Like a mummy, his head was wrapped in a bandage, down to his neck, almost covering his entire face, sparing only his eyes, ears and lips.

"Jack Duval?" The implacably immaculate free man asked, cupping his mouth and shouting above the strong winds. The shark hunter turned and said nothing. "Got a message from Captain James Newton Summerville," he further explained.

Duval remained unresponsive for a while, and then waved the stranger over. He came within five feet of the badly injured sailor and stopped.

"Dean Goldman," he introduced himself, but Duval waved him closer.

"What is it?" The sailor held Goldman on both shoulders and brought his head closer to his right ear and asked, his voice hoarse and wheezy.

Goldman now understood why the shark hunter waved him closer. The effect of the shark's bite that almost ripped out his jaw and part of the flesh around his throat, could not permit him to speak out loud. This made the Investigator upset.

"You were right," he managed to say, shaken and pitying Duval's condition. "There was evil onboard the Freedom Star. She tried to kill you because you were the only one that sensed her presence."

"She?!" in a whispery and quivering voice, Duval brought his face closer to Goldman's ears and asked.

"Here take a look," Goldman stepped backward, pulled some papers from under his coat, and gave the first one, which was the illustration from the Virginia Cardinal. "I guess you recognize her," he said when the sailor's eyes suddenly brightened. "Angela Draper Burgess, but her real name is Rebecca Drake born in Georgia to a white father and a Black woman of Latino descent. She grew up at the Cottonwood Plantation in Virginia."

Jack Duval began to tremble. With his shaky hands stretched, he walked to Dean Goldman and held his shoulders, again.

"They didn't believe me," he began to share tears. "I still remembered that paralyzing fear."

"I felt the same," admitted Goldman. "When I looked into the eyes of the portrait of her carving done by a little boy who witnessed the execution of a slave who she seduced and hypnotized, a strange dreaded, creepy and paralyzing feeling came over me.

I could not move my hands and legs until Miss Mason, a survivor of fire Rebecca Drake started a few days after the hanging, rushed upon me. She shook me and then I came to myself. Take a look at the other portraits of Rebecca Drake miniaturized by the kid whose parents left in the fire."

Listening to Dean Goldman, and then looking at the rest of the portraits, Jack Duval was more convinced of how Elijah Burgess drowned. The color purpose CEO had discovered and was devastated that the woman he married was not who she said she was.

The Findley brothers attested to the despair in his eyes when he entered the main desk where they were playing baseball. It was now clear that the distinguished abolitionist did not drown from seizure. Rebecca Drake seduced and manipulated him into marrying her, and then cast an evil spell that paralyzed him, causing him to drown when he was in the water.

It was the same evil spell that was cast on him by the phantom he saw up the cabin window. Like the flamboyant black man standing before him, the spell was disrupted when Len Dole stood over and shook him as he lay in the boat.

"What you saw that got you paralyzed when you and your crew returned from looking for Elijah's body was a grisly transfigure of herself, propelled by a powerful dark magic, which she inherited from her mother. It's Voodoo, a dark power practiced amongst Latino community. She's going to kill more people."

"So, what is the next plan of action?"

"In the next few days, I'll be sailing further west of the Atlantic at the Malagueta Coast. Roger Monroe Burgess wants the murderer of his son," Dean Goldman replied. "When I get back, I will tell you how it ended."

On his way back to Massachusetts, and then onward to New York to board the next available vessel for the West African Coast, Goldman reminded himself of what he was up against. Rebecca Drake was no ordinary person. The disfigured face of Jack Duval revealed a whole lot about the dark power she possessed.

"I think you need to see this sage before you make the trip," Handing him a piece of paper with a map and an address, Constable Richard Allington had told him. "Check this one up. It might help you with what you are up against."

The next few days, before heading for Cape Code, Dean Goldman, with the help of the map, visited the Powhatan territory of eastern Virginia where he met the sage, an old Angloquian Indian sitting on a rock looking up at the sky.

"Why do you seek to apprehend a person that murdered the white man?" the old sage had asked him.

"She kills black people, too," retorted the free black investigator. Here. Take a look at these sketches."

The Indian shone his eyes on a series of sketches of the incident at the Cottonwoods drawn by Gary Jackson, the kid.

"Such powers are drawn from the cosmos, the repository of the forces of nature," the old man said, studying the optical constellations Gary had drawn around Rebecca Drake's eyes as she gazed at Borbor Douglass on the gallows. "Only a high-ranking voodoo queen has the ability to possess such powers. It involves manipulating the heavenly bodies with the control of the eyes. A victim is lured and trapped in that effulgence of rays and he or she is instantly paralyzed. There are at least one person per generation with such powers."

"How to stop it," mesmerized by the sage's bizarre revelation, Goldman asked.

"Just close your eyes. They are the mirror of our souls as you may have heard. When one sees, he admires or detests which leads to motivation when one admires what he sees, and demotivation whenever he detests what he sees. Our souls respond to these two stimuli through our eyes. They are the pathways to our neurological faculty. Our eyes are simply the medium through which we are controlled."

"Are you saying that I will have to close my eyes to apprehend this woman, this voodoo princess with such dark powers? I would not last a second," complained Dean Goldman.

"The mind does have eyes, too," the old Indian offered, after a brief thought. "We humans have the power to look, and yet control what we want to see. The blind do move, shop, cook, do the laundry and many unimaginable things. You got to know from where they draw the ability to do these things."

"It's from God."

"It could be from God, other gods, or the spirits of our ancestors, depending on what you believe. But it could also be from the empirical order of things like the sciences. An antivenin is only effective against the specific snake bite, and so a countermeasure against a dark power from the cosmos is only effective if it is specific to the identical cluster of galaxies where that dark power is incubated."

As if it was enough for the day, the old Algonquian turned to his right, and the free black investigator noticed he was looking at a Powhatan cemetery. Then he sat on the ground, legs crossed. He first hauled out a curved wooden dagger and threw it behind him. It landed right at Dean Goldman's feet. Then he took a small hand drum and stick from under his deerskin fur cloak, and started tapping on it, at the same time crying in his dialect.

Dean Goldman knew that there was no need to bother. The old sage was in his state of mourning for the dead as many of them have recently died from diseases that the white man has brought since he set foot on their land. The mourning was a ritual to call upon the spirits of the dead to provide the living with immunity for these strange diseases.

"Thanks, old man," he muttered, not knowing what he was thanking the Indian for, without a definite answer on how he would catch the witch.

He however picked up the dagger and turned to leave, pondering over what the old Algonquian meant when he said, *'The eyes are the pathways to our neurological faculty .... 'Humans have the ability to look and yet control what they see.*

Chapter 15

The life-threatening screams from within a hut were too frightening and unbearable for Momo Shiafa. After pacing and panting back and forth at the entrance door of the village midwife hut, he sat on a stick-bench under the elves and watched three elderly women, carrying herbs. Preoccupied, they hurried past him and entered through the door.

Bendu Kiatamba was lying on a bamboo plaited mat with her hands and legs spread apart. Her body was half covered with a single lapper. She was sweating profusely. Her abdominal muscles were moving with waves of contractions. Terrified, her eyes were stretched wide open, gazing at the midwives with their serious faces and then at the inner roof.

With a wet cloth, one of the midwives was wiping her face and her chest. The other one was working her hands between her legs, at the same time administering the herbs while the third one was using a lapper to wipe the break water, pouring on the mat.

"Push harder," the one administering the herbs, commanded.

Still sweating and trembling hysterically, Bendu screamed out loud, when she gave it a try. This caused Momo to jump to his feet.

"If you do not push harder, you will lose the baby or yourself," she nagged.

"And stop giving us a hard time, too," complained the other one, who was wiping her face. "We are not the ones that lured you into Momo's bed."

The Midwife who was wiping the break water came out with a bucket in her hand to wring the soaked lapper. Momo's heart leapt, when he saw her weary face. This meant all was not good. Bendu may die in childbirth. And he will be beheaded if her father finds out.

"This is going to be bad for me," he muttered, walking up and down in front of the hut. "If I had known I would have told the truth to the people who said the governor was looking for her."

Two weeks ago, two indigenous men visited him at his selling place and asked him about the whereabouts of Bendu.

"You know Miatta, my wife, right?" In response, he asked Lassana, one of the men he knew.

"Yes," replied Lassana, feeling hopeful that his familiarity with Momo and his wife might lend some help.

"So, there you go. It is only Miatta's or my son, Shiaka's whereabouts that will concern me. Not Bendu's."

With this cheek, the men were reluctant to ask any more questions. So, they felt insulted and left. Two days later, sitting in front of his produce, a light skinned tall settler, along with Lassana and the other man, stopped by.

"Major Rudolf Crayton," the man introduced himself. "I work with the governor. We are looking for Bendu Kiatamba. We know that she's very sick and the governor has offered to help her. We also know of your acquaintance with her mother, and Bendu herself, from her childhood. We believe you may know her whereabouts."

"Oh! That was a long time ago. And Bendu is a woman now. So, she's big enough. If she's sick she knows where to go. As you can see, I make and sell my bamboo baskets. I am not a doctor."

"Remember that if anything happens to her, King Kiatamba will not spare you, and the authorities will not spare you, either, if the king uses that as a case for war," warned the colonial intelligence officer, and then left.

"I should not have listened to Bendu," he murmured, still pacing up and down. "The Colonial Headquarter has a health center. It was going to be better to take her there, than all this will not be happening. I tried to talk to her but she refused because they say they made Estella Carter a big woman now. She will kill her baby if she finds out she gave birth at the maternity ward, and nothing will come out of it."

He and his wife Miatta eyes locked. She was sitting in front of their hut with Shiaka on her lap. The toddler made an attempt to jump from his mother's lap to run to his father, but she angrily held him back.

Startled, Momo saw the suspicion on his wife's face, telling him how strange for a man to worry about another man's belly, unless that man may have something to do with it, and not being bold to admit it.

Pushing harder, and harder, Bendu began to scream out loud. The labor pain was severe and unbearable, but she was giving it her all whether she dies or not. Momo trembled to her terrifying and sustained agony.

However, a couple of minutes later, the cramps began to reduce, and her screams were gradually fading. Then they finally stopped, and there was silence.

"This is strange," now sitting on the ground with both hands on his head, Momo began to weep. "Why am I not hearing the midwives rejoicing for the newborn or mourning for the dead?" He suddenly got up and raced to the door and wailed, "What's happening inside there?!"

"Come and see for yourself," the maid-wife who was wiping the break water and washing the lapper stood at the door, responded and stepped aside to allow him to enter.

"No. Just tell me what is happening there. Why does no one want to talk to me?"

"Don't give us a headache here, *Papa*. We were not there when you were enjoying this girl."

"Stop that. It's someone's life we are talking here, even mine," he pleaded and dashed into the hut, as Miatta, who also became concerned of the sudden silence in the delivery hut, raised her eyebrow in reaction to her husband's last words.

He saw the second maid-wife holding a tiny baby in her hands. Momo gasped; the baby looked lifeless. He panicked when he looked down at Bendu. She was lying helplessly on the mat. The second woman brought the baby closer to him and presented it.

"What do you want me to do with it?" he moaned, his hands and legs trembling.

The woman smiled and slapped the baby on its buttocks. It suddenly uttered a deafening cry. Then it peed in Momo's face, causing the maid-wives to laugh at him.

"It's a boy!" bewildered, Momo exclaimed.

"You are too scared," the first maid-wife said as the other two continued to laugh at him. "And you weren't at the time of Miatta."

Momo said nothing as he could not control his cry of joy. He handed the crying baby to the maid-wife and sat on the dirt floor, beside Bendu. He looked at the first maid-wife who was still wiping her sweat and saw her assuring eyes.

"Bendu will be okay. She just needs a little rest," she said, smiling. "We were silent because the baby does not look like you. You and the mother are dark in complexion, and this baby has light skin."

"I know. Thank you very much," he replied, and wondered how the midwives could tell the difference, when all babies are born with light skins.

"Here, Bendu. Let him have some breast milk," said the second maid-wife bringing the baby to its mother, when it stopped crying and began to make the smacking sound indicating the urge for its first breast milk.

"She's weak and needs to eat, too, so she can produce enough breast milk for the baby," said the first maid-wife when she saw how the baby was latching on the nipple, suggesting that there wasn't enough milk pouring out of Bendu's breasts. "Did you prepare the kind of food we ask you to prepare?"

"Yes," Momo replied nervously, getting up and hurrying out of the hut.

On the way to his hut, he almost ran into Shiaka.

"Miatta please try to control this boy," he said, holding his son by his hands and bringing him to his mother.

"You don't want to hold your own son anymore?" Refusing to take the boy from his father, Miatta asked with suspicion,

"I have been caring for Shiaka for five years now. That girl in there is helpless and she and her baby need some food to eat right now."

Momo Shiafa continued with his son into his hut, and got the dish his wife refused to prepare. With Shiaka behind him, he brought them to the delivery hut. Bendu was helped up to sit on the mat. As the baby continued to feed, his mother was served brown rice with bitter leaf soup mixed with brown beans and enough bush meat.

Finally relieved, Momo rubbed his son's head as Shiaka stared at the tiny helpless baby, frantically concentrating on its breastmilk.

Throughout the next few months, the baby grew healthy as Bendu's breast milk increased and became more nutritious.

"Humm. I see that you have followed my advice to also add sweet potatoes, and mushroom soup to your diet," observed one of the midwives who visited Bendu to check on how she and the baby were doing.

"So, what name will you give the baby?" Momo asked Bendu one evening when she was bathing her baby. "It has been more than three months now, you haven't decided on a name, yet."

"Let's call him Gbotoe for now," she replied after a long thought, bearing in mind that when all this is over, Mr. Carter will find a suitable name for his son.

"Gbotoe is your brother's name, right? One of the king's sons by your mother. People say he is more intelligent than his other brothers."

"Yes. And he loves me so much. Sometimes I miss him."

Shortly after she named the baby, Shiaka had turned six. He became fond of the baby from the day he was staring at the tiny little infant struggling to suck its mother's breast. He was always at Bendu's hut which was just a few feet from his parents'.

"Shiaka. It's time to come home and take your bath," Miatta would go and get him when it is evening time. "Your father will soon be returning from town."

"Don't worry," Bendu would say. "I will bathe him and Gbotoe and bring him to you."

Now that it was obvious that Gbotoe did not look like her husband or any one in his family, though not entirely, Miatta had disregarded her earlier suspicion that Momo had had a hand in her pregnancy. She would forge a smile and then leave. Sometimes Shiaka would remain at Bendu's, playing with Gbotoe until his father came for him.

As the months passed, Gbotoe became stronger and so was his mother. She would put him on her back and tied a lapper around it to hold him, and strode to the edge of the nearby swamps.

"When we were small in the village, we used to follow our mother and aunts to lay baskets and fish in the creek," she told Momo on one occasion. "But when my mother sent me to live with the Carters, I did not have the chance to do all that. And I missed it."

"I hope I am wrong, thinking of what you want me to do," Momo said, studying her face.

"No. You are not. I want you to please make me some fishing nets and baskets, she pleaded. "The swamps around us look ripe to fish."

One day Momo brought her some fresh fishing nets and baskets he had made for her. As Bendu thanked him and cheered, he did not look happy. She suddenly stopped when she noticed it.

"Why are you not happy about the net and baskets, you yourself made for me?"

"Our little village is becoming crowded now. We were only four from the interior that settled here, and now we have more than 8 huts. Settlers' spies and some enemies of your father may soon start venturing here looking for you. Two days ago, the settlers' agents approached me again concerning your whereabouts. I think they have started keeping surveillance on me. That's why I come from town very late, these days."

"So, what do we do?"

"I also got a canoe for you which I hid in a secret place in this swamp," he informed her, pitying her now apprehensive face. "There's a village along the creek north of here, established by my brother, Molly, who once lived here. I will show you the route in case they finally tracked me here. Molly knows you. He's a good man. I will show you how to paddle a canoe to get to him, okay?"

Hereafter, Bendu began to venture into the swamps to lay her baskets and to fish, with Gbotoe on her back. More often she would only allow Shiaka to follow her when she became weary of his persistent cries whenever she refused. But she would make sure, with stern warning, that he remained on the ground where she could see him because some parts of the swamps had deep mud.

She would fish all morning with her nets, catching a huge quantity of sizable fresh cold-water fishes, such as the Tilapias, catfish, and the purple back river crabs found in the mangrove swamps of Stockton Creek. One morning during the mid-dry season, Bendu gathered some of the village women to help her block a certain part of the swamp at both ends, and used buckets to throw the muddy water on the banks. For every throw, fishes were fluttering on the banks.

"We never knew there were plenty of fishes in this water like this," marveled one of the women.

That day, as they threw the water out, they caught many, including a sizable amount of spring frogs. Some were dried and sold and they made enough money.

Every evening, Bendu would chop some red palm nuts into pieces, put them into her fishing baskets and lay them in the marshy parts of the swamp. At dawn, she would hurry back to the swamp to remove the baskets. Trapped in them were usually giant size crawfish. Momo would take the ones they wanted to sell to town while they consumed the rest.

One morning, with Gbotoe on her back, and a wooden tub on her head, she hurried past Momo's hut to go and check on her baskets she laid the evening before. Just then, Shiaka came outside to pee. She did not notice him and kept on until she reached the swamp. At the edge, she removed her slippers from her feet, adjusted the hem of her lapper above her knees, and walked through the cold water.

She reached to where she laid the baskets, which she remembered by the sticks she planted near them. Then she began to remove them one after the other from under the water. As she turned each outside down, she shook them until all the crawfish trapped at the bottom layer were emptied into the wooden tub floating in front of her.

Suddenly, she heard Shiaka shrieking and began to cry. Almost falling into the water, she immediately dashed one of the baskets she had just pulled, and waddled towards the direction she heard the kid screaming. When she reached him, Shiaka was stuck between the tall water grass in the mud holding his right leg.

In no time she rushed and pulled him from the mud, and saw blood oozing from a fang-like stink above his inner right ankle bone. She was alarmed and horrified, when she saw that it was a snake bite.

"Momo!" she screamed when she got to his door with the boy helplessly cradled in her arms. "Come out quick! A snake bit Shiaka!"

Both Momo and Miatta instantly dashed out of their hut.

"It's a water snake's bite!" wailed the bamboo basket maker when he inspected his son's legs.

"I did not know he was following me when I went to check on my baskets," cried Bendu. "Let's do something about this, quick!"

"I know an herbalist somewhere in Duala who treats snake bites."

"Then let's hurry there!" screamed Bendu, when she saw only the white of Shiaka's eyes showing.

"No. You stay with Gbotoe," Momo rejected, looking at his son's eyes and crying. He rushed to Miatta who was rolling on the ground, screaming. "Miatta. Get the boy and follow me to my canoe. Crying like that will not help us!"

Later that afternoon, the village dwellers were gathered at Momo Shiafa's hut, nervously waiting for the outcome from the herbalist. Some of the women were warning their children to refrain from venturing into the swamp, alone. Worried and sorrowful, Bendu was sitting on a low stool in front of her hut rocking Gbotoe who could not stop crying.

Suddenly, everyone rushed to the edge of the creek when they saw Momo's canoe appearing from the distance. When it landed, the whole place erupted into cries, when Momo disembarked the canoe, holding his son wrapped in a white cloth in his hands while Miata lay helplessly in the canoe.

"Ay Shiaka. Why did you do this to us!" cried Bendu, leaving Gbotoe on the bamboo mat she had laid for him and running to Momo.

"We got there too late," wept the dead toddler's father, upon seeing her coming towards him. "And It took us time to locate the herbalist."

By then, some of the women had rushed to the canoe for Miattia, who was still lying in it, groaning.

"Bendu! Why didn't you look back when my son was following you?" she moaned, while the women were bringing her to her hut. "My people! Please tell me. How can she carry her son and my son into the swamp, but she only brought back my son, dead?! All the time children have played in that swamp, is it only my son that the snake can see and bite?!"

"Ay my people! I did not see him behind me!" wept Bendu. "Why will I kill Shiaka who I took like my own son. Why will I do such evil to Momo who has done so much for me?!"

"Don't mind that. Go and tend to Gbotoe," in tears, Momo tried to console her.

At a brief family meeting following Shiaka's burial. Everyone was seated, including Molly who got the news late and came after the burial. Bendu was also there, sitting on the mat, breast feeling Gbotoe.

"From what I have gathered from my brother, their door is usually left half opened early in the morning," Molly addressed the family members. "He did not observe that Shiaka has been sneaking through it to come outside to pee. Just today, he got to know from Miatta herself. So, he takes full responsibility for his son's death for never caring to wonder and figure out why Shiaka was no longer peeing in bed."

"I take full responsibility," cried Momo, embracing his brother, as two other family members parted him on his back to console him.

Miatta was never herself after the death of her son. She refused to respond when Bendu greeted her.

"Stop blaming that poor girl," Momo would tell her. "We will continue to try for another child."

Three weeks after the incident, Miatta began to speak to Bendu. Gbotoe continue to grow more healthily. she would cry, thinking about Shiaka, whenever she held the baby, and felt his weight in her arms.

"Miatta. Stop crying," Bendu would console her whenever she visited and was playing with Gbotoe. "You will get another baby. And I pray that it will be another son."

As the days passed, Miatta began to forget about the episode. To help her stop worrying about her son, she and Momo decided to go to town to sell together every morning and return to the village late in the evening. She had managed somehow to venture into the swamp to lay her own basket Momo had made for her and carry the fresh catch to town.

On the other hand, Bendu was mourning inwardly. She could no longer go to the swamp to fish and lay her basket for fear of remembering Shiaka who was always there with her. She and Miatta tried it before but whenever the mournful mother heard Gbotoe playfully humming on his mother's back, thinking about her late son, Miatta would stop and then feel very sad.

"I used to make money from the fish Momo used to carry to town to sell for me," one evening she said to herself, while sitting in front of her hut, bathing Gbotoe. "Now I don't feel comfortable going to that swamp to fish anymore. And I don't want to be a liability on him while Miatta is still grieving."

She paused when she had wiped her baby's skin, rubbed it with palm kernel oil, and had put on his lapper made diaper. Then she positioned him properly and put her nipple in his mouth. Gbotoe immediately began to suck on his mothers' breast, sometimes flipping from one nipple to the other like he was confused as to which one he enjoyed the most.

"People in this village keep telling me that Bendu is pretending to have accepted Shiaka's death, and I think she still blames me," she continued to talk to herself, now gently rocking the baby as he began to doze off, though still clutched on is mother's breast. "But I will try to find my way to Molly's village this coming rainy season. Maybe when I am out of her sight, it will help her to stop grieving and blaming me, and maybe it will make her to get pregnant for her husband, again."

One evening, while all the fish sellers were finished selling for the day and were packing to leave, Lassana, avertedly bumped into Miatta while on her way to join her husband to where he sold his bamboo baskets.

"Miatta. It's been a long time," greeted Lassana. "Only your husband I often see. How have you been, and your son, too?"

"Oh Lassana. I still remember you. Long time. I am doing good," she answered.

"And your son? Shiaka? I assume he's growing quite well."

"Shiaka died last month. Snake bit him." Bendu suddenly burst into tears.

"Ah! How did it happen?! Just the other day we saw your husband and asked about Bendu, that girl who used to come along with her mother to sell farina. All Momo could tell us was he is only concerned about you and his son."

"Why asked him about Bendu?" Suddenly becoming concerned, but still sobbing, Miatta asked.

"The people she was living with are looking for her and are worried. And she has not gone to her hometown, so we thought your husband knew her whereabouts."

"Why did she run away?"

"She got pregnant."

"I see why she always refuses to come to town," Bendu said to herself, nodding and making a face that she has just learned something.

"What?! Do you know where she is?!" Excited, the colonial spy asked.

In mid-April of the following year, the rainy season started. It was a few days after Miatta and Lassana met. Early one morning, when it was still dark, it started to rain heavily and the swamps were getting full. Even up to the time day was breaking, it continued like it was never going to stop. Unable to come outside, the villagers were stock in their huts.

Momo and Miatta were still lying down wrapped up and waiting for the rain to stop so they could get ready for the market. But his wife would not be going with him because, with the rising tide, it was impossible to go and fetch her baskets she laid the evening before. Moreover, she sold all her catch the day before.

Bendu had bundled up some of her things, meanly Gbotoe's food and medicine and was lying down, her eyes up on the inner roof, waiting for the rain to slow down or stop so she should sneak out of her hut to go to Molley's village before anyone could come outside and notice.

Fortunately, there was a lull in the heavy downpour. She quickly wrapped a thick sheet of black plastic around her, covering her body from her head and stopping right above her knees. She also did the same to Gbotoe who was still asleep, also covering his head with a piece, making it look like a hood.

Satisfied, she put him on her back and tied a lapper around her waist. With her bundle also wrapped with the plastic on her head, she sneaked out of her hut and clandestinely made her way to the back. When she was sure no one was outside, she slipped into the bush ducking along a path that snaked its way to the northern part of the swamp.

In a matter of minutes, Bendu reached an undergrowth at the edge of a part of a swamp where Momo showed her, he hid the canoe. It was positioned upside down with the gunwale resting on some logs. Relieved that it was still intact, she removed the branches concealing it, and with little effort she turned the canoe on its keel.

She found a pair of paddles which Momo hid between the logs. First, she put her plastic covered bundle in the canoe, then the paddles. Next, Bendu gently shoved the stern. The canoe began to slide on the logs until it reached the edge of the water. She shoved it some more, applying a bit more effort. With her feet now in the water and above her ankle, the canoe was now fully afloat.

In no time she climbed inside, careful not to slip and fall into the water. She was nervous. With trembling hands, she grabbed one of the paddles. Just as Momo taught her, she began by first stroking the paddle gently to her right and then to her left. The canoe began to move.

"You will need two paddles; in case you are nervous and one dropped from your hands and you are unable to get it," with her eyes on the other one, she remembered Momo telling her the first day he was teaching her how to paddle a canoe.

After 20 minutes of paddling upstream, she was making progress. As her fright diminished, she became calmed, and remained close to the edge to avoid the rough current as the water flowed downstream.

Gbotoe was still asleep, which was not surprising to her. Thanks to the brown rice cereal she made and had started feeding him with it. This was heavy enough to keep him full for a couple of hours.

The rain had stopped completely and the village dwellers were coming out of their huts. Miatta had awakened from bed. She came outside to make some hot water for her and her husband to take a bath. While in the outside kitchen looking for the dry wood among the ones that were wet, her attention was drawn to a large canoe approaching from a distance.

"Good morning, Miatta," greeted Lassana, jumping down from the canoe along with Foday Kamara. "This is Mr. Kamara. He's Bendu's uncle. We came to get her."

"Oh! I was not expecting you time like this. And why bring these men along?" Maitta asked, as three other men, and Major Rudolf Crayton, dressed in a raincoat, were disembarking.

"As I told you, the last time we met, we didn't want her to get away. It's important that we get her."

"Anyway," breathed Miatta, after a moment of thought. Then she pointed at Bendu's hut. "That's where she is staying."

Lassana and the three other men immediately encircled the hut.

"Bendu," he called. "We know you and the baby are in there. We came to get you."

There was silence.

"Maybe she's sleeping. You need to knock on her door," advised Miatta.

"Let her uncle do this," said Major Crayton, and gestured to Foday Kamara who reluctantly walked towards Miatta's hut.

"Miatta," he called. "It's me, uncle Foday. You got me worried. All along I thought you had gone home. But we are here to get you. I will make sure you will not go back to Mrs. Carter's house."

There was no response. The hut remained quiet, even when Mr. Kamara knocked it harder.

"She's not in here," he turned to Major Crayton and announced.

He tested the door and was surprised that it was not bolted.

"She must have left just before we came," said the major. Turning to Miatta who stood, confused, "Where's your husband?"

Suddenly becoming worried, and more confused, thinking that Momo had escaped with Bendu, she did not answer the major but ran into her hut, shouting her husband's name like something terrible had happened.

"What is it?!" asked Momo, jumping out of his hut with his lapper still wrapped around his wrist and with no shirt on him. But his inquisitive face suddenly changed to bewilderment when he saw Mr. Kamara, Lassana, and Major Crayton standing behind Miatta. He flipped his eyes towards Bendu's hut and saw the three other men coming from inside.

"Bendu! What have you done! Did you speak to these men! Do you know what her father will do when they get her?!" Momo held his head, panting.

"Bendu ran away from me, her uncle because she was just scared of the people she was living with when she got pregnant. I have come back to get my niece. You know me to be her uncle, right?"

"You and I know very well that Kiatamba wants war. Now she has run off. If anything happens to her, the colony will be burned to the ground. That's what she is avoiding. And you people did not understand." He turned to his wife. "Miatta have you seen what your foolish jealousy had caused us?!"

"Put on your clothes. We are taking you to the headquarters," ordered Major Crayton.

"Where are you taking my husband?!" Miatta asked, panting. "Let me come along."

"No. You stay here," Lassana told her. "They are simply going to ask him some questions to enable them to find Bendu."

Miatta started to weep when the men barricaded Momo and escorted him to the canoe. The villagers who had come out were surprised. Some of them held Miatta when she attempted to jump in the water to follow her husband.

"It's my fault," she continued to weep.

Meanwhile, Bendu continued to paddle upstream, watching out for Momo's description of how to get to his brother's village.

"You will continue paddling up north until you reach a certain part of the water where it is dark green. The Mangrove are thicker than the ones surrounding us. There, the water is wider. It is like a river with smaller creeks, about three, branching off at its left. A short distance after the third one, you will see a large tree to your right. You must pass it and continue until you reach a small creek to your right and enter it.

It will take you all the way down to its banks made of white clay mud. Take a path to your left until you reach a village of plantain, banana, and paw-paw trees. Ask anyone for Molly," she listened to Momo's voice echoing in her ears.

Paddling through the dark green part of the water, it began to get breezy. The mangrove branches swung violently as the wind got stronger. Out of a sudden, darkness filled the sky. Then there were droplets of water descending from the cloud. Bendu knew that it was going to rain again and so she began to stroke faster.

A lightning flashed, followed by a terrifying thunderbolt. Gbotoe jumped from his sleep and began to scream. Bendu got antsy, more especially with the subsequent downpour which would soon fill the canoe. The current became rough and strong, slowing the canoe as it propelled against the flow, and making it difficult for Bendu to stroke faster. The baby screeched louder as the heavy droplets patterned his head and his back.

As the situation became fearful and hopeless, "Ay God! What have I gotten myself into?" She began to sob.

"When under a heavy rain and the current becomes strong, you must do what all you can to keep to the edge of the water and continue to stroke; twice on the right and left to save energy or else your arms will get tired. At the same time, you must throw out water from the canoe after every round of stroke. But some water must remain to give it weight so that the current at the edge must not pull it to the middle of the water where it will be difficult to control," she again reflected on Momo's advice.

All seemed good as she followed the instructions. Her eyes were on the branches, especially for the cascading ones whose trunks were bigger and stronger and were within her reach. She would grab and clinch unto one of them, in case she sensed that the canoe was about to capsize,

"The mangrove branches are strong enough to withstand your weight until the rain stops and you can begin to call for help as a fisherman might be paddling nearby and hear you," Momo had advised.

She managed to maneuver until she reached the first stream branching to her left. With the baby still crying on her back, she thought of entering it to find somewhere to stop and feed it with breast milk so it can stop crying. She would then wait for the rain to stop, and hope that Gboto falls asleep before she resumes.

But she decided against that idea and struggled onwards. It took her some time to reach the second one. She wanted to pass it and continue, but the downpour was getting heavier and the water in the canoe was getting full.

With lots of effort, she managed to paddle and passed by the confluence. When she did, she executed the J stroke to her left, so she could get to the other side of the edge, and turn back downstream for the current to take her back to the confluence.

As she drifted, she reached the mouth of the stream and turned into it, J stroking to her right. With speed, the canoe drifted, according to the direction of the flow. Bendu had to slow down a bit by gently executing the reversed paddle stroke.

She realized that the water became smaller and was completely cascaded on both sides by the mangrove branches with the leaves blocking most of the droplets. At a certain area the canoe began to slow down with Bendu easing the reversed paddle strokes, causing her to rest a little. With the unexpected change of the surroundings, Gbotoe had stopped crying and had started to experience hiccups. The canoe finally stopped at an edge where the bow struck between layers of thick and spacious mangrove roots.

Bendu looked around her. The place was shady and quiet, only the patter of droplets on the leaves and the occasional quacking of frogs. She reached for her plastic covered bundle, opened it a little on the side and shoved her hand inside. For a while she rummaged into the bundle and finally fished out a gourd water bottle and shook it.

Pleased that the fresh water she stored inside did not drain out, she uncapped it and drank some. Then she shoved it between the left of her hip and the hull of the port side of the canoe to hold it and gently untied the lapper from around her waist. When she removed Gbotoe from her back, she eased him between her legs which she was unable to spread wide enough because of the size of the canoe.

Then she held him, face up, on her chest. She cupped her right hand around his mouth and poured water from the gourd into her hand to give the infant some water to drink to reduce the hiccup. Gbotoe took in some, but swung his head towards her breast.

"You will not drink some more water? We still have a long way to go," she complained after several attempts to give him more water. "I know you want some breast milk now," she said and began to remove the plastic sheet from around her.

The baby had sucked enough breast milk. Bendu observed that it was asleep. Her first try to take the nipple from its mouth was unsuccessful with Gbotoe's refusal to let go as he held her firmly and stuck his face further into his mother's breast. Bendu waited for about thirty minutes before she made another attempt.

This time, she was successful.

The ripples were gently rocking the canoe, while she sat, waiting for the rain to subside. Splashes among the mangrove roots drew her attention. She saw scores of mudskippers swimming towards the upper roots of the trees to rest on them.

When they were kids, her brother Gbotoe did not like them for their protruding eyes and funny head shapes. Early every morning, they would stroll to a swamp at the back of their grandparents' huts with Gbotoe, carrying a catapult and some pebbles. As his sister watched, he would aim at the creatures, sometimes killing them, and leaving their lifeless bodies floating in the water.

One morning, they dashed out of the swamp in one piece, screaming, when they saw a giant size green iguana with yellow spots resting on the bark of a slanted tree. Bendu remembered how frightened she was when the lizard looked her way and thrusted out its long, creepy and thick forked tongues.

As it was believed, the gigantic lazard was about to pounce on her chest and drill its tongues into her nostrils all the way to her brains to lick them dry. It took her a while before she ventured along the edge of that swamp again.

The rain had subsided much to her delight, ejecting her from that brief childhood encounter. The sun ray was filtering through the cascaded branches bringing in some warm air and making the temperature conducive. Tied and now sleepy, Bindu suddenly yawned and began to doze off.

A Couple of minutes later, Gbotoe had woken up. Playfully, the baby began to twist and turn in his mother's chest. Bendu's hands lazily fell from around him as the child continued.

Few months of learning to crawl, the baby found an opportunity to turn his head towards the bow and started crawling in the canoe. He reached the bow and was now struggling to hold it to support him to stand up. Any mistake he would slip and fall into the shallow water.

Bendu suddenly jumped from her sleep when she heard her baby crying. Fear gripped her when she saw a huge man with bushy hair and beard, holding Gbotoe in his arms. Behind him stood a boy who appeared to be in his early teens, holding two cutlasses in both hands.

"The baby almost fell into the water while you were snoring," the man said. "What are you and your baby doing in a place like this?"

"Who are you?" gasping, Bendu asked.

"I am Daywein and behind me is my son, Zuannah."

"Are you Dei?" detecting Daywein's accent, she asked again.

"Yes. I am Dei by tribe."

Bendu exhaled with a sigh of relief. The man did not mind being interrogated, which meant he was not hiding anything, and may be a good man. Furthermore, he told her the boy behind him is his son, meaning he had a family.

"Please give me my baby," still in the canoe, she pleaded. "We are on our way to a village up the main river. The rain was heavy and we found this place to rest."

"You will not be able to make it," The Dei man warned in a calm voice. "The water is still full and the current is usually rougher, shortly after a rain."

"Come with us. We will take you to a place for you to stay and then we can help you find this village when the water goes down," offered his son, his eyes sparkling with admiration, staring at Gbotoe.

Bendu looked back at the narrow stream flowing from the bigger one as she weighed her options.

"This part of the swamp is very dangerous. Slave hunters have been roaming here lately. Also, one day, an old lady in my village while laying her baskets saw many large crocodiles lurking in the swamps in the direction you say you are heading. With the water now full, it will not be safe for you and your baby."

"Then what are you and your son doing here?" Bendu asked, her eyes on Daywein's. If they blink while responding to her question, it would mean he was lying.

"My little son is sick. He has worms, and so, as soon as the rain subsided, we came to cut some mangrove roots to fix the medicine," Daywein replied, still holding the baby in his hands. "If we were bad people, we were going to kill you and take the baby, or you would have woken up with your hands and legs tied."

"But you want to lure me into following you so you can abduct me later and sell me and my son."

"My wife and I are Christians. We don't sell or kill people. We attend a church. It is located in a big compound run by a nice preacher," explained Daywein. "Or if you don't believe me, you can have your baby and go. At least our conscience will be clear."

Daywein gave her the baby. Then he took one of the cutlasses from his son. "Let's go," he said.

As they ducked under the low branches further down the edge of the swamp, Bendu watched the man and his son took careful steps among the thick mangrove roots. They reached a certain part and stopped. Daywein squatted and began to dig and remove black mud from around the bottom stem of a mangrove tree, scaring away some mudskippers resting on it.

After some time, he chopped off a root and pulled it from the mud. He washed it off and chopped the cassava-like sprouts into segments. One after the other, he handed them to Zuannah. The lad received them from his father and put them in a bag attached to his waist.

Daywein and his son then started off, on a footpath that led into the bush without turning to look at Bendu, who was still sitting in the canoe. They had walked some distances when they heard rapid footsteps. When they stopped and turned to see who was following them, it was Bendu with the baby on her back and her bundle on her head.

"Please take me to this Christian compound."

Daywein smiled and then continued walking. Also smiling, Zuannah jolted his head sideways, signaling that she must follow them. The Dei man and his son resumed walking, with Bendu now trekking behind them at the same time looking around her. Gbotoe was stretching his hands for the leaves on the side of the path, sometimes leaning to grab a bush flower.

Feeling more comfortable with the strangers and wanting to break the silence, after walking for about 30 minutes, Bendu asked, "So, how are you going to fix the worm medicine with the mangrove roots?"

"My mother will split them like splitting a sugar cane and boil them. After that she would give a cup full to my brother every morning and evening for four days," Zuannah explained."

"How does it taste?"

"It tastes like warm and sour fruit juice."

"And like with a little salt inside, too," added Daywein.

"My brother's stomach was unusually swollen," continued Zuannah. "We thought it was because he likes to eat a lot, until this morning a bunch of worms flushing out of his stomach were stuck in his rectum while toileting."

That was enough for Gbotoe's mother to ask further questions. Her facial expression transmitted how terrible it was for the child. They reached a stream about ten feet wide and some twenty feet below a bridge of three long logs. A strong robe on both sides served as the rail.

Taking his time to step on the slippery algae covered single log bridge first by holding and testing the robes to his right, before carefully walking over it, "Don't forget to tie the baby on your back properly, before it weighs you and causes you to slip over," he warned when it was Bendu's time to cross when he observed that Gbotoe was leaning to her right, head-down.

About ten minutes' walk from the log-bridge, the baby was again trying to grab a leaf from the cascading branches bordering the narrow path. Bendu heard the rattle of a branch. Seconds later, she felt the ragged edge of a leaf at the back of her neck. She turned and saw the baby holding a leaf and was trying to put it in its mouth.

"No! Don't do that!" she said and jerked the leaf from her son's hand, causing the baby to cry. "Long time ago in my village, a baby, on his mother's back, pulled a leaf and put it in his mouth while on their way from their farm. By the time they reached home, the baby was dead. The father saw the leaf in the baby's hand with the dead baby's spit and slime on it. He took and inhaled it trying to figure out what kind of leaf it was, and he instantly dropped to the ground dead. The native doctor also inhaled it and died, too. Soon, scores of the villagers who came in contact with the leaf were dead," Bendu explained when Zuannah looked back at her.

After another thirty minutes of walking along the path, they entered a village of about five huts. There was a group of lads happily running after a dragonfly with a piece of bamboo stock in its tail.

Three women were in the outside kitchens. One of them was cooking while the other two were pounding cooked cassava into a mortar as three little girls, probably their daughters or granddaughters, held onto the brim to hold the mortar still. Smoke from fire hearths bellowed through the attic of every other kitchen; a sign that evening meals were being prepared.

At the north of the village, two men, one older than the other, emerged from the bush, toting sticks and fresh palm thatches on their heads. Three dead groundhogs, with their hind limbs tied together by robes hung across the neck of the older man.

They met up with Daywein. He responded when the men greeted and passed. Everyone else who saw them greeted or waved when Daywein, and his son passed, as inquisitive eyes shone on Bendu and the baby.

She felt more relieved. The village looked similar to hers, except that it was a bit far from the swamp, unlike her grandparents'. The people looked good.

"Zuannah. Give me the medicine and carry our stranger to the compound," Daywein said when they reached a yard of two small huts and a large one. "Tell your cousin, Moses, to take her to Reverend and come back here right away."

A girl, looking in her early teens bearing resemblance to the Dei man, was sitting on a log in the outside kitchen, with a winnowing fan on her lap, plucking dried beans from their pods.

"Siatta go to your aunt's place and tell your mother I have brought the medicine for your brother," he told the girl, who immediately put down the fan, got up and hurried to the next hut, a few yards to her left.

Zuannah and Bendu continued until they reached a road, much wider than the path. They turned northwest until they reached the picket gate of a compound with an inscription '**Riverside Baptist Missionary Compound, Upper Caldwell**' written in the form of an arc above the gate. Bendu saw that it was situated at the edge of a large river which she soon recognized to be the St. Paul.

"Moses," Zuannah knocked on the gate, shouting.

In no time a boy, looking older than him, hurried to open the gate. "What is it, Zuannah?" he asked, at the same time looking at Bendu.

"Papa says to bring this woman to Reverend. She came from far away, and has no place to stay."

"Come in," Moses gestured to Bendu. "Reverend is a little busy now, but I will take you to Sister Barbara Newland. She will attend to you until you see him."

"You and your baby will like it here," Zuannah assured her, and ran back towards the village, as soon as Bendu entered the compound.

"Will I see you again?" stepping back outside, she shouted.

"Yes. Sunday at church," from a distance, he stopped running, turned towards Bendu and shouted back.

Bendu observed the compound, as Moses led her to one of the buildings. There were about 6 big houses made of mud bricks with thatched roofs. The yard was planted with coconut trees sparsely apart from each other. At the back was the river. Painted white, a church stood in the middle of the compound.

There were four other offices at both sides of the hallway in the building. At the waiting area, Moses ushered her to a bench adjacent to an office at the left. He first knocked on one of the doors and then entered.

"Barbara Newland," a woman, dressed in a sky-blue dress covered with a white apron, came out of the office, with Moses following behind and greeted. "How are you and the baby? I am told you came to see Reverend, and you don't have a place to stay. What is your name.?"

"Bendu."

"And the boy?"

"Gbotoe."

"Oh okay. Let me see whether he's okay."

Miss Newland took the baby and performed some examinations that its mother did not understand and then handed it back to her. "He's okay and strong," she said, smiling. "Have you both eaten?"

Bendu nodded.

"Okay don't worry. The Reverend will see you soon. I am hurrying to teach at choir practice. Can you sing?"

Bendu shook her head, no.

"Okay. Let me leave you with Reverend now," the choir director said, pretending to be a little disappointed that she thought she had had a fresh talent. "Moses, you can stay around to wait for the Reverend's instruction.

A door to the next office suddenly opened and a tall man wearing a white shirt and black trousers with a black suspender stepped out.

"Bendu?' he asked. She nodded nervously, surprised that the man she had never met knew her name. "Don't worry. I was listening to you and Sister Newland. I am Reverend Charles Gooding III. Come in."

Bendu got up and followed Reverend Gooding in his office. He offered her a seat and sat behind his desk.

"So, I heard you don't have a place to stay?"

"I was going to my uncle who lives in a village up the creek but it was raining and I got stranded in the canoe. Daywein, a Dei man, and his son, Zuannah rescued me and advised me to come to you."

"They were correct," said the reverend, smiling. Rev. Doctor Lott Carey, the governor, asked me to run this place to help the people here. We teach local children the bible, and how to read and write."

Bendu gasped, upon hearing the name of the governor.

"What is it?" Observing her facial expression, Reverend Gooding asked.

"He sent men after me. That's why I ran."

"Why? The reverend is a God-fearing man, just like me."

"It is because of my son's father," Bendu answered feeling a bit ashamed and embarrassed.

"Oh! I see," said the Reverend, staring at Gboto. "You were living with a settler family and got pregnant by the father in the home. Well, such are becoming common these days. Don't worry. You and your baby will be fine here." Then he got up and walked to his door, opened it and peered outside. "Moses. Come carry Bendu to where she will be staying. Let Katumu bring her water to bathe and then get her some food."

"Thank you very much, Reverend," Bendu began to shed tears; It was obvious that she was in good hands.

"It's okay," Reverend Charles Gooding consoled her, patting her on her right shoulders. "We will find this village where this uncle of yours is, and inform him that you and your baby are here with us."

Chapter 16

Somewhere along the shores of South Beach, south of Monrovia, hundreds of newly recruited settlers' militia, dressed in their all-blue uniforms of waistcoats and trousers crisscross with white double sash and red Tricon hats, stood in line formations on the wide stretch of beach lawn, bordering the sand. Commander Elijah Johnson, and Major Rudolf Crayton were on horse backs facing the recruits.

To their left were Governor Carey on a white horse and Captain Ashford Capehart on a black one. The governor rode closer to the recruits with Captain Capehart riding behind. At a distance where he could be audible, he stopped to address the men.

"Today, you are called the Sons of Freedom not because of the value and love of liberty that compelled you to brave the Atlantic and landed you on these shores. It is because you chose to be the soldiers of light to shine, expose and eradicate the evil of bondage that plagued these shores of our forefathers for so long. The very evil that bundled them in ships with their necks in collards, and their hands and legs in chains. The evil that whisked them away to the white man's world where they faced the worst human degradation of unimaginable proportions.

Now with our ever-changing world, the echoes of freedom have evoked the consciousness of humankind, sprouting the righteous to muster the courage to embark on the struggle for total emancipation. This noble cause we have since pursued is predicated on the preamble that all men are born equal in the sight of God. It is therefore etched on our hearts, and flowing in our veins that the dignity of freedom is a universal human right. And as such, these convictions have led to the establishment of this colony, and it is incumbent upon us all to defend these rights.

While some of the causes that provoked this conflict are due to the recklessness of some of us, this has engendered the alacrity of those who hate us for our stance against slavery, to use that as the case for war. As you undergo these training, I want you to focus on defending Monrovia without prejudice, but with a hard message that we and those that oppose us are all from the same forefathers, and that it is on these shores their naval strings were buried.

The minds of our enemies are hard and set for battle, and the wisdom of peace will only penetrate their hearts, if they are hit very hard in the defense of our lives, and the sanctity of the freedom we uphold. The essence of which they will feel in that emptiness that arises when men with mis-judged vengeful hate soon realize that it is all vanity. It is only in such circumstances they will be compelled to embrace the path of peace."

The governor ended amid cheers from the gallant men. Among them were Derrick Hart, the sweetheart of Henrietta Patmore, the young couple who were on board the Freedom Star. Derrick told Major Crayton his grandfather was among the black men that fought the war of 1812. As the recruits continued to cheer the governor at the same time brandishing their rifles, tears ran down his eyes; like his grandfather, here he was, about to acquire the necessary training to go to war in the name of advertising the woes of slavery.

"Attention," shouted Commander Elijah Johnson when the governor had left. The group immediately fell in line, and there was silence. "Our training today will focus on how to aim for the enemy's eyes or right under the neck between the collarbones. This is because their bodies are charmed with juju to make them impenetrable to bullets. We were advised that the eyes and under the throat are their weakest spots. Major Rudolf Crayton will demonstrate the rest to you."

The major got down from his horse and walked among the lines with his hands clasped behind his back.

"Before we begin these demonstrations, we want you to bear in mind that the enemy will attack at night," the intelligence officer began. "These are people who were born, grew up and did everything in the dark. So, they will see you in the dark, sneak in on you and chop off your heads before you can adjust your eyes."

As the major spoke and studied some of the faces, he could sense fear and the second thought to quit. The legs of some of the recruits were shivering.

"But do not be deterred," he resumed. "As we have been teaching the others before you, by the time you graduate, you will know how to go for the eyes, beneath the throat, or even the testicles when confronting the enemy at night. Now, for our first exercise, I want 10 of you to line up about 30 yards from those 10 poles before you."

The first ten recruits immediately line up before the ten poles as Major Crayton instructed.

"As most of you will be forming defensive lines behind fences, and trenches, you will be shooting at the advancing warriors chanting fearful battle cries. The poles before you are about 5'11" tall, the average height of a Dei and Vai warrior. You will hit his eyes if you aim 5'2" below the forehead, or, under his throat, if you shoot just 5 feet below the forehead. And if you are lying on the ground, you can take him down, aiming for his testes, 3'8" from his feet.

At the count of three, you must get your rifles in firing positions, and after another three counts, you must fire. For today, we will practice this one, and then at our next session, we will be doing the Mamba, and Bassa warriors. We will teach you how each of them chant their battle cry."

A week later, Governor Carey had just returned from Bishop Emilie Thompson's house, somewhere on central Ashmun Street to attend to the bishop's wife who was seriously sick. The worried Bishop had informed him that Olivia had been having a strange fever causing buckets of sweat to ooze out of her body.

Earlier, he was at the ammunition dorm, somewhere on Lynn Street where for several days, he had been overseeing the stockpile of ammunition and taking inventory of them as the hostility with the indigenous grew. He had to leave early for the bishop's house, while Elijah Johnson and Major Crayton continued, and then home, to tend to his own wife who also had not been feeling well.

At about 8:30pm, tired, weary, and depressed of the task on hand to protect the colony against imminent indigenous attack, a thing he hated to do as a missionary, he was resting on his porch when suddenly Sgt. Desmond Howard, a young ground commander and head of the guard that night, rushed to him, with King Gbessagee, following behind, sweating and panting.

"We received information that Sorteh Gbayou and Kiatamba are gathering their warriors and planning to attack tonight," cried the allied king.

"How did you get this information?" the governor jumped from the recliner chair he was lying on and asked.

"My people intercepted Paye Garmugar, the Mamba and five men carrying on reconnaissance. They were asking some people about where I sleep so they can assassinate me, first, and then signal to their men to march on Monrovia," explained King Gbessagee.

"Are they still in your custody?" asked the governor, seeing that the allied king did not bring the men along.

"Garmugar and four of the men escaped. My men were able to catch one of them, but he died after he confessed to their plot."

"I guessed after he was tortured," the governor mumbled, closing his eyes, but dismissed Gbessagee's inquisitive eyes that he meant nothing. "We need to get to Commander Johnson at the ammunition dorm to ready the men at once," he said to Sgt. Desmond Howard, instead. "Send one of your men to Captain Capehart and tell him to join us at the ammunition dorm and then the rest of you must remain stand-fast and watch over my wife."

Seconds later, Governor Carey was galloping down the hill from his Mamba Point residence, through the dark Benson Street corridor with King Gbessagee sitting behind. Minutes later, they reached the arm dorm. No one was outside, and so the governor got down from his horse, took a small lantern hanging on one of the reins on the right side of the horse's neck, and lit it with a match.

King Gbessagee had also gotten down from the horse and was walking behind the governor. They reached the gate of the picket fence. The guard minding it was not around. He had gone to escort his indigenous girlfriend who often visited him from the nearby community. Annoyed that the ammunition dorm was left vulnerable, he flunked the gate open.

"No, governor! Get out of there!" he heard Commander Elijah Johnson's voice, amid footsteps racing up Lynch Street, but it was late; Governor Carey had entered the yard holding the lantern before him. He stumbled on some piles of ammunition on the ground and fell. The lantern dropped among them and there was an explosion. The force from the blast also sent King Gbessagee to the ground. He had stopped about three yards from the gate when he saw Commander Elijah Johnson, Major Crayton and a number of colonial militiamen racing up to them.

While some of the ammunition were still popping, Commander Johnson, and the major hurried into the yard, lighted by parts of the blazing fence and the branches of a mango tree in the yard.

"We need a stretcher," cried Major Crayton.

Two militiamen carrying a mat stretcher rushed into the yard. Governor Carey, unconscious, with massive burns covering his face and body was laid into it and taken out of the yard.

"Take him to the health center now!" screamed Commander Johnson.

"O Jesus. What happened?" Wailed Captain Capehart who had just arrived, jumping down from his horse.

"We saw the governor rush into the yard with a lantern in his hands, and there was an explosion as you can see," Major Crayton explained.

"Old Ernest Cheeseman unexpectedly brought in fresh consignments, soon after the governor left. He said two of the indigenous men with him just disappeared with some quantities before it got dark and so he thought to hurry here with the ones he had already produced. We went down to the regiment quarter to get recruits to help load them in the storage. On our way back, we saw the governor hurrying into the yard," Johnson further explained.

"He didn't know the ammunition was on the ground," said Major Crayton.

"He had hurried here to warn of an attack on Monrovia, tonight," interjected King Gbessagee, weeping.

"Crayton, Capehart assemble the men, including our new recruits, to secure all the entrances into the city. Sgt. Harris, take a few men to put out the fire. At day break, we will deploy in other parts of the colony," instructed Commander Elijah Johnson. Then while looking around him, he suddenly froze. "Where is Corporal Davis, the guard?"

Everyone stood looking around.

"Ay Galaypor! Ne Batou o," suddenly shouted King Gbessagee in Bassa; 'Ay God! My Friend," he meant, as Governor Carey was rushed to the colonial clinic.

The colonial city of Monrovia was tense. People were moving from one part to another; scores of settlers' families were leaving their settlements at the outskirts of the colony for central Monrovia while some indigenous who resided in the city were leaving for the hinterland.

Despite the rumors of an imminent indigenous attack, after the explosion at the ammunition dorm, and the subsequent deployment of colonial militia in settlements outside of Monrovia and at strategic parts in and around the city, some settlers families, living a few miles outside Monrovia, organized armed vigilantes to mind and protect their settlements. The colony was bleached with the gloomy aura of war.

"Seems like the struggle for freedom never ends, no matter in which part of the world," remarked Dean Goldman, riding through Water Street in an open top two wheeled coach, observing the apprehensive faces of pedestrians.

"This one will be slightly different, when it ever comes, sir," said the coachman, a settler who worked in the transport department at the colonial headquarters, now on an assignment to pick up Goldman, a guest who had just arrived.

The Richmond black community crime investigator lay backwards in the seat and looked up at the sky. Like he had just remembered he left something in the left bottom pocket of the dark brown vest he was wearing, he fished into the pocket, got his pipe, and inspected the chamber to make sure the tobacco was still inside. He put it in his mouth, and lit it. After some draws, he gently breathed a faint cloud of smoke out of his nose.

"What's your name?" he asked the coachman.

"Ellis. Vincent Ellis."

"So, how is this one going to be different, Mr. Ellis?"

"This struggle is about freeing the natives from themselves and saving this sweet land of liberty. If they continue to sell each other into slavery, they will risk a self-inflicted annihilation, and eventually the British and the French might claim and seize this territory and divide it among themselves. We, as the descendance of those who were sold from these shores, will not allow that to happen. But I don't think there will be any war. Governor Carey has been fostering peace between us and them. He's a good man."

"And if the British and French do seize this land, the scary question is, where does that put the free American Negros? With the natives persistent refusal to back down on the slave trade, time seems not to be in the colony's favor."

"That's the point, sir. So, what brings you here, then?"

From looking up at the sky, Dean Goldman turned his eyes on the coachman. He took a few draws of the pipe and this time, puffed out a thick plume of smoke. Anticipating a response, Vincent Ellis slightly turned and caught the guest's eyes.

"I am here on an excursion."

An excursion in the middle of a looming crisis? Pondered the senior chauffeur. There was no need for further questions. As the response did not make sense, the guest was simply telling him to mind his business. Sensing that Ellis had gotten it with his sudden silence, Goldman smiled and continued puffing, as the coach neared the colonial headquarters.

The guest was ushered into the waiting room of Deputy Governor Ebenezer Butler's office, who was now the officer in charge. Two weeks now, Governor Carey has not yet recovered from the blast. There was an emergency security meeting taking place in the conference room opposite Butler's office, attended by Commander Elijah Johnson, Captain Capehart, Major Crayton, Charles Deshields, and Councilman Samuel Brisbane. As Dean Goldman sat smoking his pipe and listening to the conversation from the conference room, which is directly opposite Butler's waiting room, the meeting sounded like it was an interrogation going on.

"Can you explain why you did not show up for work, the day before we were informed of an attack on the colony?" he heard someone ask.

"I went to the interior to visit a little sister of mine who lost her baby in stillbirth," a man, sounding indigenous answered.

"Before we employed you, you told us your family lived at Bassa Cove, but you were spotted crossing the St. Paul, two days after the blast and when the attack did not take place, you crossed back into the colony. Also, a day after the arrival of the Freedom Star, you crossed the river to attend the meeting between kings Gbanjah Kiatamba and Sorteh Gbayou which was held in the Gola Forest. So, we have reasons to believe that you were the interpreter at that meeting." There was silence. After some time, the interrogator declared. "Mr. Deshields, your staff is the mole we have been looking for."

"I am disappointed in you, Witty Peter. You were my best interpreter," Deshields was heard saying. "Now you will give us the names of the rest of you."

The conversation continued in low tone and then there was a heavy argument which lasted for some time and then the meeting was over.

"With Butler the officer in charge, this colony is now acephalous," roared Councilman Brisbane storming out of the conference room. "Why will he say the deployment of our militia in and around the colony is causing panic when there's evidence of an attack? I am afraid that he is unfit to run the colony."

Goldman watched the fair colored man glance at him, in his fate of rage, as he passed him and pushed open the exit door. Commander Johnson came out, followed by Witty Peter, who looked like he was closely guarded and escorted by two other men in militia uniforms, and then Major Crayton, walking closely behind. Also were Deputy Governor Butler, and Captain Ashford Capehart. They all, except Witty Peter, and the two men escorting him, greeted or nodded at the guest, as they trooped out of the waiting room.

"Dean Goldman?" Deputy Governor Butler walked to the guest and asked, extending his hand.

"Yes, Dean Goldman," the Richmond base investigator got up, also extending his hand.

"Deputy Governor Ebenezer Butler, Officer in Charge. Nice to meet you, and welcome to Monrovia."

"Welcome, sir. Charles Deshields, Director of Settlers-Indigenous affairs."

"My office, please," the deputy governor motioned towards his office door, and then to Deshields and the guest.

"I am here in pursuant of the cable, I believe you received a few weeks ago from the Color Purpose Organization of an investigation we are conducting." Goldman began when he was offered a seat in Deputy Governor Butler's office.

"Yes. But it did not say what the investigation is about," replied Butler.

"It is a matter of confidentiality. There was an arson attack on Cottonwood Plantation in Fairfax County, Virginia, which resulted in the death and destruction of almost the entire plantation, slaves and the owners alike, except two persons. The perpetrator fled and was one of the passengers on the Freedom Star. A murder was also committed on the vessel. Elijah Burgess did not drown."

"And who the murderer might be?"

"Mrs. Angela Draper Burgess."

"His widow?!" exclaimed Charles Deshields.

"That woman is not who she says she is. She practices Voodooism, the dark art. She seduces her victims, manipulates, and kills them under mysterious circumstances, just how she killed Elijah Burgess."

Deputy Governor Butler turned to Deshields who was sitting opposite Dean Goldman. "Of all the new arrivals, I never met this woman. Was she part of your Settlers-indigenous Integration program?"

"No," Deshields breathed with fear. "Bishop Emilie Thompson vouched on her behalf that she couldn't attend because she was still mourning her husband. She was not at the welcoming ceremony, either."

"Where is she staying?" asked the Officer in Charge.

"The bishop might know exactly. He told me she was building a cottage somewhere near the newly declared settlement of Bensenville."

"This is strange. That place is isolated. It is not yet declared safe for settlement," the governor frowned. "Anyway, let me speak with Major Crayton to have some of his men accompany you to apprehend this woman. As you may be aware, we have a crisis on our hands; a fortnight ago, the governor was severely injured in an accident orchestrated by the fear of an indigenous attack, and we are expecting the attack, any time. The areas surrounding Bensenville may be dangerous now."

"I will prefer only one person, Governor Butler. The woman we seek, if alarmed can be far more deadly, than I just described. I will stop by the bishop to learn a thing or two about where she lives."

"Okay. Major Crayton is due in my office anytime from now."

"I'll wait, governor."

It took about fifteen minutes before Major Rudolf Crayton entered the office.

"Got something, Major?"

The intelligence officer nodded.

"Okay. But first I want you to find one of your trusted men to accompany our guest, Mr. Dean Goldman from Color Purpose to Bensonville. He's on a special assignment." Than to Deshields. "Prepare a Communication to notify the Bishop about Goldman's visit."

"Please follow me, sir," Major Cryton motioned to Dean Goldman, who got up and followed him out of Butler's office. After ten minutes, the intelligence officer was back.

"We managed to break Cho Vuyougar. He's only aware of one messenger. His name is Garsuah Togar, commonly called Abraham Garsuah. Whenever the Santa Amelia is ashore, this Garsuah makes contact with the captain, and takes a message to King Gbayou. He uses the Du and Junk rivers to navigate his way to King Gbayou's territory. All this time we didn't know that the Santa Amelia was a Portuguese slave trading vessel. Edwardo Gomez, its captain, has been trading in slaves with the Bassa king for many years."

"We must alert the American Naval captain about this!" exclaimed the acting governor. "The Santa Amelia is currently en route to Monrovia and is expected to be anchored on our shores anytime."

"Yes governor, I will mobilize and deploy our watchmen along Garsuah's navigational course.

"That will be good, Major."

"Thanks, governor," noted the major, with a sheen of appreciation, soon overtaken by a faint expression of concern. "So, what's the special assignment with our guest from Richmond?"

"He's here to apprehend one of the new arrivals who came with the Freedom Star. An arson was committed on a plantation killing almost the entire inhabitants, and this suspect murdered Elijah Burgess, too. This one is a matter of top confidentiality, and here's the next one; Bendu Kiatamba is currently in Caldwell. Reverend Charles Gooding informed us this morning, when he came to see how Governor Carey was doing. She is staying at the missionary compound, he's assisting the governor to run, and she and her baby are doing well."

"No wonder why the attack hasn't started yet. She didn't go to her father."

"Yes. And that's why I suggested that we must scale down our deployments.

"Brisbane is batty about that," the major noted, his tone emphatic, and sounding more or like a warning.

"And I am aware of what he's planning now. He's galvanizing support from the rest of the voting league to vote and declare me unfit to act in Carey's place."

"Is he going to get this?"

"Sure. With Councilwoman Comfort Dixon Wallace still abroad, Councilwomen Dennis and Dunn are likely to vote in my favor while Councilman Russel, Horton, and himself will obviously vote against me."

"That would make it a tie," observed Major Crayton. "Brisbane himself, Russel, and Horton are on one side, while you, Councilwomen Dennis and Esther Haywood Dunn are on the other side."

"Don't forget, Major. Deputy Governor Estella Carter will vote against me, too. Remember she was heavily supported by these very councilmen when she was nominated for that post."

Realizing this fact, Major Crayton wrinkled nervously as a fresh dose of sweat dripped from his face.

"As this administration sinks deeper into this crisis, you gotta act now to prevent Abraham Garsuah from slipping into Gbayou's territory, to inform the hostile king who would see it as the right time to attack. Also, we must catch Captain Gomez by surprise. And we will now have to depend solely on the American Navy, as the British have been slowing down their assistance lately.

"Yes, they are now preoccupied, expanding their colony from Sherbro Island further east into the Mano River region. They have realized that if they continue to help us to rescue these besieged tribes, we would gain more of the indigenous trust which would allow us to expand the colonial administration and prevent further territorial encroachments by the Crown." Major Crayton said.

"Without direct involvement of the American government in the affairs of the colony, the British see this as an opportunity to absorb us without problem. And with the French also moving fast towards the Cavalla from the east, and thrusting from the Guinea Highlands at the north, eventually, we risk being enveloped. We are faced with another threat."

"With this war on our hands, we have no time to prepare for that one, governor."

"If we must survive, and protect this land, we must first have to think about the unthinkable to stop this war, and prepare ourselves to live with the harsh consequences. We will have to take some tough discussions, even if it would mean instituting the last resort to defend the colony," breathed Governor Butler, slightly shivering with the horror of the thought he had in mind. Then he looked up at the major. "And another thing before you leave. How's the interrogation with Corporal Davis?"

"The old guard has put himself under a self-imposed hunger strike. He is still berating himself for leaving his post as soon as we went down the regiment's quarter for help to haul the stock pile of ammunitions into the armory. Says he will commit suicide if Governor Carey dies."

"And this indigenous girlfriend of his?"

"She's clean. Her visit was a mare routine. But she came late that night because we did not leave the ammunition dorm early."

"Okay, let her go. And as for old Corporal Moses Davis, let him remain suspended. If an attack ever occurs, arm and send him to the battle front. Defending the colony might ease his guilt."

About fifteen minutes later, Vincent Ellis was driving down Ashmun Street from the Colonial Head Office with Dean Goldman in his coach as dust swirled on the dusty road.

"Here we are," announced Corporal Levi Gardea Gray, the uniformed guard Major Crayton had assigned to the guest, when the coach halted in front of the wooden gate of the Methodist compound, hosting Bishop Thompson and his family.

At the gate, they met an indigenous man, looking in his late forties. Dean Goldman handed the communication. Recognizing the colonial seal at the back of the folded letter, the man immediately raced towards a brick house, a few feet from the church. He returned without the letter, opened the gate, and ushered the guests into the compound.

"Welcome, sir. You can have your seat," said Emily Thompson, motioning to the stranger, at the same time staring at the guard at the door "And you, too, sir."

"Thanks. I'll be on the porch."

The investigator took off his hat and sat in a chair. Studying the elaborate living room, he fished in the bottom pocket of his vest, and pulled out his pipe. Catching Emily's eyes, and then switching his to the portrait of the Lord ascending to heaven at the Mount of Olive hanging on the wall opposite him, he became embarrassed and shoved it back into his pocket.

"My dad, the bishop will be with you, shortly," pretending like she did not notice his embarrassment, or, it would have been impolite to a guest, Emily informed Goldman.

Then she went into the hallway and stood before her parent's door. Her face suddenly changed into sorrow and her eyes turned red and teary. She wanted to cry. But trying to be calm, she fought it, despite a flow of tears that ran down her cheeks. Emily hesitated for a moment before she knocked on the door. Pausing again for a while, she opened it and entered.

Mrs. Olivia Thompson was lying in bed, with the bishop sitting beside her. She was shivering, and her teeth were rattling. Her lips were dry, scaly and split with sores. Her eyes looked bruised and red, and were focused towards the ceiling. Sweat profusely oozed out of her body, as a nurse wiped her head, neck and chest with a soaked towel.

She was trying to tell her husband something, but her voice was hissy and quivery, disrupting her speech and making it difficult for the bishop to understand what she was trying to say, even when he laid his head sideways to her chest so that his right ear should get closer to her mouth. He heard the door open and looked back. It was his daughter who had entered the room and nodded to him.

"Take the guest to my study, " he told her, and looked at his wife. Holding her wrist and squeezing it gently, he whispered, "I'll be back."

Dean Goldman was seated across the bishop's desk when he entered. He watched the fair skinned towering clergy man remove his coat and hung it on a rack on the wall. Bishop Thompson first reached for a bottle of communion wine with two vials on a cabinet next to the rack before idling towards his desk.

Sitting behind his desk and adjusting his cravat, "Communion wine?" he offered.

"Just a little, Bishop," responded Goldman, at the same time taking from his breast pockets, and unfolding the portraits of Angela Draper Burgess. "I am here for this woman."

"Lord have mercy!" whispered Bishop Thompson, looking at the portraits spread before him with horror as Dean Goldman explained the intent of his mission.

"Where is she?" asked the investigator, pouring the sacramental wine in one of the vials.

"Let me change into something for the road," horrified and shaken, the bishop said and hurried out of his office.

After a sip, Goldman sat the vial back on the bishop's desk, took the portraits and folded them.

Emily Thompson was on the porch observing the colonial militia guard and the gateman standing at the gate, having a conversation. The militia man looked young, intelligent and immaculate in his uniform. When he noticed her, he excused himself from the gateman and walked to her.

"You look familiar," she said.

"You are correct. I attend the Methodist Church."

"Then you are supposed to know me."

"Yes, of course. You're the altar girl."

'What's your name?"

"Levi Gardea Gray."

"Gardea?!" Emily asked, emphasizing. "It sounds indigenous."

"I am a grandson of King Gray. When I was little, my parents sent me to live with a settler family. They trained and taught me to speak good English."

"That's nice," Emily tried to smile-it was her first; since that day she had been worried as her mother's condition worsened.

"Miss. Have you seen your father?" They were suddenly interrupted by Dean Goldman who came rushing outside.

"No. I don't understand. I thought you both were in his study."

"Yes, but he left to change his clothes when I told him to take me to Angela Draper Burgess."

"Let me check in his room," Emily said and hurried inside. "He's not in," she told the visitor who met her in the hallway when she came from the room.

"Where does he keep his horses?" Goldman asked, his voice quivering a little.

"Why?" Emily asked, frowning, instead of a response.

"Your father has gone to Mrs. Burgess," replied Goldman, panting. "She's not who she is. That's why I am here. The bishop will be in danger."

"What?!"

"You got to take me there now. Ever been there?"

Emily nodded nervously. Right away, with the visitor following behind, she raced towards the back door, and flung it open. She was appalled. Standing before the stable, her father's horse was gone.

"We have to go after him, now!" cried Goldman. "Mrs. Burgess is wanted for the murder of many persons back in the United States. She also murdered Elijah Burgess. Your father will be risking his life, if he confronts her about this."

Few minutes later, Emily was riding along with Dean Goldman, and Levi Gardea Gray in the coach as Mr. Ellis lashed the horses. The chariot was in full speed, heading towards Crown Hill.

"Two weeks ago, my father visited her to inspect the cottage she was building. He came back with a herbal tea he said she grew in her garden. We drank it, and my mother is seriously sick," Emily explained, with tears rolling down her eyes.

"The tea was a spell meant for your mother," said Goldman, watching Gardea Gray inspecting his raffle. "Maybe your mother has become suspicious of her lately."

Bishop Emile Thompson was galloping through a Sinkor dirt road at the edge of the Mesurado River. His face was tense and full of anger. When the visitor revealed to him who Mrs. Burgess really was, it became like the spell that clouded his thought of raising any suspicion concerning the death of Elijah Burgess, was broken. The mysterious shark attack on Jack Duval at Cape Verde, her refusal to attend the welcoming ceremony when they arrived, her reluctance to attend the settlers-indigenous program and even her lukewarm attitude towards going to church, all now made sense to him.

"Why doesn't our widow go to church?" Olivia Thompson asked her husband while having supper on the evening of their first Thanksgiving Day.

"She still mourns her husband," shrugging, the bishop answered, defensively. "She needs the help of a specialized doctor, but we don't have that expertise around here."

"Elijah Burgess died many months ago. We have all gone past that unfortunate incident. Her continuous morning now looks odd to me. I think she needs the word of God to deliver her from whatever abyss she's entrapped in."

Bishop Thompson said nothing and continued with his supper. Surprised that as a bishop well versed in the word of God, and counseling, her husband was suggesting a psychiatrist, instead of the word of God to intervene in Mrs. Burgess' situation.

"What sin have you committed that's weighing heavily on your consciousness that you think the Lord cannot forgive, if you go to church and pray, and ask for his forgiveness?" Mrs. Thompson asked Mrs. Burgess, while they both were alone, in the widow's kitchen peeling freshly harvested sweet potatoes from her garden, when the family once visited her temporary wooden house, shortly before the construction work on the new one began.

"The only sin with a catastrophic consequence my late mother once told me about is what kills the cat," Angela responded, and threw one of the potatoes she had peeled and shaped into the form of a cat, into the frying pan. Then she offered the clergyman's wife an ominous smile, as they both watched the potato fry until it burned in the hot oil.

"Curiosity!" Olivia Thompson gaped. She swallowed hard, as the word whispered in her heart, and shivered in reaction to the widow's threat.

"People who detest the house of the Lord dwell in darkness," she cautioned her husband while on their way back home, later that evening. "I will never step foot here again. Hope you got that, Emile."

"You surely won't, anymore," standing in her living room behind her curtains, Mrs. Burgess whispered in Mrs. Thompson's ears as the voodoo princess watched the coach of the Thompsons leaving her yard.

At home, the whisper continued to filter in Olivia Thompson's ears until she got sick.

Pondering over all of these, about an hour later, the bishop reached Mrs. Burgess' fence. He jumped down from his horse and stepped the gate open. Clad in his full garment, he pointed his crucifix towards the front door of the cottage.

"Angela Draper or whosoever you are, come out now and confess your sins or face the wrath of the Lord," he called in a loud and chilly voice.

Then, there was a sudden gust of wind blowing across the yard, flapping the bishop garment, rattling and cracking the surrounding trees, and blowing away the roof of the old frame house Mrs. Burgess was staying in, before building her cottage. This startled the bishop's horse and it went galloping away.

"Neither storms nor torrents will stand in the way of God's judgment," still pointing the cross forward, and bracing firmly to prevent the wind from toppling him, the clergyman shouted.

The breeze suddenly stopped. Afterwards, with a heavy force, the door of the cottage flung open. Mrs. Burgess, dressed in a white transparent garment, stood at the door. Her hair was covering her face and reaching her shoulders. But it parted around her nose, mouth and cheek, making them visible. Like a possessed breaking free from an exorcism, she descended the stairs, barefooted. As if she was in a trance, she went gladding to the back of the cottage with the hem of her garment sweeping the dirt on the ground.

Shocked and horrified by the ghostly appearance of the woman he had known from the beginning of their journey from the New York harbor to the Pepper Coast, Bishop Thompson dabbed his forehead drenched with sweat with the sleeves of his cassock, and took a deep breath.

"The lord is my Shepherd, I shall not want," he recited the first verse of the 23rd Psalm.

After mumbling the other verses, and taking one step after another toward the back of the cottage, like he had renewed his faith and gained confidence, he shouted, this time louder than when he first accosted her. "Yea though I walked through the valley and the shadow of death I fear no evil, for thou art with me. Your rod and your staff, they comfort me."

When he got to the back of the cottage, he suddenly froze, terror stricken; the faith and confidence he had exerted had disappeared. Mrs. Burgess was standing, with her garment half way down her hips, before a voodoo shrine she had built. It was partially enclosed in a fence in the form of an arc made of sticks covered with neatly plaited palm branches, adorned with horrific looking masks, sculptures, skulls and the horns of animals.

What startled him the most was when he saw a doll among the many that were lying on the altar, surrounded by jars with portions of different colors in them. It was neatly carved out of soft wood with the hair made of strands extracted from palm branches. The doll resembled Mrs. Olivia Thompson. It was clad in an impeccably wedding dress; the same one the bishop's wife wore at the time of their wedding, 16 years ago.

"Attempting to intrude into the real person in me, reaps a horrid consequence," Mrs. Burgess said, her voice, eerily smooth, sounding like an opera playing on a gramophone. "So was Elijah Burgess," With her back still turned to him, she went on, and took the Virginal Cardinal Newspaper lying against one of the bottles of red wine and flung it at the bishop's feet. "My husband read the dreaded headline and knew who I was and so I killed him."

With a fresh dose of fear, the clergy man gaped and swallowed hard, as his Adam apple roved up and down his throat. The headline, "**Murder at Cottonwood Plantation, near Gunston Hill**," flashed in his face.

"The inquisitive are vanquished Just like what I am about to do to Olivia, lovely Olivia," she spoke again, her tone now sorrowful. Then she bowed down, the garment completely slipping down to her knees, exposing her rear and arousing the erotism of the cleric. He suddenly flushed.

Mrs. Burgess drew a large jar, sitting on the altar closer to her with water inside. She went for one of the wines, and unscrewed it with her teeth. She took a sip and spat it on the doll. Then she poured some of the wine into the jar and the water turned, first, blue, and then orange and red. She waved her both hands over the jar and it immediately turned into flames. Immediately, the portion in the jar began to boil.

Olivia Thompson started screaming when Mrs. Burgess dropped the doll into the boiling glass jar. The nurse attending to her ran out of the room when she saw red rounded blisters appearing on her patient's skin, bursting and causing sores. Emily's mother's skin got so hot that the beddings she was lying on caught on fire. Bishop Thompson could hear the screams of his radiated inflicted wife almost deafening his ears and her agony piercing his heart. The effect caused him to drop to his knees, shutting his ears with both hands at the same time holding the left side of his chest.

The pains and screams lingered for some time and then they stopped, abruptly. The bishop knew right away that his wife had died. With a sudden vigor, he rose to his feet, with his cross once more stretched forward. But he again flinched, his eyes on the voodoo diva, standing before him, now completely naked.

"In the name of God, the Father, the Son, and the Holy Spirit," shutting his eyes and shaking his head violently, as he struggled to fight off the temptation of the eros flickering into his mind, he raised his voice. "Let fire from hell consume thee."

When he opened his eyes, Mrs. Burgess was still standing before him with no fire from hell consuming her. Bishop Thompson now stood, entrapped in the devil's snare. Absolutely dreaded, he quivered in anticipation of what was coming.

"Oh mine! You have forgotten the story of your prophet Elijah; it is from the mouth of the pious, shall fire rain down from heaven," she crooned, and then snared. "But never from the throngs of hell. How dare you tread into where you profess you do not belong."

The last words of Mrs. Burgess referred to the theme of a sermon, 'Hell is not where we Belong', he once preached many years ago as a young reverend. But now, instead of heaven, he was calling fire down from hell, the paradox of which has played into the hands of the agent of the devil.

Now realizing that he was dealing with a woman with a strange power he could not match, the bishop was perplexed, and trembling. The dreadfulness of which, galvanizing his fear.

"Oo! Frightened now?" she said, her tone softening but creepy. "The prophet himself feared the wrath of Jezebel, you poor old dunce."

Mrs. Burgess took another jar from the altar filled with giant size bees. She uncapped it and unleashed them on the bishop. Chased by the swarm of bees plaguing him with vicious stings of acidic enzymes that tore into his garment, reaching and peeling off his skin, the clergy man ran towards the front of the cottage, screaming.

Vincent Ellis had driven Dean Goldman, Emily Thompson and the colonial militia guard at Mrs. Burgess' gate. They saw Bishop Thompson running out of the yard. His garment had completely melted on him. Like a leper, his skin was covered with sores.

"Daddy!" screamed his daughter.

"No, Emily! Don't!" Goldman wailed, grabbing her, before she could jump down from the coach to run to her father. "She has unleashed a deadly spell on your father. You will get infected if you touch him."

As the coach raised into the yard, the leprosy riddled bishop, with his hair, ears, nose and lips eaten up, including the flesh around his fingers, heard his daughter's voice and ran past them into the bush.

"Gad damn-it!" exclaimed Vincent Ellis, uttering a common settler's idiomatic expression of bewilderment as he pulled the reins, and halted the horse. *"Let me get my boonka out of here."*

Before he could turn the coach around, Mrs. Burgess appeared before them. With its forelimbs in the air, the frightened animal jolted and neighed, causing the coach to flip over, throwing its occupants to the ground. With her transparent garment back on, her hair stood, and her face brightened. One again like the universe, the sparks in her eyes were spinning, just like the encounter with Percy Macadam and Jack Duvall. She stretched her hands holding two jars filled with human blood.

"Turn your face to the ground, and close your eyes!" cried Goldman. "Do not look into her eyes or else she will connect to your souls, through which she will unleash her spells. "No!" he screamed as Levi Gardea Gray positioned his raffle and fired.

The bullet hit one of the jars, shattering it. The blood-portion wasted on the ground, and began to foam into steaming hot bubbles. With the other jar still in her hand, the voodoo princess stepped closer and stood over the colonial militia guard. She turned the jar outside down and wasted the portion, but before it could land on Levi's back, Dean Goldman sprung on top of him and the portion landed on his back, instead. As the substance began to boil, it consumed the fabric of the coat he was wearing and peeled the flesh on his back.

"You three must get out of here now!" Goldman screamed at the same time keeping his eyes shut and hauling the dagger, the old Algonquian Indian gave him, from his side.

He stabbed Mrs. Burgess several times on her left foot, until the dagger pierced through and bore the ground.

With Emily and Mr. Ellis following behind, they ran towards the gate. But the militia guard stopped to pick up his gun from the ground, reloaded it, turned around and closed his eyes to shoot the witch again.

"No!" Goldman screamed again. "You will not be able to aim with your eyes shut. Get out of here before we all die!"

"You heard him! Let's go!" cried Emily, running back and pulling Levi.

The voodoo princess attempted to run after them but Dean Goldman, screaming as the acidic blood portion tore into his back, pressed the knife further into her flesh at the same time clinching onto her legs to prevent her from moving.

While Levi and Emily were far ahead as Ellis trekked behind, out of a sudden, two tribal warriors emerged from the bush, and sprang on the coach driver, taking him to the ground. Soon there were more of them sprinting from the nearby bushes and picking up the chase after Levi and Emily. He turned and saw the two warriors sitting on Vincent Ellis's back while one of them was pulling his arms behind him to tie them.

"They are Gbayou's men; the slave catchers!" cried Levi, aiming his musket at them. "Run faster!" he screamed at Emily who had stopped to see what was going on.

The colonial Militia fired. A warrior was caught in the head. He swayed backwards and dropped to the ground, dead. Before he could reload again, three of the warriors chasing them were on him. Within minutes, Levi Gardea Gray was thrown on the ground.

"Get out of here, Emily!" he screamed at Emily who had stopped and looked back to see what the warriors were doing to him.

Back at the cottage, Mrs. Burgess had pulled Dean Goldman from the ground. Weakened by the excruciating pain on his acid stained back, she brought him closer and looked straight in his face.

"From your comfort in Richmond, it's going to be so exciting to see your carcass in the jaws of the hungry Jackals of West Africa, Goldman," she said, in her unusually eerily melodic tone. "Elaine Mason will be nowhere to save you, this time. What a pity."

"You tried to stop me at the plantation you destroyed, while looking at Gary Jackson's carvings," Goldman said, his speech sluggish due to his dizziness. "That little boy survived. Even if you kill me, he will hunt you, so long Eli's family is still on the face of the earth."

"You sound so weak and defenseless."

Goldman got his pipe from his coat pocket, lit it and began to take a couple of draws. He coughed, as the fumes flowed out of his mouth and nostrils. Then he opened his eyes and looked into her face. For a while she said nothing.

"You see. With all your powers and vicious spells, you are the one who's so weak, seeking this part of the world to hide. But the people you have hurt will hunt and find you."

When he could no longer puff and when the smoke filtering out of his nostrils and mouth had reduced, Mrs. Burgess flung the investigator towards the edge of the bush. He began to scream as wild dogs appeared and devoured him.

Angela Draper then hurried back into her cottage. Minutes later, she came back outside wearing red and white stripy guayaberas, and brown dungaree pants tucked into a black saddler leather knee-high boots. A group of warriors had gathered in her yard with Levi, Vincent Ellis and some indigenous tribesmen, with their hands and necks tied together with robes, like war prisoners. She right away knew that the raids had begun, and Monrovia would soon be attacked. Wearing a Fedora straw hat, with her hair braided in a ponytail, she descended the stairs, as three warriors rushed to her with robes in their hands.

"She's evil! She'll kill all of us!" cried Ellis.

Looking in her eyes and attempting to grab and tie her hands with the robes, the warrior nearest to her, froze. The spiraling sparks, and the spinning stars like a galaxy, had him spook and hypnotized.

"Take me to your king," she demanded, and offered a faint smile when the hypnotized warrior signaled his men to stand down.

She pointed to the horse, standing at the right side of her fence. It was still attached to the coach. Immediately, another warrior ran and loosen the reins from the coach. Holding it, he hurried back to her with the animal trotting behind him. Mrs. Burgess gently tapped the horse on its side, and rubbed its forehead. It suddenly got down on its belly, and stood back up when she sat on it. Guarded by two warriors, with one of them holding the reins, she appeared like a slave master riding behind his subjects, as the warriors, along with their captives, trooped out of the yard in single file.

Deep into the forest, with tony weeds tearing her dress and latching her skin, Emily Thompson ran aimlessly. With her parents no more, she wept as she scurried into the bushes, shouting and calling for help. When they captured Levi Gardea Gray, two of the warrior's slave catchers continued to pursue her, but she was far ahead of them.

Despite the noise of the low branches rubbing against her and the scrunching of dry leaves she trampled on, she could still hear similar rustlings at the far distance behind her, indicating that the men were getting closer, no matter in which direction she ran.

She decided to slow down and take her time to avoid wandering aimlessly and be caught by the men who knew their terrain well. Luckily, she found a suitable place to hide and waited. Just as expected, the rustlings stopped; the slave catchers have lost track of her position and were waiting for her to resume running and shouting for help, so that they can again pick up the chase after her, using the noise of the low branches that will brush her body and the dry leaves she will trample on to pinpoint her location and track her down.

Emily took a deep breath when a thought came to her. Instead of running, she began to dock, avoiding low branches and tramping on dry leaves. She continued until she reached a stream, and followed it southwards. Bearing in mind that it may take her all the way to the coast where she could find help, she resumed running again.

About an hour and a half later, giggling and splashes in the distance ahead, like children playing in the water, caught her attention, causing her to slow down. Now taking her time, she crept closer. From her position, she could see girls, some of whom looked around her age, playing in the water while some of their mates sat along the banks, playing the flip, gather and catch game with fresh palm nuts.

She was a bit relieved when she saw that the girls were covered with white chalk all over their bodies. The chalk was washed off the skins of the ones playing in water. But when they got tired and came out, their friends would rub the chalk, in patterns of designs, all over their bodies. Emily had seen such girls, loitering around the outskirts of Monrovia, especially around the settlement of King Gray. She was watching a group of *Blunjous*.

One of the girls who was playing the game had won, when she flipped a palm nut high in the air and swiftly gathered all the ones on the ground, before catching the one she threw up with the same hand. She had jumped to her feet, jubilating when she turned and saw Emily.

"How did this settler girl get here?!" puzzled, she asked.

Surprised, the rest of the *Blunjous* got up and walked to Emily.

"No. Don't scare," one of the girls who looked the oldest, said in broken English, when Emily attempted to run. "The bad men in the bush will catch you. Come to us."

Uncertain and nervous, Emily hesitated, and repeatedly looked at her real to see whether the warriors had caught up with her. When they heard the bush shaking in the distance, the older *blunjou* motioned to her again, gesturing appealingly that she will be safe with them. Frightened, and in no time, Emily hurried to them. Less than three minutes later, the two warriors raced towards the group of half-naked *Blunjous,* careful not to look at them, or stop to ask questions, as it was forbidden.

A particular *Blunjou* looked scared when the men were passing by them. Twice her eyes sparkled with apprehension when one of the warriors twice glanced at her. Fortunately, she slowly breathed with relief, when he did not recognize her. Now full of gratitude, Emily Thompson regarded the older *Blunjo,* as she watched her pursuers hurrying past them.

Chapter 17

The cold dry harmattan wind blew across a village picking up dry leaves and particles from the ground forming dust devils about 10 ft high. It was a small village with three thatched roof huts surrounded by a thick forest. At the back of two of the huts were two outside bathrooms made of round pole sticks forming a circle, and covered with palm thatches. A hen and its six weeks old chicks, harassed by a large red rumbling rooster, were foraging at the edge of the village yard near the bush.

An outside kitchen made of four sticks shaped like a square with thatched roof, stood a few feet to the right. A boiling pot full of cassava was sitting over the fire hearth as a young girl, sitting on a wooden stool, tended to the blazing firewood.

On a sooty bamboo dryer near the fire hearth, lay two dried groundhogs partially covered with wild plantain leaves. A large calabash bowl with some rice inside was lying between an emptied winnowing fan and another one, filled with fresh bitter balls, okra, and pepper. The bowl was spinning and was being dragged by the wind.

"Ah! Is this how strong the Yahni-paypay can be on this side?" using the local word for the hash harmattan wind, complained the young girl, rubbing her eyes with the tip of her lapper, when the arches and sparkles from the fire, stirred by the wind, blew into her face.

Still dabbing her eyes, she got up and hurried after the calabash bowl when she heard it dragging. Holding her side, she took her time to bend over for the bowl, mindful not to press her bulging stomach against her upper thigh. She however managed to retrieve it and took her time, and wadded back into the kitchen.

"So, this girl couldn't allow me to prepare this evening meal for my son," mulled an old lady who came from one of the huts dragging a worn-out fishing net. "And she knows that my son will understand that her pregnancy is well advanced."

She had no clothes covering her upper body. Only a short lapper was wrapped around her hips. She sat on a piece of stool log in front of her hut, and looked the girl's way for a while. When the girl looked back and smiled, meaning that she was okay, the old lady returned her smile and turned to inspect her old fishing net.

When she discovered the spots where the net was torn, she put it down and stretched her right hand for some fresh palm thatches lying on the ground close to her feet. She got them and began to pluck out the midribs and laid them on the ground in bundles. Later, the green stalks would get dry and turn hard and brown. Then, she would make yard brooms out of them.

But her mean aim was to mend her nets. So, she peeled off the leaves into tiny segments, rolled the tip of the short lapper all the way to her abdomen, and repeatedly rubbed each tiny segment on her wrinkly thigh, until they formed into threads.

"Aww!" she uttered, disappointedly. "The threads will not be enough to mend this fishing net." Then she looked towards the other hut to her left. "Laynumah," she called.

"*Naywa*: Yes mother," in Kpelle, a male voice responded from the back of the hut, just as the sound of the chopping of branches with a cutlass died down. "*Lay pay keh*? What is it?"

"The fresh thatches you brought are not enough to mend my fishing nets."

Few minutes later, a boy, looking in his late teens, came from behind the hut toting a pile of palm branches on his head, and dumped them before the old lady.

"I was still chopping off more branches," breathed the boy, brushing off dry leaves particles and tiny red ants from his skin. "I had to take time because the red aunts were too many."

"But you brought more than enough. I only need a little more to patch this my fishing net."

"I know. The other day I went to the creek where you always go fishing. My fishing line could not handle the large ones I caught. Grouped together, that old fishing net will not be able to hold them. That's why I brought more of the thatches enough to fix a new one."

"But it will take me time to make a new one, Laynumah. The dry season is well advanced and creeks are getting drier. The fishes are swimming far off for the deeper waters. Before I finished fixing a new net, they would have long gone."

"Okay. Use the ones you want. I will come back to collect the rest to enforce some areas around your bathroom."

"Thank you, Laynumah," the old lady said and smiled as she watched her son walk back behind the hut.

Then she looked towards the kitchen with lines of concern running across her forehead. The girl was scooping over the fire hearth, trying to take down the pot. When she did with ease, the old lady resumed manufacturing her thread.

She paused when she heard rustlings up her roof. Giant size dark brown salamanders were dropping to the ground and running heather scatter. She almost jumped from her stool, when one crept under, and made its way for the bush, startling the hen and her 6 weeks old chicks, causing the aggressive mothering fowl to chase after it.

"Laynumah," the old woman called again. "*Furleng-nga-da ker ta myamie,yo!:* The Salenanders are getting plenty, again."

"I have already scaled off the smiley tree bark. I will boil them and waste the liquid on the roof to drive them away," the young man responded from behind the hut, amid the cessation of what sounded like he had reverted to brushing the back yard.

The old lady remained silent for a while like she was trying to digest what her son had told her. Then she looked towards the kitchen again. The young woman was now picking the cooked cassava she emptied from the pot into the emptied winnowing fan. With a knife in one hand, she was splitting the tubers from head down in her other hand, and removing the fibers from the middle.

Sneaking behind her, Laynumah came tipping-toe into the kitchen, and snatched a lump of the cassava. Before the girl could notice and pretend to knock his hand with the back of the knife, the lad had run back behind the hut, giggling.

"Beware that you have just stolen your own potion of evening meal," the girl warned, jovially.

Then she continued with what she was doing, further splitting the steaming tubers into pieces and putting them into a mortar. Amused by the little quip between the girl and her son, and that all was proceeding well for the pregnant young woman, the old lady once more focused on preparing the threads to patch her fishing net.

"Laynumah! Come at once!" she called. Something caught her attention when she lifted her head and looked straight into the bush ahead of her. "Laynumah! Hurry up!" she called again, now dropping the fishing net and the threads, and jumping to her feet.

"What again," he returned with his cutlass in his hand.

"Look straight ahead of you. Something is lying under that tree like a leopard!"

"It looks wounded! And it can be dangerous like that!" said Laynumah, seeing the leopard lying helplessly by the tree. It was not looking his way. "Let me get my spear."

Laynumah ran into his hut for his spear and came back outside with it. He looked at the young woman in the kitchen. She was now pounding the cassava in the mortar with a pestle. It was best not to notify her about a wounded Leopard close by. Least she caused a stir and alerted the animal. So, he motioned to his mother to be calmed. With his spear in the lancing position, he began to take careful steps towards the query.

The animal was in his clear view, when he was a few feet within its reach. He was about to throw his spear, aiming for the neck region but suddenly paused, gapping. It was not a Leopard, but someone dressed in its skin and pretending to be one. It was a trap.

The branches of an overhead tree shook. He looked up and saw three men dressed in similar fashion, leaping from the branches and descending on him. He soon realized that they were enemy Leopard warriors. In no time he positioned his spear intended for two of them to land straight into it, and get pierced. But the one who was pretending to be a wounded Leopard suddenly leapt forward, charging at Laynumah with a powerful spear taking the youngster to the ground, just in time his colleagues landed without harm.

"Laynumah!" screamed the old woman ceasing one of the palm branches and charging at the Leopard warriors on top of her son. But one of them ran towards her. He grabbed her by the neck and began to strangulate her as her son screamed. As the old lady convulsed with her eyes stretched, the warrior hauled out from his left side a small knife and thrust it into her stomach.

"Nawoe!" screamed the young woman who was pounding the cassava, leaving the mortar pestle and running to the old woman, now lying on the ground bleeding. "Der *ne nu a keh?*: What have you people done?!" she cried in Bassa. "These people are my in-laws. They are not your enemies!"

Standing over the dead old lady with the bloodied knife in his right hand, the Leopard warrior looked at the young woman weeping over the corpse and pulled her up by her hair.

"How dare you lay with the enemy," he grunted and gave her a nasty back hand slap across her face, sending her back to the ground. "Take them," he ordered, and immediately a group of other Bassa warriors jumped from their hiding places and took Laynumah and the young woman away.

The three Leopard warriors then entered into the three huts. Seeing no one, they came back outside, very alert. Two of them inspected the thatched roofs for some time while the other one hurried into the kitchen for the two dried groundhogs, wrapped them neatly in the plantain leaves and solved them into a bag made of leopard pelt pulled from beneath his leopard outfit. Having tasted a couple of them, he also wrapped the cooked cassavas into the leaves, and put them into his bag.

A sudden noise from the hen startled him. Taking him for a leopard, the chicken was alarmed. He made a decision to go after it too. But judging from its distance it will take a little time to catch it, and it was time to get out of there. The next moment, they sprinted out of the yard and disappeared into the bush.

Meanwhile, Yallah Koliemenni was wandering into the bush under the descending sun as the wind blew his face, burned his nostrils, and caused a dry throat. He did not like the harmattan season, and he has never gotten used to it. With his Kinjah on his back, the young hunter was on his way to a particular area where, for the past three months, he had been observing the prints of a particular animal.

Lately, he had been focusing on setting his traps rather than hunting, and so the first time he came across these animal tracks, he observed that it was a Bush Cow. Studying the size and depth of the foot prints, he determined that it was an adult, probably a male. Usually, he would set his trap right in the animal's path, at a certain spot where no matter what, it would pass, but because he wanted to see whether it would grow bigger than it is, he covered the tracks and waited to see how long it would take for it to reappear. This would tell him the exact time the buffalo would trek on that particular path.

Every day, Kolliemenni would inspect the animal's path to see whether the foot prints would appear. Afterwards, he would plant a piece of stick in the ground to keep track of the number of days he inspected them before the prints reappeared. He continued this routine until the prints appeared at the 21st stick.

Surprisingly, the hoof prints have gotten bigger and deeper, indicating that the animal had grown heavy and meaty. He covered the tracks again and observed it for another 42 days. The size and depth of the foot prints did not change within these days. The young bush cow had fully grown into a beast, and it was time for the former warrior spearman to set his trap.

Months earlier, it would have taken him days roaming the forest to track and kill it, but because Saydah did not like it when he stayed too long in the bush, since the day she had gotten pregnant and had moved in with him, he has reverted to setting traps where he will only have to go out into the bush and return late in the evening.

They have been seeing each other since the day they met at the upper Farmington where they made their rendezvous. And whenever they met, he brought her some of his kills. One time, she prepared fufu and soup with a ground hog he brought from his trap, and the crawfish she caught, which he struggled to swallow, as it was his first time, but enjoyed Saydah's dish. Another time, she was surprised to see that he had built a temporary kitchen of sticks and palm thatches. That same day he brought some rice and fresh meat. She happily cooked them and they ate and rested, lying on a neatly plaited bamboo mat under the perfect shade of the kitchen. As always, when it was approaching the evening hours, they parted ways.

It had now become habitual; she would cook and they would eat and lie down, and sometimes taught each other their dialects, the excitement of which began to diminish Kolliemenni's suspicion. As his trust grew gradually, Saydah would play in his hair, picking lice and scratching dandruff flakes with an afro comb with 3 teeth fashioned out of a dry wood.

But the former warrior spearman was mindful not to follow her to take bath in the river which she likes to do. He still harbors the fear that there could be Neengins waiting under the water to snatch him.

One day, she scratched his dandruff which he enjoyed and fell into a deep nap. She got up, found his spear hidden in the roof of the kitchen, and ambled down the river with it. Minutes later, he jumped from his nap. Sitting on the mat, he did not see Saydah. He immediately reached for his spear and did not find it, either.

He muttered a curse; the woman he was beginning to trust wholeheartedly, has sold him. He should have reminded himself that she was a daughter of the enemy, and he had been too foolish to allow her to lure him with her charm. With his heart pounding, he went ducking down to the river, at the spot where she usually bathes. Reaching, he crept behind the rocks to see what she was up to. Maybe she was arranging with neengins.

He was suddenly shoved from behind. Kolliemenni yelped, and went down into the river. Standing on top of a rock was Saydah, holding his spear and laughing at him.

"All this time you don't trust me yet?" jovially, she asked. "Here take your weapon and kill the Neengins." She threw the spear in the water, and continued to laugh. "Over there! One is under your feet. Look!"

Sheepishly, Yallah Kolliemenni stood in the water, reaching the level of his knee, with an expression that all alone he had been wrong about her and he was sorry. She suddenly stopped laughing and jumped into the water.

"You are the man I want to be with," she said, slouching closer to him. "Why will I kill you or have you killed, Kolliemenni? I took your spear to lure you here. If I had not done it, you would not have come looking for it. I have gotten matured and ready to show you my love, now."

She took his hands and put them on her breasts helping him to caress them. Getting on her knees, she gently pulled him down with her until they sat chest high in the water. With his hands still on her breasts, Saydah reached between his legs and smoothly messaged his genitals causing Kolliemenni to utter some faint groans. When she felt his penis swollen and stiffened, she got up holding his hands, and led him to one of the rocks with a flat surface. She was the first to climb on top of it, and then she urged him on. When he did, she removed her lapper, lay down and spread her legs.

Yallah Kolliemenni immediately loosened his *Bumbor* and laid on top of her. After some hasty efforts, including lubricating her genitalia with his spit, he inserted and glided his long-hard erection into her.

"*Ahh! een nay*: Ahh Mama!" At his initial amateurish and forceful thrust, she screamed and pushed him off.

Sensationally charged and on his knees, the spearman appeared sheepish, and apologetic.

"It's my first time," Saydah said, her voice trembling, but sounding lazy and lascivious. With her eyes on his dangling genitals, "I want us to do it. But please take your time," she pleaded.

She stretched her mouth wide open, including her eyes up at the sunny skies at the same time clawing at the surface of the rock in reaction to the pain, fear and pleasure as Kolliemenni stroked deeper into her in his frenziedly boyish manner.

The spearman himself, having stroked for a couple of minutes, an erotic ecstasy suddenly took hold of him, causing him to convulse and distraught his rhythm; he was about to have his first climax. Mid-way through, he felt he wanted to urinate and attempted to get off, but Saydeh, also feeling hers coming, grabbed him and couldn't let go. Next, they were fuming, groaning and screaming, their voices reverberating across the forest. Then it was all over.

After that episode, they lay side by side, none looking at each other, and none saying a word. But both were breathing an air of satisfaction, with Saydah, conveying the display of a dutiful woman while Kolliemenni, the pride of exhibiting an active manhood. They relaxed on that memorable rock for the rest of the day, and then parted ways.

Minutes later, Sinegar crept down from a tree, furious at what he had just witnessed. Many things have happened in these parts of the forest, while he was away on an assignment for the meeting between King Gbayou and King Kiatamba.

Fuming with rage, the hominid crept to the rock where a daughter of the Bassa people had made love to a Kpelle warrior, their sworn enemy. With his large red eyes popping and stretched, he spotted a blood smear mixed with semen on the spot where they made love, and gently dabbed it with his index finger.

He raised it in the air and studied it. Then he suddenly screeched, throwing himself on the rock, rolling all over, almost falling into the water below. An abomination has been committed; a daughter from their tribe has been impregnated by the enemy.

Saydah and Kolliemenni however continued to meet and copulated regularly. But for almost two months, she stopped coming to the water side until one day she came with a bundle on her head. Her

Shores of our Forefathers

stomach looked swollen. Kolliemenni knew right away what had happened to her and took her for the first time to his village where she has since been living with him, Nawoe his aging mother and Laynumah his junior brother.

The former spear man now stood in the animal path, figuring out what kind of trap to build to suit the size of the bush cow. Contemplating on the size of the buffalo, he disregarded setting the single stick foothold trap in which the animal leg will be caught and jerked up, or, the time-consuming body grip trap, which will ensnare the entire body of the quarry when it falls into a pit which he will have to dig, followed by a huge log which he will have to cut and suspend above the pit to fall on the animal as soon as it lands into it. Instead, he decided to build the cage-like type, in which the animal will simply enter through a trapdoor.

He sat his Kinjah on the ground, and rummaged inside for the materials needed to set the trap. After an hour and a half, he was finished. Satisfied, Yallah Kolliemenni started home, in his usual tactical manner to ensure he wasn't followed, in case an enemy might be lurking around to stalk him. He will return to inspect the trap, after 21 days. And when it catches the buffalo, he would kill it in the cage. With Laynumah's help, they would haul all the meat and have enough for more than a month.

He has reached a certain part of the bush where the low semi-deciduous trees grew among the tall evergreen ones. With his spear in one hand while his cutlass in the other, he trimmed the low branches cascading along the path on which he was walking.

A branch suddenly rattled and a dry stick, followed by smaller pieces of dry wood fell to the ground. Usually, he would stop and gather the fallen sticks for firewood, but he disregarded that, remembering that he and Laynumah had gathered enough, the previous week. So, he didn't pay attention and continued walking.

A few meters away from that spot, he suddenly held his stomach, stroking it lightly, and made a face like he was feeling the urge to defecate.

Kolliemenni swayed to his right and scooped under a low bush and pretended to ease himself. Within seconds, he sprang back out and rolled on the ground, with his spear in his hands. On his feet, he threw it with all his might high up in one of the low semi-deciduous trees, standing between two evergreen ones.

Something suddenly screeched. Blood was pouring down from the branches. Kolliemenni saw the hominid-like being holding its badly injured chest, and then struggling to climb on one of the high evergreen trees to properly camouflage itself before the Kpelle warrior strikes it again.

Before Kolliemenni could reach for his weapon and finish the creature that has been stalking him since the first time he met Saydah, Sinegar had disappeared into the high branches. Tracing the blood smear dropping on the low branches and on the ground, the spearman picked up the chase after him. It would not take long to get him, because where the hominid was heading, the semi-deciduous trees were many. That was the purpose for which he chose this part of the bush.

Frightened, Sinegar desperately jumped from branches to branches of the endless leafless trees, like a wounded primate fighting to conceal himself and safely get away or become an easy target for the

Kpelle assailant. He soon realized that he was completely exposed and trapped among the sea of semi–deciduous branches. With no way to camouflage himself, he had given up hope and clunked on a branch. The arboreal enemy scout looked down at Kolliemenni, his eyes sparking with bewilderment as the spearman positioned his javelin to strike him.

Like a sudden sign of relief, Sinegar suddenly rolled his eyes to the right, and then to the left of Kolliemeni's position. His assailant also followed them.

Before Kolliemennni could second-guess the creature-like being's sudden relief, a large net was thrown on him, the weight sending him to the ground. Despite his pain, Sinegar uttered a triumphant sound and then continued to move between the branches, his urgency no longer fearing the enemy, but for the life-threatening wound he had sustained.

Kolliemenni knew that he had been caught in the net of the enemy. The hominid was not alone. So, he quickly pulled his small hunting knife from his side to tear the net open, before the Bassa warriors who threw it on him came out of their hiding places.

Despite the sharpness of the blade, he tried to cut the robes but it couldn't. He became frightened, but he quickly managed to calm down. He was entrapped in a special kind of net the Bassa warriors use to catch their victims, and so it required a special blade to cut it. Whosoever threw such a net on him may have that kind of blade to cut loose his captive, before binding his hands or feet to take him away.

The young hunter lay on the ground and pretended like he had fainted out of the shock of being captured, killed or taken down the coast and sold as a slave. After a few minutes, a huge warrior from the Leopard society sec emerged from the bush and crept towards the net. He knelt over his catch, and hauled his knife, a long black dagger from his side to cut through to get out the strong looking Kpelle warrior.

He had pulled Kolliemenni out and signaled to the others when the cunny Kpelle spearmen launched at his neck, grabbing and securing it into a headlock. Both men remained on the ground with Kolliemenni under, wrapping his legs around the men's wrist to tighten his grip. Then he stretched his free hand for the warrior's dagger which had slipped from his hand and gently stabbed him on his left side, around the rib cage, at the same time still holding the Leopard warrior tight. He thrust the blade deep inside, until the base of the wooden handle pressed against his skin.

Yallah continued to hold onto the enemy warrior with all his might, pressing his opponent's face close to the ground to muff his screams. As blood and water oozed out of the Leopard warrior's punctured rib cage, with the blood splashing all over Kolliemenni, the dying man uttered faint groans.

Another Leopard warrior emerged from the bush to see what was taking his colleague long to remove the net and bind the unconscious enemy. But Kolliemenni caught his position through the corner of his eyes. He pushed the dead one from on top of him and rolled over for his spear. From a distance of about 30 feet, the warrior was struck on his neck, the force from the thrust, sending and smashing him against a tree. The spear bored through his neck, above his Adam's apple, and came out from the back. It had him stock on the tree. He convulsed as fresh blood drained down his chest.

With his face covered with blood, the spearman hurried to the man. With one jerk, he pulled his spear from his neck. The Leopard Warrior fell to the ground, dead. Kolliemenni looked around him, readying himself to face any one who would emerge from his hiding place. Seeing no one, which meant there were only two of them, he resumed chasing after the wounded hominid. He traced Singar's blood all the way out of the semi-deciduous part of the forest to the evergreen trees, but the enemy spy had managed to escape.

For some time, he continued to search for the wounded giant chameleon turned enemy scout, until he reached further down the rapid prone flow of the upper Farmington, but he did not see him. Disappointed that a valuable enemy had managed to escape or may be lying somewhere dying and vast information lost, Kolliemenni hurried back to his village.

He suddenly sprang under a low bush when he heard voices and what appeared like a scuffle in the distance ahead. It continued for some time and then it abated. Covering himself with leaves and branches, he chopped off to conceal himself, Kolliemenni waited as he lay flat on the ground. Soon there were footsteps of a group of people coming his way.

As they got closer, he heard the cries of women and children. It sounded like Kpelle people. Then he heard the groaning of men, also sounding familiar. As this grew closer, he slightly lifted his head to look on the path a few meters from his position.

A group of about 20 Leopard warriors passed. With their eyes sparkling with alertness, their machetes, spears and bow and arrows were drawn. Then, there they were, walking in a straight line with their hands tied behind them, his kinsmen and their families, about 25 of them, captured from their villages. They were being taken down the coast by Bassa raiding parties. The hominid had been scouting and locating all the villages around the upper Farmington.

The former spearman thought about his own village. Saydah, his mother and his little brother, Laynumah, were in danger. He waited until the slave caravan passed. Then he got up and raced towards his village. He arrived late in the evening, but unfortunately, found no one.

He dropped to his knees when he saw his mother, dead. Her eyes were stretched open and her tongue was lolling out of her mouth, indicating that she was strangled. He also saw her gashed stomach. The raiders did not take her captive because she was too old. They killed her to destroy evidence. But they took Saydah and his brother.

Kolliemenni wept for a while and then buried his mother. After that he sat on his mother's stool, his gaze at the blazing fire in the kitchen, pondering over the fate of Sadah and his brother. Then, there were the rustlings on the roof. The giant-sized Salamanders were falling to the ground and dashing across the yard. He sensed that something was not right.

He immediately grabbed his spear and raced into the kitchen. He took two blazing firewood from the health and raced back towards the hut. He threw them on the roof and waited, with his spear in striking position. The thatched roofs caught on fire and were soon blazing with the aid of the wind.

After a while, there were rumblings coming from within the roof. Then there were screams, and the smell of burned human flesh. A Leopard warrior jumped down screaming. His body was covered with thatch and it was on fire. Kolliemenni hit him with the side of his spear, sending the screaming warrior to the ground. He pressed the spear against his body to hold him on the ground so that he should burn to arches. Another two jumped from the roofs of Nawoe and Laynumah's huts. With the fire heavily blazing on them, they remained on the ground until they burned to ashes like their colleague.

The day before, Kollimenni and Layumah were out in the bush. Saydah had accompanied Nawoe down to the running creek to fetch drinking water. The Leopard warriors used that opportunity to sneak up the roof and buried themselves in to lie in wait, until midnight to conduct the raid on the village while Kolliemenni and family were asleep. Because the spearman had left early to set his trap, they remained put in case their colleagues missed him on his way back. Sineguy had warned that the Kpelle warrior was smart and elusive.

When the three huts were completely burned to the ground with three more bodies of the enemy among the ashes, Kolliemenni was sure that the enemy warriors were all dead. He saw the rooster and the hen with its four chicks coming from the bush apparently for what was left of the yummy salenders and roof bugs amongst the ashes.

He sighed with relief that the abductors did not steal Saydah's presents given to her by his mother in appreciation for her expected grandchild. He took his time to chase after them, caught and put them in two chicken coops; the hen and her chicks in one and the rooster in the other. Then he carefully hid them in the bush a few meters from the outside kitchen. Afterwards, he began the long race to the headquarters of the Kpelle people at Kakata to inform the authorities of what he had seen.

Sometimes resting, he ran all night. At dawn, he was within the vicinity of Kakata.

"Don't go on your farms, if they are very far from here," he immediately warned when he bumped into some people. "The Bassa warriors are in the bush raiding our villages and taking our people as slaves. You must turn back now."

"We know," replied a man. "Our warriors are being mustered further down the road."

Surprised, but a bit relieved, Kolliemenni nodded and then hurried past the family. It didn't take too long before he met a large group of his kinsmen jubilating and ready for battle. Walking among the horde of warriors, he made his way to where the spearmen were gathered. Seeing both the veterans and the new recruits together, he became invigorated. His people were taking the campaign very seriously; everyone was out for the battle to free their people from Sorteh Gbayou.

"Yallah Kollemenni," he heard a familiar voice from his rear. "We are happy to have you join us."

He turned around, and it was Kokulo Jawo, his long-time comrade, fully clad in his warrior attire, walking to him with open arms. Both men's fathers were town criers who later became spearmen. Due to their marathon abilities, a trait they inherited from their fathers, Kokulo and Kollemenni were among the first that were recruited by Flomo Zawolo. They fought side by side during the last days of Tokpa Gbowee and early, during his daughter Lango, reign.

"Her majesty will be happy to see you," Jawo told his friend after they embraced for a while and then gestured with his right hand to follow him.

Lango Gbowee was seated on a stool surrounded by a band of warriors. The successor of the late hawkish King was attired in a red sleeveless gown made of country cloth bedecked with cowrie shells. Her face was painted with brown chalk, making her difficult to recognize. Exposing her round and flat face, her hair was plaited all down, dog ear style. When she saw Kolliemenni, the huge and heavy bodied woman got up from the stool to meet her former spearman.

"Your Majesty and great daughter of our land. I, Yallah Kolliemenni, son of Barworor Kolliemenni, have come once more to avail myself for battle with our enemies," bowing, Kolliemenni said.

The Kpelle ruler nodded and stretched her hand. A huge warrior immediately brought a spear and gave it to her. Lying in both hands, she presented it to Kolliemenni. With both hands stretched forward, the spearman knelt down and received it.

"With your vast knowledge of these jungles, I decree that you lead the charge of the spearmen," she said. "You will be assisted by Kokulo Jawo." Then she turned to the huge warrior that brought the spear. "Take Kolliemenni and have him consecrated."

About an hour later, Yallah Kolliemenni appeared before Her Majesty the ruler, fully decked-out in his warrior outfit.

"Kolliemenni, Kolliemenni, Kolliemenni, "shouted Kokulo Jawo, brandishing his spear in the air, and immediately the other warriors repeated after him.

This continued for a while until Lango Gbowee raised her hand in the air, followed by the sound of a horn. A wave of silence spread across the thousands of warriors.

"I don't have much to say," she began. "But our actions to free our people and put an end to the Bassa King, will speak for themselves. By raiding our villages, and taking our people captives to sell to the white man, the coward has foolishly invaded a beehive, and the swans are about to unleash a venomous and devastating sting. A sting his generation and the generation after him will painfully remember, if there will be any left. I order you now to begin the onslaught to annihilate Gbayou and his people forever."

There was a large noise as the warriors shouted battle cries followed by the clattering of machetes, and the hammering of the end of the shafts of their spears on the ground. In the next moment, they were matching east, towards the upper Farmington.

Chapter 18

Clouds of dust filled the air and descended on the branches, along the dirt road leading to the off sketch of the partially inhabited settlement of Bensonville. A group of colonial militiamen, led by Major Rudolf Crayton, were galloping, with their guns raised high in the air. Their faces were partially covered with handkerchiefs to prevent the dust from entering their eyes and nose.

Minutes later, they reached an intersection where to their right, the narrow trail to Mrs. Burgess cottage, branched off from the main road. They slowed down and entered. With the heads of their horses thrusting forward in unison, they trotted along the trial. Rocking with the motion as the animals moved gently, each militiaman had his weapon pointed and ready to shoot as they surveyed the trees and into the undergrowth where hostile warriors might be lying in wait.

Major Crayton suddenly raised his rifle, bringing the party to an immediate halt. A few meters ahead was Bishop Thompson's horse with its straddle still intact. With its eyes widened, and flaring nostrils, it would occasionally stomp its hoof in the dirt. The animal may be frightened, he observed.

The militia intelligence commander got down from his horse and slowly walked to the stallion. He gently held the reins, looked back and signaled to one of his men who came trotting to him. The major handed the robes to him, and watched the militiamen tie it to his own horse and then trotted back into formation. After that, they resumed trotting.

15 minutes afterwards, just upon reaching the entrance of Angela Burgess' yard, the bishop's horse suddenly neighed and jerked, startling the troops. Major Crayton raised his rifle again, another time stopping the party.

"From this point, we continue on foot," he informed his men, when he got down from his horse. "But remember one thing. Lately there have been several indigenous attempts on our settlements. The bishop and his daughter along with corporal Gray and Vincent, and a guest to the colony may be abducted by indigenous warriors when they came here. And these warriors may still be around. Keep your ears sharp and your eyes open."

The militia men got down from their horses. Ducking, they encircled the yard when they got near the gate. With their rifles pointed, they took careful steps as they advanced towards the cottage. The first thing the colonial intelligence officer saw was the coach, still turned upside down. He motioned to two of his men, who cautiously circled around the coach to inspect it.

"Nobody's here, sir," surveying the deserted yard, Private Derick Hart, one of the men, informed.

"Okay everyone. Let's look around for anything that may be a clue of what happened here," instructed Major Crayton. "And don't touch anything when you see it. Just call me. Do not get near a spider web if you see any; it could be an indigenous bobby-trap sprayed with venom, whose smell causes blindness and death in a matter of seconds." One of the men saw Goldman's dagger on the ground, covered with dust. "I repeat. Don't get near or touch anything unusual. The owner of this cottage is a witch." Frightened, the man suddenly swayed away from the knife.

To the right of the picket fence, Major Crayton noticed that some planks were missing, and suspected that they were removed by the warriors who sneaked into the yard, especially when he saw the pieces lying on the ground. Getting closer, he saw the prints of what looked like wild dogs. Startled, he suddenly gapped, struggling to suppress his reaction so that his men should not notice him and be frightened.

The shredded coat of Dean Goldman, smeared with blood and traces of human organs was lying a few meters behind the open space of the fence. Right away, he deduced that Goldman was dead, eaten alive by wild animals.

"Over here, Major," Private Derick Hart suddenly called, his voice chilly and apprehensive.

The major hurried to the left side of the entrance of the yard, a few meters into the surrounding bush.

"Bishop Thompson," breathed the young colonial militia, when his commander joined him.

Under a tree, lie the body of Bishop Thompson, completely deformed and decayed. They could only recognize it by his Cossack and his cross still in his hands.

Major Crayton looked at Derrick, and nodded with an expression, appreciating the young Private for only notifying him, or else it could have frightened the other men.

"Get the medics here, right now," he ordered. "At least they are used to seeing such a horrible thing like this."

Derick hurried for the two medics and came back with two older militiamen. "Wrap him up, and then the other one near the fence at the left side of the yard in separate cloth. Derick, you stay with them to prevent any of our men from getting close."

The Major came back in the yard and made his way to the back of the Cottage.

"Jesus," he whimpered, seeing the Voodoo shrine and the doll of Mrs. Thompson. Mrs. Burgess is indeed a witch, he thought, and looked back towards her door which was open. "She killed the bishop and his wife. She may have fled, and probably joined ranks with the hostile ruler, King Sorteh Gbayou."

At high speed, soon five militiamen came galloping in the yard. One of the men, a young corporal named Harmon Walker immediately got down and asked for the Major.

"A word from Governor Butler, sir," he said, handing the Major a piece of note he took from his uniform pocket.

"Santa Amelia has arrived!" The note read.

"Our medics are all set, Major," Derrick interrupted while Major Crayton was digesting the message.

"Okay, boys. Let's saddle up."

In the bush, about a few meters away from the entrance gate, half of a figure was standing behind a large tree, its white painted face was watching Major Crayton and his men as they saddled their horses and were about to ride out of the yard. Then it stepped from behind the tree, exposing itself. It was the lead Blunjue.

"Marpue," she called, and Emily Thompson, in her full Blunjue attire, now with her hair shaded, also stepped from behind the tree, as the rest of them followed suit.

Weeping, her eyes were red and teary, watching the two medics wrapping her father's corpse, and then strapping it to the back of his horse. She opened her mouth to scream and attempted to jump out of the bush to run and hold onto her father's body to cry more loudly, but she was prevented by the lead Blunjue, at the same time covering her mouth with her hand.

"This is not the way of the Blunjue," holding her hand, the older Blunjue said, calmly. "You are part of us now. We are trained to master the virtues of womanhood. To endure as with enduring labor pain. To bear the sting when a husband, or a child dies. To exert the courage to accept a new wife in the home. To cope with hardships when they do come as it is the mandate to stand with your husband, and never abandon the home. We must always be prepared to see the good things the world brings as well as the evil it dispenses. Our strength as Blunjues is to look at evil as natural and face it. We must see and yet determine how we view what we see."

As she spoke, Emily stood, convulsing, weeping little by little, and finally stopped sobbing. To her disbelief, she had taken control of herself. Just how she witnessed Dean Goldman smoking his pipe, regardless of being in the snare of the witch, and the excruciating pain she inflicted on him, he was calmed, and courageous to look in her eyes.

"Now tell me. What are you seeing now?" asked the lead Blunjue.

The settler turned Blunjue took a deep breath when the horse, carrying the corpse of her father and what was left of Dean Goldman's, rode past them.

"I no longer see the mutilated body of my father," she answered. "All I am now seeing are bundles of firewood on the back of a house."

"You are now learning the ways of a Blunjue," the lead Blunjue smiled.

Leading the rest of the troop, they came out of the bush and walked into the yard. Emily stood, still calmed and composed, as the others searched the place. Then she saw Goldman's dagger. She took and concealed it under the shisha skirt she was wearing.

"I know where the bad men took your friends," the older Blunjue came to her and said in a comforting tone. "Come let's go."

A day after the Santa Amelia arrived, Garsuah Togar, aka Abraham Garsuah had successfully paddled out of the middle eastern part of the Du River. With only two days to connect to the Junk River, and then the Farmington to reach the territory of King Gbayou, he entered a narrow creek, an offshoot of the Du, in the forest of Garmaymu village to commence the twenty minutes course for the middle Junk River. This time, his distance was a little longer than previous journeys, because settlers' spies have recently stepped up their patrols along these bushes.

Moreover, his friend, and market mate, Zoegar had been observing him suspiciously since the last time he conveyed the hostile Bassa King's message. But with his unmatched knowledge of this locality, the route he was now using was the best option to evade them. Feeling relaxed and satisfied, he landed his canoe at a clearing, hauled it partially out of the water and disembarked. He first grabbed his cutlass and then a bamboo basket.

The variety of palm trees spread across this vast land, produced juicy palm nuts. Because it was uninhabited, and many hunters did not frequent this part of the forest, the trees would bear to the extent that over ripe palm nuts dropped to the ground. To Abrahan Garsuah's delight when he first discovered this place, luscious opossums, in their numbers, were scurrying for the nuts. That day he managed to kill only one by knocking a stick on its head while the others ran into their dens. Since then, whenever he came this way, he had been setting small traps and catching many.

With time still in his favor, he swaggered along the 20 minutes partially covered path, he himself made, to the palm trees to check on his traps he set, the last time he came here. Even though it had taken a little while, and some of the rodents caught in the traps may have died and decayed, there was a possibility that some caught in his other traps could still be alive. Just as he expected, but with a little surprise, he got there and having inspected his traps, he was able to find four large ones, caught, but still alive.

He realized that they may have been feeding on the palm nuts, because the twine he used to set the foot trap was long enough, allowing the forest rats to roam some distances. With his cutlass, Garsuah chopped them on their heads. Then he loosened the dead rodents and put them in his basket, glossing over the thought of a nice fufu and soup Wlaymar, his friend and stranger's mother, will prepare later that evening.

Garsuah Togar returned to his canoe and put the basket and his cutlass in it. He was about to push it back into the water, but froze.

"*Gulay ay, ne mba:* Good afternoon my friend," coming from his rear, greeted a masculine and confident voice in Bassa.

"*Hay ne mba, na gee*? Hey my friend. Good evening," pretending to conceal his astonishment, he turned and responded to a muscular man, standing with his arms folded.

The man who greeted him was wearing short pants with a sleeveless shirt, V-neck style. It was made of country cloth, stopping above his naval.

"*Deh ne sor keh*? Where are you from?" The man, Gaye Geezy, observing a line of consternation appearing on Garsuah's face, asked.

"*Ne sor lay Garmaymu*: I am from Garmaymu," he responded, becoming more baffled, as the question simply meant that the man was probably a settler spy. How in God's name did he find this place?

When the settler spy remained silent and glared at him suspiciously, "As you can see, I came to check on my traps and I am on my way back," he explained, reaching first for his cutlass and then the basket to show to Gaye.

"I have been in that village for three days now, but did not see anybody like you there?"

"Well," Abraham Garsuah swallowed, figuring out what explanation to offer, at the same time putting only the bamboo basket back in the canoe. He was now pondering on the possibility of a physical confrontation, a thing he had always prepared for. "I am actually from *Dubor*, and returning to my village to see my people. But why all these questions? Let me be on my way to my other traps. It's getting late. Maybe you can stop by my family house. My grandmother will prepare a nice opossum soup."

"It is because you are lying. We know that you are Gbayou's informant. You are on your way to him to deliver the white man's message."

Fully aware that he had been made, Abraham Garsuah immediately pointed his cutlass at Gaye.

"Leave me be, or I kill you right now," he warned, his voice full of desperation.

"*Oh! Mon kay von?*' Oh! you want to fight now?" asked Geezy, unfolding his hands and walking to Garsuah.

"Only if you stop that kind of lie," the informant replied evasively. He turned to haul his canoe in the water when Gaye Geezy stopped.

Climbing in, he was again startled to see two other canoes with two men in each, coming towards him.

"*Hey Jou guy. Deh ne mu er keh:* Hey you there, where do you think you're going?" one of the men in the lead canoe, demanded.

He immediately sensed that he was in a serious predicament. With his cutlass raised, he turned to Gaye Geezy and charged at him. His goal was to get the muscular man out of his way with a single and decisive strike on his head. And while he was lying on the ground, bleeding and fighting for his life, he would escape into the bush before the men in the canoes reached the shore.

Unfortunately, the wrestling champion was upon him, grabbing his hand before he could strike. Both men were soon engaged in a scrimmage, with Gaye Geezy still holding the hand with the cutlass, and sometimes swinging Garsuah around. A thorny tree, about 4 1/2 yards stood at his opponent's rear. Careful not to allow Garsuah to see it and guess his intentions, he used his strength to shove him towards the tree.

He thrust Abraham Garsuah against the thorny tree trunk, the impact causing the sharp thorns to piece his back with some of them breaking off. But he pretended like it was nothing. Not allowing his opponent some breathing space, Geezy pressed him harder against the tree, whilst repeatedly smashing the hand with the cutlass, and rubbing it against the thorny tree trunk, causing them to bore into the flesh and veins at the back of his hands.

Abraham Garsuah was forced to drop the cutlass. But as an expert wrestler himself, he right away went for his opponent's testes to grab and squeeze them with all his might. Sensing this, Geezy thrust himself backwards, increasing the length and making it impossible for Garsuah's hands to reach his Scrotum.

For a moment, the scuffle was focused on both accomplishing a specific objective. Knowing very well it is the weakest spot of even the strongest, the cunning informant's aim was to grab the strong man's nuts and squeeze the hell out of his testis, while Geezy was preventing that from happening.

Garsuah felt a nasty left knee under his cheek, rattling his teeth and causing a bruise on his upper lips. He groaned, but in a controllable manner, feigning that it meant nothing, and it would not deter him from accomplishing his objective.

There was another groan, this time a little louder than the first, when the settlers' spy gave him another one, which landed between his upper lip and his nostrils, splattering fresh blood. While Garsuah Togar wrestled with the pain in his nose and mouth at the same time trying to mentally assess the level of bruise he had sustained, Geezy gave him a bear hug. His groans became clearly audible, as Geezy squeezed his ribcage with his large and powerful arms, causing Garsuah to gasp for air.

Twice, he tried to head-butt his adversary, but each time the canoe maker would dodged by tilting his head backwards. Gaye Geezy suddenly swayed sideways, reaching his left hand between Garsuhl Togar's legs at the same time his right hand around his neck. The informant was instantly lifted and raised high in the air and slammed to the ground with a large thud. Gaye Geezy quickly gained central ground control by sitting on Garsuah's chest, his heavy torso pinning and preventing him from breathing properly. He was pressing both knees on Garsuah's arms, at the areas around the elbows.

"*Mber-lay von. Eh?* You know how to fight. Eh?" Gaye Geezay said, giving Abraham Guasuah some solid ground poundings.

By then, the men in the canoe arrived and jumped out. Garsuah Togar was pulled from the ground and made to stand up with two of the men holding his hands. He uttered a loud cry when Geezy gave him a back heel step in his groin. "*Ne mon-lay von*? You still want to fight?" He asked, again.

"Garsuah Togar," he then heard a familiar voice.

With blood oozing from his mouth, he raised his head. He was surprised and frightened to see his friend and fellow fish seller, Zoegar.

"Search in the small bag attached to his wrist. The thing the white man always gives him to take to King Gbayou will be inside."

"Tie and let's take him to King Gray," Gaye Geezy ordered when he pulled the small raffia bag from Garsuah's wrist, looked inside and found Captain Gomez's pin.

"*Ay ne mbar. Mon Bassor yon o*, Ay my fellow kinsmen. I am a Bassa man o," Garsuah Togar cried as the settlers' spies bound his hands and feet and shoved him into the canoe.

Chapter 19

Yallah Kolliemenni had led his men along the banks of the upper Farmington, almost three days' walk south from where he first met Saydah. After several hours of combing the surrounding forest, they reached a place at the edge of the river. There were rapids downstream with rocks jutting above the surface. Having observed, with his eyes sparkling and alert, how the rocks were spread out in a sequence of intervals, especially the ones in the middle of the flow, he raised his spear in the air and the massive Kpelle warriors immediately came to a halt.

"This is where we cross," he said, turning to Kokulo Jarwoe who was standing behind him. "This place seems ideal to construct the monkey bridges," he continued, as he deduced the distance and formation of the tree lines on their side of the banks and the ones directly across the river.

"Shall we now assemble the bridge builders?"

"Yes," he initially agreed, but suddenly exclaimed, when something flashed in his memory. "No! Not now, Jarwoe!" With lines of consternation forming across his forehead, he explained. "This spot looks too ideal to be real and suitable to lay the bridges. This river bed may be full of neengins with some of them hiding in water holes underneath those patterns of rocks you see leading to the middle of the river. Any attempt to let our bridge builders swim across, will be disastrous."

"I see," Kokulo Jarwoe's eyes suddenly brightened, as he glared at the rocks. "The formation of the rocks seem pre-arranged and the intervals appear to be at equal distance which can lure anyone to swim towards them and rest, and be snatched under, before thinking about swimming to the other side. This particular formation looks different from the other ones we have seen in other parts of the flow."

"Which means, some of the bravest warriors with swimming abilities will have to swim to those rocks and try to fight the neengins out of the waterholes, if they encounter any, to clear the way for our bridge builders to swim across the river and begin the construction. But I fear that we will lose most of them in that process."

"The *Tallers* can take care of that, Kolliemenni," Jarwoe said, beaming.

"The *Tallers*?" Kolliemenni asked, clueless.

Kokulo Jarwoe smiled. "They are a special surprise package Lango Gbowee has for the Bassa King. Watch and see what they will do," he explained.

He then signaled to a warrior who was watching them from a distance behind a tree overlooking the river. The warrior looked behind him and uttered a squishing sound. Few seconds later, a group of about 50 warriors, in groups of four, were toting long wooden poles shaped like cones, towards the river banks.

Amazed, Kolliemenni watched how in less than a minute, the men assembled the poles which laid about a hundred feet on the ground. Then their comrades helped them to insert their legs into the poles. When that was completed, each man was given two long spears of about the same length as the hollow poles and was lifted back on his feet. Soon what looked like a company of *Gio-devils* holding and balancing themselves with the long spears stood before the river.

They formed straight lines. After that, they were braced together by strips of reeds attached to their left and right and tied together with strong robes. Then there was another group of fifty of these men hurrying to the river banks carrying the same poles, and assembling them. In about thirty minutes, facing the river, was a formation of 150 Tallers, forming three columns with an interval of five feet apart.

"The Tallers are ready," Kokulo Jarwoe turned to Kolliemenni. "It is now your call."

"You have been preparing for this, Kokulo. It's supposed to be your call."

Kokulo nodded and signaled to the lead Taller at the first column to the left. Like giant centipedes, the columns stepped into the water, one after the other. When they were a few meters from the banks, forming a straight line from the left to the right, another group of warriors with about six inches long catapults hanging around their necks, raced towards the banks.

"They are the backers for the Tallers. Each of them are expert bird hunters with the ability to aim at a height of 100 feet. They were trained to convert that into an aim of equal ground distance," Koluko Jarwoe informed Kolliemenni.

Each Taller backer removed the catapult from around his neck, and took smooth pebbles from a small sac around his waist. Then, they dipped the stone in a dark liquid, poured from a small calabash on the other side of their waists, and inserted the stone into the pouch. They stretched the bands at chest length, and were ready to strike at anything that would jump out of the water.

"Whose idea is this?" impressed, Yallah Kolliemenni inquired.

"Lango Gbowee herself. A few months ago, she visited Nyenla Suah, the powerful daughter of Menepakai Suah, the aging ruler in central Kpelle land on the occasion of the ceremony when the king announced her as his successor. Also invited was King Gunganu of Gompa, a close friend of Nyenla. The Mano king brought along his tall mask dancers to perform at the ceremony. Reflecting on the challenges our warriors faced when crossing the Farmington in pursuit of our enemies during the campaign of her father, that was how our ruler brainchild the idea of using the craftsmanship of dancing on long sticks into military use."

"So, the Mano king agreed to share such splendid craftsmanship with us?"

"Yes. Nyenla Suah has a great deal of influence over him. In their plans to protect all Kpelle lands, Nyenla made the proposal on our wise leader's behalf, and Gunganu agreed."

By now, the columns of Tallers were deep into the flow. The current was surprisingly gentle which to Kolliemenni, was artificial. Experienced swimmers would turn back when approaching the middle of a river if they notice that the current is dangerously rough. Because of this, the Neegins have devised means to control and lessen the water current to lure their targets to continue swimming to the middle where it would be too late to turn back when one finds himself in the middle of a dangerous current. Then, they would strike, snatching their victims from underneath.

For every step the Tallers took, they would juke the pointed edge of the spears into the river bed along their path and around them to pierce anything that would be underneath. When they got near a rock, they would tap the surface and juked around it to make sure that it was not a trap. They all became alerted at the first sign of blood oozing from under the water. A partially naked body with face painted white, emerged and was floating down stream. In the next moment, the water surface became bloody, and more bodies were floating.

"It is working!" exclaimed Kolliemenni. "We need to stop the bodies from floating down so that this does not alert our enemies. Remember we want to surprise them."

"We also had that in mind," assured Kokulo Jarwoe.

At that moment, another group of warriors raced further down the banks. They were carrying large fish hooks fashioned out of bones, attached to long robes. As soon as they reached the edge of the river, each swung the hooks a number of times, and threw them into the water. The floating corpses were hooked from their rib cages and necks and pulled out of the water.

The column of Tallers reached the middle of the water, where the current as Kolliemenni expected, began to increase, but not strong enough to sway the leg-like poles as they slouched through the water. Thanks to the reed strips that were bracing them together and the spears, anchoring deep in the river bed.

The lead Taller reached the first rock and tapped it on its side. It suddenly sank. Like dolphins, four neengins, with cutlasses in their hands, jumped out of the water in an attempt to cut down his pair of leg-poles, so that he would fall and then his entire column. But they were struck on their foreheads by the pebbles propelled by the catapult units. This caused bruises which allowed the flowing into their blood streams, the toxic venom from the dark liquid the stones were dipped in. It paralyzed the neengins, instantly. Within seconds, they were dropping back into the water, dead.

"The stones are poisoned with the vernon secreted from cassava snakes.

After several attempts on the other columns, scores of Neegins sneaking out from underneath the rocks were floating motionless. As their bodies drifted downstream, the men with the fishhooks pulled them out of the water.

"It's time we send the first batch of bridge builders," ordered Kolliemenni when the lead column eventually crossed the river.

As Kolliemenni and Jarwoe watched the last two columns in the water providing a protective corridor for the bridge builders, the first team of ten builders, with ropes tied around their waists, swam across.

Coordinating with their colleagues on the other side of the river, they immediately began with the construction of a monkey bridge.

Within two hours, the first Monkey Bridge was built and hoisted over the middle upper Farmington. Now gaining complete control of the river, the first batch of Kpelle warriors crossed over the bridge. An hour later, a massive assembly of warriors were concentrated on the other side.

The second bridge was constructed further down the flow allowing other groups of warriors to cross. Now approaching the early evening hours, Kolliemenni and Kokulo Jarwoe were among the last group that crossed, using the first bridge.

"We are now in the territory of the enemy. It is guarded by Gbayou's Leopard warriors. We must rest quietly tonight. At dawn, we will call in the Coo," hissed Kolliemenni.

Just after midnight, the Coo, comprising a large group of men, specialized in slice, burn and felling of trees with less time, had encircled a large portion of the forest, believed to be where the Leopard warriors were lying in wait. Within minutes, they were clearing the bushes with axes and cutlasses which blades their blacksmiths designed with noise muffs.

Other groups of Kollimmenni's men formed two layers of circles around the Coo. The first were armed with machetes and diamond-shaped shields while the second comprised the archers.

When day broke, the Leopard warriors guarding the western flank of the Farmington were taken unaware of the clearing of huge acres of forest that shielded them. Only the potion where they were concentrated, remained.

A group of them were borrowing under the roots of large trees while some were positioned on the branches monitoring the advancing Keplle warriors. Realizing that they were being encircled, they immediately came out and charged at some members of the coo who were advancing closer to them. They retreated as the enemy pursued. Unfortunately, the Leopard warriors were lured into the ambush of the first line of the circle, comprising the men with the machetes and shields, who were hiding under the chop off branches.

There was a clash as the men from both sides fought. Heads and arms were chopped off as blood splattered on the faces of brave Kpelle warriors. Within minutes, the Leopard warriors were dead. Overwhelmed, some of their enemies however managed to retreat and were running back, but they were struck by the arrows of the Kpelle archers, holding the second circle.

At the last portion encircled by the Coo, the battle was tough, lasting several hours. 50 of them, attempting to narrow the circle from all sides, lay dead in a pool of blood with about half that number wounded when the Leopard warriors sneaked out and slew them.

"They are using guerilla tactics to hold their last line," breathed Yallah Kolliemenni, himself smeared with the blood of his wounded men he had to drag to safety.

"It seems to be the best of their men, remaining at that last portion," observed Kokulo Jarwoe.

"Order the *coo* to halt their advances. And the rest of the circle must pull back. It's time we send it the *Nyagois*".

For a while, military activities around the perimeter of the last remaining portion was halted. The Leopard warriors who had successfully held the advancing enemy back, sensed that they may be retreating, but they were not enough to pick up the chase after them. Most of their men have been killed.

One of them, perfectly camouflaged, lying flat on the leafy branch of a tree, became alert when he saw below him a group of about 6 young men, wandering into their territory. They looked in their teens. Hanging across their backs were bags with tools inside.

Having keenly observed the young men, who appeared lost and were trying to find their way back to their units, he deduced that they were the ones directly behind the men who were cutting the bush. Their role was sharpening the tools the *coo* was using to slice their way into their territory.

He quickly signaled to his comrades, lying in similar manner on other branches. A huge net was thrown on the youth, and they were immediately captured. They would be subsequently interrogated to disclose the position of their men.

As the young men were attempting to disentangle themselves, about ten Leopard warriors, attired in their outfits made of Leopard skins covering their bodies and wearing face masks designed like the animals', climbed down from the branches, and surrounded the captives. The others watched as one of them cut the net and pulled out one of the captives. Three of his colleagues joined him to hold him on the ground on his back. Like how the apostle Andrew was laid on the X cross, they stretched his legs and hands.

Holding a spear whose head was shaped like a Manual Post Hole Digger, one of them stood over the frightened captive. Like a mortar pestle, he raised it in the air to thrust it down into the young man's chest to pluck out his heart so that his colleagues can see that they mean business when it comes to extracting information.

Before he could land the digger, he suddenly cried out loud and dropped his weapon. With his eyes stretched, he watched the tip of a spear thrusting about 18 inches out of his chest. His colleagues realized that it was a spear of an enemy, but it was rather too late. Kolliemenni, Kokulo Jarwoe and a group of their men emerged from the undergrowth and attacked them. A scuffle ensued.

In the next couple of minutes, the Leopard warriors were reduced to one who was engaged in hand-to-hand combat with a Kpelle warrior. Both were locked into a stale-mate as they unsuccessfully tried to tackle each other, physically.

Eventually, Keleku Kermue, a hairy warrior overpowered his opponent and slimed him to the ground. Immediately, Kokulo and another warrior stepped on both of his hands, when Keleku Kermue laid on top of him and held them stretched on the ground. The warrior screamed when both men thrust their spears in his palms while another two held onto his legs.

The frightened enemy warrior watched how Kolliemenni scoop over the captured youths, pulled the special black blade from his side and cut through the nets to get them out.

"You have done a great job," he told them, smiling.

With awe the man realized that he had been tricked, when he saw that the boys who he thought were lost, smiled at him. They were not just the ones who were sharpening the cutlasses and the ax used by the Coo. They were the *Nyagois*. With their frail and innocent looks, they were a group, specialized to lure the enemy out of their hiding places. With their popping and sharp eyesight which earned them the name *Nyagoi*, they have the ability to operate in the dark to spot the enemy's location.

As he remained pinned to the ground, an old man, wearing a *bomber* with his body painted with white chalk like a fetish priest, was accompanied by two warriors. He squatted down at the warrior, and took from a bag hanging across a chest a folded leaf and opened it. He took a black paste and robbed it from under the warrior's eyes down to his chest. Then he gently pulled out a huge black scorpion from the bag and laid it on the men's chest.

"Now tell us where and how you Leopard warriors hide yourselves or else, the scorpion will do the following to you: 1. It will crawl on your chest and leave an acidic substance in its tracks that will cause an everlasting sore. 2. It will crawl over your face, sting your eyes, and release a very painful venom which will make you blind. And 3 the venom will continue to the back of your head and cause an everlasting headache," warned Kolliemenni, speaking the little of the Bassa dialect he learned from Saydah.

Within minutes, the Kpelle warriors had bulldozed their way into the remaining encircled portion, seeking out from their hideouts, the formidable Leopard warriors who were posing problems for them. In a brief bloody battle, Kolliemenni and his men slaughtered many of them.

However, some managed to escape by sneaking out of the hollow of tree trunks or beneath the roots cleverly made into dens which were going to be difficult to spot had it not been for the information extracted from their captured comrade. Expecting this, the Kpelle spearmen chased after them and struck them down, one by one.

One Leopard warrior, protected by his comrades who were sacrificing themselves by standing in the way of every spear to prevent the Kpelle javelins from striking him, was sprinting and leaping, covering a distance of about a quarter of a mile.

"Kpelemou! That warrior has seen how we fight! Make sure he doesn't get away or our tactics will be compromised!" screamed Kolliemenni.

The fetish priest nodded, and quickly took a two-inch cup made from the dry stem of a reed. He uncapped it and immediately a black and yellow *Vonvon* flew out and hovered around his head. Kpelemou rubbed off a portion of the yellow chalk from the face of a dead Leopard warrior with the tip of his index finger and raised his hand slightly above his head. The beetle landed on the tip of his finger.

While it buried its face into the yellow chalk, Kpelemou inserted a tiny piece of bamboo stick into its abdomen and gently blew the insert off. As he chanted, with an unimaginable speed, the high-flying bug flew into the direction the Leopard warrior ran.

Wee Gongar, the Leopard warrior who managed to escape, had run for hours. It was now early in the evening. Due to his incredible knowledge of the forest, he had successfully evaded the enemy's pursuit. As a member of a special group of their sect, he was trained to observe the enemy's tactics and whenever they were overwhelmed, he would escape with the valuable information to be used by the hierarchy of their battle planners to devise countermeasures.

There were only five in the group that were guarding the portion that the Kpelle had cleverly infiltrated. Four of his comrades were killed. Three of whom, severely wounded, had to sacrifice themselves to allow him to escape. The enemy spearmen pursuing him had to slow down to pull their spears from his dead colleagues. By the time they resumed their chase, he had gained more distance.

He was now exhausted because he had to burn more energy to outrun his pursuers, who themselves were the best runners of their sect. So, he needed to find a suitable place to hide and rest, mindful not to do so in ways already disclosed to the enemy.

A large contingent of his men were concentrated at a village further south, and it will take a day's run to get there to inform them that the defensive lines both at the upper Farmington and the territory to the west had been breached. The Kpelle are matching down south with a huge and organized army, and massive reinforcements are needed. Because he had seen how they fight, he would be best suited to lead the counteroffenssive to halt the enemy and push them back across the river.

Wee Gongar ran on top of a hill covered with a low bush and tall grass. Convinced that the enemy will not be aware of such a hiding place, he used his Post Hole Digger spear to dig a hole between and under the tall grass, making sure that none is removed. He was about to creep in under the grass and cover himself with the dirt in such a way that he would not suffocate, he felt like a mosquito bite on the left side of his neck.

He rubbed the area just at the same time a *Vonvon* flew off. Obviously, it was just an insect bite, but just when it occurred to him that a *Vonvon* does not sting, he was alarmed and suddenly became dizzy and fell off.

Early the next morning, he was awakened by the humming of an insect hovering around his ears and nose. When he opened his eyes, it was the same *Vonvon* that stung him. Terrified that he did not find himself in his hiding place, he immediately sprang to his feet, but soon realized that he was surrounded by the enemy.

"Did you sleep well?" smirked Yallah Kolliemenni, the tip of his spear pointing at Wee Gongar's vocal cord. "But the choice is yours to sleep forever, if you don't tell us what we want to know."

"*Ne mein, yo, ne mein, yo, ne mein, yo,* :I am dying, o, I am dying, o, I am dying, o," breathing little by little, Sinegar grunted as he lie on a mat, his eyes stretched wide open, looking straight in the arctic of an open thatched kitchen at the Fetish Priest corner on the out sketch of the King's quarter.

The wound caused by Kolliemenni's spear was severe and life-threatening. Wheigar, a herbalist and Fetish Priest, specialized in treating the wounds of warriors from the battlefield, was carefully examining it.

Furious, King Sorteh Gbayou paced up and down the thatched kitchen with his hands folded behind him. In the middle of executing his slave hunting campaign, his principal asset who had mapped out all the remote Kpelle villages along the upper Farmington that has so far provided his men the opportunity to raid about half of them, was dying. The triumph of successfully snatching about a 100 of his enemies was aborted when the hominid was brought before him, fatally wounded.

"Ne jelay de ne njay gee, ne doyon won gee, ne mlana won de cone yon: My eyes can't see but my ears can hear and my nose can smell the power of my herbs," Wheigar, considered the best in Bassa land, repeatedly chanted as he prepared his most trusted herbs to administer to the hominid.

He was a slim old man who as an infant, refused breast milk, preferring rice pudding instead. His hair was reddish brown and picky. His vision was blurry, because his milky-cloudy eyes were full of cataracts. His name meant 'dead body" in the Bassa language. When he was a 3 weeks old infant, it was thought that he died for about 3 hours, because he was suffocated by a handful of red rice pudding his mother was hand feeding him.

The king's face sank with grief when Wheigar squinted, and sadly shook his head; indeed Sinegar, having served his father for many years, and now him, was dying.

While Sorteh Gbayou was reflecting on the circumstances surrounding Sinegar's birth, and how he was useful in the second war with Tokpa Gbowee, at the time the young Gbaryou was a brave warrior fighting alongside his father to slow down the vicious Kpelle ruler's onslaught, he was interrupted by the sound of the Doo-doo bird. The Santa Amelia was anchored at sea and Captain Edwardo Gomez and his men were now rowing into the mouth of the Farmington to collect another consignment of slaves.

"Bring him along," he ordered the Fetish Priest. "Before he dies, let him see the fruit of his labor."

Accompanied by his men from the Leopard warriors sect, the king was escorted to his slave trading center. Sinegar, still grunting but now faintly, due to the effect of a concoction administered by Wheigar, was carried in a small hammock, hoisted on the shoulders of two of the Fetish Priest acolytes, dressed in sisal skirts with their upper arms tied with fresh palm thatches and their bodies dotted with white chalk.

At the slave trading post, the king descended his shoulder-carried carrier and strode between the rows of bamboo made cages where the Kpelle, abducted from their farm villages, were kept. The men, with their feet and legs tied with strong robes, were separated from the women and children. Also, the pregnant women were separated from the rest of the women while the elderly and the aging, who did not die along the way, were removed from among them and slaughtered. They were too old to be sold as slaves.

Sinegar suddenly screeched like a frightened young primate, at the same time pointing his tiny index finger at Saydah when the king stopped in front of the cage where they held the pregnant abductees. Mourning her mother-in-law, she was sitting on the floor weeping and lamenting in Bassa.

"So you are that traitor who betrayed your own people," inquired the king when he got closer to the cage. His eyes were full of fury, staring at Saydah's stomach. "Because of your foolish actions, the man who put that abominable thing into your stomach has harmed someone I love dearly. Where are you from?"

Sitting on the ground with her head bowed, Saydah lifted it up a little to look at the king.

"I am Saydah, from a village about five days walk northwest from here. I lived with my parents but they sent me away when I refused to disclose the owner of my pregnancy," she said and then got up, walked to the cage, and held it with both hands like a prisoner behind bars appealing to her arresting officer. "I am not a traitor. At my age, I know neither of your enemy nor your wars. The man responsible for this pregnancy and I share a love and happiness beyond the animosity of our respective tribes. Our example could be a symbol of peace and co-existence between our two peoples. O king. See this as a way out of this conflict."

"How dare you to lecture me about peace and happiness?!" snarled the King, stepping away from the cage as Sinegar screeched more deafeningly. Saydah's statement has increased his temperament and caused his wound to hurt him more.

"Your love and happiness is a daydream whose end will be your death." Then he turned to the Fetish Priest who was now dabbing Sinegar's chest wound with some herbal potion because it had worsened due to his continual screams. "Weigar. By the time I conclude my business with the white man, I want you to grate that abominable fetus from her womb, and let her feel the pain Sinegar is feeling, and she must watch it pounded into a mortar." The King instructed and then turned to the men guarding the cages. "Separate her from the rest." And then added with a strong warning. "Let this be a lesson to your sisters and daughters."

While the men were removing Saydah from the cage, one of the King's lieutenants came rushing to him.

"We have a visitor with the son of King Gray as a captive, and a man who looks like a settler," the man breathed, excitedly.

Surprised, the king hurried to his court where he always receives his guests and sat on his throne. The news of the kidnapping of King Gray's son was good. He hoped that he must be the one who is a settler militia.

As he sat on his throne, he watched from the direction from the west, the caravan of a strange woman riding on a horseback. And there he was, Levi Gardea Gray, whose description matched the information provided to him by his spies. With his hand tied behind him, he was guarded by two warriors.

"Where is Garsuah Togar? He should be here by now," The king asked, minutes after the caravan with Angela Draper Burgess reached the platform and stopped.

"He has not yet arrived," replied his Lieutenant. "King Gray's men are patrolling along the Du and Jink Rivers, compelling Togar to take a longer route to get here."

"Oh! The white man is within sight along with Vuyougar," The king said, looking in the distance down the river as the Portuguese rowed closer to the banks. "Let our guest have her seat," gestured the king, opening both hands in a welcoming manner, his eyes beaming at the most beautiful woman he had ever seen. "Bring her two captives forward and let them kneel before me," he instructed as Mrs. Burgess, assisted by two of the warriors who were accompanying her, climbed down from the horse. "How dare you follow your father's advice to join the evil army to kill your own people," he then addressed Levi Gardea Gray. "I will return your head to him as a reward for siding with the settlers."

"O King, the most powerful in all Bassa land, here comes our stranger," the head of his elder suddenly announced when Captain Edwardo Gomez and his entourage, including Cho Vuyougar appeared before him and bowed.

"You are welcomed my friend," said the king. Then he looked towards the bamboo cages. "As you can see, we have more than enough of the specimens of slaves you have requested. "I also have an important guess from the side of our enemies, who wish to share a proposal with me. While our men inspect the captives, Vuyougar will interpret what she got to say"

Captain Gormez bowed slightly to the king, struggling to wrestle with the concern appearing on his face.

"The king forgot to return my pin, as it is with the protocol," he whispered to Witty Peter.

"Oh! Great King of our land," the interpreter bowed. "Our stranger requests his pin."

"Oh yes. Togar is still on his way, as you may be aware, King Gray's men have stepped up their patrols in the forest north of his territory. He is just a bit careful."

Gormez nodded when Vuyougar relayed the King's response.

Isso não parece certo This doesn't seem right," on their way to inspect the captives, he whispered to one of his men in Portuguese. "Ready our big guns and tell the men to bring the King's mechanize. We must load the cargo into the boats at once and hurry the hell out of here."

"Our enemies, the settlers, seek to exterminate this woman because she has constantly warned them about their ill-treatment of our people," Witty Peter interpreted to the King as Angela Draper Burgess spoke. "She has come asking for protection in exchange for the son of King Gray. She has great knowledge of the strength and weakness of her people which she has offered to share."

"She has presented her case well," King Gbayou responded, after consulting with his council of elders. "So, it's a deal, provided she remains a valuable asset to our cause."

"All hail to you, O wise King for understanding the significance of this deal," proclaimed Mrs. Burgess, her voice taking the Bassa King and his subject off balance as they marveled at her extraordinary beauty. "I will demonstrate to your advantage my own unique capabilities as we see this deal through."

"It is my wish," replied the King. "Take these two away. The settler must be part of the white men's cargo, and place the son of our enemy king among the captive deem for execution," he ordered his men.

At the cages where they held the captives, Vincent Ellis, who could not believe what he had just witnessed as one of their own entered into an agreement with the hostile King, watched in horror as the warriors took Levi Gardea Gray to the cage meant for those that will be executed. As the men led him to the cages where the Portuguese were inspecting the captives, the fear of once more becoming a slave overwhelmed him.

"Please tell the King that I would rather die, than to be sold into slavery," he pleaded, weeping, with his eyes on Cho Vuyougar. "Let the king execute me."

As Levi was shoved into the cage cell meant for the condemned, he saw the Blunjues, standing a few yards away in their usual straight line. His eyes suddenly beamed at the one who stood directly behind the lead Blunjue. Then there was the sound of a strange battle cry, coming from the surrounding bushes, causing confusion among King Gbayou's warriors. The ones who were guarding the cages became alerted and drew their weapons. Levi saw the Portuguese, with their rifles raised, and swords drawn, rushing into their boats with few of the captives.

As the sound of battle advanced closer, the Blunjue matched towards Levi cell. The others stood watching, as the second one in the line pulled out a dagger from under her sisal skirt and cut the robes that were binding the stick and bamboo door. Levi Gardea Gray looked at the knife. It was not locally made. Then he remembered seeing it with someone. It was Dean Goldman's dagger.

"Emily!?" He gasped, astonishingly, when he recognized the Blunjue.

"For now, I am Marpue. Kpelle Warriors have invaded this slave trading post to free their people. We must find a place to hide until the battle is over," she said and flung the door open.

A group of Kpelle warriors led by Kokulo Jarwoe had bulldozed their way into where their abducted kinsmen were held. The Bassa warriors guarding the bamboo cell were soon surrounded. Jarwoe shouted a loud ominous cry and immediately he and his men charged at the guards, slewing the first three in their way. As more of them were dropping dead or wounded, some took to the bushes to flee but they were ambushed by Kpelle archers and spearmen lying in wait.

"*Gee Wua kay mu* let's get out of here," hissed the lead Blunjue, addressing Levi, as the Bassa guards were being slaughtered. "You are the son of a good King. We got to protect you."

"No," replied Levi, looking at the bodies of his kinsmen strewn on the ground. "I must find a way to end this bloodshed or else the Kpelle will kill all our people."

"No, Levi. it's too dangerous," cried Emily as the settler militia ran towards the remaining Bassa warriors who were still stubbornly defending the cell while most of their comrades lay dead or wounded.

"I am Levi Gardea Gray. Son of King Gray," he called to his fellow kinsmen in their vernacular. "You are surrounded and King Soteh Gbayou has fled along with the white men. Stop fighting now or the Kpelle will kill all of you. You need to drop your weapons and you will be spared or else you will see your wives and children no more."

To his surprise, the warriors immediately stopped fighting. He raised his hands in the air and walked to them.

"We thought you were a settler," one of them said.

"No. I am a Bassa man just like you. I was sent to live with the settlers and I have studied their ways and have learned good things from them. Now history will judge you rightly if you save the lives of your men. The mightiest don't always win on the battlefield, but the most noble victory is the one that is won with the ethos of peace. If you take me as a son of a King, you will throw down your weapons and go to your families."

Jarwoe, sensing what was happening as the Bassa warriors dropped their machetes and raised their hands in the air, ordered his men to halt the attack. Levi then took one of the machetes from the ground and began to cut the robes binding the doors of the other cells.

"Let's help him," the lead Blunjue said, and the rest joined Levi.

The cells of the elderly captives were opened and they were released one by one. "Now your people have been freed, please spare our lives and let us go," Facing Kokulo Jarwoe with his hands in the air, Levi said.

With his machetes drawn, Kokulo Jarwoe came close to the Bassa prince, and set his blade on his right shoulder causing Levi Gardea Gray to shut his eyes. "Remained where you are, and don't try to save me or they will kill all of us," he told the Bassa warriors and the Blunjue.

One of the old men who was released from the cage cell walked to Kokulo Jarwoe and held him on his shoulder.

"He's a good man. His own people wanted to kill him," he said and turned to leave.

Marpue, with appealing eyes, suddenly knelt down and the rest of the Blunjue followed. Jarwoe looked at the strange girls dapped with white chalk over their bodies and the man whose neck he was about to chop off. Then he looked at his elderly kinsmen who they had released.

"Let them go," he muttered.

The warriors surrounding them immediately open a corridor. Seeing this, Levi walked to Emily, unsure as to whether he should touch her as the tradition forbids until she has graduated from the league.

"My sisters will take you back to your father," she said.

Meanwhile, On the other side of King Gbayou's slave trading post, mainly the area a few meters surrounding the platform, Yalleh Kolliemenni and his men were heavily engaged into a fierce battle with the Leopard Warriors guarding the King. With the swing of each machete, warriors on both sides lay dead.

But the Kpelle lead warrior had managed to close the gap on King Gbayou, further cornering the once feared Bassa ruler. Sanding by him, Mrs. Burgess knew that it was just a matter of time for the Kpelle to capture her ally. She took a small sickle, shaped like a NAZI symbol from a brown bag hanging across her chest, and stretched it towards the advancing Kpelle warriors.

"Seek and slaughter," she hissed to the object. Then she sent it, spinning in the air.

As if guarded by a remote control, the zigzag blade flew with high speed, spinning towards Kolliemenni and his men, slitting the throats of some of them. Convulsing, ten lie on the ground holding their slit throats to stop the bleeding.

The Voodoo Princess stretched her hands, and the spinning sickle flew back to her. She grabbed it with her naked hand, causing no laceration. Anticipating her next move, Kolliemenni and his men stood in readiness.

"Spare no one and let their blood soak the ground," she said, this time audible as the Bassa King watched with a grin of relief on his face.

Again, the sickle flew spinning, this time faster than the first, making it difficult to see with the naked eyes.

"My spear!" yelled Yallah Kolliemenni, standing before his men, as the sickle spun their way.

The warrior who kept his spear whenever he was not using it, immediately threw it to him. The lead spearman leapt in the air and grabbed his weapon, just when the bewitched object whizzed nearer. Any moment it was going to slit his throat and then the rest of his men. Yelling with all his might, he thrust the spear in its path. It collided with the sickle. Like a magnet, the blade stuck on it. Still spinning, it slid down the shaft. Kolliemenni trembled to the vibration. The blade was descending very fast, and was nearing his hands.

"Kpelemou! Do something or we will all die here!" cried Kolliemenni.

The warrior Zoe, who had cradled his way from the rear and was standing directly behind Kolliemenni, was holding and chanting to an antelope horn bedecked with beads attached to red thread. As he did, Kolliemenni, still yelling, would jerk several times like fresh power was injected into him.

He suddenly pivoted and threw the sickle back towards the direction it came from. As if the blade was interrupted by a more powerful remote control, it spun back towards Mrs. Burgess. She dodged it before it reached for her throat. The blade flew past and stuck deep into the trunk of a cotton tree behind the platform.

Immediately, Kolliemenni and his men resumed their advances towards them. As Kpelemou continued to chart, she made several unsuccessful attempts to conjure the blade from the tree. Startled that her power was challenged for the first time, her fear and desperation grew.

She suddenly turned and faced Kolliemenni and his advancing men. Her face became bright and her eyes turned to the color of the universe and spun like the heavenly bodies. Looking into her eyes, Kolliemenni and his men froze. Soon they were becoming spooked and paralyzed. One after the other they were dropping to the ground.

"Kill all of them," King Gbayou shouted to his warriors.

Kpelemou, who was also lying on the ground, paralyzed, suddenly sprang to his feet. Whiling in a strange tone, he horridly took a straw and a ball made of palm nut chaff and breathed on it. The chaff ignited into a tiny flame. Then, there was a glow, followed by a huge black smoke pouring from the chaff and bellowing into the air.

Like an Olympic torch bearer, the warrior Zoe ran into a circle as the smoke swirled around Kolliemenni and his men, thus blanketing them. As it grew thicker, the voodoo princess could no longer see ahead of her, preventing her eyes from connecting to the souls of the Kpelle warriors.

Leopard warriors on the move to execute their King's order had reached a few meters from the smoke and began to cover their eyes and noses as it covered their faces. Kolliemenni and his men, suddenly springing to their feet, emerged from the smoke, grabbed and pulled their enemy warriors back in.

The Bassa King was suddenly plunged into bewilderment upon hearing the groans of his men being slaughtered in the ring of billowing smoke. As they advanced further, the cloud of smoke also protected them. Nearing the enemy warriors, the Kpelle would sprang out of the smoking ring and charged at them.

The King turned to run, but Kolliemenni leaped out of the ring of smoke and threw his spear. It caught him in his right leg, to the thigh region. He fell to the ground, but one of his men immediately pulled it out as he screamed. Then he was helped up and carried by two of his men.

Following a trail of blood dripping from the King's legs, Kolliemenni and some of his warriors ran after them, while Kpelemou and the others ran after the Voodoo Princess who had also fled in another direction.

Saydah was standing in her cage cell holding the stick bar with her face pressed against them shouting Kolliemenni's name, when a fleeing Leopard warrior approached the cage, with his machetes in his hands. With rage, he got closer to her, but Marpue suddenly appeared from behind the cell and stood in his way.

"Get out of my way or I slaughter you both," angrily, the warrior warned, but the settler-Blunjue did not move. "How dare you side with this traitor?" He asked, but she said nothing and remained blocking his way. "You have lost your value, then," he snarled and raised his machetes in the air to strike her, but he was suddenly tapped from the back by another warrior.

"Have you forgotten that it is forbidden to strike the purest of our *Grebo Bush Birds*? Have we not had enough disaster on our hands?" he asked.

Marpue recognized him to be one of those whose life the Kpelle warrior spared when Levi intervened.

"*Mom Zulu yon*?! Are you stupid?!" he asked and pulled his comrade towards him. "The Kpelle warriors are right at our tails! Let's get the hell out of here!"

While Levi and the rest of the Blunjue waited at a safe distance in the bush, Marpue turned to Saydah. She took her dagger and cut the robes binding the cell door, and yanked it open. As soon as Saydah came out, beaming with gratitude, a strong wind suddenly swept them off their feet, sending both of them to the ground unconscious.

Saydah felt being pulled and lifted from the ground. When she opened her eyes, she saw herself being carried in the arms of a Bassa warrior. Ahead of them was the witch, the wicket settler woman slithering into the bush.

"Kolliemenni" she began to scream with all her might, her voice reverberating into the bush, when she realized that she was being abducted, again.

Yallah Kolliemenni heard her screaming. He straightaway stopped pursuing the wounded king, and urged his men to continue the pursuit. Then he turned and ran into the direction he heard her voice with an impressive speed.

Marpue was awakened by the screams. She immediately grabbed the dagger and ran towards the direction. On the way she bord up with Kpelemou and Laynumah, who he had just freed. Wasting no time, she pointed into the direction Saydah was screaming and ran.

"*Loqui lee kpeleh yo!* A brave little girl!" remarked the warrior Zoe, looking at Emily racing ahead of them.

"The girl who is screaming is my in-law," informed Laynumah. "She's been abducted.

"Your in-law?!

"Yes. She's carrying my brother's baby."

"Okay I am going after them," Kpellemou said. "Go and find your brother and direct him to where I am going."

"Laynumah!" Koliemenni came running to them.

"They killed Nawoe," cried Laynumah as he and his brother embraced. "Now they have taken Saydah."

"I know. And we are avenging our mother's death now." he said, easing himself from his little brother's grip. "But you have to be strong now." Then he turned to Kpellemou. "Where are the screams coming from?"

"That way but it seems far now," responded the talisman of the Kpelle warriors.

"We must do something to save the girl, now. You have to locate their position fast. She is carrying my child."

Kpelemou's eyes suddenly sparkled with urgency. He immediately uncovered the small wooden cup where he kept the *Vonvon* and let it out again. Humming with its usual *Vonvon* sound, it immediately flew into the air. "Let's follow the bug," he commanded.

"The battle has ended. We have defeated our enemies," came running Kokulo Jarwoe. "Lango Gbowee will be proud. Where is the head of the Bassa King?"

"He fled, wounded, but Keleku Kermue and some of our men are after him. Search and slaughter the stubborn among their remnants. I am pursuing the settler witch on a personal matter."

"We don't have time," suddenly shouted Kpelomou, holding the tip of his left ear, listening to the humming of the *Vonvon*. "This way," he pointed to a direction.

Deep into the forest, Mrs. Burgess conjured the warrior toting Saydah, who had given up screaming to stop and laid her on the ground. Then she ordered him to leave at once. The warrior initially stood perplexed and wondering what the Settler ally intended to do with the traitor, and then he reluctantly turned to leave.

He had not gone too far and turned to look back, but the settler witch suddenly stretched her right hand towards scrubs of wild vines growing around a tree which immediately disentangled themselves, slithered towards the frightened warrior and wrapped around his legs. The vines crept up to his neck and choked him. With his eyes stretched and popping out, the warrior fell to the ground, dead.

Now with no one around to see what she was about to do, Mrs. Burgess turned to Saydah who had fainted when she saw what had happened to the warrior. She knelt before the pregnant girl and spread her legs apart. Pieces of hibiscus petals were sprinkled around Saydah, forming an outline of how she was lying on the ground. Then, the voodoo Princess suddenly rose to her feet, looked towards the sky and raised her hands in the air.

"O ye who possess the power of the cosmos," she called out loud, her voice once again sounding like an opera on a monograph, but only this time extremely desperate. "I invoke your power of rapture to transform and transcend me into the soul of the fetus lying before me." This time her voice became louder. "I beg of you, O ye force. The daughter of your faithful servant seeks to be reborn into the hidden freshness of the embryo of the one I have chosen as a perfect place to hide, to incubate, to rejuvenate and to grow with the power consistent with this part of the world so that I can more effectively administer your will."

Suddenly there was a storm, swinging the trees and shaking the bush. Mrs. Burgess was raised a few meters into the air like she was seized by a powerful force. Her hair stood and began to wither into plumes of faint dark smoke; she was now transforming and any moment her entire body will transfigure into the dark plumes. Like a serpent, it will glide its way between Saydah's legs and enter into her uterus.

"Dean Goldman was right!"

The voodoo princess was suddenly Interrupted. Stunned, she stopped, so was the strong wind, and the invincible force that held her suspended mid-way into the air, which pulled her back to the ground. She looked in the direction she heard the voice. Emerging from the undergrowth was Marpue.

"Seeking this part of the world to hide into the fetus of an innocent blood means that your powers are weakening," said the settler Blunjue, as Mrs. Burgess looked at the strange indigenous girl who spoke perfect English.

A cold breeze blew past, touching her head. She immediately felt it, and realized that her head was stripped clean; her hair, transfigured into thin dark plumes, had disappeared.

"He was right," continued the strange Blunjue, stepping closer to Mrs. Burgess. "With all the evil spells you cast on Elijah Burgess, Jack Duvall, and my parents, you have now been forced to hide yourself."

Bewildered, the settler witch's eyes sparkled with recognition.

"Emily?!" she swallowed, her voice quivering.

As if she had realized that she had prematurely acknowledged that her power has weakened, she quickly feigned her usual fearful posture.

"That you wish to see the faces of your parents, your folly has led you into the alley of death," she said. "The wrath that will inflict you will ravage and vaporize your soul."

"That befitted those who attempted to know you, order than the actual you. But I do know who you really are."

"Well then. This curious little pussy cat will have to die with such knowledge."

"Rebecca Drake," Emily Thompson chortled, just as Mrs. Burgess stretched her eyes to unleash her deadly wrath. "The daughter of the Voodoo Queen, Maria, by Admiral Charles Norman Drake, once a slave trader in the Caribbean. At the age of 13 you were sent to the Cottonwoods. The evil you inherited from your mom cajoled and led Robert Bob-bob Douglass to the gallows. Then you seduced Perry, murdered the entire Cottonwoods and burned down the plantation." Emily paused, her heart rising with excitement, and now taking bold steps towards the witch, as Rebecca Drake's face blushed with awe.

The altar girl had listened keenly to Dean Goldman as he responded to the many questions she asked him when they were on their way to the cottage to rescue her father. Moreover, with the little time she spent with her Blunjue friends, learning more of the virtues of womanhood, she had managed to guess the meaning of the phrase of the old Algonquian Indian, Dean Goldman told her about; "*The mind has eyes, too: We humans have the power to look, and yet control what we want to see.*"

That was the secret. Just how she viewed her father's corpse appearing like bundles of firewood on a horse back, she will look into Rebeca Drake's eyes, but cloud her mind with other unrelated things to break the transmission of the dark power from the cosmos, from penetrating, capturing and controlling her soul.

"With nowhere to hide from the cries and vengeance of the blood you spilled, you seek to hide into the soul of the unborn." Now directly facing Rebeca Drake, she asked. "Remember this?"

Spell-bound and terrified of such a revelation in the least manner she expected, Rebecca Drake suddenly gasped. Then she felt a sharp object thrust into her stomach. Dropping to her knees, she looked down and saw Dean Goldman's dagger buried deep beneath her navel with blood pouring out.

"Your vengeance is soiled by an everlasting guilt for failing to save the child and its mother," cried, the voodoo princess.

Rebeca Drake pulled out the dagger from her stomach and crept to Saydah who was still lying unconscious. Just as a bug flew past Emily and circled around the settler witch's head, kneeling, with both hands, she raised the dagger in the air to stab the pregnant girl in her stomach. Within that moment, with Kpelemou, and Laynumah following closely behind, Yalleh Kolliemenni came sprinting from the bush. The spearman leapt into the air and rolled several times on the ground when he landed.

Rebecca Drake screamed with pain when Kolliemenni thrust his spear at the base of the back of her head, driving it deep, until the pointed edge came out through her mouth. Then he stepped on her back and pulled his weapon out, causing the voodoo princess to fall to the ground on her stomach.

She convulsed and squirmed for some time. Still holding the dagger, she resumed crawling towards Saydah. Right away Emily scooped and ceased it. With all her might, she drove the knife into Rebecca's Norman's temple, instantly killing the dark princess.

For a while, Kolliemenni looked at the strange girl with appreciation and then ran to Saydah. He shook her until she came to herself and was surprised to see him beaming at her.

"Yallah," she whispered with a faint smile.

"You're safe now," he said.

After embracing him for a while, "Laynumah!" she cried when she saw her brother-in-law and ran to him.

Careful not to press her stomach against his, she embraced him, and held unto each other for some. Then she turned her head to her left, when she saw Emily in the corner of eyes and recognized.

"I will forever remain grateful to you, kind stranger," she said, easing herself from her brother-in-law and walking to the settler Blunjue.

"It's time to get out of here, and join the pursuit of the enemy king," announced Kpelemou, retrieving his *Vonvon*.

"Laynumah. Take Saydah and follow the others all the way to Kakata," Kolliemenni instructed his brother. "The rest of us will remain searching for the Bassa king and have him executed to prevent further trouble for our people."

"What about our village?"

"I burn it down along with the people that killed our mother. But you can go there. I left Saydah's hen and chicks in their coops beneath the roots of the large Red wood tree at the right of the outside kitchen.

"We've been waiting and I was worried," Levi said when Emily re-joined them.

"Oh my God! It is you, the bishop's daughter!" crooned Vincent Ellis, who was rescued by Levi. "You joined these Grebo bush girls to save our lives?"

Emily nodded. "And I have avenged my parents' death, too. The witch is no more."

Levi exhaled with relief. Then he looked down the river, and then at the lead Blunjue.

"Take me down to the beach where the white men fled with some of the captives. I want to see his Vessel and convey the description to the authorities in Monrovia," he said in Bassa.

Disappointed that he did not have the time to take enough of his precious cargo, except a few of them, Captain Gomez however managed to snatch Sinegar who was left lying on the ground screaming as Weigar, the Fetish Priest and subjects fled from the Kpelle attack. He and his men successfully escaped from the scene. They were rowing back towards the mouth of the Farmington. In case he encounters any problem along the way, the hominid will aid their escape into the bush.

Before rowing out at sea, when he reached the river's mouth, his heart leapt when he spied into his telescope. The Santa Amelia was guided by two frigates carrying American flags. He focused on the desk and saw his men kneeling down with their hands on their heads with the rifles of American men of war pointing at them.

"Our boat has fallen to the American Navy," he said, almost weeping. "They will find the hidden area where we keep the slaves."

"Someone has sold us out," declared Jose Dos Santos, the young expeditioner, standing to his right and looking into the telescope handed to him by the captain. "What do we do now?!" he then asked, perplexed.

"Why did Abraham Garsuah not show up at the King's trading post?" Captain Gomez turned to Witty Peter who was standing behind him and asked, at the same time drawing his pistol from the back of his trousers. "How come the Americans know that the Santa Amelia is a slave trading vessel?"

"Maybe he was apprehended by settlers' spies and may have told the intelligence officers about the vessel," replied Witty Peter, with traces of quivers in his tone.

Captain Edwardo Gomez's eyes suddenly turned red. He had sensed betrayal in the way his interpreter spoke. With rage he pointed his pistol at Cho Vuyougar's temple.

"Garsuah has never entered the Santa Amelia. Only you," snarled the captain.

Just then, the bushes on either side of the river began to shake. Soon afterwards, settler militiamen were lining up on the banks with their rifles pointing at the Portuguese boats.

"For trading in slavery, you have violated the laws of the colonial administration. We are therefore placing you and your men under arrest," with his pistol swinging in his hand, Major Rudolf Crayton stepped forward and spoke. "You are commanded to row your boats towards our forces along the banks of the river or we will be forced to open fire."

"*Vocês estão falando sério, caçadores de guaxinins*? Are these Raccoon hunters serious?" Captain Gomez smirked in Portuguese, and then facing his men. "*Mate os bastardos*: Kill the bastards," with furry, he ordered.

His men immediately positioned themselves on both sides of the boats and opened fire on Major Rudolf Crayton and his men. The militias returned fire as they retreated back into the bush to take cover behind the trees. Scores of them lie along the river banks, dead.

The Major was lying on his stomach facing the Portuguese boats, and returning fire with his pistol. Then, there was a loud explosion. A cannon was fired from one of the American frigates that had sailed a few knots directly to the river mouth. It hit one of the Portuguese boats. The flaming ball landed and tore through the floor, causing water to rush into the boat.

Another cannon was fired, creating another hole into the stern. More water was rushing in, and the boat was sinking fast. In the next moment it sank; goods and bodies were floating over the river.

"Come out and shoot," yelled the Colonial Intelligence officer, seeing that the Portuguese were in disarray; one of their boats, the one with the Kpelle captives, had turned back up the river with the Portuguese desperately rowing towards an elbow to evade the pounding from the frigate.

A unit of settler militia, led by Derick Hart ran after the boat at the same time firing. The five Portuguese inside were shot and killed. Now unmanned, the boat slowly turned towards the direction of the current and began to drift back down the river mouth. Then it was struck by another cannon fire, and it too began to sink.

Crayton's men were hearing the cries of people in the boat, with one of the captives thrusting his head above the gunwale, crying for help. Immediately, some militia men, aided by a group of friendly Bassa men, got into canoes to rescue them before the boat sank. As they brought the captives on shore, the militia men on both sides of the banks began to shout triumphantly.

Gomez, Dos Santos, and three of his men were docking in his boat as settler militia on both sides were taking aims which looked like target practice. The American frigate was now directly facing him, putting the slave traders' boat in some sort of an envelope.

"What the hell do you think you're going," cried the Portuguese captain when he saw that Witty Peter was about to jump out of the boat into the water.

He fired, but the interpreter was quick. He had plunged into the water. From ducking Gomez attempted to get up to fire into the water, but a militia bullet missed him by an inch, forcing him to duck back inside the boat.

"Keep an eye on Witty Peter," docking for cover behind a tree, Major Crayton instructed. "Make sure he emerges where you will be waiting for him." Then he turned to another group of his men. "Throw the robes, and pull the boat on shore."

When the frigate had maneuvered on its portside, ready to fire at the Portuguese slave merchant, if he tried to post any more threats, the man then threw large hooks attached to robes into Gomez's boat, and began to pull it to shore. When it landed on the left side of the banks, the Portuguese captain and his men were met with tens of rifles pointing in their faces.

"Who among you is Captain Gomez?" asked Major Crayton, climbing into the boat.

"Him," pointed Cho Vuyougar who was brought by two militia men who pulled him out of the water when he swam to the same side of the banks.

"Major Crayton!" shouted Levi, who came running from the bush with Vincent Ellis behind when they heard the shootings and explosions. "Thank God you got here in time," he breathed.

"Levi?! Ellis?!" surprised, the Major asked. "We thought the witch had you."

"Yes, she did. But they rescued us," he replied, turning to look back into the bush at the same time pointing at the *Blunjue*, who, from a distance, were standing in their usual formation.

"And the witch?"

"She's dead, according to her," still looking back at the *Blunjue*, Levi answered.

"According to who?"

"Emily Thompson. The bishop's daughter. She was rescued by the Sandi Bush girls, and she's part of them now. That's how they found and rescued us."

"Is she among them?"

"Yes. But she will not join us now. At least after graduation."

Major Crayton watched as the *Blunjue* turned to leave, beginning with the last on the line. Following them were the captives who were rescued from the sinking boat which Mapue had volunteered to turn over to the Kpelle warriors who might still be around looking for King Gbaryou. As a boat from the frigate rowed towards them, the major then instructed his men to tie the hands of Captain Gomez, Jose Santos and his three remaining men.

Jose Santos suddenly fixed his gaze at the lead *Blunjue* who also stood staring at him. He recognized the face. She was the one that stood looking at him from the high banks, the last time they rowed into the Farmington when their interpreter warned them to stop staring or be blinded.

"The United States Navy have charged you for engaging into the slave trade," he was suddenly interrupted by a young Navy officer as two other officers took them away. His eyes full of tears, Jose Santos looked back at the lead Blunjue, who then turned to join her league.

They all were alerted to sudden eerie screams from within the boat. Immediately an American moved closer to it, his rifle pointing forward, as everyone else docked for cover or took aiming positions.

"Over here Lieutenant," the soldier called when he looked into the boat and saw Sinegar lying on the floor. "Found something!"

"What is it?" the Lieutenant asked as everyone came out of cover.

"Don't really know, sir," cried the soldier. "Could be a creature, a being. I don't know."

"Get him out," ordered the Lieutenant.

The soldier got closer and looked into the boat. "Could be a being, but kind of weird."

The hominid was brought out of the boat, looking scared.

"I'll be damned!" whispered Vincent Ellis, bewildered.

Thinking that he was going to be turned over to the colonial militia officer, Sinegar began to scream when the soldier handed him over to his commander who took him in his arms and walked towards Major Crayton.

"He's also under the custody of the United States Navy," the Lieutenant informed, and turned to leave.

Major Cryton hesitated for a while and then nodded.

"As it always is with the white man," he muttered. "Confiscating such extra-ordinaries for the purpose of research."

The hominid stopped screaming when it became clear that he would not be turned over to the settler and subsequently be persecuted for serving as a spy in the hostile Bassa king's army. As the Lieutenant and his soldiers made for their boat, Sinegar looked up at the white man to try to detect any mischief in his eyes.

On the contrary, the naval officer took a piece of bacon from his breast pocket and gave it to him. Initially hesitant, the frail warrior spy stretched his tiny hands for it. First, Sinegar brought it to his nose and smelled it. Then he bit a portion and began to chew

Chapter 20

The Vai King had begun the '*Keh ba*'; the great battle, to reclaim all the lands occupied by the settlers across the St. Paul River. He led phase one, by marching into Banjor with a large group of his warriors, battle clad, with their faces and their upper bare bodies painted blue.

Like a tsunami they smashed the Dei forces loyal to King Golajor. He fled but was captured, attempting to cross the mouth of the St. Paul River for the territory of Duala. His canoe was surrounded by the invading forces' and he was brought back to Banjor, a prisoner of war.

"Today Golajor ceases to be your king for siding with the enemy from across the Atlantic. And, as you all know, these people have taken and desecrated our land," King Kiatamba told the people, who were made to gather at Banjour main square where they had King Golajor kneeling with his hands tied behind, and his head resting on the crossbar of a log built like an abattoir. "As the conduit through which the folly of bridging our indigenous solidarity was brain-child, and the betrayal of trust that ensured, I will therefore chop off his head to relieve his body from such malady so that he can be honorably buried."

Just as the Via King announced the sentence, a huge warrior, wearing the mask of a masquerade, raised a large machete in the air with both hands. With a single swing, King Golajor's head was instantly chopped off from the rest of his body. Like a coconut, it went rolling on the ground. Later, it was displayed on a spike.

After that, King Kiatamba announced. "I will now present to you a trusted ally as your new ruler. He is no different from you. He's your own son, Jahtono. And I will spare the lives of your sons and husbands who rose up against me to defend Golajor, on one condition; if they join me, and your new king to liberate our land."

At the edge of the upper St. Paul was a huge build up of Kiatamba's forces, ready to execute phase two of the Keh ba. Jebbeh, the mother of elephants, was standing in her winnowing fan full of white rice powder. Her face was pasted with white chalk. With her both hands stretched forward, she was facing the river with a fixed gaze towards the other side of the banks.

Beside her were the two old ladies, painted with white chalk with line patterns that ran from their hair to their wrists. It continued all the way down to their feet after a break with the black country cloth with white linings tied around their wrists. They were holding grayish clay pots in their hands.

The priestess stretched her hands down towards the winnowing fan. Immediately, the two elderly women moved closer to her and dipped the clay pots into the fan, filling them to the brim with rice powder. When Jebbeh stretched her hands again towards the river, the old ladies also did with the clay pots. Then, they put their free hands into the clay pots, collected portions of the rice powder, and sprinkled them into the water. After the third sprinkle, the winnowing fan began to slide by itself from the banks. With Jebbeh still standing inside, it floated some meters into the water.

Mysteriously, the rice powder did not get soaked, as water seeped into the tiny spaces underneath the winnowing fan. When the two old ladies stepped into the water and waddled behind their master, the winnowing fan stopped floating, when the water level reached their necks.

The priestess then uncoiled the ivory trunk of a young elephant from around her neck. She twisted a little, and the fan spun towards the opposite bank. A loud sound reverberated across the forest, when she blew it.

"Let your men make way for the beasts or else they will trample on them," she addressed the lead warrior.

A tall man waved his hands in separate directions to a heavy and rumbling sound coming from their rear. Within minutes, with Kiatamba's men out of harm's way, troops of large elephants came rushing out of the forest, and tumbling down towards the banks.

A large stretch of the river banks were lined up with hundreds of the gigantic beasts, thrusting their tusks into the river. After drawing a large volume, the elephant would put their tusks into their mouths, and drink. Within a couple of minutes, the water level began to recede as it gradually dropped from the necks of the two old ladies to their breasts and so was the winnowing fan.

Whenever the water level reached below their knees, with the two old ladies following, and still holding the grayish clay pots and sprinkling the rice powder, the winnowing fan would float further towards the middle of the river, where it was still voluminous. They would stop when the water level reached their necks, again. The elephants would also move forward, and continue to drink.

Within an hour, the entire river bed was visible. Startled as to the sudden drop in the water level, fishes struggling to swim and fluttering about, would leap into the air in a frenzy. At ankle high, the priestess and the two elderly women were now across the river.

They turned back to facing the warriors. Jebbeh then waved, which meant it was now safe to cross. The next moment, the massive forces of Kiatamba were marching through the river bed with some among them catching the fishes and putting them into baskets hanging on their backs. Within minutes, they successfully crossed to the other side.

The priestess and her two subjects then crossed back to where they started. Then, she again blew the ivory horn. Immediately, the elephants began to release the water back into the river bed, and the volume began to rise. The lead warrior watched how the water level increased within the same time it receded. There was another sound of the Ivory horn, and the beasts trooped back into the forest, fulfilling one of the assistance the priestess offered to the Vai King at the meeting with King Sorteh Gbayou.

"There is no turning back now, as we move to reclaim our land," facing his men, the lead warrior addressed them. "Raise the signal to our messengers," then he instructed a warrior who initially surveyed the trees along the river banks for a suitable one to climb so his comrades, the messengers on the other side of the river could clearly see him.

He saw a suitable one and climbed it. At the top of the highest branch, he waved a fresh palm thatch. The two town criers saw it and immediately picked up running southwards towards Banjor to inform King Kiatamba that his troops had successfully crossed and they were now in the bushes of the settlement of upper Caldwell.

"As we march southwards, we must keep our eyes open and our ears sharp. The Dei on this side of the river are allies to the settlers. There are many of their farms along the way. If you encounter any of them, make sure they are detained until we accomplish our mission. Lest they run back to town and inform their masters, and our position compromised," the lead warrior continued to address his men.

King Kiatamba's strategy was to lead his forces north and southwest of Monrovia. His men, marching from Caldwell after pillaging all the known settlements, would cross the Stockton Creek and continue marching down towards the eastern territory of Duala. Having secured Banjor, he himself would cross the mouth of the St. Paul by way of the beach, lay waste to a settlement at the eastern tip of the river estuary and join his forces from Caldwell. Then they would march together towards cape Montserrado.

King Sorteh Gbayou will join forces with King Garmondeh and both will dislodge the weak forces of King Gbessagee at New Georgia and march down south towards Via Town with some of their men using the mangrove swamps to enter the colonial headquarters.

Subsequently, the combined forces will encircle the settlers, pestering them from all sides, until they are cornered towards the beach. This will put them into a situation which will require them to negotiate their way into the American Navy Vessels anchoring along the shore to ferry them back to where they came from.

Councilman Samuel Brisbane had successfully advocated for early election, when Butler failed to convince Captain Willman of the US Navy to provide artillery support, if the hostile kings attack the colony. Monrovia was cramped with the families of settlers from its outskirts. These included the men and their aged sons who initially remained to defend their settlements, but were forced to retreat to the city for fear of Kiatamba's eminent raids, after learning that he had captured Banjor.

"How about lending us three of your big field cannons to be mounted at the eastern, northern and western flank of the colony to ward off hostile indigenous warriors, since you cannot lend us your artillery support from your vessels on grounds that this conflict is an internal matter?" Ebenezer Butler had asked the captain.

"The United States government stands to be accused of aiding and abetting a potential genocide against an indigenous population, if we allow you to use these deadly guns," Captain Willman had replied. "Like I told you, we were only involved in capturing Captain Gomez, because our government does not support slavery. However, we will only support any peace efforts between you two peoples."

"This is a diplomatic ineptitude at the highest level for failing to secure a much-needed military support from a traditional ally in the time of a crisis that has the propensity to wipe out the entire colony! As Governor Carey's condition worsens, the survival of this colony is left with what I am afraid to say, the mercy of the natives!" capitalizing on this setback, the councilman had argued, prompting an election between the Governing council which he won.

Early the next morning, he was in his study scrawling on a sheet of paper, at the same time dictating to himself. It was still dark and so his Lantern was on his table, burning. Balls of roughly crumpled sheets of papers were lying on the table and on the plank-floor, evident that he had been up all night, preparing his acceptance speech when Butler turned over the mantle of authority to him, later that day.

He was wearing a dark brown overhaul dungaree with a thick beach sweatshirt. His pistol, well oiled, was lying on the table.

He finished another draft and read over it. Dissatisfied, he crumpled the sheet and threw it on the ground. Because he was a bit overwhelmed with the elation of finally assuming the governorship, he was finding it difficult to arrange his thoughts.

The governor elect got up, grabbed his pistol from the table and walked to the wooden window, overlooking the offshoot of the St. Paul on which edge he built his wooden frame two storey residence. He unbolted the inches, and used the nozzle of the pistol to gently open the window.

It was still dark outside, but he could still see. Two of his twenty armed personal guards and one of the three settler militia assigned to him were standing at the side gate of his picket fence, keeping guard. At the inlet, he could see his locally made wooden boat, and two small canoes at his mini dock.

The house and the rest of his yard were quiet. For a week now, he had sent his wife and children to Central Monrovia for safety. He also let go of the five indigenous working in his yard. Only he and his security guards remained.

After eye-sweeping his back yard and seeing nothing unusual, he strode to his cabinet and searched for his favorite bottle of moonshine. He poured half a glass and when he had watered-down the liquor, almost emptying the glass in one gulp, he felt his ecstasy simmering down, providing him a clear head to think. Then he sat back behind his desk and resumed writing his speech.

Just when daylight was appearing, Othello Johns, one of the private guards, heard someone whispering his name outside the fence.

"Who is it?" he asked, with not much of a concern because the voice sounded familiar.

"It's me," it responded, now a bit louder, but still a whisper and with a sense of urgency.

Raising his lantern, Othello strode to the fence which reached the level of his neck to peek outside. Just as he expected, he recognized Dwannah, one of the indigenous boys who was responsible for the laundry and cleaning the councilman's yard. He was hired by Martha Brisbane, the councilman's wife, but he was sacked, just before the tension between the settler and the indigenous heightened.

This happened one day when Councilman Brisbane complained of five pieces of dollar bills missing. He remembered leaving them in the pocket of a particular trousers he sent to the laundry, a wooden structure facing the river at the back of the house.

Othello Johns was asked to investigate the matter, but Dwannah repeatedly denied ever finding the money in the trousers and deliberately refused to turn it over. After five years of diligently serving Brisbane, he was let go.

Still protesting his innocence, Dwannah left the yard in tears. Three days later, Brisbane found the money in another trousers. Furious, Martha Brisbane sent for Dwannah to return to work. Unfortunately, she was informed by his neighbors that he had left for the interior.

The laundry man was standing under a plump tree with his hands behind him like he was hiding something. His face was painted blue, and his head was tied with fresh palm thatches. His sparkling eyes, cold, creepy, and mean, shone in the dark hazy shadow of the tree. With his hands still behind him, he stepped forward.

"Dwannah! What are you doing here this early?!" demanded Othello, raising his lantern higher to see clearly. "Remain where you are and answer me. Don't come closer."

Dwannah continued to step forward.

"Have they found the money and was Mrs. Brisbane looking for me to come back to work?" he asked, his voice cold and empty.

"Yeah, but she's not here now…Hey! You heard me! Remain where you are!"

The laundry man was now completely out of the dark, standing before him; only the fence was separating them. Then he took his hand from behind him, revealing what he was hiding.

"*God-damn-it*!" Othello Wailed.

"What is it?" Joseph Holt, the head of the councilman guards, and one of the militia assigned to him, came rushing when he heard Othello yell.

"Othello!" he called, when he saw the guard froze, jerked, and then dropped the lantern.

"Enemy!" he shouted when Othello turned, and staggered towards him. A machete was stuck deep into his forehead with fresh blood all over his face.

The other guards came running with their rifles and muskets pointing forward. Soon the fearful cries of warriors erupted. Dwannah climbed over the fence and jumped into the yard. Three guards ran past Holt, opening fire on him, but they were startled. The bullets were falling off his skin as he scoped down to pull his machetes from Othello's skull.

"*Sonovabitch*!" Joseph Holt suddenly screamed, aiming for Zwannah's eyes and then fired.

The bullet penetrated his right eye and came out of the back of his head, taking with it a portion of the occipital bone, instantly killing the laundry man.

"John, Elliot, James, Alphonso, Patmore and Blake. Take your positions down to the docks. The natives might be using the river. And the rest of you, at the western fence," instructed Joseph Holt, moving about in a frenzy. "And make sure you aim for their eyes. If you miss, then aim for their nuts; these are the weak spots for bullet proof."

Councilman Brisbane heard the shootings, and then the dreaded battle cries of warriors coming from the west of his fence. He immediately jumped from behind his desk and ran to his rifle cabinet. He grabbed two of them, with some ammunition. When he loaded them, he swung one of the rifles on his back and tugged his pistol at the back of his pants.

Then he hurried back to his window. He could see dozens of canoes in the distance with three fearful looking warriors in each, paddling toward his boat ramp. Another group was mobilizing a few yards outside of the fence. They were doing the war dance and chanting battle cry.

"Jesus," he hissed and ran down the plank stairs, racing through his hull way. In no time he was at his entrance door.

"Hold your fire until they get within 15 yards!" shouted Joseph Holt, still moving from one end of the fence to the other. "Aim for their eyes, or if not, go for their nuts. I repeat! Aim for their eyes or their nuts!"

"Holt!" Councilman Brisbane came running to him. "How many are they?"

"40, 50. Maybe hundreds of them."

"Where is Nathaniel?!" he asked, though unmoved, but his voice, full of urgency.

"Sir," responded a young Militia, who had the nozzle of his rifle pointed between a space of the picket fence.

"Get my horse and ride to town to Captain Capehart. Tell him we are under natives' attack. We need some troops here; about 100 men, armed to the teeth." Brisbane instructed. "From what you are witnessing now, you must stress on the number of men we need."

Nathaniel immediately left his position and ran to the stable at the east of the yard. He trotted out a horse, mounted it, and galloped out of the yard through the main entrance gate at the north side.

For some time, the indigenous warriors chanted their battle cries and performed some mystical gymnastics. Then, out of a sudden, the battle cries got louder, electrifying, and fearful. Brandishing their weapons in the air, like swarms, they charged towards the fence.

"100 yards, hold your fire," eccentrically moving about, announced Joseph Holt, his voice loud enough, so that his men should hear him above the enemy's deafening battle cries. "50 yards, hold your fire; 30, keep holding. No one fires until my signal… 25, 20, FIRE!"

When the enemies were within their firing range, like thunder, the guns of Councilman Brisbane guards roared. Some were hit on all parts of their bodies and were dropping dead, but their comrades who were still standing, advanced closer. After another wave of shooting, more warriors were dropping dead or wounded. Some of the guards were even shooting the wounded, finishing them once and for all.

"Do not waste your bullets on the wounded!" shouted Holt, kicking Frederick in his buttocks when the young guard landed two bullets into a wounded warrior. "Councilman Brisbane. We need to open the armory now!" he turned to the councilman who had joined the guards, firing. "And you need to stay away from the fence!" With a nasty stare, he roared at the councilman. "It might be too risky! Leave the fighting to us!"

Brisbane smirked, his facial expression conveying a thought. For now, he will listen, but later, he will have to ignore this tantrum-prone guard of his.

The councilman was fond of Joseph Holt. It was he who recommended to Captain Capehart to assign the colonial militia guard to him. One day, at the colonial office, after a governing council meeting, he noticed this energetic militia guard moving about and issuing commands. His comrades were referring to him as '*Crazy Holt*.' When he was later interviewed on his new role to serve the councilman, Brisbane immediately took to liking him when he observed that his no nonsense attitudes matched his nickname.

"Frederick! Load and assign to each man a rifle," Holt instructed, when Councilman Brisbane came pulling a cachet of rifles and ammunition in a wheeled carrier. "Make sure you reload when the others run out of ammo. Cole and Eugene. Join Frederick. Amos. You're a better marksman. Take Frederick's position. The natives have noticed the inaccuracy of his shots, and may plan to concentrate their thrusts in his direction."

The indigenous warriors were beaten back with scores of them lying dead. As they retreated, they toted or dragged their wounded along. At a distance out of the firing range of Holt's men, they were mobilizing, again. When they gathered more men, mostly from the ones who were in the canoes, they chanted their battle cries louder, performed more war dances and this time, like buffalos on a stampede spree, they charged again.

Several of them, waving cow tails bedecked with white and brown cowrie shells with fresh palm thatches and tiny snail shells tied around their heads, necks, knees and ankles, were in the lead, forming straight lines, shielding their battle-charged men.

The ones who remained in the canoes were paddling towards the mini dock. Some of them, with their bows and arrows drawn, were kneeling at the bow. Their objective was to capture the dock to give them the opportunity to swoop into the councilman's bark yard and flank the guards who were halting the advances of their comrades at the western part of the fence.

The dock appeared to be abandoned and so the warriors were advancing rapidly and without caution. Before they could realize it, John, Elliot, James, Alphonso and the other two, concealing themselves behind the huge pillars logs supporting the boat ramp, were taking them out one by one with precision. As several of them were floating in the water dead. The rest were forced to turn back, thus thwarting what was going to be an indigenous amphibious landing, south of the colonial councilman's fence.

"Good job, guys," Joseph Holt, who came rushing to the dock to see what was going on, commended them. "But next time, let your bullets bow through the hall so water can seep into their canoes and sink with them."

At the western side of the fence, a group of lead warriors who were waving the cow tails, were charging towards the position Frederick formerly held, just as Holt expected. When they got within firing range, they were dropping to the ground dead. With precision, the guards, knowing that they were the ones with the bullet-proofed bodies, were aiming for their eyes or below their groins.

Certainly, the ones who were shielded, because they did not possess the bullet-proofed charm were now exposed, and gunned down. Sensing that the enemy guards had discovered their latest strategy, once again, the warriors halted the advance and pulled back.

Let's chase after them!" screamed councilman Brisbane. "We got to finish them!"

"No!" rejected Joseph Holt. "We are not many. The best way is to hold them the way we are doing until the reinforcement comes!"

In full adrenaline mode, Private Joseph Holt was racing up and down, inspecting the front gate and the eastern part of the fence. The entire neighborhood was quiet; the people who live outside of the councilman yard were either indoors or had fled.

The battle cries had stopped. And the guards were reloading their weapons. Three rifles each were now assigned to the best of the marksmen, while two each were assigned to the rest.

"It isn't over yet. They are strategizing," Holt announced as he moved about the yard. "The natives have been planning this for months."

"Can anyone hear that?" Brisbane suddenly asked upon hearing what appeared to be a whooshing sound, prompting the guards to be attentive and trying to figure out what it was, when it got louder.

"Has anyone seen movements, anything?!" He asked, again.

Having peek through the spaces of the fence, and observed the terrain outside for a while, one after the other, each guard shook his head, no.

"They must be using frightening tactics to scare us. But lock your ears and remain focused on your shots…"

Before Holt could end his words, fireballs were swooping down in the yard. Some were landing on the house and setting the roof ablaze. Others were smashing against the fence, splattering hot flaming wax which were spreading the fire. Amos, Frederick and one of the guards standing next to him were instantly set ablaze with the hot wax peeling their faces, when a fire ball made of dry coconut shells landed on their heads.

"The dock is ablaze!" retreating with Elliot, James and Alphonso, shouted John. Their colleagues, Blake and Patmore were rolling on the ground, screaming and blazing with fire.

"They are using slings to throw the fire balls!" frightened, Amos screamed, when they reached Holt who had raced up to meet them.

"The fire balls are dry coconut shells with a flammable wax drained inside," explained the commander of the guard, struggling to remain composed.

"They would pick the coconuts, let them dry and remove the husk. Then they would throw them amongst the red aunts which would eat the meat inside, Dwannah once mentioned," added one of the guards who joined them, with Councilman Brisbane walking behind.

The west side of the fence, engulfed in flames, fell to the ground. The yard was now exposed from the west, rendering the guards' position vulnerable. A horde of warriors were amassing again with a more dreaded and vicious battle cry. With their target now in a clear view, they were ready to descend upon their enemies. Away from the fallen fence, the remaining guards, now 15 in number, formed a shield to protect Councilman Brisbane.

Just as the throng charged, a group of them were gently swinging the slings with coconut shells, this time producing huge, thick, grayish smoke clouding the atmosphere, distorting the guards' vision, and prompting them to fire in all directions. Three of them were stocked by flaming enemy arrows.

"Pull back! Pull back!" screamed Joseph Holt when he heard the three guards who were struck down by the arrows, screaming when the blanket of smoke glided over them. Next, their heads came rolling out to Holt and his men.

Councilman Brisbane ran to the stable for his horse. Before he could pull the double wooden door open, three of the fireballs landed. One on the roof, the last two, on the wall of the left elevation, instantly gutting the barn.

A chunk of fire dropped on the councilman's right shoulder setting his sweatshirt on fire. Joseph Holt threw a bucket of water, sitting near the burning door, on the screaming councilman, immediately putting off the fire.

"At the front gate!" whirled the Commander of the guard, pulling Brisbane with him. "Don't leave your weapons and ammunition behind. Our priority now is to protect the governor elect. The colony must have a head to run it!"

While running towards his entrance gate, **S**amuel Brisbane could hear the snorts and squeals of his horse as the stable was burning down. When he was out of his yard, he briefly stopped to watch his house completely in flames. The roof, wooden window and the plank frame were all falling down.

Three warriors circled around the house from the left and picked up the chase after him. Holt fired twice. Two of them dropped dead. At that time, one of the guards, bruised from the face and chest, also circled around the house, sprinting towards the third warrior. He grabbed him from the back. When the warrior turned to face him, both were engaged in grappling. But the guard was suddenly lifted in the air and knocked to the ground with a heavy thud.

On top, the warrior was struggling to free his hands, which were locked between the guard's arms, so he could grab his neck and choke him to death. Within that time, the entire left elevation of the house, heavily ablaze, fell on them.

As he ran out of the yard with the councilman, Holt heard the screams of the warrior and the guard in the flames. He could also hear the screams of his remaining men being slaughtered at the back of the house.

He fired several times at another group of warriors, dropping 3, when they emerged from behind the house and put up a chase after them. To find a shortcut to get on the main road to Monrovia, to board up with the reinforcements, with Brisbane following closely behind, he dashed between the huts. The warriors followed, spreading themselves into the community and searching every hut.

Upon seeing the two settlers with guns in their hands, running between the cluster of huts, and the warriors pursuing them, some indigenous dwellers ran indoors, screaming. But a woman, standing in front of her hut, was shouting in Vai, calling the attention of two warriors who came running her way, when she recognized Brisbane.

Holt looked behind and saw the two warriors advancing closer. He fired, but they dodged by docking behind a hut.

"Keep running and don't look back!" he told the councilman who was becoming exhausted.

Not looking back, the councilman ran for some time, struggling to keep up with his pace. Extremely exhausted, and hearing only his footsteps, he stopped by a hut. Holding his wrist with both hands, and breathing heavily, he leaned against it.

Not seeing Holt, he became worried. He was about to resume running when the two warriors circled around another hut and caught up with him, face to face. In no time he hauled out his pistol from the back of his trousers, pointed it at the warrior closer to him and squeezed the trigger.

Frightened, the two warriors suddenly shrieked and dropped to the ground, but the gun did not fire. In desperation, the councilman tried again but, it was futile. Brisbane's face sank with horror when he remembered that he did not load his pistol. It was only the two rifles which he disposed of when the bullets in them were depleted.

Sensing this, the two warriors immediately sprang back to their feet while their enemy was desperately searching in his pockets for ammunition. One grabbed the colonial councilman by his neck with one hand while he held onto the hand with the pistol.

Joseph Holt suddenly rounded a hut and appeared on the scene just before the other warrior could join the scuffle between his colleague and the settler. Opting not to shoot to expose his location, he grabbed the other warrior from behind, and covered his mouth in a firm grip. Aiming for his left ventricle, Holt thrust a dagger into the upper left side of his ribs. A volume of dark red blood poured out as the ventricle contracted. Seconds later, the warrior, emitting faint sounds escaping through Holt's fingers, was dead.

"*Ahh Kammei*," the other warrior who almost had Brisbane, cried out in Vai, "Ahh God!," when he felt a dagger drilled into the left side of his shoulder, puncturing his jugular vein with blood gushing out like a fountain. "*Ah-h-h Kammei, kammei …*" looking into the sky with his eyes stretched wide open, his cry was now a whisper, as his life rapidly faded away.

"I have seen that woman with Martha! The one who was pointing at us!" Astonished, Brisbane cried at the same time rubbing his neck to relieve it of the tension from the warrior's choke. "Several times she has come into our yard to ask for food, and money. How can these people be so ungrateful and cruel?"

"This is war, Councilman. Everyone Chooses the side he or she belongs to," replied Holt. "We have to move now. Next time when I say keep moving, keep moving."

Councilman Brisbane, still bewildered, blinked his eyes and turned to leave. "And don't forget to load your weapon," Holt reminded him and threw a sock full of ammunition to the councilmen.

After wandering several times, they finally got on the main road to Monrovia, somewhere around what is now Point 4 Junction.

"Oh, thank you Jesus!" The councilman suddenly cried out loud, dropping to his knees and raising his hands in the air, when they saw a large contingent of settler militia in the distance ahead of them.

"A large group of Vai warriors are at our rear," breathed Joseph Holt, immediately after they safely reached the contingent.

"Kiatamba's men," muttered Captain Capehart, who along with a group of Militia Cavalry and Nathaniel had galloped to meet them.

"What took you so long, Capehart?" as if it had just occurred to him, Councilman Brisbane raged. "Had we not escaped, we would have been slaughtered."

"We were proceeding cautiously, Councilman," replied Captain Ashford Capehart.

"Proceeding cautiously with these savages? A boy we knew led warriors in my yard and burned down my house. A friend of my wife showed our enemies the route through which we were escaping. Are these the kind of people to take time with?"

"The governor elect is not to himself. Take him to the clinic," ordered Capehart. Turning to Joseph Holt as the councilman was ushered into a two-wheeled chariot and whisked towards Monrovia, "What to expect?" he asked.

"The mode of their attacks suggest a long-time planning. With devastating effects, they are using slings to volley rapidly combustible coconut shells fireballs at us. They have also devised means to blur the vision of our marksmen by blowing thick dark smoke into the air."

"Well," inhaled Captain Capehart after a brief thought. "We will need barrels of water from the Mesurado River to counter the fireballs. As for the billowing smoke, the direction of the strong wind blowing from the ocean will divert them. Take some of our men and King Gray's men who are fighting alongside us to the river to get the water." Then he called a militia officer on a house back, right next to him. "Quartermaster Marshall. Provide Joseph Holt with the necessary logistics; wagons, barrels and anything they can use."

Chapter 21

Riverside Baptist Missionary Compound. It was early on the morning of the indigenous' all-out attack. Reverend Charles Gooding III was in the middle of a morning prayer, following an all-night tarry held in the church's edifice to intercede on behalf of Governor Carey as his health continued to deteriorate. Sister Barbara Newland, the drummer Nathaniel Giddings, Bendu Kiatamba, Daywein and his son, Zwannah were among the thirty-congregation of indigenous and settlers, who were present.

"As you said in Psalm 91:1, our governor has dwell under the secret place of the most high, so, shall he abide under the shadow of your Almighty, O God," prostrated before the sanctuary, which window was a portrait of Jesus ascending to heaven, Reverend Gooding prayed. "Let your healing power restore the health of Governor Carey. Just like you restored the health of King Hezekiah, not letting him die while in his prime to continue to do your good works, so it must be for your faithful servant, a good Shepherd, who came to take care of your flock on this side of the world. As your prophet Habakkuk prayed, renew the wonders and the many miracles we have heard, to see them in our time, O Lord, more especially at this time when we are calling upon your healing power to manifest itself in the life of our dear Governor."

Also in attendance was Moses, Zwannah's cousin, the one who ushered Bendu into the missionary compound the day she was brought in. He came out of the church to go to the lavatory at the back of the compound to urinate. Just when he was through, he suddenly froze, becoming attentive, when he thought he heard a howling sound.

After listening for a while and making a face that it was nothing, he stepped out of the urinal and was about to close the door of the lavatory when he heard a different one, a Whooshing sound coming from down the river. Then, he saw warriors circling the compound.

"Fire! warriors are burning down the compound," thunderstruck, Moses screamed, as he ran to the church when he saw fireballs raining down into the yard. "Reverend. They are attacking the compound and burning it down," his eyes stretched with bewilderment and breathing heavily, he entered the church and announced.

"Who is attacking what?" Reverend Gooding asked, jumping to his feet.

Before Moses could answer, the roof at the rear of the church was torched and began to blaze.

"Everyone out!" immediately, Reverend Gooding ordered.

Terrified and screaming, the congregation ran out of the church. In the yard, they ran into Kiatamba's warriors. In the next moment they were encircled. Each warrior with his weapons raised, was closing in on them.

"If you are not an indigenous, step aside from the others," the lead warrior said in Vai, but no one moved. "I will chop off the first few heads, if I have to repeat myself," with a fearful face, he warned.

"What's going on?!" asked Reverend Gooding, running out of the church, after making sure that everyone was safely out, and seeing some members of his congregation separating themselves from the others. "We need the men to run down to the river to get water to put the fire out."

A warrior suddenly grabbed him at the back of his neck and started shoving him towards the lead warrior. Bendu Kiatamba, who was standing with the indigenous congregation with Gbotoe on her back, ran to the warrior.

"No! Don't treat that man like that!" she said in Vai. "He's a good man. All he does is teach people to be good."

"Are you with him?" another warrior asked her. She nodded, "Then you both will die together, traitor."

He then grabbed her by the back of her neck, and jolted her forward.

When he was brought before the lead warrior, the reverend was shoved on his knees and was made to put his hands on his head. They ripped his shirt off, exposing his bare upper body.

"Having stolen our land, you are now stealing the minds of our people to believe in a strange God that tells people to love their enemies?!" unbelievably, the lead warrior asked, his huge and monstrous body towering over the reverend. "Your head will be the first one on the spike."

He pulled Reverend Gooding by his neck, swung him around to face his congregation, and then pushed him among the settlers. Just at that moment Bendu was brought before him with Gbotoe on her back, crying. The once hostile appearance on his face immediately turned bright with astonishment when he recognized her.

"Bendu?!" he asked.

"Gbotoe?!" also astonished, she asked, instead, pulling herself from the warrior's grip and walking to her brother.

"Yes. It's me," he said, with a chilly voice, and almost weeping.

The siblings held each other's hands, avoiding to hug, which is forbidden for a woman to embrace a warrior, when he is consecrated and clad in his battle outfit.

"What are you doing here?! And whose baby is on your back?"

"Seeking refuge," she retorted. "I got pregnant by the man whose house I was staying at. Fearing retaliation from his wife, Mama's friend whose care I was entrusted with, I fled." Then she loosen the lapper from her back and flipped the baby in her arms. "This is your nephew; I named him after you, Gbotoe, because I missed you a whole lot."

"And he looks just like me, too," he observed, smiling, taking the baby from his sister's arms. "Papa held me in the bush preparing me for this war the whole while. So, it was difficult for me to contact you."

"Where is Mama?"

Gbotoe breathed, the expression on his face compelling Bindu to flinch in awe; her brother's response will not be good.

"When she got well, Papa refused to let her come to him. He was vexed with her for letting you live with the settlers. We heard that they killed you because you are his daughter. So, just before I was sent to the bush, I accompanied Mama to our grandparents' village."

"Papa was wrong and had been wrong all along. Your nephew's father is a good man. He did not deny the pregnancy and sent me away, just like that. I was scared, and so I had to leave. And as you can see, the man you were about to behead has been taking care of us."

"Not knowing you were here, I could have had you and my nephew, my namesake, killed."

"And if this war continues, his father might be killed as well."

With his face now pale, his expression shaken, and remorseful, he looked in the faces of the people he thought to be his beloved sister's companions; the settler he almost had killed, and the compound that hosted his sister and her son, he had set ablaze. He was full of sorrow.

"What do we do now?" asked his sister, sensing that it was the right moment for such a question.

"Put off the fire," he commanded his men. Then he turned to Reverend Gooding who was still spellbound by the sudden change of developments in the last few minutes, "Give my men your buckets to help you put off the fire," he said, and turned to his sister. "Hope they do this in time to hurry to see Papa before this war gets any further."

"Reverend," Bendu called his attention, and interpreted what her brother had said.

As if he was snapping out of a dream, "Yes-yes!" he responded. "Tell your brother to leave this to us. What is urgent is to hurry to the king at once."

The lead warrior nodded, and then handed his nephew back to his mother. Gbotoe's eyes were now flooded when his namesake started to cry again as if he liked being with his uncle.

"Papa will not be happy with you, for trying to tell him to stop the war" Bendu cautioned her brother, her eyes also flooded.

"I know," Gbotoe agreed. "But I must tell him that I no longer see my nephew, his grandson's people differently."

Putting Gbotoe back on her back, Bendu watched her brother lead his huge group of warriors down the river matching along the banks towards Duala.

"Take care of my nephew," he stopped, looked back at her and called.

Then, she felt a hand on her left shoulder. She turned and it was Reverend Gooding.

"The compound!" she gapped, holding her breath.

"Don't worry," the reverend assured her. "The men are doing well. We will save the church. We were lucky it is the only structure in the compound that was torched."

Initially overwhelmed with relief, she embraced Reverend Gooding. While in his arms, she burst into tears.

"O my brother. I am afraid that my father will punish him cruelly for disobeying his orders-aborting his plans he had been conceiving for years."

"Don't cry," the reverend tapped her on her back. "God will be with your brother. Have faith; it is not by coincidence he met you here today. It was God that brought you here."

"Reverend. The fire has been put out," running to them, drenched with water dripping from his clothes, Moses announced.

"God is great!" raising his hands in the air and looking up at the sky, Reverend Gooding raised his voice.

The men, exhausted, had joined the women in front of the church. Sister Barbara Newland raised a song and they all joined her, clapping and singing praises to God.

At about mid-day, King Gamondeh had gathered his forces and were marching from what is now southwestern Mount Barclay, using the forests of present-day Louisiana for the territory of King Gbessagee. At a certain point, he will be joined by the forces of King Gbayou trooping from the east. With this gigantic force, they would attack Gbessagee, who would be no match for them since he had reduced himself to a mere chief when he turned over his territory to the colonial authority. While this is happening, King Gbayou's neengin warriors will creep into the surrounding mangrove swamps, lying in wait for the signal from the forces of King Kiatamba, swarming in from the west and they all will descend on Monrovia.

But the Bassa King was antsy. After two hours of waiting at the rendezvous where the two forces were to meet, Gbayou's warriors did not show up. On the other hand, Gbessagee, with prior knowledge of King Gbayou's defeat, became emboldened, and launched a pre-emptive attack on his enemy. Had the colonial militia who were to fight alongside him had not been withdrawn to beef up the strength of the contingent deployed at the western front to halt King Kiatamba, King Gamondeh would have been easily crushed. But the battle was fierce and there were huge casualties on both sides.

"What makes Gbessagee so brave to attack me now when the last time he ran to the settlers with his tail in his butt," a bit taken aback by his rival's sustained attack, King Gamondeh wondered, "And he is attacking me without the militia. Any words from King Gbayou? Are his warriors in sight?"

"No, my king," answered one of his men who was part of a team on the lookout for his ally.

"Bring Garmugar to me at once."

"We are still awaiting the Neengins, my king," responded the Mamba, when he appeared before the king. He was part of a five-men team stationed at the edge of a distributary of the Du awaiting the Neegins to arrive, ferrying warriors in their submergible crocodile watercrafts. Then they would head straight for the mangroves of Stockton Creek, parts of the Mesurado and the southern Du Rivers. And when they land, Garmugar and his team, with knowledge of the terrain of Monrovia will lead them into strategic parts of the city.

"Gbessagee knows something we don't," pacing up and down, the king declared, after a long thought.

His attention was suddenly drawn to one of his messengers sprinting from the direction of his headquarters. Then he saw the one monitoring the battle with Gbessagee, also sprinting towards him.

"O king," catching his breath, the one from the battle front whirled. "Gbessagee is breaking into our defensive lines. Our casualties are rising. Any moment, our defense will be beaten."

While King Gamondeh was pondering over this, the second messenger, sprinting from the north, arrived. "The news is bad, O king, "he said, when the King looked up to him for information. "Lango Gbowee has crossed the northern Du. Her forces are matching towards Carey's Burg."

Out of trepidation, the King's knees suddenly buckled, and he was reaching to the ground. But his men quickly held him, and brought him to his crown stool.

"King Gbayou has been defeated," apprehensive, the king now realized, when he came to himself. "His neegins were to be minding the northern Du to prevent the Kpelle warriors from crossing. With Gbessagee now breaking through our defenses from the south, she is now advancing from the north. My headquarters are now vulnerable."

"Our strategy seems to be crumbling," cried Garmugar. "It seems we will lose the war and everything."

"We are going to make our headquarters the last stand against the Kpelle. We must pull back our forces," instructed the King.

Before long, a group of his warriors came running from the direction of the battle front, some of them severely wounded, and were leaning on their comrades. Battle ridden and denigrated, the remnants were pouring. King Garmondeh knew right away that his rival had beaten the last of his defense, and was pursuing his retreating men.

"We have lost the war O king," cried his lead warrior. "We were surprised by the ferocity of Gbessagee's attack as we least expected." Looking around him he suddenly became concerned. "Where are our allies?" he asked.

"Beaten as well," the king replied.

"What do we do now?"

"We wait for our enemy and then accept our defeat," Garmondeh said. "Gbessagee is not the dangerous one now. We got Lango Gbowee to confront. The Kpelle are a more vicious land-hungry sect."

In a couple of minutes, the forces of King Gbessagee were in sight, cautiously approaching their defeated enemies. The victorious king, looking fearful in his royal warrior outfit, was ahead. His defeated rival could see the glee of victory on his face, and the unbelievable triumph which, had it not been for King Gbayou's defeat, was going to be marred with cowardice and fear.

"This is his day," breathed the defeated king. "Everyone drop your weapons," he instructed when Gbessagee forces were about a few yards away.

Seeing this, the beefy victorious King raised his hands, bringing his warriors to a halt.

"We accept our defeat," King Garmondeh said, after both kings stared at each other for a while. "My term is to no longer be hostile to you and your ally."

"Your condition?" requested King Gbessagee.

"Allow me and my forces unhindered withdrawal to our territory to defend it against the Kpelle ruler currently marching towards my headquarters."

"But your men are weary and demoralized."

"We will rather surrender to you, our kinsmen, than to coward before the Kpelle. It's best for our pride that we die defending our land from such people."

Upon hearing this, King Gbessagee surveyed his defeated kinsmen. The wounded were on the ground, groaning. Some of them were dying. Blood was all over the bare ground. The expression of his able-bodied men, though a sizable number, did not portray warriors with the gusts to fight another war.

He could see the strain of war in their eyes. Secondly, it will be best to his interest that he will no longer have to worry about protecting his territory from Garmondeh which will give him the leverage to join forces with the settler contingent at the western front engaging King Kiatamba.

"I accept your proposal, but not without a price. Hand Garmugar over to me. I want him to pay for his attempt on my life."

King Garmondeh had no alternative but to use the Mamba as the sacrificial lamb. It is better he dies, than the destruction of his headquarters in which many of his people will die. Or, it will be appropriate to give Garmugar the chance to amicably settle his matter with King Gbessagee.

"Garmugar," he called, but the Mamba was gone. "He was right here standing by me. Where did he go?"

"He wouldn't be far, I guess," offered King Gbessagee. "Go and bury your dead and attend to your wounded. Leave the scoundrel to me."

"I'll hand him over, if I find him in my territory."

King Gbessagee nodded, as he watched his counterpart and the remnant of his forces depart after some friendly exchanges amongst the men. Then it occurred to him that he must do something to help his former enemy. After all, he is a fellow Bassa man like himself.

Governor Butler hasn't turned over to Brisbane yet. He will prevail upon the outgoing governor who had established a contact with the Kpelle ruler to abort her offenses. Garmondeh was no longer a threat.

Meanwhile Garmugar was paddling into a small stream that joins the Du, feeling betrayed by the man he supported against his own King. Gbessagee's request, he reasoned, was King Gray's ploy to get at him in retaliation of his disagreement with the manner in which the sale of Mamba Point was handled.

With King Garmondeh's surrender, and his reliance on his former enemy's influence on the settlers who may prevail upon the Kpelle to halt their advances, he was now vulnerable and on his own. His next move is to disappear deep into the hinterland and probably resurface, if aging King Gray dies.

"That will be too long to wait," he muttered. "Garmondeh will eventually find me and turn me over."

His thoughts were aborted when he heard from his rear, the usual sound of the ripples when paddles are slicing through water. Alerted, he looked to his right and his left, seeking a perfect place to hide to see who was coming after him.

Luckily, he spotted a narrow cove-like passage cascaded by mangrove trees, and gently steered his canoe into the tunnel-like channel. A few minutes later, he watched, through the spaces of the cascading branches, three canoes with warriors that looked like Gbessagee's men, paddling past his hideout. He lowered his head, when one of the warriors in the last canoe looked his way.

He waited for about thirty minutes. And when the strokes of the paddles had faded, suggesting that his pursuers had wandered far off and probably lost their way, Garmugar hurried out of the channel and took another course heading southwest, which would lead him to somewhere in Sinkor. Initially debating and finally agreeing to his next option, sneaking in on Charles Deshields was the best he had to consider.

Chapter 22

In the early afternoon hours, the Vai and Dei warriors, trooping from across the mouth of the St. Paul at Banjor, were converging on Duala. From there, they were marching towards Monrovia. In the middle of the throng was King Gbanjah Kiatamba, attired in the war-like version of his gorilla outfit riding on his horseback with his gorilla fist staff, stretched forward. His stern look, coupled with his body language, conveyed a posture that he meant business.

He made a stop at the crossroads to Caldwell to be joined by his Son, Gbotoe, who was marching with his forces from that direction while the rest of the forces headed on.

The advance team, led by Kandakai Goyah, continued marching onwards, until they reached what is present day freeport. He sent word to King Kiatamba informing him of not seeing the warriors of Kings Garmondeh and Gbayou who were expected to swoop in from the north and cross the Stockton Creek to join them at that point.

"We will address the tardiness of our allies later. For now, right before you is Vai town. Move in, gather the support of our kinsmen, and continue with our plan," the King replied.

Before reaching the Vai town, Kandakai Goyah brought his forces to an immediate halt. Settler Militia, apparently in a smart move to prevent Vai warriors from entering into the town and mobilizing their tribesmen, had moved in earlier, and secured the town.

When the chief warrior relayed this new development, especially when it appeared like King Gray's men had joined forces with the enemy, "Begin the assault," the King replied, and then warned. "Any more messages back to me order then the progress of the battle will require your head in response."

At the colonial militia fortifications in the center of the town, Captain Ashford Capehart, ahead of the lines, was galloping horizontally from edge to edge of the dirt road as dust from the hoofs of his horse swirled into the air. He was focused on the advancing indigenous forces who had suddenly halted and formed battle lines when they saw his forces.

"They seem surprised," he observed. "They were not expecting us here."

Then, there was the sound of the swinging of the slings.

"They are about to unleash the fireballs!" Joseph Holt, standing by the captain, alarmed.

"Ready the water bearers," instructed the captain.

Immediately the water barrels, each minded by ten abled bodied men, most of whom King Gray's men holding two small wooden buckets were lined-up on the sides of the road and between the structures and huts of the town. Like a barrage of shooting stars falling to the earth, the fireballs dashed in on the militia position, igniting the perimeter around them. But the water bearer unit, hauling buckets of water from the drums, was putting the fires out before they got mature and became difficult to contain.

"Clever," mused Kandakai Goyah, after consulting with his war council. "But Let's see how you will handle this one."

The second barrage of fireballs were launched and at the same time a band of warriors charged at the enemy. Their ploy was to attack while their opponents focused on putting the fire out. But the militia opened fire, aiming for the eyes and groin of the charging warriors. The few militia who were composed were taking out scores of Vai warriors with the aim to the eyes or the groin, but the majority of them managed to break into the lines of the enemy, swinging their machetes at any one in their way.

After firing several successful rounds with his rifle, he quickly dropped it when it ran out of bullets and hauled out his pistol and continued to shoot. A brave warrior dashed and docked under the captain's horse, grabbing his legs and pulling him down, causing the startled animal to neigh and gallop out of harm's way. While sitting on top, the warrior raised his machetes with both hands to bring it down in the middle of Captain Ashford Capehart's forehead to split it into two, but the commander of the militia guard was swift to stick the nozzle of his pistol in his opponent's right eye and fired. The impact threw the warrior off, and dragged him a few meters away. The next moment he was dead.

"If you can't aim from a distance, let them come close before you take them out!" shouted Captain Capehart, grabbing his rifle, jumping to his feet and reloading it.

For a moment the two groups were engaged in close combat at not more than two yards from each other, sometimes resulting in hand-to-hand combat and wrestling. While under fire, some of the warriors with bullet proofed bodies got close to the militia, grabbed their rifles and a tussle ensued. In that commotion they wrestled each other to the ground. Some of the militia were stabbed in the chest by a warrior on top while some warriors' eyes were blown off and died instantly.

One warrior suddenly screamed, breaking himself free from a scuffle between him and Joseph Holt, and jumping, holding his groin as blood poured from below his lower abdomen. The cunny militia guard had pressed the nozzle of his pistol against his groin and fired into his genitals. Fluttering, the warrior turned and staggered towards his group. Midway, he fell forward and died.

As the first group of Vai warriors leading the offensive began to sense that they were becoming increasingly outnumbered, they started to retreat, but Captain Capehart, Joseph Holt and some militia chased after them. At a certain point they heard the whooshing sound and turned to run back. As they did, fire balls were flying over them and hitting the positions of the militia.

"They are now hitting us with accuracy!" alarmed Joseph Holt, observing the precision in which the fireballs were landing.

Running, docking and yelling instructions to the water bearers as some of the fireballs were hitting the sides of the drums igniting the wooden staves in an attempt to destroy the wooden barrels and spilled the water, Captain Capehart's attention was drawn to some youths of the town, mainly boys between the ages of 12 and 15 lurking between the huts on both sides of the road, holding fresh palm branches. For every fireball that landed accurately, they would raise the palm branches in the air.

"They are using the kids to direct the hits!" the major screamed. "After them," he commanded and immediately he and his retreating men dashed between the huts for the boys.

"They are coming after us!" whirled one of the boys in Vai and immediately he and the others took to their heels.

The pursuing Militia soon noticed that some warriors had sneaked into the town, and were standing at an interval of about 50 feet from each other. They realized that they were the ones relaying the information from the boys to the men throwing the fireballs. When they saw the captain and his men after the boys, they too took to their heels. Captain Capehart fired a shot. One of the boys was caught in his left foot and fell to the ground screaming. Out of fear, another boy ran to his colleague and sat on the ground crying for his friend. Captain Capehart, Joseph Holt and the others arrived and picked them up.

After two and a half hours of battle with the indigenous forces now losing accuracy in the throwing of the fireballs, following the apprehension of their young target spotters, there was a lull in the fighting.

Commander Elijah Johnson had arrived at the battle front to assess the situation. At the highest point of Cape Montserrado, he and Governor Ebenezer Butler were at the observation post, set up to monitor the buildup and movements of King Kiatamba warriors. Appalled by the gigantic buildup, they hastily requested an audience with the American Naval Captain.

"With a force of such a gargantuan proportion, our kind risks annihilation, and the purpose of establishing this colony, a dream of our founding fathers, yours as well, will go down into the abyss," the governor had told Captain Willman, offering him the telescope to see for himself.

Surrounded by militia guards, Elijah Johnson was sitting on a stool in front of a hut. Captain Capehart sitting next to him, was appraising him of the situation on the battlefield which included information extracted from the youthful indigenous targets spotters in their custody.

"The situation in Duala is dire," the commander told Captain Capehart. "The group we are fighting now is meant to wear us down until the Vai King comes marching upon us with his huge reinforcements."

"Have the Americans seen this?"

"I think they have, though Captain Willman did not look into the telescope when the governor handed it to him to see for himself."

"So what became of the meeting?"

"It was inconclusive. This time around the Americans neither reject nor agree to lend us their field cannon."

"I suspect that with their silence on the matter, they are waiting for this dire situation to present itself to legitimize any countermeasure as the last resort."

"Which will not present itself, until we create an opportunity in such a way that it does not turn on us," agreed commander Johnson. "This is what we are going to do," he said, after taking a deep breath.

Having re-adjusted their strategy, based on what they had gathered from the first two waves of attacks, Kandakai Goyah was preparing for the decisive onslaught. To their advantage was the huge built-up at Duala which significantly outnumbered the settler militia. Secondly, they were aware of the slow time it takes for a militia to reload his rifle which they will use to their advantage.

Their first line comprised about 150 warriors with the bullet proof who would draw the enemy fire and deplete their ammunition. Within the time it would take the enemy to reload their weapons, the second line, the slingers, would begin to volley the fireballs. Then the last line, the one with about a 1000 men, along with the bullet proof unit, will join the attack, to wear down the settler's defense. With the defensive lines of the militia weakened, the colossal re-enforcement, led by the Vai king himself, would bulldoze their way through.

While in the final stages of planning this attack, Kandakai Goyah forces were unexpectedly besieged from the right and left. Settler militia and some of King Gray's men had infiltrated their position from between the huts, and from the beach. King Gray's men who managed to haul the water barrels with them, were throwing water at the fireball slingers to extinguish the glowing ball before they could launch them.

Taken aback, Kandakai Goyah struggled to push them back, but the militia, many of whom with pistols, some with two, were firing at close range, taking out the bullet-proofed units with remarkable precision. Seeing that his casualties were rising astronomically, when a fresh influx of militia arrived, the Vai warrior chief sent his battle messenger to the king for reinforcement.

As the setters' pressed on, Kandaikai Goyah and his men began to retreat, a ploy to lure more militia to pursue them as more were pouring into the battle. Near what is now point-four Junction, the militia immediately stopped chasing them, when they met up with the first batch of Kiatamba's reinforcements.

"All units, retreat!" On his horseback racing towards his men, Commander Johnson shouted.

"They have seen the might of our king!" cried Kandakai Goyah. "After them, even if they dig their own graves and bury themselves, dig out their corpses and toss them into the sea!"

Like invading army worms, the Vai warriors pick up the chase after the retreating settler militia. Spears and fireballs were thrown. Corporal Victor Digs, the militia guard whose mother hurt little Esmond Baryougar for picking almonds in her yard, suddenly shrieked when a spear bored him from his back and came through his stomach.

Holt heard the militia, whose suspension was lifted, screaming far behind. He looked back and saw the corporal on his knees holding the tip of the spear. He was immediately surrounded by three warriors.

One of them stepped on his back and pulled out the spear, causing the militia to scream louder. Anticipating what was coming, Holt fired three rounds from his rifle with all three hitting the warriors, but only one dropped dead. The other two had bullet proof.

Then, the warrior with the spear dropped it and sat on the young private's back. He reached for his head and tilted it. The next instance he was reaching for his cutlass on his left side.

"This is how we slaughter our goats," he said and ran the blade across Private Digs' throat with fresh blood gushing out.

Like meteorites falling from the sky, sparkles of fire-balls landed on scores of militia, instantly setting them on fire and causing them to run hither-scatter, screaming. Some of the water bearer units chased after them to put the fire out.

More spears and fireballs were thrown and more militiamen were taking hits and were being set ablaze. A young militia lost its way. While circling around a hut, he bumped into a huge and muscular warrior. The blue painted face held him by his neck and raised him in the air.

"Jesus!" The militia shrieked, when the mammoth thrust his spear below his abdomen. From his stomach, it passed through his neck, until it reached his skull, and pierced through it, killing the young militia instantly.

Commander Elijah Johnson had galloped to Vai Town and reached the place where they initially formed the defensive lines. He swung his horse around to face his retreating men, Captain Ashford Capehart, and Joseph Holt among them. At their rear were the massive reinforcements of Kiatamba's men.

"We will hold them here!" cried the commander, when the captain and Holt joined him.

"With that massive force, we will not last, sir!"

"I know, captain," admitted Commander Johnson, trying to steady the nervous horse and ducked when a fireball lobbed closely over his head. The frightened stallion neighed, kicking its forelimbs in the air, almost toppling the commander.

"We just need to buy a little time, and hope for what will happen next," Commander Johnson managed to say, while still struggling to steady his horse.

Within the firing range of the settlers, the massive Vai warriors were taking hits. Some of them were dropping dead or wounded, but many marched on, launching fireballs, throwing spears, and shooting arrows.

As they got closer, the militia casualties were rising. Captain Capehart looked at Commander Johnson, signaling that the tide was now turning against them. Any moment, their defensive lines will be beaten.

"Do not retreat until I return!" said the commander, turning his horse around and galloping towards the Mesurado River.

When he arrived, he stopped at the edge, hauled out his telescope, and unfolded it. He pointed it first towards the observation post up at Ducor and spied into it. The spherical image of Governor Ebenezer Butler appeared on the front lens with himself spying into his own telescope whose nose was pointed in the direction of the battle. Charles Deshields' also appeared on the Commander's lens, standing behind him stretching his neck as if to say he wanted to peep into the telescope.

Governor Butler suddenly shifted his telescope towards the ocean. A boat rowing towards Commander Johnson's way, was focused on his lens. Four US Navy personnel were inside, including old Ernest Cheeseman and Corporal Davis, the guard at the ammunition dorm. Also, was the outline of what appeared like a field cannon covered with tarpaulin.

Seeing this, Commander Johnson exhaled with deep relief. The American Navy, monitoring the battle from the sea, has seen the danger. The colony was about to be destroyed, and the free black slaves and their descendance faced total annihilation.

Commander Elijah Johnson swung the horse around to face the direction of the battle and spied into the telescope. The situation was getting desperate. More of his men were dying. Kiatamba's men were about to smash the militia defensive lines.

"Get me a wagon," he ordered.

Immediately, a militia man, keeping guard at the warehouse at the dock, ran in and hurried back with a two-wheeled cart, attached to a pony.

"When the boat arrives, gather some men to load the field cannon into the wagon," he instructed.

The boat finally arrived. Immediately, some militia men, with urgency and desperation on their faces, raced towards the edge of the river to get the field cannon out of the boat and rolled it into the wagon.

"Remember the terms," one of the navy personnel reminded Commander Johnson, who nodded, and watched the sailors row back to sea.

Old Earnest Cheeseman, who had not been himself since the blast at the ammunition dorm, mounted the wagon. Commander Johnson was a bit surprised when he looked in his ammunition maker's eyes and saw the bloody urge for revenge. Then he looked at Corporate Davis. The guard looked reluctant. He was not paying attention. One of the cannon balls slipped from his grip and fell to the ground while helping to upload it.

"You got to be focused, Corporal! Helping to end this war will save your life, and enable you to marry that indigenous girl of yours." When corporal Divis shot him an assuring eyes," Follow me with the wagon," he commanded, spun his horse and galloped towards the battle front.

When he arrived, Kiatamba's men were about less than 20 yards from the colonial militia defensive lines, shifting it further away from its original spot. As they advanced, some of them were dropping dead, but a sizable number were wobbling closer to the militia as bullets bounced off their skins.

Tono, the warrior who was displaying his mystical wits by uprooting a tree with his bare hands at the time of the meeting between King Kiatamba and King Gbayou, managed to maneuver his way towards Captain Ashford Capehart. Within reach, the muscular warrior suddenly leapt and gave him a spear. The captain staggered backwards, but quickly gained his balance and did not fall. Tono gave him a bear hug, twisted sideways, and finally brought the captain to the ground, his huge body almost covering the lean head of the militia guard.

With both hands Captain Capehart went for the warrior's massive neck and squeezed it. In an attempt to compel his opponent to release his neck, the warrior grabbed the handle of his cutlass, hauled it from a sheath made of sheep wool hanging across his wide chest, and brought it down horizontally, with the blade upwards, to press it above Captain Capehart's Adam apple. Just as he expected, the captain immediately released his neck to block the cutlass before it reached his throat.

Pressing both hands against the newly sharpened blade, the warrior continued to apply more pressure to force the cutlass down on Capehart's throat. He did not care that it gashed his palms, as his blood dropped on the captain's face.

With great effort, Captain Capehart winced and pumped his jaw, and with clenched teeth, he struggled to prevent the dull edge from reaching his throat. Unable to resist the warrior's strength, his elbows began to bend, and the steel was gradually nearing his throat. Within seconds, it was now touching his chin. He began to scream.

"Fall back behind the cannon! Fall back behind the cannon!" suddenly shouted Commander Elijah Johnson, maneuvering his horse between his men.

With his pistol drawn, he was shooting in the air and at the enemy, whenever they attempted to get closer to him. Behind him was old Ernest Cheeseman, Corporal Davis and the three militia that rode in the wagon with them. They turned the mouth of the big gun towards the enemy, rolled a cannonball in and fired.

Suddenly, the combatants on both sides froze. There was an explosion that shook the ground as the cannonball, emitting excessive heat and smoke, tore into the massive reinforcement of Kiatamba's men.

The aftermath was horrific. Body parts of Vai warriors were scattered on the dirt road with many of them smoked, fried, and disfigured beyond recognition. Some of the settler militia who did not make it behind the cannon in time were caught up in the blast, their bodies or parts, also dismembered.

Except for his eyes, sparkling with terror and bewilderment, Tono's body was smeared with thick black steam, when the cannonball hummed over his head. He immediately dropped his cutlass, and got from on top Captain Capehart. Like a Zombie, he went wobbling away from the battle front.

Captain Ashford Capehart, reeling out of the sting of death that missed him an inch, grabbed a pistol lying by a decapitated militia, and sprang to his feet. With rapid strides, he walked behind Tono, pointing his pistol. But he suddenly lowered the barrel, when he saw other warriors getting up one after the other, and backing away from the battle.

Tono stopped when he approached a corpse, charred, lying stiff and stretched. Recognizing that it was Kandakai Goyah's, he knelt before it, sobbing. He gently pulled a chain of stained beads from around its right ankle, and continued wobbling.

It was then that Captain Capehart realized the devastating effect of the cannon. Bodies of the enemy, and some of his men, crisped and baked, were lying everywhere. The battlefield looked like a mummy dumping site.

As he walked among the corpses, he would kick the side of every fallen settler militia. A few of them who were not hit, would gain consciousness and get up. Disoriented and dazed, they too would turn away from the battle and walk back towards the direction of the cannon.

"Reload the cannon!" wailed old Ernest Cheeseman. "The enemy is getting up to regroup. What are we waiting for?!"

Perturbed by the bloodbath, Corporal Davis and a militia at the canon refused. With rage, the ammunition maker shoved the militia away from the cannon and went for another ball.

"The war is over!" cried Commander Elijah Johnson, galloping toward the cannon. "We must respect the terms or we risk being accused of genocide."

Ignoring the Commander, Cheeseman continued to struggle with the cannon ball as he tried to insert it into the firing chamber.

"Gad damn-it, Cheeseman! " screamed Commander Johnson, jumping down from his horse and grabbing his ammunition maker by his collar. "The war is over! It's over!"

As if injected with a fresh dose of consciousness, Cheeseman immediately came to himself. Shaken, the old man dropped the cannon ball which went rolling out of the wagon. Then he dropped to his knees, and began to weep.

"They were going to wipe us out," he lamented.

Just before the cannon was fired, Charles Deshields, expecting what was coming when he saw the field cannon driven to the battle front, hurried away from the observation post, leaving Governor Butler sitting on the floor, when he himself was not sure whether he was going to bear seeing the aftermath. Right at the corner around his house, someone called his name. He turned and looked and saw Paye Gurmugar, the Mamba standing between two houses.

At first, the Settler-Indigenous Affairs director did not recognize his persistent complainant. Dressed like a Mandingo trader, many of whom had made central Monrovia their safe haven to avoid being mistaken for Vai sympathizers, Garmugar was completely disguised.

"I seek asylum from the colonial administration. I need your help to take me to the governor," he said.

"Just after the tide has turned against you?" Deshields asked, his tone, sounding like he was not surprised.

"King Gray seeks my head."

Deshields said nothing. Expressionless, he waited for more explanation.

"If the governor likes, I will subject myself to the investigation."

"The governor is preoccupied with the battle currently being fought at the Vai town."

The Mamba also waited, his expression desperate, and his eyes appealing.

"The war has not yet ended, "Deshields said, his voice suddenly shivering, apparently thinking about what was going to happen any moment on the battlefield. "When all is over, we can begin from there."

It was right after he said this, when they heard the roar of the cannon, followed by the earth trembling beneath their feet.

"What happened?!" Wailed the Mamba, as people ran out of their houses.

"You need to get out of here now before someone recognizes you. You will have to disappear for a couple of months and then come to my office."

"Will I still get my money if the investigation finds me innocent?"

Deshields nodded, and waved him to leave at once. More people were now trooping on the streets. In no time, Garmugar disappeared between the houses with the hard truth that King Garmondeh was the most valuable witness on his mind. He would testify on his behalf that he had no dealing with the slave trade.

Out of the piles of dead bodies, King Kiatamba crept out, his body covered with stains of blood and liquid from the sores that ooze out of burned human flesh. Caused by the blast, pieces of what was left of his gorilla pelt war-like outfit, stock on his skin like tattoos. Strangely though, with his gorilla fist staff still in his right hand, he struggled to his feet.

He was enraged. With clenched teeth, he was looking at the churned corpses of his men who fell on top of him to protect their King before the cannon ball landed. Thick but tiny flow of blood ran from his ears, the right corner of his eyes, his nose and the left corner of his mouth.

"The king is alive," shouted Tono, leading the remnants who were wobbling away from the battlefront.

The warriors immediately hurried to their king. The ones who still had their weapons held them in protective position, while the others scurried among their dead comrades in search of whatever weapon they could find or what was left of them.

Suddenly, they were all alert, and were ready to protect their king to their deaths. But they became calm. It was the king's horse neigh that got their attention. Seconds later, they watched the animal galloping to its master. They helped King Kiatamba to mount it. Then they formed a defensive column around him. With Tono holding the reins, the group of war-ravaged warriors marched with him back to Banjor.

At the crossroads of Caldwell, they met the group of warriors led by Gbotoe Kiatamba, who heard the blast and was hurrying to the battle front to rescue his father or retrieve his corpse, if he died.

"Papa!" rushing to meet his father, he exclaimed.

Shaken with guilt for not marching his troop in time to prevent his father from going to war, he fell to his knees, weeping.

The king rode on and stopped when he reached his son. He gestured to be helped down from the horse, and then walked to Gbotoe. With tears flooding his eyes, he extended his hands. Gbotoe took them. With a gentle pull almost staggering him backwards, the king helped his son to his feet.

He looked above Gbotoe's shoulders. His eyes were on the huge contingent he had brought, fresh and ready to continue the battle. For a while, both were locked into a gaze and none spoke.

"We can't keep fighting, Papa," Gbotoe said, waiting for his father's reaction, but didn't see any, only tears were now rolling down the king's eyes. "The weapon just used on us will wipe us out if we continue; our tribe, and our heritage risk obliterating if we go on fighting."

More tears were rolling down the king's eyes, a thing his son had never seen since he was born. This caused him to shiver with emotions. Then, Gbotoe saw the opportunity to tell his father the most obvious truth, the reality that is poised to gnaw at the king's conscience to see reason to give in to defeat. A defeat not only on the battlefront where his dependable ally did not show up, but to avoid the absurdity if he still wants to fight, when he hears what his son was going to tell him.

"Bendu, your daughter is alive with a son whose father is the people we are fighting," Gbotoe broke the news, himself, now with inundated eyes. "I almost burned down the place where she and Gbotoe, my baby nephew, are sheltering. I could have had them killed."

The king flushed, his staff almost dropping from his hand.

"They were seeking refuge, and cared for by a settler priest, when she fled the settler authorities who she thought wanted to apprehend her because of our hostilities towards them. But she later realized that it was to protect her as a gesture to you to refrain from going to war."

The king's face, always stern and resolute, now seemed remorseful.

"Bendu is fond of these people. She has lived among them," Gbotoe continued. "The settler authorities will be glad if we send her as our emissary to pave the way for a meeting with them. Maybe we can lay out our concerns, listen to theirs and find a balance, the equilibrium that we can hang on to foster our coexistence. With the white man on their side, evident by the terrible weapon that was fired at us today, we can't go on fighting…"

"I can't do that," with his usually firm voice, like he wanted to hear no more, the king interrupted.

Thinking all along that he was making sense, Gbotoe Kiatamba was immediately taken off balance. His father was not buying into his suggestion. Continuing to fight to the last man was still on his mind. Gbotoe looked at his men, sizable, fresh and ready for battle, and then the remnants of his father's, ravaged and war weary. Then he looked in the king's eyes, and saw the usual defiant mode of the intent to continue fighting, despite the enemy who will not relent to use the big gun and more, should they march towards Monrovia, again. Gbotoe was thunderstruck; his father has gone insane!

"But you can," the king offered, instead. "I was born a warrior and grew up to be a leader to protect our land, its people and heritage. Since the coming of these settlers, I have made a vow to never consider peace until they are driven or wiped out of these shores, the sacred place of our forefathers."

The king watched his son's face illuminated and then suddenly turned pale. Gbotoe knew his father had changed, but not without a consequence.

"You and your sister were born different," King Gbanjah Kiatamba continued. "We are now at the crossroads where peace often reigns after the brutality of war. You both are the shovels filling the void of the emptiness, that hopelessness that arises when men have fought and killed each other, and realize that there is no meaning to it, at all. You must now fill in that void, a new king of peace, Gbotoe."

"Papa!" Gbotoe swallowed, realizing that his father was turning the crown over to him at the same time suspecting that the king had something unfavorable in mind. That which he was not prepared to accept.

"Take me back to Banjor," the king said. "That's where I want the ceremony to begin."

Chapter 23

A week after the dreaded battle, there were no signs of hostile indigenous activities. But the colony was still tense for fear of the tribal warriors recuperating, regrouping, re-strategizing, and renewing their march on Monrovia. With the devastating effect of the field cannon, which also cost the lives of a number Vai Town dwellers, appalling, the American Navy was yet to rate the huge death toll as a genocide.

The fear was, if Kiatamba launched another attack, would the US Navy be willing again to lend and authorize the use of the field cannon? With no sign of an offer of truce from the hostile Vai King, Governor Ebenezer Butler was not entirely satisfied with reports from colonial spies that there may be no more indigenous attacks.

When the tension seemed to be dying down, he along with the rest of the colonial authority paid a visit to Councilman Brisbane. The governor elect had been discharged and taken to his family residence at Mamba Point, but had not still recuperated from the shock and trauma from the vicious warriors' attack on his residence. His wife and kids were not sure he would be able to serve at the colonial council again. After all, they would not venture back to their home across the Mesurrado River.

That same day they visited Governor Carey at the health center to appraise him of the situation. The ailing governor twinkled and blinked his eyes as he slowly opened them in his reaction to the good news from the battle. The bed-ridden governor wiggled his bandaged fingers, prompting an impression that he was recuperating and would live. But reflecting on the large scale of the death toll, he forced a faint smile, which was cut short with a wince like he was experiencing some pains.

Councilwoman Esther Haywood Dunn and Irene Wilmot Dennis suddenly wailed when the governor could not shut his eyes, and was no longer wiggling his fingers. While the two women were crying, the men in the room took off their hats. They turned to the wall and closed their eyes when the head nurse, Mrs. Matilda Gibson rushed into the room, grabbed Governor Carey's left hand, checked his pulse, and shook her head. She suddenly sank to her knees, weeping. The missionary had finally died.

A week later, there were still no signs of indigenous hostile activities and rumors of war. The colony continued to mourn. The funeral service for the fallen governor was put to halt due to looming uncertainties of renewed hostile indigenous attacks. At the beginning of the following week, three boats bringing Major Cryton and his men docked at the wharf at the mouth of the Mesurado River. Among them was Cho Vuyougar.

Though in his custody, the interpreter had been cooperating with Major Cryton in seeking the whereabouts of King Sorteh Gbaryou. With the help of the *Blunjue*, they accompanied the Kpelle they rescued from the Portuguese to join their kinsmen who were still roaming the bush in search of the defeated Bassa King.

They met Yallah Killimenni and his men. A tacit alliance was forged, when Levi Gardea Gray turned his people over to him. Afterwards, they jointly searched for King Sorteh Gbaryou. Few days later, they met three of the King's main elders.

"Gbaryou is no more," Old man Garbala, presenting himself as the Chief Elder informed the joint search group.

"Where is his body?!" Vuyougar asked, interpreting Major Crayton's question.

The old man signaled to one of the elders who then raised the king's blood stain garment in the air. "We found these at the edge of the Mycline River. He was severely wounded and drowned while trying to swim across."

"Did you find his body?" the Major pressed on.

"We are wounded, and the fatigue of war has made us too tired to search into the deep bottom of the river in search of his body," Garbla responded. "We are overwhelmed with the anxiety of seeking peace with you and the Kpelle so we can have time to bury our dead and rebuild our lives."

As key stakeholders from the defeated king's territory, they were brought along to negotiate its annexation to the colonial administration. Regarded as a Bassa royalty, Levi Gardea Gray was designated to negotiate the terms on their behalf.

That day, there was a ceremony commending the brave men that defended the colony. Among them were Commander Elijah Johnson, Major Rudolph Crayton, Captain Ashford Capehart, Private Joseph Holt, Privates Derick Hart, and Levi Gardea Gray, etc. In private, a ceremony was held in honor of Old Ernest Cheeseman to avoid angering the indigenous for the many lives that were lost when he fired the field cannon.

Privates Derick Hart, and Levi Gardea Gray were promoted to 1st Lieutenants while Private Holt rose to the rank of Captain. Captain Capehart was promoted to Major while Major Crayton was elevated to the post of Deputy Commander of the Colonial Arm Militia.

"Today you have proven yourselves as the true sons of liberty, by laying down your lives to defend this colony, and the land beyond," Governor Butler praised the men. "For ages, your gallantry, bravery and valor will be remembered in the annals of our history. You are the proud sons that stepped up our efforts to weed this coast of the slave trade by apprehending Capt. Edwardo Gomez and his collaborators for engaging in this evil trade along these shores.

As we look forward to a total end of fighting, and forged out peace between us and our indigenous brothers and sisters, we promised a bigger ceremony in which all who contributed to the protection of the colony would be decorated."

Two days later, Governor Butler and his security team were having a meeting in the war room at the colonial headquarters. With him were Commander Elijah Johnson, Deputy Commander Crayton,

Major Capehart and some intelligence officers assessing the possibility of an end to the war, when Charles Deshields rushed into the office, breathing heavily with excitement.

"We have a guest," he announced.

"Let the guest wait, Deshields," responded Governor Butler. "As you can see, we are in the middle of our security briefings."

"Gentlemen! The meeting can wait. It's important that we know who this guest is and what she has to say."

"She?" asked the head of intelligence.

Charles Deshields nodded, turned to the door entrance, peeped into the adjacent hallway and gestured to someone. Reverend Charles Gooding III entered, wearing a long-sleeved black shirt with a white cravat and a black trousers. A bible was clung under his arm.

"Charles. As I told you, discussions surrounding Governor Carey's funeral will have to wait. The security of the colony remains paramount."

The Baptist prelate said nothing, but instead, looked towards the door and gestured. Immediately, Bendu Kiatamba stepped into the room.

"Gentleman. We are pleased to present her excellency Bindu Kiatamba, an emissary of the Vai King, Gbotoe Kiatamba," Charles Deshields announced.

"Are you serious?" whispered Governor Butler.

"King Gbotoe Kiatamba?" asked Commander Elijah Johnson, mesmerized by the sudden change of opulence of the indigenous maid of Deputy Governor Estella Carter and her husband, Thomas. She was now adorned in Vai royal clothing; a white woven country cloth with black linings with her hair well threaded in a special way, and her neck, waist, and ankles worn with ivory chain and beads, respectively.

"Greetings, gentlemen," she spoke, her voice business-like and assuring, causing the eyes fixed on her to snap out of their gazes. "On behalf of King Gbotoe Kiatamba, the new ruler of Vai-Gola and Dei lands, I bring you the prospects of peace and reconciliation between our two peoples."

"So shall we accept such noble recommendations, Madam Kiatamba," responded the governor. "Kindly have your seat"

Bendu nodded, and gestured to Reverend Gooding to take his seat, to which he gestured that she should be the one to sit first. She hesitated, then smiled and took a seat near Deputy Commander Crayton.

"We had no intention to hold you hostage the day we went looking for you, Madam," he said, slightly bowing his head, when both of them looked at each other.

"Understood," she replied, smiling.

"We could work out a peace conference to cement this peace deal, but we need a little time to bury our late governor," Governor Butler recommended.

"While we await the day of this conference, the king also expresses his condolences to the colonial authorities. I am a witness to what I saw he intended to do to prevent the war when I came here to see my uncle, Foday Kamara."

"We are highly grateful for that, Madam Kiatamba."

"Thanks, Governor. But before I leave, I have a personal request."

"And what is that?"

"Kindly release Momo Shiafa, the man you arrested for hosting me when I ran away from the Clinic."

The governor looked at Deputy Commander Crayton who nodded. Then he looked at Bendu.

"He is well. consider your request done."

The Emissary looked at Reverend Gooding who nodded, suggesting that it was time to leave. Then, both of them got up. "We must leave you now," Bendu announced.

She and the Reverend were at the door, and were about to step out.

"So, if you may. What happened to the old king?" Asked Commander Elijah Johnson, having in mind that he must have died during the battle.

Bendu stopped. Reflecting on the encountered few hours after the deadly cannon was fired, she closed her eyes.

When Gbotoe left the compound to meet his father to put an end to the fighting, she was worried for her brother. She wasn't sure the king was going to like it, and that he might execute his son and continued the march on Monrovia. Her fear grew when she thought of the many persons that would die as she imagined that the colonial headquarters was jammed packed with people fleeing adjourning settlements. Reverend Gooding had called for prayer, and while they were praying for peace at the same time crying, and rolling all over the sanctuary, they heard the explosion.

They suddenly stopped. They were frightened.

"Cry to the Lord. Lay your plea at his feet, and pray until you can pray no more," Reverend Gooding pleaded.

About two hours later, no one knew what was going on. Caldwell was quiet. Expecting the worst, because it was an enclave where the indigenous and the few settlers had managed to coexist, everyone was indoors. Then people began to flee from the compound when they saw the warriors who had left early that morning, returning, but without Gbotoe Kiatamba. Sensing that her brother may be dead, and that her father the King has sent his men to arrest her, she remained lying on the floor with her son by her side. Slowly, for the first time she began to recite the 23rd Psalm which she learned at the Carters'.

"The warriors are here for you, Bendu," she heard Reverend Gooding's voice.

Bendu got up, holding her son in her arms. Just as she thought, the warriors have come to apprehend her and her son. Her brother was dead. She and her son were the next. She should not have had a child by the enemy.

"Even though I work through the valley of the shadow of death, I'll fear no evil," she said in Vai, when two warriors entered the church.

"The King has summoned you at once," one of the warriors said. "You and the boy."

She nodded, and turned to Reverend Gooding. "He sends for me," she said, weeping.

"I'll go along."

"It's dangerous," she sadly shook her head.

"I insist," the Reverend grabbed his bible and held her hand.

"Your brother demands to see only you," one of the warriors said.

Bendu froze. She did not believe what she had just heard.

"My brother?" astonished, she asked.

"Yes. Your brother the king. We must hurry now. Your father, the old king, must see you and his grandson before he takes the journey to his ancestors."

"His ancestors?" again, Bendu asked, now spooked, but overtaken by the unbelievable elation that her brother was now King; this was too quick.

While Bendu Kiatamba stood, still processing the sudden change of event, the warrior who spoke said nothing else. They both stood, arms folded, their expressions seemingly impatient.

Alone with Gbotoe, she was taken to her brother at Gbanjor. She met him at the main square in his full royal regalia, sitting on the movable throne his father once sat on.

It was full of people. Some were crying for their relatives and loved ones, who died in battle, as warriors ferried from across the river, the bodies of their fallen comrades wrapped in large banana leaves, and laid them before the new king. Herbalists and Zoes, specialized in identifying disfigured corpses, were summoned from across Dei-Gola and Vai land to perform this ritual.

Bendu ran to her brother when their eyes met. He immediately jumped from his throne, and also ran to meet her. They embraced and wept for some time. "I don't see the staff of the king," she whispered, her voice conveying a little concern but at the same time, tears of joy flooding her eyes.

"Papa said I shouldn't have it. It's a staff of war, and now I am a king of peace. Too many people have died."

Bendu breathed with relief, but unable to withstand the too much of wailing from the people as more bodies were hauled from across the river.

"Our Dei ally risks losing an entire generation. Too many of their people died," the new king informed his sister. "They made up the huge number that led the attack."

"Why?" she asked, her voice now hoarse in reaction to the increasingly unbearable situation.

"From one part, they were the fiercest and the bravest while at the same time acting on a mandate of 'Do not return without victory or your heads'."

"Papa," crooned Bindu.

"Well, it's all over now," the king said, reaching for his nephew on his sister's back. "Let me hold my nephew. Hey Small Gbotoe. Look at you; our ambassador between our two peoples."

Later, the new King ushered her to their father who was in a hut surrounded by warriors.

"You have a beautiful son," he said as soon as she entered the hut. "And you are a mother now. Your mother did not tell me she took you to stay with our enemies."

"She knew you wouldn't allow it."

"Your brother told me you always wished to live with these people when she first took you to Monrovia." The king was suddenly shaken. "Too many of our people have died. I have to take the journey to our ancestors to account for this. Be your brother's keeper. The ones before him may be envious. But such is the time for such a king."

"He will be a wise king, Papa," Bendu began to weep.

Few minutes later, with his eyes flooding with tears, the new king entered with four Zoes. He took his little nephew from his sister. Then, he gestured that they should leave the room. Weeping loudly, Bendu shouted and fell at her father's feet.

She attempted to hold onto them, but was prevented by one of the Zoes. With Small Gbotoe, they waited outside while her brother returned into the hut. For a while, the room was quiet. Then, suddenly, her brother shouted in a loud voice. After some time, he came out, shaken. Soon the Zoes followed with the corpse of the old king wrapped in the royal burial customs, the gorilla fist staff lying on top of the corpse.

The king held his sister's hand and marched behind their father's body as the four zoes, and another one who was ahead, carried it on their shoulders. Ahead of the lead Zoe was a drummer with a talking drum clung under his left shoulder, beating the drum in the tone of the royal requiem.

Also accompanying the fallen king were a group of warriors with fresh palm thatches tied around their heads, and wrists with their bodies dabbed with blue dye. As a certain distance, the zoe leading the procession changed the tempo of the talking drum, and stopped. Then, he blew a small antelope horn hanging around his neck, bringing the entire procession to a halt.

After performing the rituals to bid the fallen king farewell to his final resting place, sobbing, his successor and the rest of the warriors waited while the zoes continued with the body, and then disappeared into the forest.

"When you have served your people well, get old and die, will you be buried this same way? Will your relatives and children never know your grave?" Bendu asked, sobbing.

The king looked at his sister and smiled. "You are talking about a long time from now," he replied. "By then, times will change. It may no longer be the same way."

Standing at the door, wiping a tear from her eyes, Bendu turned to the men in the room.

"To make way for peace amongst our peoples, my father had to voluntarily embark on the journey to his ancestors."

About three weeks later, Reverend Charles Gooding III was on the pulpit of the first Baptist Church on Ashmun Street as preacher of the funeral discourse of Governor Carey, a request of the dying missionary. Governor Butler, Councilman Samuel Brisbane, and all the colonial council members and staff of the head office were present. But the governor elect, complaining about no longer having interest in colonial administrative matters, left earlier..

Captain Willman and a few of his officers of the US Navy were also present. With Momo Shiafa sitting right next to her, Bendu Kiatamba, occasionally weeping, was also in attendance.

"We have come a long way though the many dangers, toils, and snares to fail," he preached. "It is through the works of God Almighty that we have survived as a people. It was by the power of the Holy Spirit that raised such men like Reverend Doctor Lott Carey from the arches of slavery to the virtue of humanity to bring light to the dark world.

One day he told me, initially he felt that the good old Lord had stopped him from adequately doing his missionary work when he assumed the governorship of this Colony. While pondering over this, he heard a voice saying, 'Reverend! You have come a long way to fail for our Lord and Savior Jesus Christ will be by your side. Through your efforts, a nation will be born, and it will be the symbol of African Liberty. A nation that all men will be equal in my sight, no matter if you're an indigenous or a settler.' And from that day, Reverend Doctor Lott Carey understood the work he was called to do.

He is lying here today, because he did not fail. His death was not in vain indicative of a peace conference in the coming days, where indigenous and settlers alike will have the opportunity to drink from the foundation of coexistence and tranquility. A conference whose success I envision, will entreat the spirits of our ancestors who died on these shores, in slavery, and along the perilous journey to be sold as slaves, to dance to the songs of freedom.

With God above we must continue to forge our desire to exist, and coexist. With this, we can pledge all hail to a new nation in sight, springing from the highlands to the north, with the bright and early morning sun rising from the east, and setting to the west, the effulgence of its rays revealing the glamor of a beautiful country. A beauty unfathomable, and the glamor of the Atlantic Ocean excitedly dropping its waves on a bright and flourishing West African coast. In God we trust."

After the sermon, a unit of colonial officers, headed by Major Capehart, marched ahead of the coffin bearing the mortal remains of the governor, mounted on a wagon driven by a white pony. Led by Reverend Charles Gooding III, the clergy from all the denominations in the colony, followed by a joint choir of all the Baptist churches, and the rest of those who came to pay their last respects, marched behind the coffin.

The group paraded down Ashmun Street, towards a plot of land to the right side of the church. A tomb stood in the middle of the yard decorated with flowers. In it the body of Reverend Doctor Carey will be laid to rest. Nearing the tomb, the choir, led by Barbara Newland, sang the song "On the Day of Resurrection"

The peace conference began three months after the burial of Governor Carey. It lasted for a week, beginning with general discussions with each party outlining their respective claims and issues. After painstakingly finding common grounds, a preamble was crafted and interpreted in Bassa, Dei, Gola Vai and Kpelle. Copies of the documents were shared amongst the tribal rulers with their interpreters explaining the points stated in the preamble.

After some clarities, and concurrence, a validated version was endorsed. Then, it was agreed that the best place it must be read before the parties and signed was on Providence Island.

The Island was jammed packed with people. There were cultural performances by the Bassa, Dei, Gola, and Vai traditional maskers. Among them were the Gbatu, and the Nafai. Guykpwee, the Blue Diamond Afro Mask Dancer was also there, performing his usual display of traditional rock dances and drawing crowds.

The colonial authority and the Americans were present, including the tribal rulers. They were King Gbotoe Kiatamba, King Gray, King Gbessagee, and King Garmondeh. Lango Gbowee, with a few of her council of elders were also in attendance. With her was Yallah Kolliemenni, who brought Saydah and their 6 months old baby along.

Colonial Militia, which included the Kaki attired indigenous ones, supervised and commanded by Major Capehart, and 1st Lieutenant Levi Gray, respectively, were ensuring that security was intact.

Director Charles Deshields was seated next to Emily Thompson who was now working with him as an assistant, charged with the responsibility to foster Settlers-Indigenous Integration in the southern Farmington region. She was recently brought back to town when she completed the *Blunjue* traditional school as a full flesh member. Because of this, she was given such a task.

With admiration, she was watching Levi Gray, well clad in his military attire, gently making his way towards them. When he was within reach, he leaned forward and whispered something to Director Deshields. Surprised to see Emily, he smiled, slightly bowed and left.

Deshields left his seat and walked over to where Governor Butler, Captain Willman, and a US Navy officer, Commander Elijah Johnson and Deputy Commander Rudolf Crayton were sitting. He whispered, passing on to them what the 2nd Lieutenant had told him. With a gloss of excitement on his face, the governor nodded. Then the Director for Settler-Indigenous Affairs mounted the podium.

"Ladies and Gentlemen, we are pleased to announce the arrival of the Mandingo King from the northwest," he announced.

After that an entourage of warriors accompanying a huge man with white long beard, wearing a black country cloth gown beautifully adorned with linings, entered the platform. He was ushered to where the other traditional rulers were sitting. After some greetings and pleasantries with his counterparts, he waved his staff to the crowd and took his seat.

Governor Butler observed that the Mandingo King looked unusually weary and tired, then the last time he visited the coast. Three months before the hostile indigenous attack, he sent Falllekou, commonly known as *"The Konianke Trader"* for his vast knowledge and experience in trading between the Guinean highland through the dense Belle Forest and the coast to the late Governor that he would pay the colony a visit, to hear some of the complaints and claims by the hostile kings.

Unfortunately, he was delayed. While on his way he was attacked by Kponkay at a crossing of the St. Paul where the tip of the southeastern part of his kingdom met the tip of the northwestern part of Gola land separated by an island.

The vicious Gola warrior chief held the forces of the Mandingo king for days, preventing them from crossing, as both forces fought a fierce battle. At one point, there was a stalemate, which subsequently led to a loll in the fighting.

In order to determine Kponkay's weakness and outsmart him, the crafty Mandingo King sent his best spies to sneak into the camp of the Gola Warrior Chief. He chose Fallekou to lead this special assignment. They saw how Kponkay was preparing for his final assault.

"Behead the Mandingo king like we did Jaingkai for his dealings in the evil trade," much to their interests, they heard the enemy chanting this slogan.

When Fallekou reported back to the King, he immediately proposed and a parley was arranged. The Mandingo King met Kponkay, a stocky man whose hair and beard look green due to months of roaming the jungles, and eating fresh leaves and vines. He convinced the Gola war lord that he was not a slaver, and that he was on his way to the coast to put a final stop to some kings who were dealing in this evil trade, and that both men were on the same side.

"For this treachery, Jebbeh will pay with her head, no matter how deep she hides in the forest," grunted the Gola raider, saddened by the number of deaths caused by the ill-advised war he orchestrated.

Kponkay eventually pulled back his forces. Relieved, the Mandingo King finally crossed the St. Paul and made the journey down to the coast.

Elated, Governor Ebenezer Butler, flanked by three interpreters of each of the concerned tribes, mounted the podium and unfolded the document to read to the crowd.

"Today before men, and the Divinities of our ancestors, and the Almighty God above, we the settlers have agreed with our indigenous counterparts to coexist upon these truths," he began.

"1. That we are all descendants from the same forefathers comprising those that were sold in slavery and those that sold them, and that the same blood of our ancestors runs through our veins. 2. Upon this truth, we hereby denounce the evil trade of slavery, and that we must coexist in the principles of oneness, irrespective of our culture and religious affiliation. 3. That upon these truths, the strength of this coexistence is dependent on our indigenous brothers and sisters acknowledging and recognizing us settlers as descendants of their forefathers who were sold as slaves and our acknowledgement and recognition of them in a like manner. 4. That all issues regarding the purchase of land from our indigenous brothers and sisters must be settled amicably," the governor paused amidst cheers and jubilations.

Director Deshields saw Germongar, the Mamba sitting at the far back end of the platform, cheering. Both men locked eyes, with the Mamba offering a broad smile, his eyes utterly appreciative.

"Number 5," the governor resumed. "That there shall be no forced acquisition of land from our brothers and sisters rather than through a transparent and fair negotiation, predicated on their willingness. 6. That any colonial expansion into the hinterland must be of negotiation for the purpose of integration, not necessarily for the purpose of land purchases influenced by greed and an uncompromising ownership by title which usually leads to mis-understanding and segregation of our two peoples."

There was another applause, mainly from the indigenous. Councilwoman Irene Wilmot Dennis and Esther Haywood Dunn were also applauding. Remembering the Late Governor, both wiped a tear forming at the corner of their eyes.

"Brisbane should hear this," quipped Councilwoman Dunn, nudging her colleague on the side.

"Number 7," now charged with euphoria, Governor Butler continued. "That all traditional rulers integrated by such expansion must retain the right to administer the affairs of their people, our people, but in consultation with the colonial authority. Number 8. That such integration must be one of culture sharing or assimilation. 9. That all religions indoctrination must be one of conviction through teaching, but not by force. 10. That inter-marriages must be encouraged. 11. That education must be for the children of our both peoples. 12. That the security of these shores and the land beyond must be the burden of our two peoples. 13. And in order to trust the colonial authority to extend its jurisdiction into the hinterland, our indigenous brothers and sisters have recommended that some changes be made at the helm of our authority . They would prefer I Governor Ebenezer Benedict Butler remain the head, and that the head for the department of commerce must be changed with someone with a persuasive character since the collection of fees and fines within the colonial administrative jurisdiction is a burden imposed, and that it needs a great deal of persuasion to collect," the governor paused as the interpreters explained in Bassa, Vai, Dei, and Gola. Again, there was another round of applause, this time with the beating of drums and blowing of traditional horns.

When the interpreters were finished, the document was laid on a table. The governor signed on behalf of the colony, then Captain Willman of the United States Navy. King Gray was the first to affix his thumb on the part that bore his name. Next were King Gbessagee, King Garmondeh, King Gbotoe Katamba and followed by Lango Gbowee. The last ruler who stuck his thumb on the document as a witness was the Mandingo King.

After that the festival continued. There was "country cook," organized by Director Deshields in which indigenous and settlers alike displayed and shared varieties of dishes.

"Happy to see you alive and beautiful, more especially in the ways of our culture," said 1st Lieutenant Levi Gray who approached Emily Thompson who was chatting with her "Blunjue" friends, also at the festivals. The once all white chalk painted girls, dressed in beautiful lapper suits, looked different.

"Thanks," replied the newly appointed Settlers-Indigenous Relations Assistant, smiling. "Well, how sincere it is, for the beauty you profess I have, to lie in the eyes of the beholder?"

Trying to figure out what Emily meant, the lieutenant frowned, and then burst into a laughter when he had understood. "Simple," he said, shrugging. "It was the admiration I saw in your eyes the first time we met, the sincerity of which captivated you to track my captives, and rescue me from that slave cage."

Emily laughed, and then they were joined by Yallah Kolliemenni and Saydah.

"Thank you, my brave friend for saving the lives of my son and I," Saydah said and then looked at Yallah Kolliemenni at the same time taking the baby from her back and giving it to Emily.

"I highly appreciate it. Thank You. Ooh! Look at you. You are so big!" Emily crooned, taking the baby and lifting him in the air.

"My husband and I brought some gifts for you."

"That will be nice," said Emily, giving Saydah her baby.

Saydah gestured, pointing her hand towards the country cook fair, and they all trudged in that direction.

"Emily? I'm damned!" A voice suddenly shouted. It was Mrs. Pricilla Findley sitting behind drums of liquor she brewed and brought to the festival. "I heard about your parents. I am so sorry."

"Mrs. Findley!" Emily exclaimed, bending over and embracing her.

"Poor child. Not knowing all along in that vessel, we were riding with the devil's daughter. Oh! Poor old Burgess."

"How's Joel and Harold?" Emily managed to ask after a brief sadness, thinking about how her parents died.

"Those two little devils are out to sea. I sailed with them from Bassa Cove. But their captain couldn't let them stay. The old rascal said they were sailing down the mouth of the Cavalla. Ever heard about it?"

Not sure what it was, Emily shook her head.

"Never mind, poor child. Aberdeen. Serve Emily and her friends some of the best brews we brought. And make sure they have some dough, too."

On the other side of the Island, Bendu Kiatamba, her uncle Foday Kamara, Reverend Charles Gooding III, and Momo Shiafa had returned from the waterfront from seeing King Gbotoe Kiatamba and his entourage off.

"I hear that Miata is pregnant for you," she enquired.

"Yes. It is in its third month."

"Thank God, "breathed the Emissary. "And thanks for listening to me by forgiving her."

Momo Shiafa frowned, reflecting on Miatta's behavior, but offered a smile when he caught Bendu's eyes. He immediately called her attention when he pointed at Thomas Carter, and his friend, Cornelius Caesar walking to them.

"Hello Bendu," greeted Mr. Carter. "I am happy to see you, and I am impressed with your role at these occasions."

"Hello, Mr. Carter. And thanks for the compliment."

For a while both didn't say a word, but kept staring at each other.

Thomas Carter took a deep breath. "Look Bendu," he then broke the silence, his voice apologetic, and appealing.

"Mr. Carter. You are a nice man. You didn't do anything wrong to me. I know it's about your son. He's safe. You can visit him anytime you like at the Riverside Baptist Missionary Compound in Caldwell."

"Thanks for the understanding, Bendu." Carter said.

Bendu nodded, with a smile. "For now, he's spending some time with his uncle the king and his grandmother. Mr. Kamara will inform you when he's back with me. Where is your wife?"

"She traveled to the states. She and Agnes. She's gone to seek medical attention. Only Jeremy is here with me."

"I am sorry she lost her job. The people say they don't want her."

"That's okay," breathed Mr. Carter. "At least she will have time to check on her own health."

"Well," breathed Bendu. "I am still enjoying the festival. And before I forget you need to thank Reverend Gooding. He's been a great help to Gbotoe and I"

"Gbotoe?!"

"Yes, that's your son's name."

For a while, Mr. Carter stood pensively. Like he had just remembered he was supposed to do something, he turned his attention to the reverend, and Both men nodded to each other without a handshake.

"How's my friend, Monconjay, Mr. Caesar?"

"I haven't seen her since. But I am sure she's doing well."

"Okay," Bendu sighed. "Enjoy your time on the Island.

Bendu and Momo Shiafa, her uncle Mr. Kamara and the reverend walked past them as both men looked. Thomas Carter's face was full of sadness as memories of the encounter with him, Bendu and his wife, Estella Carter flashed in his memory. Mr. Caesar tapped him on his shoulder and shook him a bit to assure him.

"She's a good girl and a strong woman, too," he told his friend. "But anyway. Be thankful that you still got your family and your little boy."

Later at the cultural fair, Reverend Gooding met the Roberts family. Jason and his wife Mary and their son Daniel greeted him with excitement. He introduced Bendu to them, briefly telling them about her bravery that led to this day. Daniel Roberts had grown a little taller, towering over his parents.

"I am told they sent someone to investigate Burgess' death, reverend" inquired Mary Antoinette Roberts, resting her hands on her son's shoulders.

"So, I also heard," replied the reverend.

At the platform where the Mandingo King sat, he and Ebenezer Butler were having a conversation with the governor explaining through an interpreter the circumstances surrounding Governor Carey's death.

"In three days, I will have a word with all the rulers." the king said, after a moment of silence. "And I request that the main traitor be handed over to me. The one who is an interpreter. We have to institute a deterrent."

When he and Deshields had negotiated with the Mandingo king more on this matter, the Governor finally agreed to turn over the traitor.

"The preamble that you all have agreed to is in the interest of our peaceful coexistence," the Mandingo King addressed the kings on the day of his meeting with them. "The French are to our north and east, and the British are to our west. Their intentions may not be good for us and so we must rally with the settlers to hold together to protect our land or else we will be absorbed and partitioned among them," he paused, allowing that to sink in and then resumed. "Anyone of you who will stir up trouble again, will have to answer for your actions in the direst term. And I do not need to remind you of what I will do," he ended with a strong warning.

Each ruler spoke, reaffirmed their commitments to upholding the preamble. When he was about to make the journey back to the northwest, a group of Colonial Militia led by Lieutenants Joseph Holt and Derrick Hart, brought Witty Peter to him. As soon as Cho Vuyugar saw the Mandingo King, he immediately fell at his feet.

"O king! Please forgive me. I also contributed to the end of the war. Please don't behead me!" he cried. "*Ay e Fai, e joe*: Ay my father, I beg of you," he continued in the little Mandingo he knew.

The two colonial officers turned to leave as two of the Kings' men held Witty Peter's hands and pulled him from the ground.

"Ay *Allah! E joe*: Ay God! I beg You," he wept when the men were taking him away. "Where is Governor Butler?" he turned to look at the two Lieutenants, his eyes full of tears. "Where is Deshields? Who will talk on my behalf? They are going to chop off my head."

The king stopped, turned and walked back to him.

"Let me see his hands."

The men held and stretched them before the king. One of the warrior guards standing by the king, stepped forward and felt them. Then he looked up at the king and sadly shook his head.

The king nodded. He laid his right hand on Willy Peter's head, his heavy and large palm almost covering it.

"If you want to save your head, it is up to you to strengthen your hands for the toil that awaits you."

End.

Epilogue

Ashmun Street, July 31, 1850. This was a week after the 3rd independence anniversary of the new Republic. Liberia, as the former colony was now called, declared its independence on July 26, 1847 with Joseph Jenkins Roberts its first president.

Riding down Ashmun Street on his horseback, Reverend Charles Gooding III was returning from a meeting held at the Providence Baptist Church to establish a Baptist missionary school on a parcel of land situated about 2 and a half miles across the St. Paul River. Soon after a brief drizzle, the sun was up and scorching. As he galloped down the street, the glitter of the gold ring he was wearing on the 4th finger of his left hand occasionally flashed in his face, whenever he pulled the reins to slow the animal down.

He looked at his watch. It was nearly 2:30PM, and so he needed to hurry before the end of school day at the First United Methodist High School. At the back of his straddle was a parcel of neatly woven country cloth he was taking to Gbotoe Carter.

Reverend Gooding reached the school just before the school belt rang. Seconds later, students were rushing out of their classes to make their way home.

"Can any of you kindly find Gbotoe Carter and tell him Reverend Gooding is here to see him?" assuming they were Gbotoe's classmates, he trotted towards a group of students in their senior year uniforms and asked.

"There's no such name as Gbotoe Carter in our class," a student responded.

"The only Carter in our class is Leroy G. Carter," added another student.

"Okay. Leroy G. Carter," sighed Reverend Gooding, appalled as to why Gbotoe has changed his traditional name to Leroy, just 3 years after he had left Caldwell to live with his father. "What's your name, son?" he then asked the second Student who corrected him.

"Joshua Samson."

"Okay Joshua. Can you please find Leroy for me?"

The student nodded and left. In a few minutes Gbotoe was ahead of him as they both joined Reverend Gooding and the group of his classmates who were waiting for him. The Reverend watched his stepson, now bearing so much resemblance to the king, trudging towards him.

"You can leave us now, sons," he said as soon as Gbotoe reached him. "And thanks Samson. Hope you all will go directly home and do your homework before going out to play."

"Good afternoon, Reverend," Gbotoe Greeted as soon as his classmates left.

"Good afternoon. And by the way, your classmates do not know your Gbotoe name."

"Leroy G. Carter sounds good, Reverend."

"Your Gbotoe name is noble. Your name sake is a man of peace. I guess that's why your mother named you after him."

"Yes, Reverend. My mother always told me that. That's why I am keeping it as my middle name."

"Okay. Your mother wanted you to have this," the Reverend said and then handed his stepson the parcel. "Your uncle the king sent them as your independent day gift."

"Oh well," Gbotoe chirped, shoving the parcel into his book bag. "He always shows me kindness. And my mother, too."

Reverend Gooding did not say anything else, but stood watching how fast Gbotoe had grown. He has just turned 21 and was in his senior year. Most of his primary and elementary days were at the missionary school he ran in Caldwell.

"Thanks Reverend. Greet your wife for me. Got to catch up with my classmates," Gbotoe Carter said and dashed out of the sight of his stepfather.

The Reverend watched his stepson skipping towards Gurley Street to join his classmates. From Gbotoe Carter to Leroy G. Carter, he mulled over the change of name, a fresh sign that it was going to be the norm in the new republic.

The President was a Methodist, and so was the school, an institution where the children of the new administration, predominantly of the same denomination, sent their children. It was one of the best schools surpassing all the ones run by the other denominations.

Though this was a cause for concern, Reverend Gooding wrestled with the reason that there was a need to give the new country a chance. The administration, settler dominant, was burgeoning. It has a lot more to learn to gravitate from running a small colony to a whole nation that is expected to expand.

But he speculated that had it been Governor Carey, he would have done it differently. Maybe, the reverend considered, he would have focused more on the Setter- Indigenous integration part, thereby fostering reconciliation and coexistence. For example, names like Varney, Gbotoe, Garmonjue and other indigenous names were going to be heard amongst the Samsons, Woods, Johnsons, and Dennis, etc. in the first Methodist school.

As the clergyman trotted down Water Street, another issue seeped into his mind. A week before Independence Day, he visited a new elementary school established by the administration for all. Located somewhere around Clay Street, yet again, it was settler dominant.

The administration blamed the indigenous parents' lack of interest in having their kids who were supposed to be helping with daily chores and farm work, rather than standing before some crabby settler spanking them because they do not know how to recite and write the white men's language.

Inquiring further, the authority responded that awareness on the importance of education for the indigenous can wait.

Appalled, this was the first time the Reverend's heart leapt, more than the day he saw warriors torching the chapel at the missionary compound. From that day, he began to pray that the future of the new country should not be bleak, more especially, this should not extend to the generations many years to come.

Acknowledgement

My special thanks and appreciation to the following persons:

The late Hon. Thomas Doe-Nah, former Commissioner General, Liberia Revenue Authority (LRA) for positively rating and promoting my first book, "SASSAYWOO: Trial by Ordeal" which encouraged me to publish "Shores of our Forefathers: The Sacred Coast of Patriotism, Gallantry & Liberty." Because of the fresh impetus you injected into me, I am almost done with "Outbreak of the Hemorrhagic Fever." May your soul rest in peace.

Mr. & Mrs. Lawrence V.C. Dennis for your highly needed support, commitment and encouragement.

Thomas M. Sako, for encouraging me to pursue my calling as an author, and for your continued support.

To Mr. Varney Arthur Yengbeh, Chairman of the Board of Trustees, Bomi Community College, Tubmanburg, Bomi County. Thanks for your technical advice, and for our discussion a few years back about the need to publish a book on Liberian history from the perspectives of the settlers, the Americans and the indigenous people. Though this is a fiction, it did mirror our history based on these three perspectives.

Mr. Thomas Kaydor, a publishing author, and Associate Professor at the University of Liberia for believing in my work and for ushering me into the publishing world.

To my interpreters, I commend you for taking time with me as we went through the manuscripts.

To my sister Miss Dehdeh W. Zeze of the Liberia Institute for Statistics & Geoinformation Services (LISGIS) for accompanying me on a tour of most of the scenes described in this book.

Finally, to my loving and caring wife, Mrs. Mosesetta Bedell Zeze, and our children, Jamalla, Josetta, and Princess, for your understanding and patience and continuing to make the sacrifices to have Shores of our Forefathers published.

About the Author

The author, Joseph Akoi Zeze was born and raised in Bong Mines, Fuamah District, Lower Bong County, Republic of Liberia.

He published his first book "Sasaywoo: Trial by Ordeal" in March 2023, and is being sold on Amazon and other online bookstores. He is currently working on his 3rd novel, "Outbreak of the Hemorrhagic Fever: code name 'Jack 'O Lantern'"

Mr. Zeze earned his Bachelor of Arts Degree from the University of Liberia.

He is married with 3 children.

The author currently lives in Monrovia.

E-mail address: joseph.zeze@yahoo.com

Cell #: (+231)-886571107

Milton Keynes UK
Ingram Content Group UK Ltd.
UKHW051842141024
449461UK00023B/98